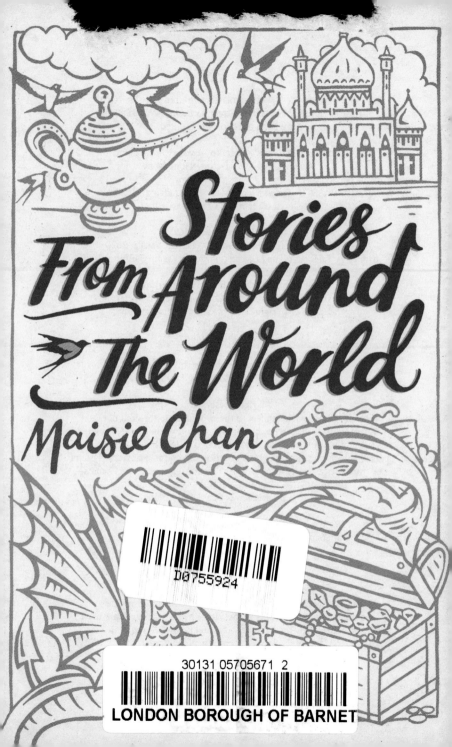

Stories From Around The World

Maisie Chan

Published in the UK by Scholastic Children's Books, 2020
Euston House, 24 Eversholt Street, London, NW1 1DB, UK
A division of Scholastic Limited.

London – New York – Toronto – Sydney – Auckland
Mexico City – New Delhi – Hong Kong

Text © Maisie Chan, 2020
Cover and chapter head artwork © David Wardle, 2020
Irish Fairy Tales, Myths and Legends extract © Kieran Fanning, 2020

ISBN 978 1407 19646 6

A CIP catalogue record for this book
is available from the British Library.

Printed by CPI Group (UK) Ltd, Croydon, CR0 4YY
Papers used by Scholastic Children's Books are made
from wood grown in sustainable forests.

1 3 5 7 9 10 8 6 4 2

www.scholastic.co.uk

Contents

Introduction

Fairy tales, myths and legends have existed for thousands of years across the world, but they haven't always been written down. In their earliest forms, they were shared by spoken word, passed down as cautionary tales for children to enjoy and learn from. The stories within this book have been collected from far and wide, using early versions of these tales as inspiration to create a varied collection specifically written for children today.

For Santi and Alma

Mulan

CHINA AND MONGOLIA

Mulan is one of the most famous legends in China. The earliest records of Mulan were found in the "Poem of Mulan" (sometimes called "The Ballad of Mulan") which was written anonymously and undated. It featured in an anthology compiled by Gui Maoqian, who claimed that the poem was created in the sixth century. In that version, the word "Khan" was used instead of "Emperor", which suggests that Mulan was from an area nearer to Mongolia than China.

Once upon a time in China, a baby girl was born. Her father called her Mulan after the beautiful wood orchids that blossomed around their home. Like those flowers, Mulan grew into a fine young woman. She was strong and quick-witted, with beautiful long hair the colour of ebony. Her mother taught her many useful skills that girls were supposed to know back then, like sewing by hand and weaving on the loom. But Mulan was bored. She wanted to be outside in the fresh air, training in martial arts – just as her father had done. She secretly wished he would teach her how to fight and how to use a sword, and she couldn't understand why everybody said that combat was just for boys. However, she never told anyone about this, as she didn't want to upset her mother, who wanted her to be the perfect lady.

One day Mulan couldn't keep quiet any longer and begged her father, "Please train me so that I might have adventures like you. I don't want to stay at home and sew!"

"I'm afraid your mother will never agree to it," was his reply.

"But father, just because I am a girl, that does not mean I should only be able to do things girls are supposed to do. Why, I am as strong as Liao who lives down by the stream. He is older than me but I can lift him over my head."

"Mulan, I know you are eager. And yes, you are very strong. But usually it is the son of the family who learns martial arts."

"It's not fair," said Mulan, sulking back on the table, her unfinished sewing hanging with loose threads. Her glum face could not be ignored, and Mulan's mother noticed how sad she looked every time she sat down with the needle and thread or at the loom. Eventually, her mother relented with a smile.

"If you are going to huff and puff around the house so much then I will let your father train you. It will be good exercise. BUT only as long as you help with other chores around the house."

"Oh, mother, thank you so much! Whatever you want me to do, just ask!" Mulan could not contain her glee. Now she would show the village boys that she was every bit as good as they were.

Training began immediately. Mulan's father knew that Mulan was an eager student. And just as he suspected, Mulan always listened carefully when he told her to practise a move or how to hold a sword properly. When he taught her how to use a bow and arrow, she instinctively knew how to adjust the bow according to the wind. Even when she couldn't do something the first time, she never gave up, and she was kind and gentle but determined. Soon Mulan had learnt many new skills, including the ability to tame and ride the wild horses that wandered on to their land.

Time passed in much the same way, until one day Mulan's mother gave birth to a baby boy. The family rejoiced and soon settled into their new routine. Alongside her warrior training, Mulan continued to help around the house, looking after her baby brother when her mother was tired. Five more years passed, and the monsoon rains came bringing with them a sickness to the house. Mulan's father fell sick, and soon he was unable to leave his bed. Worried for her father, Mulan helped around the farm, feeding the animals and gathering the crops. If she had time left after her chores, she would try to practise her martial arts alone as best as she could.

One day, while walking in the market with her younger brother on her back, Mulan noticed a notice

being pinned to the doors of all of the public buildings. Gently placing her brother on to the ground,
Mulan stopped to read one of them.

BY ORDER OF THE EMPEROR:
EVERY FAMILY MUST SEND A
MAN TO JOIN THE ARMY.
ANY FAMILY WHO DOES NOT SEND A
MAN WILL BE PUNISHED BY DEATH.

A list of names appeared underneath. She scanned
the sheet.

"No! It can't be true!" she gasped.

Her father's name was on the list – Hua. The rest
of the notice declared that war was imminent and
soldiers were needed, so no family could be spared.
Mulan felt terrible. Her father had been sick since
the monsoon season with pain and fever. There was
no way he could go to war. Her heart throbbed as
she thought of what going to fight would do to him.

"What's the matter?" asked her little brother. He
did not understand why his usually brave big sister
was crying.

"Father has been summoned to fight for the Emperor
and the men must leave for camp in two days!" Mulan

knew her father would not be better by then.

"But he's ill in bed," said her brother. "He can't fight."

"I know. Now *shhhh*. I need to think of what I can do to help him," Mulan replied. Her mind reeled – if he went, her father would be killed instantly by the enemy, as he was too weak to even lift a sword. Her brother was far too young, and they had no other sons that would take their father's place. But if no one went from their family, then the Emperor's men would come to the house and the family would all be punished.

Mulan thought hard on the silent walk home, wracking her brain for a solution. A plan dawning on her, she decided that the only way to save her father was to take his place and pretend to be the soldier the Emperor needed.

The next day, working quickly and in secret, Mulan gathered supplies that she would need for her journey to the army camp. She found her father's old armour and some food in the cupboards, and she took materials from her mother's sewing table to wrap up her long beautiful hair. Knowing that she couldn't take a horse from the farm, as her family needed them, she went off to market in search of a new steed for herself. There she bought the cheapest horse that nobody wanted. He was a wild stallion – a horse nobody could control. But Mulan knew that the horse's fighting spirit could be useful, and with the skills her father had taught her, she would be able to tame any horse. This wild horse would have speed and courage that the older, steadier horses did not.

Whilst her family slept peacefully at dawn the next day, Mulan tied up her hair, winding it into a tight knot. She placed her father's armour over her body, padding it with scraps of her mother's fabric. Then she packed her meagre belongings on to the horse and sighed, her heart was breaking at the thought that she might never see her family again. But she knew what she was doing was the only way to save them from the Emperor's wrath. Determined, she silently bid them farewell and hoped that one day she would see them all again. As she crept away, she saw her little brother at the bedroom window, his eyes wide at the sight of his sister in armour in the early morning light. She waved to him and then put a finger to her lips, hoping he would not wake their parents. He nodded and went back to bed. With a sadness in her heart, Mulan turned away and set off on her new adventure.

Into the night she rode, along the Yellow River towards the camp where new soldiers signed away their lives to the Emperor's cause. Mulan's pulse quickened with fear as she arrived at the base camp. She stood last in the long line, hoping that everyone would see just another soldier, not a young girl who had run away from home.

"Next!" shouted the officer taking registration.

"Hua," she replied, her voice an octave lower than usual. Making her gait wide and shoulders squared, the officer accepted her as a man without question.

"Put your mark here," he asked.

Mulan's fingers trembled. She took a deep breath and then made the mark of her family name. The deed was done. To all who met her, she was now her father, and a member of the Emperor's army.

Mulan soon began the rigorous training to become one of the Emperor's elite soldiers. Combat was easy for her, as her muscles were used to years of sparring with her father. Her feet were swift, and her aim was sharp. Her fellow soldiers were in awe of her skill and talent. She wielded her sword like no one else for miles around and her fear of being discovered as a girl disappeared as she became known as the best and most fearless fighter in the army.

Soon théy marched off to war, and death and destruction was all around. Mulan was very lonely because she was afraid to make friends in case her secret was revealed. She spoke little and kept her head down, not causing any fuss. But eventually, she befriended a kind soldier named Wei. He came from a small village, too, and they often joked and laughed together about their old lives.

Mulan was happy to have someone to talk to. She tried not to give too much away about her family life, but she told Wei about the farm where her parents lived and the stream that flowed by. Soon the pair became inseparable, fighting side by side. When Mulan was made General, she made Wei her second-in-command, and they fought valiantly in each battle and led the armies to success after success, until finally, victory belonged to the Emperor..

Despite her success, Mulan was tired of fighting and longed to return to her family. Twelve years had passed and she wished to see her little brother and her parents more than anything in the world. After many long years, Mulan thought it was time to put down her sword.

The Emperor himself called for Mulan, recognizing

the part she had played in his victory.

"You have fought for this kingdom for many years. You have led great armies to victories. Tell me, what can we do to honour you?"

The soldier known as Hua replied, "Your esteemed Excellency. I only wish to take my steed and ride as fast as the wind to my homestead."

Despite being puzzled as to why the General hadn't asked for wealth or a high-ranking office, the Emperor smiled and declared that General Hua was released of his position in the army with full honours. Now free, Mulan's service to the army was over and she could return home.

Back at home, the sun was setting over the farm when a figure appeared on the horizon. As the horse drew closer, the soldier took off their helmet and shook their head. A head of jet-black hair flowed down.

"It can't be! It's my Mulan!" Mulan's father hurried towards his long-lost daughter.

"Father! Mother! Brother who is not so little any more! I am home!" she shouted, getting off her horse and running towards her family.

They embraced, tears streaming down their faces. They were sure their daughter must have perished in the thick of war. Mulan was overjoyed to be home in the arms of her family.

"Come, come! Let us feed you!" her mother insisted.

"I'd like to change my clothes first," Mulan said. "The years of wearing this heavy armour has taken its toll. I wish for lighter robes."

With that, Mulan was led her to room, where she took off the armour. Her robes and hairbrushes had not been moved. Even her bed was neatly made and a fresh orchid bloomed on the table. She could see the love her family had for her everywhere she looked. Sitting down on her bed, she let out a sigh. *Home at last*, she thought. Mulan brushed her long hair slowly with her jade brush. Her father put the armour back into his trunk.

Years passed peacefully while Mulan took up her old chores on the farm. Then, one day, unexpected visitors arrived. It was Wei, her friend from the army. He was with a few of their other comrades, all of whom had fought together in the war.

"We've come to pay our respects to General Hua. Is this the right farm?" Wei asked. Mulan's little brother ran inside, calling for her. The soldiers were shocked beyond belief when, instead of stern General Hua, beautiful Mulan appeared, long hair down around her face and dressed in her old flowing robes. Her face was familiar to them, but everything else was different.

"I am the one you seek," she said.

"But it can't be!" Wei exclaimed, recognition dawning as he looked into the face of his friend.

"I am the person you knew as Hua," Mulan explained "I am your General. I am still the same person who fought alongside you all. I was a woman the whole time."

The men stood wide-eyed with their mouths open, and they stepped uneasily apart from Wei and Mulan. But, taking off his helmet, Wei dismounted his horse and stood in front of Mulan. He raised his arm and saluted his general, and when the other men saw this, they did the same.

"I owe you my life," Wei said. "Man or woman, you are my hero."

"You are our hero too!" said Mulan's little brother, who was proud of his big sister.

That night Mulan's mother and father put on a feast for the soldiers who had fought alongside their daughter.

"We now know that even though you are a woman, you were the best warrior our kingdom had ever seen," said one of the soldiers as he lifted the rice bowl to his face.

"Thank you," Mulan replied, accepting his praise graciously. "I hope you have learnt that women are at least as strong and clever as any man," Mulan smiled, and Wei nodded, raising a toast to Mulan – the finest warrior ever seen in the kingdom.

John and his Magical Violin

BRAZIL

This story is a retelling of Dr Sílvio Romero's story "Historia de João" ("The Story of John") featured in Contos Popularares do Brazil (1885). This tale is similar to many European fairy tales, such as "The Pied Piper of Hamelin" and "The Golden Goose", but the location and exotic animals make it very much a Brazilian story.

Once upon a time, there was a boy called John whose father had sadly passed away. His father didn't have much in the world, and so all he passed on to his son was a cat, a dog, and a patch of land filled with banana trees. John knew that he wanted to travel and seek his fortune, so he sold the cat and the land, and kept the dog for company. Before he left on his journey, he went to a stall in the market and bought something he had always wanted – a violin! He put the violin under his chin and held the bow with his other hand. He wasn't sure how to play, but as soon as he touched the bow to the strings, it was as if his arms had a will of their own! The violin played a melodious song and the boy was astonished.

"How can this be?" he exclaimed. He lifted his arms again and the violin played another song and then another. The sound was more beautiful than anything he had ever heard.

The owner of the stall smiled at John, and told him that the violin had belonged to a wizard who loved music so much he had enchanted the instrument, saying that when the right owner came along, the violin would play happily by itself. John couldn't believe his luck and continued to play as he and the dog set out on their journey.

Although John could now play wonderful music on the violin, he needed to find a job because the rest of the money he'd earned from selling the cat and the land would soon run out. So he and the dog walked for miles and miles until they came to a city. *Surely I will find a job here*, John thought. He asked about work at the ironworks and in the marketplace, but was told he was not needed. He knocked on many doors to ask if he could play his violin to earn his keep, but each one was slammed in his face. Finally, he asked if he could tend to the king's sheep, but the king already had many shepherds and did not need another one.

Defeated, John and his dog found shelter in a nearby forest. He sat against a tree and took his violin out of his case. Caressing the bow across the strings, he began to play. The sheep that had been sleeping in a nearby field heard the music and found themselves drawn to the sweet sound. They gently made their way deep into the forest until they arrived at the John's resting place.

Back in the field, the shepherds also heard the

music, but could not find out where it came from. The harder they tried to follow the tantalizing sound, the more lost they became, walking around in circles and losing their way in the forest. Afraid of never finding their way home, the shepherds gave up their search and returned to the rest of the flock.

John was happy to be surrounded by the sheep. He could see how they loved his music, and he found that as more and more sheep came to listen, the songs the violin played became more joyful. He, too, was feeling less sad and lonely. As the music became even more joyous, the dog started to dance on its hind legs. Then the sheep started to sway to the rhythm. John stopped playing for a moment to see what would happen. The dog and the sheep stood still, eagerly looking at him, their eyes begging for him to carry on playing. He was delighted to see that his music made even the animals happy and continued to play into the night.

The next day, John, the dog and the sheep walked for miles and miles across the land, the boy playing the violin at the front of their strange procession, as the animals marched in time behind him. When they came to an area near the rainforest, a cluster of monkeys appeared, swinging through the treetops.

They too were enchanted by the wondrous music that was being played by John and his violin, and they gibbered away with glee and waved their hands. But their noise almost made it impossible for the music to be heard.

"Excuse me, monkeys. Could you please stop chattering so loudly so that everyone can enjoy the music?" he asked politely. And the monkeys quietened down as they did not want the music to end. They swung from tree to tree following him. After journeying for so many miles, tired and thirsty, John sat beneath an *amapá* tree to rest a moment. The animals gathered around him and waited for him to play again, and very soon he was ready to move on.

With the violin resting under his chin, and his right arm weaving back and forth with the bow, John and his band of animals danced through the rainforest, the violin's beautiful melody ringing out through the trees. Soon a tapir joined the gathering. The four toes on its front feet and the three toes on its hind feet began tapping. It was enchanted by the music and joined the procession.

An armadillo that had been curled up into a ball released its heavy armour and found itself moving its feet and nodding its head. The music was just too enticing to ignore. Next to join the procession was an anteater, its nose shaking up and down so much that it forgot about sucking up ants. A wild cat stalked alongside for a while until eventually it too joined the happy crowd of animals. It was too busy dancing to notice the sheep who normally would have been its supper.

An anaconda slithered silently down a tree, wishing it had legs that it could dance and stomp with. Instead it slithered from side-to-side, hypnotized by the weaving magic of the violin. Birds of every colour flew through the sky, diving and looping in time to the song through the forest canopy.

On and on they went, passing rapids and waterfalls. The landscape changed and John found he had led the animals to a great rock formation. Little did he did know that they had arrived at the edge of the forest, where lived a king and his daughter, the princess.

The princess was bored. She had been cooped up in the castle for her entire life. Everything about the place was grey and dull and she was listless and unhappy. Wanting his daughter's life to be joyful, the king had declared that anyone who could make his daughter smile or laugh would have the gift of a chest full of gold. Unfortunately, the inhabitants of the area were not known to have a sense of humour and were particularly bad at telling jokes. Although there were many who tried, not one of the locals could make the princess smile.

One day, the princess was looking out of the window just as John passed by playing his violin. She could not believe her eyes. She blinked again just to make sure she wasn't dreaming. Eyes open like saucers, she saw the dog dancing on its hind legs, the sheep shaking their rumps, the monkeys waving their arms in the air, the tapir tapping its funny-looking feet and the armadillo nodding its head. A wildcat was bobbing along to the music side-by-side with the animals it would usually eat for breakfast. And best of all, birds of every colour were zooming around the sky – they looked like beautiful fireworks, swooping this way and that. The princess let out a merry laugh and her father nearly fell off his throne. Could it really be? Had his ears deceived him or did his daughter really just laugh? But no, he hadn't imagined it – she was smiling at the scene below her window, finally happy.

The king ran to the see the commotion outside

and spied the odd procession. He called out, "You there! Come, come to stay with us. You shall have a house of your own and a chest full of gold if only you play your violin here!" John and the animals changed direction and marched into the huge grey castle.

The boy named John who had been travelling for miles across the land had finally found his fortune. He had seen the cities, the rainforest and the mountains, and all of that travelling had made him a little tired. He was glad he no longer had to knock on doors asking for jobs because now he had found a new home. He enjoyed his new life, and the animals all stayed close by. When he played his violin the princess smiled and everybody danced with abandon. People flocked from all over to the land to hear him play and watch the animals dance. When he was old, and had finished playing his last tune, he carefully placed the violin back in its case and passed it on to his granddaughter so she could carry on playing music and spreading joy throughout the land.

The Snake Prince

PUNJAB REGION

The Punjab region is an area that overlaps India and Pakistan and is a place of many myths, rivers and fairy tales. The word Punjab means "five rivers", and like those twisting and flowing rivers, it is also the home to many different kinds of snakes, which are a common feature in tales from this region. This story would originally have been told in Punjabi – one of the languages of the people who live there. An English translation of this story first appeared in The Olive Fairy Book *(1907) edited by Scottish folklorist Andrew Lang.*

Once upon a time in the land of the five rivers, there lived an old woman who was very poor. The only food she had left to eat in her entire house was a meagre handful of flour. Sighing at her bad luck, the woman decided to go to the river – at least there she could bathe and fill up her drinking pot, even if she didn't have any food to eat. And if she brought a little water home then she could mix the flour and water to make a small amount of *roti* to eat. Her tummy rumbled to think of it, but she was filled with dread as she did not know what she would eat once the flour was gone.

After a long walk, she arrived at the river and undressed, neatly folding her clothes and laying them on the bank next to her water pot. She left her brass pot on the side of the bank, covering it with a light cloth to keep to keep the flies and dust out. Entering the cool and refreshing water, the woman felt instantly better. Even if she didn't have much to eat, at least she would feel clean and have water to drink.

After she bathed, the woman climbed the river-bank, dried herself and was about to fill her brass pot with water. She took off the cloth and nearly dropped the pot in shock. Inside she saw the glittering scales of a deadly snake. It filled the pot with its black and green-flecked skin. The woman was terrified, yet, she was able to think clearly enough not to disturb it in case it awoke and attacked her. She held the cloth tightly over the opening of the pot, making sure she did not drop it. What should she do? She thought hard.

"If I kill it at home with the club I have, then maybe I can sell its skin to make some money to buy more flour, perhaps some vegetables," she told herself. Holding her pot at arm's length, she hurried towards her small house. However, when she got home, she uncovered the pot and discovered not a deadly snake, but a beautiful necklace made of gold and precious jewels. Red rubies, emerald green stones and blue sapphires dazzled her as she held the necklace up to inspect it. Confused and alarmed, she studied the necklace. But before long she began to smile at her good fortune.

"Well, if someone has given me this precious necklace then I will not waste this chance to change my fortune," she told herself, delighted with such a surprise.

For a long time she simply stared at the necklace, thinking about what to do next. A necklace such as this could not be sold in the common market-place – it was too precious! And she could not wear such a fine piece of jewellery herself, as she would be robbed in the streets. No, only a person of royalty would wear such a necklace. So, with determination, she folded the necklace in her cloth and hurried off to the palace, hoping for an audience with the king himself. The old woman travelled for hours to the grand palace, and after telling her tale, was granted an audience with the king.

Bowing politely, the woman slowly unwrapped her cloth. The king's eyes bulged when the necklace was revealed. He had never seen anything so beau-tiful. The way it sparkled mesmerized him, and he knew he had to buy it for his wife, the queen, so that everyone would know he owned the most beautiful and precious necklace in the world.

"I must have it," the king told his advisor. "I will show our neighbours that we only have the finest gold and jewels in our land. Go, give the old woman some money." The advisor did has he was told. He gave the old woman five hundred silver pieces in exchange for the necklace. She thanked him and went on her way, rejoicing in her fortune.

The queen was besotted with her new gift and the necklace was placed in a private chest in the royal bedroom. The king wore the key to the chest around his neck so that no one could steal the necklace.

Soon afterwards, word came that the royal family in the neighbouring region had given birth to a baby girl. The king and his wife were invited to a great feast to celebrate the happy occasion. The queen knew it was the perfect occasion to show off the beautiful jewels that her husband had given to her. Delighted, the king obliged and opened the chest, but when they reached inside, the necklace was gone. In its place was a healthy baby boy, his skin smooth, his smile infectious. He lay on his back laughing up at the pair. The queen gasped. She and the king had for many years been longing for children of their own, but had not been blessed by the gods. And yet, suddenly, here was a baby boy who seemed not to belong to anyone. The king told the queen, "We have long been heartbroken by our lack of children, and here now is a blessing from the gods. We should take this baby as our own."

"Are you mad?" the queen replied. "We don't know where this baby came from. And even if we did. . ."

But then the queen gazed into the baby's eyes and was instantly taken with his beautiful gurgles. The queen's heart melted and she scooped up the baby in her arms, knowing instantly that he was meant to be her son. "I take it back. He shall be our son," she exclaimed, tickling him under the chin.

Instead of going to the neighbouring region to celebrate the birth of the new princess, that night they had a feast of their own to celebrate the arrival of their new prince. There was much rejoicing in the streets, with flashing fireworks lighting up the sky, musicians playing, and food given out to the people. Nobody questioned where the baby had come from, nor why the queen had not appeared pregnant.

Time passed happily in the kingdom until seven years later. One warm summer's day, the young prince was playing in the garden of the palace when a slithering black snake slid close to his side. The prince was alarmed and yelled out, "Snake!" to warn everyone around. But instead of the word coming out of his mouth, the prince shimmered for an instant before shrinking into the shape of a small green snake. Horrified, his mother was beside herself. She rushed to get a pot and put her son, now in the shape of a snake, inside it. The king and his advisor found out what happened and summoned the most famous snake charmer in the land.

"Save my child!" the king demanded. The snake charmer examined the snake thoroughly, and when he was finished, he knew that an enchantment had taken place. With a heavy heart, he told the king and queen the news.

"This is the work of the snake queen. He should change back into a boy soon, but I'm afraid there is an enchantment placed upon your son. I can see that he is bound to the snake world in some way. I fear that one day, the snake queen will come for the prince," he said. "In that case, only true love will break the spell. If one who loves him will stand in the way of the snake queen despite his curse, he will be free to choose whether to remain a snake or a human." The snake charmer gave strict instructions to the family on what to do when that time came, urging them to keep their son's fate a secret. The king and queen agreed, and once their son had turned back into a boy, they forbid him from uttering the word "snake" again and swore him to secrecy, for they were fearful that no one would want to marry a prince living with a curse.

Many years passed by and the two neighbouring

kingdoms agreed that their prince and the princess should marry. The wedding took place with great festivities and the kingdom rejoiced.

But all was not well. The old woman who had sold the necklace to the king had realized that the arrival of the prince was exactly the same time as the necklace was sold to the palace. The emerald eyes of the prince reminded her of the jewels that had glistened that day in her brass pot. Although she had no proof that the prince was connected to her snake necklace, she could not keep the gossip to herself. The rumour spread like wildfire. Soon it was on everyone's lips that the prince was not all that he seemed. "The Snake Prince" became his new nickname, and people shuddered as they passed by the palace, saying they could hear him hissing from outside the gates.

Although the king and queen tried to keep the rumours quiet, the princess learnt of the stories and was puzzled. That night, she asked the prince to tell her the true story of his birth. When he said he would not, she was heartbroken and, feeling that the prince did not trust her, grew cold towards him. Many months went by and the tension between the couple grew and grew. Torn between pleasing his parents and making the one he loved happy, the prince decided that he couldn't bear it any longer. He had to share his secret and tell his beloved the whole truth.

So he took her to the river where the old woman had found him and said: "I will show you my secret. However, it comes at great risk. You may lose me and never see me again. But there is one chance to hold on to me, if you love me enough, so listen closely. In a moment, I will reveal my secret – in doing so, I will no longer be myself. Despite this, you must be brave, and take me to our bedroom tonight. Place four bowls of milk into each corner of the room. When the time comes you must face the one who will come for me – refuse to give me up and you will have your husband back. If you are too scared or cannot utter the words, then I might be lost for ever."

"I will, I promise," replied the princess. She was scared about what was going to happen, but thankful that she would finally find out the truth about her husband's past.

Drawing a heavy breath, the prince began his story, "I was cursed, a creature first made into a necklace, and then turned into a baby to woo the royal family, the thing they most desired in the world. The one who did this to me will come to reclaim me.

Her plan has been for me to take over the throne of my father, but be obedient to her. We must stop that from happening. I'm sorry, my dear, but I have to say the word ... I am a snake prince." As soon as the words left his mouth, the prince began to writhe and wriggle, his body shrinking. His clothes fell to the floor in a heap. The princess stood still, scared to move. Out from beneath the holes of his tunic slithered a snake, the colour of emeralds with ruby flecks. The princess wept, terrified. But she knew that her husband's life rested in her hands. Pulling herself together, she carefully picked up the snake and took him back to the palace.

Working quickly, she did as her husband had asked and placed four bowls of milk into the four corners of the room, hoping that this was going to be the right thing to break the curse. Then she sat down to wait. Sure enough, once night fell, the windows of the room flew open and a huge red, purple and black snake appeared. Its tail rattled loudly and it hissed wildly: the queen of snakes had arrived.

The queen of snakes slid around to the side of the bed, eager to take her prize. Using her son, she planned to rule both the human world and the snake world and was sure nothing could stop that from happening. But here was the princess, who loved her husband even though he was a snake, standing firm in front of her.

"Give me back my husband!" the princess demanded. She stood tall, chest puffed out, pretending to be brave. Even if she felt scared inside, she did not show it. She knew she had to fight to keep her husband by her side.

The snake queen swayed as the power of the princess's words caught her off guard. She could feel her spell weakening and hissed wildly. Again, the princess spoke: "You will not take my true love. I am his wife and I refuse to let him go!" The snake queen writhed in pain as the princess's words broke the spell and it backfired, rebounding against her twofold. With a mighty swipe, the princess chased the cowering snake queen from the room.

When she returned, the prince was returned to his human form once again. He reached out to his princess, crying tears of happiness that her love for him had been strong enough to withstand the snake queen's curse. The pair never kept secrets from one another again and not a single snake was seen in the palace from that day on.

The Nsasak Bird
and The Odudu Bird

NIGERIA

This traditional story would originally have been passed down from generation to generation of the Efik-Ibibio tribe. In the region that the tribe live, the Nsasak bird was said to be the hardest bird to hunt as it was so fast and hard to catch. Any small boys from that tribe were presented with a prize if they managed to shoot one with their bow and arrow. This story of the clever Nsasak bird was written down by Elphinstone Dayrell in Folk Stories from Southern Nigeria *in 1913.*

One hot scorching day, the king of Calabar was sitting on his throne when a tribesman rushed in with the sad news that the chief of the birds had died. The king set about finding a new chief the very next day for the king must have a chief for each of the animals at all times. In order to pick the best bird for the job, he asked if any bird was brave enough to come forward and accept a challenge he would set in order to win the title.

On hearing this, the Odudu bird, a bird as large as a magpie and as brown as dirty water, was excited for he wanted to prove once and for all that he was the most superior bird in all the land. The Odudu bird was very proud of his large size and his strength and liked to tease his neighbour, the Nsasak bird, who was very small.

"You might have bright feathers that burn red like the sun at sunset and green like the tall grass, but I am much bigger and stronger than you!" the Odudu bird trilled, preening his muddy brown plumage proudly.

The Nsasak bird tried to remain calm and not get upset by the Odudu bird's taunts. But the Odudu bird never knew when to stop and continued to torment the Nsasak bird. "You are puny and weak; you will never be the chief of all the birds!"

"We'll see," muttered the Nsasak bird under his breath. He was small but he was clever.

"Nsasak bird!" the Odudu boomed from his tree. "All you do is strut around with your pretty feathers and eat palm nuts. That plume around your neck will not help you. You are too scared to take up the king's challenge. You know you would lose, and soon you will bow to me when I am made chief of the birds."

Calmly and with no frills, the Nsasak bird looked over from his tree.

"Dear neighbour, I will show you how wrong you are – though I am small, I, too, can be mighty. I will take the king's challenge and defeat you!" Now, the Nsasak bird was only pretending to be brave – he knew that if the king's challenge involved strength, then the Odudu bird would most likely win. But fortunately for him, the king set a challenge of stamina rather than strength.

The king declared: "You will both build a house in that tree over there and the bird who can stay inside for the whole week will be my new chief. If you leave before the time is up, you will forfeit the competition."

"That sounds easy enough," the Odudu bird boasted.

"You will have no food and the opening will be closed so you will not be able to fly around," the king added.

"It may sound easy to you, dear Odudu bird, but I assure you, it will be anything but," the Nsasak bird said, already thinking about the cramped conditions and how difficult it would be not to fly around for a full week.

"Your challenge begins now!" the king boomed.

Both the Nsasak bird and the Odudu bird began gathering their supplies. Up and up they carried pieces of bark and moss for their new houses. The Nsasak bird thought furiously about what the king had said. He knew that if he was to have any chance of winning this test, he would have to use his brains. So, as well as having a hole at the front, he also created a small opening in the back of his house and covered it with twigs. While the king had said they couldn't use the entrance to their house, he had said nothing about creating another exit! This way the Nsasak bird could still leave the house to search for food without breaking the rules of the contest.

The Odudu bird made a larger house next door and he exclaimed that as he had more room to rest and exercise, he would be the one left standing at the end of the challenge. When both houses were fully completed, the two birds ducked inside their houses and the king had the entrances to both houses boarded up. The Nsasak bird closed his eyes and sat quietly. He knew he had to conserve his energy until nightfall when he could slip outside and fly to his heart's content. The Odudu bird, on the other hand, felt he needed to keep himself busy and paced up and down in his new home. He talked to himself to try and keep himself company.

"I am going to win. I am the best bird. I am the Odudu bird!" he would shout out.

"Be quiet and conserve your energy," replied the Nsasak bird. He kept as still as he possibly could and talked little. Then, when the guards outside were sleeping he would sneak out of the back entrance and find palm nuts to eat and fly for hours until the dawn. Before daybreak, he would return to his house and hide his secret entrance once more with twigs.

Day after day nothing changed. The Odudu bird was feeling more and more agitated by being cooped up inside the house without food and unable to fly. Little did the Odudu bird know that next door, his small neighbour was using his hidden exit at the back to go out each night. He would make sure no one was about and, quick as a flash, would dart through the sky, eating his beloved palm nuts, soaring and having fun. The Nsasak bird made sure he scratched a mark for each day of the challenge, which was easy for him because he could see when dawn and dusk approached, unlike his rival who was in the dark.

The Odudu bird sat on the floor of his house. The darkness was getting to him. He missed seeing daylight and breathing in fresh air. His house smelt bad. He started to wonder whether starting this challenge had been a good idea in the first place.

The Odudu bird started to mutter to himself. "What if they have forgotten all about me? I can't remember how long I've been in here without food or company." He was so hungry he couldn't remember how many days he had spent inside his prison, and he felt himself getting weaker and weaker as the days wore on.

Another day passed and the Odudu bird lay still on the floor of his house. He rested his head upon his chest. Only four days had passed by, but the Odudu bird's mind was so foggy that he had forgotten what day it was.

"They've surely forgotten about me. Something is wrong. Why has no one come to tell me that I am the winner already?" He was getting more and more irritable and angry; being cooped up was no fun at all.

He became so frantic with worry that he had been forgotten that he burst out of his house and into the daylight. The king's aide, who was standing watch at the front of the houses, immediately informed the king that the Odudu bird had forfeited the competition and had not lasted the full seven days.

The king arrived and declared the Nsasak bird the winner and the new chief of birds. The Odudu bird fell into a heap on the floor, bitterly disappointed but too weak to protest. The Nsasak bird flew around with joy as he had outwitted his old rival.

"Tell me, little bird, how did you manage to win this task?" the king asked.

"Your Royal Highness. I have to admit, I was unsure at first. But I am a bird of quick mind and cunning. You did not say in the rules that there only had to be one opening. And so I made a small hole in the back of my house."

The king laughed at the Nsasak bird's wily trick.

"This is true, and even though you are miniature in size, you make up for it with cleverness! You will make a good chief."

The Nsasak bird was proud of his achievement, but knowing how it felt when others were boastful about their skills, he remained a humble and kind leader for the rest of his days.

Fionn mac Cumhaill and the Salmon of Knowledge

IRELAND

Fionn mac Cumhaill was a legendary Irish hunter-warrior who had many adventures. Many tales of this heroic Celt are told in The Boyhood Deeds of Fionn, which is a medieval Irish book written around the twelfth century. The Salmon of Knowledge is one of the most famous myths that features Fionn mac Cumhaill and tells how he became the wisest man in Ireland.

Centuries ago, in the island called Ireland, there lived a fish. It was no ordinary fish, though – it was the Salmon of Knowledge. Legend foretold that whoever caught the salmon and had the first taste of its flesh would gain all of the knowledge and wisdom of the entire world. This is the story of how one man accidentally had the first taste and so became the wisest man in Ireland.

Ireland was in the midst of a period of war, with battles raging between many different clans. The leader of one of the mighty clans was called Cumhal, and he doted on a pretty girl called Muirne. Her father was a druid, who was very upset when he found out about their relationship. He didn't want his daughter mixing with fighters. However, Muirne was in love and decided she would marry her burly warrior, no matter what her father said. The two ran away and, not long after, Muirne realized she was expecting a baby. She was filled with joy and hoped that the baby would be a strong character like his father. But just before the baby was born, during a terrible battle, Cumhal was killed by another warrior who wanted to lead the clan. Muirne was all alone and her baby was due at any moment. She needed to get away from the clan and its new leader, who might harm her new baby – the rightful leader of the clan.

Muirne ran and ran until she came across a wooden cottage deep in the woods. The two women who lived there were kind and helped Muirne give birth to her healthy baby boy. The two women were called Bodmall and Liath. Bodmall was a herbalist, a woman who worked with herbs to make medicines, and Liath was a fierce hunter. For a while, both woman helped Muirne raise her baby until, one day, Muirne heard that the clan leader who had killed Cumhal was looking for her. With a deep sadness, she knew she must leave her boy in the care of the two women who had become family to them both. For if the new leader found her with a baby, he would know it was Cumhal's son, and her beautiful baby boy would be killed.

Bidding him farewell, she entrusted her son's care to Bodhall and Liath, who now became his only guardians, they called him Fionn, which meant "fair". They taught him how to fight, how to hunt and play and be kind – all the things a child should know. Fionn was strong and healthy and grew well in the deep, dark forest, hidden from any who meant him harm.

When Fionn was a young man, news came that the new clan leader had heard rumours that Muirne had given birth to a boy, one who had grown up to be big and strong, and was now living somewhere deep in the forest. Bodhall and Liath knew that Fionn wouldn't be safe with them for much longer, and so they packed him a bag with his favourite foods and, with tears in their eyes, told him to seek out a man called Finnegas. "Go and be safe with Finnegas, dear boy. You will find him along the River Boyne," said Bodhall.

"He is looking for an apprentice," Liath added. "He is a wise and peaceful man and no one will think to look for you there. He has spent many years walking the banks of the river, looking for a salmon."

"A salmon?" Fionn asked, stooping to hug the pair of old ladies.

"He's obsessed with it! He's been trying to catch a certain salmon for seven years." Bodhall laughed. "He may be a little odd, but you will be safe with him."

The boy hugged his beloved guardians and began

his journey following the River Boyne, puzzling at the thought of a man being so obsessed with catching a particular fish.

Fionn walked for miles and miles until he came upon an old shack next to the river. He could see fishing rods stacked high against the side of a rickety fence. A man with a long beard and a grey robe was muttering to himself as he starred into the water. His hands gripped tight to a rod dangling over the river. Fionn stood back and watched for a moment. He didn't want to interrupt the man, who was staring at the water with complete focus.

When Finnegas finally propped the end of his rod into a wooden Y shape stand made out of a tree branch and sat back, Fionn slowly walked over and introduced himself.

"Hello, sir, I am Fionn. I heard from my guardians, Bodhall and Liath, that you would like an apprentice. I am a hard worker and will do as you bid."

"Yes, yes, I have been expecting you. A hardworking boy is all I need to help me carry things, prepare my rods and stoke my fire. I also have a large collection of books that need dusting now and then."

"I can do that, sir," Fionn replied.

"Grand. You can sleep in the corner next to the hearth."

"Thank you," Fionn said.

"Now, go put your stuff in your corner. I am busy!" Finnegas waved his arm to dismiss Fionn. The strange man watched the water where his float bobbed up and down. There was no sign of a bite.

Fionn entered the cottage and saw it was crumbling, but it was warm as the fireplace was well stocked. In one corner was a bookcase filled with many scriptures and manuscripts. Fionn couldn't read any of them, but wondered if Finnegas might teach him one day to read.

Then he heard a mighty splash outside. Running towards the river, Fionn found Finnegas in the water, soaked from head to toe, waving his arms about and wailing. Fionn rushed over to help him, and together they hauled Finnegas back on to the riverbank, where he continued to rant and rave.

"I nearly had him! The Salmon of Knowledge! He was almost mine!" screamed Finnegas while Fionn looked on wide-eyed.

"Sir, why is that fish so important to you?" he asked tentatively.

"Don't you know that the person who first tastes

the flesh of the salmon of knowledge will gain all of the knowledge in the world? I have read many books and know many things, but I crave more wisdom. Think of what I could do with all of the knowledge it would give me! I will be able to advise the leaders of Ireland and guide us to a peaceful future if I can catch and taste the fish." Fionn raised his eyebrows – he had never heard the story of the salmon of knowledge before and felt determined he would help Finnegas to catch it. He helped Finnegas dry off. Tomorrow, he would help his master try again to capture and taste the famed Salmon of Knowledge.

The next day, Finngas woke up Fionn at the crack of dawn. Groggily, Fionn ate some bread and then was tasked with setting up four fishing rods along the riverbank.

"With you here I can put out even more rods to catch him!" Finnegas laughed.

The day passed lazily by. Fionn cut down some branches, dusted the books and went to check on the rods with his master. By mid-afternoon, there was still no sign of the salmon, only small perch and the occasional freshwater eel. Fionn had just gone back inside to add some more fuel to the fire when he heard a shout.

"Boy! Come here! Come here!" Fionn ran outside.

"I've got him, he's on the end of my hook!" Finnegas was standing, his heels digging into the dirt. He pulled back with all of his might. "He's the one, I can tell by how heavy he is. He's a monster of a salmon! I ... will ... not ... let ... you ... go!" Finnegas roared. With all of his might he pulled back his rod and Fionn watched as a mighty silver salmon with glistening streaks along its belly flew out of the river and hit Finnegas in the face! Fionn ran over and grabbed the fish, which was flailing and flapping all over Finnegas, covering his face with slime. Finnegas leapt to his feet, suddenly appearing to have the strength of a much younger man. Joy written all over his face, he cried to Fionn, "Quick! Take it inside and put it on the spit. I will eat it as soon as I have washed my face, put on my special robe and prepared myself for such a momentous occasion. When I tell you I am ready, bring the fish to the table."

"Yes, master," Fionn replied, wondering secretly if this really could be the fish his master had been trying to catch for seven years, or just some normal fish. It looked pretty much like every other salmon Fionn had ever seen, apart from it being bigger.

"Oh, it's finally here! The day I have been waiting for!" Finnegas chortled to himself as he made his way back to his bedroom to prepare his robes.

Fionn took the heavy fish inside and prepared it for the spit roast. The fire was blazing, so Fionn carefully placed the fish on to the spit and began turning it. He wanted to impress his master by showing him that even though he was not worldly, he could cook a fish.

Fionn was left by himself. He turned the spit, making sure the fish was getting nice and brown on one side. Then he would rotate the handle some more. The fish was releasing a wonderful aroma, and Fionn started to feel hungry. His stomach was rumbling too. Yet, he knew that to keep his position as apprentice, he was not allowed to even have one bite of this salmon until Finnegas had had his fill. He might be lucky to get some leftovers.

"Master, the fish is nearly ready!" Fionn turned the spit one last time to brown the skin a little more, but as he did so, a speck of hot fish fat popped up and scalded his thumb. Without thinking, Fionn immediately stuck his thumb into his mouth to cool it down and ease the soreness. He felt woozy for a moment. And then he stood up – straighter than normal. He blinked his eyes. Things seemed a lot clearer.

Just then, Finnegas came into the room. He was wearing a bright green robe and a red sash belt. His beard swung to the side. He looked at the fish, which was ready to be devoured. Then he looked at his apprentice, who was standing quietly and saying nothing. A shot of fear rushed through Finnegas. "Have you eaten any of my fish?" he demanded.

"No, master! I would never do such a thing," Fionn exclaimed. "I know how important the fish is to you," he finished, rubbing his thumb as it was still very sore.

"Something has changed about you, boy. I can see it. You stand taller than before. Your eyes are clearer; they know much more." Finnegas looked at the salmon to see if any meat had been taken from it. He examined the back as well as the front, but the fish still looked whole.

"Master Finnegas . . . I never. . ." Fionn sucked his thumb again, trying to ease the pain.

"Why are you sucking your thumb?" Finnegas asked.

"I burnt my finger when I was turning the salmon on the spit. I sucked my thumb to ease the pain. . ." Realization dawning on him, Fionn, now the wisest man in the whole country, knew exactly what had happened! "Master, it was an accident. My thumb . . . I was the first to taste the salmon . . . I'm so sorry!"

Finnegas held up his hand. Fionn expected his master to weep, but he didn't.

"If you are the first to have tasted the Salmon of Knowledge, then fate made it so. There is no coincidence that I caught it today, the day after you arrived. It must have been waiting for you all along, my friend." Finnegas came and hugged Fionn, and told him that now he would help him use his knowledge for good. Despite being disappointed, he could not be angry at the young warrior, for now Fionn was not only strong and brave, but destiny had chosen him to be the wisest man in all of Ireland. And with Finnegas's guidance, Fionn went on to be one of the best and wisest leaders in all the land.

The Farmer, His Sister and the Open Door

PAKISTAN

Local storytellers from the Pakistani region would have gathered around a campfire and told this comical tale of stubbornness and pride. The first known publication of the story is by Reverend Charles Swynnerton, who was the senior chaplain to the Indian Government and collected the stories he heard in his time in India and Pakistan in an 1892 book called Folktales from the Upper Indus.

Once upon a time in a small village in Pakistan, a farmer and his sister sat down after a long day's work to eat their supper around the fireplace. Both of them were hungry and in their rush to grab something to eat, neither of them had bothered to shut the front door. It stood gaping open with the dark night outside. The brother noticed a cool breeze was making his food go cold.

"Sister, I think you forgot to shut the door."

"I think you have it wrong, dear brother, it is you who forgot to shut it."

"No, no, you are definitely wrong. I am sure you came in after me and, as so, it is your duty to shut the door behind you."

"My duty? You forgot to shut the door when you came in, not I, and so you must shut it."

This went on for some time with neither the farmer nor his sister relenting. As they argued, the door remained wide open and the house became colder and colder. The fire started to die and the embers turned to ash as the wind ripped through the house. The brother was wondering what he could do to get his sister to shut the door because he was sure he had not left it open. He knew she loved a competition and so he came up with an idea. He would make a bet with her and then, if she lost, which he thought she most certainly would, he could get her to do all of his chores for a whole year.

"I am going to go to bed. If you will not shut the door and I am not going to shut the door, then let's have a bet. Whoever is the first to speak will shut the door, and the loser also has to do the other's chores for a whole year," said the farmer.

The farmer's sister was especially happy that her brother had set this challenge, as she was very good at keeping quiet. Her brother was the town gossip and so she was sure he would be the first one to speak. The idea that her brother would do her washing and carrying for a whole year was very appealing. The sister was sure she was going to win and agreed readily.

"I know I will win because I am the oldest and always beat you at any game," said the brother.

"Nonsense! I will surely win because your mouth is like a river and your words like water, always flowing out of you!" The sister folded her arms across her chest and glared at her brother, who she lived with, worked with and spent most of her time with. He was always trying to get her to do his jobs. But this time she was not going to give in.

"You will lose because you are always losing things, like yesterday when you lost your scarf!" her brother gloated.

"That does not make sense! And you will lose because . . . well, because you will!" the sister huffed from her chair to the stairwell.

"So shall we begin?" the farmer asked, following up the stairs.

"Indeed we shall," the sister replied. She turned to look at him.

"On the count of three, we shall no longer speak. The one who utters the first word must get up and shut the door," the farmer replied. "Are you ready? One, two, three." The sister pulled an imaginary lock across her mouth to indicate that her lips were well and truly sealed, turned her back on her brother and went up to bed.

They lay in their bedrooms shivering. A cold ache was creeping into their bones, their toes were like ice blocks, and yet still neither of them would get out of bed and shut the front door.

Suddenly, they heard a sound in the kitchen.

Silently, they both crept downstairs and saw a huge brown dog eating the food from their cupboards, his great big paws leaving marks all over the floor. Both used their hands to shoo the dog out. The farmer almost shut the door behind the dog, but remembered their wager at the last moment. He would most definitely not be the one to shut the door. He sniffed when he realized he had almost done the very thing he was trying not to do.

The sister smiled. She knew she had almost won. She turned and went back upstairs to bed. The farmer lay on the floor in the kitchen to make sure the big dog did not return. He woke in the middle of the night, his teeth chattering and his back aching.

The next day the door remained wide open.

The farmer's sister took some grain to her neighbour's house to have it made into flour that she could sell in the market, as the two of them were in need of money to replace the food that the dog had eaten. Meanwhile, the farmer had an appointment with the barber, who came to the house once a week to cut his hair and trim his beard. The farmer sat down on the wooden bench and the barber took out his scissors.

"How would you like your hair today?" asked

the barber. The farmer could not think clearly after having such a bad night's sleep. He shrugged his shoulders. The barber thought it strange that the man was not uttering a word. He began to cut and hoped the man would tell him when to stop. However, the man did not utter a single word, and soon the barber had taken all of the man's hair off his head. His head looked like a shiny boiled egg.

The barber hid his confusion and asked, "Do you want me to trim your facial hair?"

The farmer, drowsy but determined not to say anything, nodded his head. But he had meant to shake it. The barber began trimming the beard of the farmer. He had cut most of it off when the farmer realized what the barber was doing. Standing up quickly, the farmer put up his hands to protest, rage written large across his face. The barber stopped what he was doing, frightened at this strange, silent and very angry man.

Trying to think of something that would calm the farmer down, the barber asked if the farmer would prefer some black colour painted on his bald head to tone down the shininess. With the farmer *still* not saying a single word, the barber began to paint on dye. The black dye started to burn the farmer's head as soon as it touched his scalp, but he could not protest without speaking. So determined was he not to lose the bet with his sister, that instead of telling the barber what was happening, he began jumping up and down, grimacing and moving his hands like he was possessed.

"Is it too hot? The door is already wide open. What would you like me to do?" the barber asked, concerned that things were getting out of hand.

The farmer ran to the bucket in the corner and doused himself in water.

The barber was horrified. He didn't understand why on earth the farmer wouldn't speak and was looming over him, drenched, bald and covered in dye which was dripping down his face.

"I want my payment and I shall be on my way," the barber said, his voice quavering. The farmer shook his head firmly. He had no money until his sister came back with the proceeds from the sale of the flour.

"I want my money!" demanded the barber. Again, the farmer shrugged. Now it was the turn of the barber to be angry. He wanted his money and he wanted it now! The barber stood menacingly over the farmer. He was a big man and the farmer felt afraid. Stumbling to his feet, the farmer got up and started to run around the room as the barber chased him. He would get his payment whether the farmer liked his hairstyle or not. Round and round they ran, the farmer dodging the barber, who was trying to whip him with his towel.

"Come back here, you fiend!" the barber shouted. "I want my money!"

In the open doorway, the sister appeared. She saw her brother in a very sorry state being chased by the blustery barber with his hot towel. She couldn't help herself. It was such a sight! She burst out laughing.

"What in the world has happened to you?" she asked. But instead of telling her about the terrible morning he'd had, the farmer shouted out, "Ha! You spoke first. Now shut the door!"

"With pleasure, dear brother! Here barber, take these coins for your trouble." She handed the barber his payment as he grumbled out of the front door. Then, she shut it behind him!

"I am the winner!" the farmer boasted, jumping into the air and clapping his hands.

"Are you? Are you really?" The sister held up a mirror to her brother's face. He looked at his reflection and then burst into tears.

"What a fool I have been!" he said. "Look at my shiny bald head! And my precious beard is no more."

"Come, let's make a fire and we'll not fight any more," the sister said, giving her brother a squeeze on the arm.

The two of them lived together for a long time, sharing the chores, and both of them always made sure that the front door was shut behind them.

The Girl they Called Pigling

KOREA

*European readers may recognize this as a similar story
to our own "Cinderella". Indeed, this tale can be found in
different variations all around the world: in Vietnam it is
"Tam and Cam"; in Nigeria, "Chinye"; and in Iraq, "The
Little Red Fish and the Clog of Gold". The first English
translation of this Korean version was a William Elliot
Griffis retelling that was published in* The Unmannerly
Tiger and Other Korean Fairy Tales *in 1911.*

*L*ong, long ago in ancient Korea lived a girl called Pear Blossom. She lived with her ageing mother and father in a large house, which was made of wood pillars and beams. On the roof, grey tiles lay in lines, the corner edges curling up slightly to ward off evil spirits. But such measures could not stop death visiting the house, and one day Pear Blossom's mother was taken by fever, leaving Pear Blossom and her father alone.

They missed her terribly. However, time continued to pass and Pear Blossom's father watched her grow into a fine young woman. But Pear Blossom knew her father missed his job travelling on important business, the job he had given up to raise her once her mother had died.

"Father, please go back to work. I will be fine alone here," she begged him, hating the feeling that she was holding him back.

But her father thought otherwise.

"You are still too young to be left alone. I've been thinking – it might be time to find a new wife. That way you will have someone to keep you safe while I am away." Pear Blossom was unsure, but she wanted her father to be happy. And so he consulted a matchmaker. In the neighbouring village, a widow was looking for a husband; she had a daughter the same age as Pear Blossom, called Violet. Pear Blossom's father was content with the match and the pair married swiftly.

Within a few weeks, Pear Blossom's father prepared to go away for business. "Be good for your new mother," he bid his daughter. "Do as she asks and I shall see you when I get back." He embraced his family and left on horseback.

Sadly, it did not take long for things to sour. The two sisters shared the bedroom, and Pear Blossom noticed that Violet would watch her when she was brushing her hair, or when she was putting on her make-up.

One morning, she saw her stepsister whispering into her mother's ear. Immediately, her stepmother spoke.

"Violet cannot sleep properly with you in the room. You snore," she proclaimed. Pear Blossom was sure that she did not snore, but remembered that her father had told her to do whatever her stepmother asked of her.

"You will sleep in the hay next to the pigsty; they will not be disturbed by your snoring," her new mother told her. Pear Blossom was shocked but she had no choice, for she knew she must obey her stepmother. That night, she slept in the hay next to the sty with only a thin blanket covering her. She shivered in the night, wondering when her father would come home.

The next morning as Pear Blossom served breakfast, Violet began to sniff the air. Then she held her nose as Pear Blossom walked past with the rice. "Pear Blossom, you will now be called Pigling as you smell like a pig," Violet said, sneering at Pear Blossom's beautiful face.

"I am your elder, and as the oldest sister, I should have all of the best things in the house. Not only will I have your bedroom, but I shall take your clothes too." She threw a ragged old dress at Pear Blossom to wear. From then on, Pear Blossom was known only as Pigling: little pig girl. Pear Blossom missed her father desperately and hoped every night that the next morning would bring his return, and with that, her release from her new place as a servant in the family.

A few weeks later, an invitation arrived for the family to a wonderful celebration. The magistrate of the village nearby was looking for a new bride. To celebrate, there would be three days of feasting, starting with a procession on the first day, a picnic on the second day and a dance on the third day. All families of good breeding who had girls of marriageable age were invited.

"Oh, this is so exciting!" said Pear Blossom as she read the letter.

Violet snatched the letter from Pear Blossom. "Do you think the magistrate would want a bride dressed in rags?" she sneered. Her mother nodded in agreement. Pear Blossom knew that Violet was jealous of her beauty and would want nothing more than to get rid of her so she could marry the magistrate.

"Well, no, but the letter says everyone in the family can attend and I would love to see the procession."

"Dearest Pigling, I'm afraid you will not be able to go unless you finish your chores," her stepmother told her. She bought in a huge jug that came up to Pear Blossom's chest.

"You will fill this pot to the top with water from the well," her stepmother said.

"But this jug leaks – look here at this hole the size of my hand," cried Pear Blossom. She pointed to the gaping hole in the side.

However, her stepmother only laughed, and Pear Blossom was left to fill a broken jug as Violet and her cruel mother finished eating and got ready for the procession. They walked out of the courtyard and did not look back. Pear Blossom could hear them still laughing as they went.

"It is no good. I can never fill this broken jug. I will never get to see the magistrate's procession."

Suddenly, a mist of black soot swirled out of the fireplace and dived into the centre of the jug. A loud croaking sounded from within. Trembling with fear, Pear Blossom peered cautiously inside the jug. Inside the large jug was a grey frog-like creature looking back at her.

"Do not cry, Pear Blossom, for I am a Tokgabi, and I will help you," it said. Pear Blossom had heard of the magical soot sprites that lived in the flumes of chimneys and had the ability to shapeshift. A Tokgabi played pranks on people it didn't like, but they also were known for helping kitchen maids with their work.

He proceeded to work as fast as lightning, smoothing clay with his webbed feet to mend the cracked pot. It soon looked like new. Then the Tokgabi hopped to the well and in his mouth he held a massive amount of water which he poured into the jug, filling it to the top in seconds. Pear Blossom watched with disbelief as the water overflowed. The impossible task was complete in just a few moments.

"Thank you!" she cried, astounded at the Tokgabi's kindness.

"Now go, go see the procession!"

Stammering her thanks, Pear Blossom rushed off over the hills to the village. Ashamed of her ragged clothes, she hid in a tree to watch as the colourful procession marched through the streets with flags and musicians playing wonderful songs. She was filled with joy. She ran back home and arrived at the same time as her step family.

Violet and her mother could not believe their eyes. How had Pear Blossom mended and filled the jug so quickly?

"This is not right! Tell me how you did it!" screamed Violet, inspecting the jug with confusion. But as she clutched it, the jug started to shake. Violet tried to pry her hand away, but before she could let go, the jug tipped up and soaked her! Pear Blossom put her hand to her mouth to conceal her smile.

"Mother, she's laughing! I am drenched! It's all her fault!" Violet yelled. Her mother quickly ushered her into the house to dry off, looking back at Pear Blossom suspiciously.

The next day was the day of the magistrate's picnic at the meadow. Pear Blossom prepared food for everyone, including herself.

"There is no point you making food for yourself as you will have to stay at home to finish your chores," her stepmother said.

"And who would want someone smelling like you at a picnic?" sneered Violet. "The magistrate is bound to notice me today, not a smelly pig girl."

"Come, Pigling, you have a big job ahead of you and so won't have time for the picnic." Her stepmother dragged in three large sacks of rice to the kitchen.

"You must take each grain of rice and remove its husk. I want to see only polished white rice by the time we return," demanded the stepmother. "Remember, you have to do as I say or your father will be displeased." The stepmother was content to know that Pear Blossom would be trapped at home. She knew Pear Blossom was much prettier than her own daughter, and so wanted her nowhere near the picnic. She and her daughter left with their baskets full of the fine food that Pear Blossom had prepared.

Pear Blossom felt sad that she would not be able to join in the picnic. She so wanted to meet the Magistrate and have fun like everyone else. She sat on the floor and wondered how she would be able to complete the seemingly impossible task. But then with a *whoosh*, out of the chimney flew the black soot sprite, who swirled once more around the kitchen. The Tokgabi had returned! This time it transformed into a flock of small, tweeting sparrows. They tipped over the bags of rice and began to remove the brown husks from each grain with their tiny beaks. Pear Blossom watched with baited breath as the birds fluttered this way and that, and in no time they had unhusked the three full sacks of rice, which lay in pristine mounds on the ground.

"Thank you! Thank you!" Pear Blossom called out to the Tokgabi as the birds flapped away through the door and sat in the trees.

"Go to the picnic!" the Tokgabi urged. Pear Blossom grabbed a small parcel of food and ran to the picnic. She sat near the stream and watched as families ate and laughed in the sunshine. Soon the magistrate emerged from his grand home at the foot of the park. Pear Blossom smiled to see such a handsome man – she was sure she would have no chance of being his bride dressed in rags, but today she was happy to be free from her chores and out in the open like everyone else.

On their return, the evil stepmother and Violet could not believe their eyes.

"How can this be? You will tell me now! How did you unhusk three whole sacks of rice in one day? It's impossible," declared Violet in a rage.

"It was the birds – the birds helped me," Pear Blossom replied, smiling as she wondered if they would believe such a fantastic story.

"Lies! She is lying! Bird do not shed husks, they eat rice." Violet said. She was so enraged that she strode outside to the birds to shoo them away. The birds flew high above her head and happily sent droppings on to her fine gown and hair.

"Arghhh, I don't know how, but the little Pigling did this to me!" cried Violet, running indoors. This time Pear Blossom could not contain her laughter. She ran to the birds and thanked them. Like before, they turned into a black mist which flew into the fireplace.

The next day was the day of the dance and the final day when the magistrate would choose a bride. Violet and her mother put on their best gowns and made Pear Blossom tend to their hair.

"Pigling, oh dear Pigling. You may go to the dance today, but only when you have pulled up every weed on our land."

"Dirty Pigling will never be able to do that. Mother, you are so clever," muttered Violet happily. The land that Pigling's father owned was vast. It would take her weeks to pull up every weed and unwanted plant. Violet and Stepmother left in their fancy outfits for the dance, and poor Pear Blossom tried not to feel sad that she couldn't go as it was her last chance to meet the magistrate. But she thought to herself that perhaps it was for the best: she no longer had any beautiful clothes to attend the ball as Violet had taken all of hers.

Pear Blossom wept and wept as she got her gardening equipment ready. She knew this task was impossible and she would never be able to go to the dance.

However, just as before, a swirl of black soot flew from the chimney and a black oxen suddenly appeared before her. It looked Pear Blossom straight in the eye and then began chewing the weeds like a speeding train. He ate all the weeds in the field to the front, then he pulled all the weeds from the fields at the side and finally he demolished all the weeds from the back of the house. When he was finished, the oxen led her back to the house. Inside the kitchen on the table was the most beautiful gown and sandals Pear Blossom had ever seen.

"Go, now – wash and put these clothes on. You shall go to the dance!" said the Tokgabi.

"Oh Tokgabi, how can I ever thank you? This is so wonderful! I can go to the dance!" said Pear Blossom, excited to see the magistrate and all the nobles in their exquisite clothes.

The Tokgabi disappeared in a familiar cloud of black dust and flew up the chimney. Pear Blossom washed and changed into clothes that the Tokgabi had given to her, and ran quickly along the river, breathing in the fresh air and marvelling at the beauty of the land around her. It had been so long since she had been clean and worn fine clothes that her heart was full of joy.

"Ow!" shouted Pear Blossom, lifting her foot up in pain. Something small and hard dug into her foot. She stopped by the bank of the river to remove her sandal, discovering a large pebble trapped inside. As she was bending over, a grand procession approached. Four men were carrying a palanquin between them, the chair high on their shoulders.

Pear Blossom did not know that the magistrate was inside, but he looked out of the curtain and saw her. Struck by her beauty, he told one of the guards to ask her to stop. But the guard had a gruff voice and called out in a stern manner. "You there, stop a moment!" and Pear Blossom feared that her stepmother had sent him to take her back home.

She decided to run away, but in her haste, one sandal fell into the river. Pear Blossom did not look back – she took off the other sandal and ran barefoot towards the town as quickly as she could. The magistrate watched her fly past his palanquin and knew that despite all his searching for a wife, he had found no one as beautiful as the mysterious girl. He ordered his guards to fish the sandal from the river in case he could use it to find her.

At the dance, which was held in the village hall, the stepmother and Violet saw Pear Blossom arrive panting and shoeless, and they scowled.

"I can't believe it! What is she doing here? And where did she get that gown?" Violet huffed, crossing her arms in front of her.

They could not understand how the fields and gardens had been weeded in such a short time. They approached Pear Blossom, who was looking radiant despite having to run to the dance in her bare feet. She was holding one sandal in her hand.

"Why are you here? Surely you have not completed your chores," asked the stepmother with a look of disdain on her face. "I think we better go home and check you have done your work. Violet, you stay here and wait for the magistrate to arrive. Be sure to dance with him."

But it was too late. With a flurry of trumpets, the magistrate arrived and announced to the whole room,

"I have found my perfect bride. I saw her by the river, and I must find her." He brandished Pear Blossom's sandal proclaiming, "Whichever woman is the owner of the other sandal will be my bride."

Pear Blossom could not believe it. She was about to move towards him and show him that she was the one who had lost the sandal. But Violet grabbed the sandal from Pear Blossom's hand and waved it at the magistrate, pushing her way through to the front.

"It is my sandal," she lied, smiling sweetly at the magistrate. She sat down on the floor and tried to force the sandal on to her large foot. The magistrate watched, puzzled. He was certain that it wasn't this young woman who he had seen by the river.

Just then, a rumble in the chimney grew louder and louder. A bellow of black soot exploded out of the fireplace and black ash landed all over Violet. She was covered from head to toe in black soot. The sandal lifted itself into the air and flew towards Pear Blossom.

"No! Not Pigling! She doesn't deserve it!" screamed Violet, bashing her hands on the floor. Her stepmother ran over to Violet, who was having a tantrum.

"Come, get up off the floor, Violet! We must get out of here! Everyone is looking!" The two of them hobbled away chased by the Tokgabi. who transformed into a swarm of buzzing bees and sent them running back to their home village, away from Pear Blossom and her house.

Pear Blossom sat on a chair and put on the sandal. The magistrate came over and placed the other sandal on her foot.

"It's you," he said softly, gazing into Pear Blossom's eyes. "The girl by the river."

"I am!" she said shyly.

Pear Blossom could not believe it. How her luck had changed thanks to the Tokgabi. She knew the magistrate was the perfect match for her and sent a silent thanks to the Tokgabi for all his help. She stood up and the magistrate held out his hand. She took it and they spent all night dancing.

Soon after, her father arrived back from his business trip. He was happy that Pear Blossom was to marry the magistrate, but was horrified to hear how Pear Blossom had been treated in his absence.

"I am sorry, my sweet daughter. I promise, you will never again be called Pigling," he told her, and he shook the hand of his new son, the magistrate, thanking him for looking after his daughter. Together, Pear Blossom and the magistrate lived a long and happy life, blessed by the Tokgabi, who watched over them, never letting any harm befall the pair.

Little Thumbelina

DENMARK

Thumbelina was written by Hans Christen Andersen and first published in Fairy Tales Told for Children *in December 1835. It is believed that Andersen was inspired by the English tale of "Tom Thumb", which was one of the very first English fairy tales. Other tales from around the world that feature thumb-sized characters include: "Le Petit Poucet" (1697), published by Charles Perrault in France, "Garbancito" (Little Chickpea) from Spain, and as "Issun-bōshi" in Japan, which were found illustrated in the* Otogi-zōshi *(collections of writing produced between 1392–1573).*

There once was a woman who desperately wanted a child of her own to love and cherish. After many years of loneliness, a kind fairy who was passing the woman's house saw her crying. Taking pity on the poor, sad woman, she asked her why she was so unhappy.

"I would dearly love a child to look after, but I have none," the woman replied. "Is there anything you can do to help me?"

The fairy was moved by the woman's story and so gave her a small yellow seed.

"Plant this special barleycorn in a pot, cover it with soil, and tend to it regularly with water and love. When the time is right, what you wish for shall appear." With a smile at the woman's tears of joy, the fairy bid the woman a fond farewell.

Each day the woman did as the fairy had told her and watered the seed and talked to it, hoping that it would help it grow. At first she was unsure that the seed would grow at all, but she wanted a child so much she was willing to try anything. In the early days, the green shoots that sprouted from the seed were short, and the woman wondered if the fairy was playing a joke. Surely this small plant could never turn into the child she longed for. But she kept tending to the plant until one day it stood tall, with deep red velvety tulip petals sitting atop a single green thick stalk.

When the flower bud began to open, the woman was astonished to find a small girl, no bigger than the size of her thumb, curled up asleep inside. The girl awoke and, stretching her arms wide, she spoke. "Are you my mother?" asked the girl.

"Why, I am!" the woman replied.

"What is my name, dearest mother?" the girl asked.

"You shall be called Thumbelina, for you are no bigger than my thumb!" she exclaimed, smiling at her new daughter. The woman felt a great happiness that her longing was finally over, and she was overwhelmed with love for Thumbelina. Thumbelina's mother got to work straight away making a bed from a walnut shell, which she lined with moss and rose petals to make it soft and cosy. Then she began to make Thumbelina some tiny clothes from old silk handkerchiefs and stockings. The woman sang as she worked and she was astounded when the tiny girl opened her mouth and joined in – for Thumbelina had the most beautiful voice that the woman had ever heard. The pair sang and laughed together, and their days passed by happily.

One afternoon, when Thumbelina was having a nap in her walnut shell bed, a large warty grey toad hopped through the open window. He had seen the girl with her lovely bright smile and beautiful voice and wanted her to be his bride. Grabbing Thumbelina, he bounded out of the room and into the garden. The toad hopped down the path towards a dense thicket bordering the forest where Thumbelina lived.

"Please take me back home!" Thumbelina cried, but the toad ignored her pleas. After some time, they arrived at the muddy pond which was the toad's home. Thumbelina closed her eyes, hoping that it was all a bad dream. But when she opened them again, she discovered the toad had placed her on a water lily leaf in the middle of the pond as his prisoner. From the muddy bank, the toad croaked out, "Sing for me!"

"Never!" Thumbelina declared.

"If you refuse to sing for me, then I shall leave you alone on that leaf until you change your mind. I shall return tomorrow and I am sure you will have a different answer after a cold night in the middle of the pond!" and with that, the toad leapt away.

Thumbelina looked around the pond for a way she might escape. There were no sticks nearby to make an oar, and no one to help. She had never been alone before and everything was so big and scary outside. Her mother had told her to sing when she felt worried. So Thumbelina began to sing a song.

> *Trapped on this island*
> *Scared and unsure*
> *Is there a way*
> *I can escape before dawn?*
> *Toad is unkind*
> *And I want to go home*
> *Can anyone help me?*
> *Or am I all alone?*

A group of little fish were swimming nearby and heard the beautiful song. They felt sorry for the poor, sad girl and decided they would help her. Working together, they began to gnaw at the stalk that attached the water lily to the bottom of the pond. Before long, the job was finished and they pulled the leaf holding Thumbelina safely to the side of the pond.

"Thank you all so much for rescuing me!" Thumbelina cried, stroking the fish to say thank you. "Now I must get home to my mother – she will be so worried about me!" The fish watched as Thumbelina ran off into the forest toward her mother's house as fast as her little legs could go. But as she was so small, everything looked the same and she couldn't remember the exact way the toad has brought her.

Alone and afraid, Thumbelina ran and ran. The forest was a strange and dark place now that dusk had arrived: the trees were huge and she spied many creatures that she had never seen before crawling, scuttling and buzzing about. She wept, knowing that her mother would be missing her, and despairing that she would ever return home to her cosy bed and her mother's love.

As the night grew closer and Thumbelina was no nearer to home, she knew she must make ready to stay in the forest overnight. Working hard, Thumbelina made a shelter against the rain and wind under a large dock leaf using long blades of grass as her bed. It was a cold and dark night and Thumbelina slept fitfully, worrying that she would never return home again.

In the morning, she awoke to birds of all kinds chirping and tweeting, and she saw them flying up above her head. She marvelled as they soared in the sky and wished she too could fly as high. Then, maybe, she could find her way back home again.

As many days passed and autumn approached, Thumbelina was no closer to finding her way home. The leaves began to change from green to brown, crumpling into pieces as she tried to forge a roof each night to sleep under. Food was becoming scarce and few of the wild creatures in the forest wanted anything to do with her.

When snow began to fall, Thumbelina knew she could not stay where she was or else she would freeze to death. She searched and searched for somewhere she could go. One day, on the edge of a field, she found a little door in the side of a hill. She knocked and hoped whoever lived there would help her. An old field mouse answered and saw the girl shivering in the cold.

"Good gracious, you must be freezing out there! Quickly, come in. My home is warm and you can rest your weary body." The mouse seemed very friendly and Thumbelina gratefully accepted.

"Thank you so much," replied Thumbelina, who

was tired and hungry. The mouse fed Thumbelina and showed her a place where she could sleep on some moss.

"Now, I don't mind you staying for a few days, but I'm afraid I only have enough food for myself over winter. But my neighbour Mole is very rich and will be coming over tomorrow. He might have room for you to stay all winter, and you can entertain us. Do you know any stories?"

"Not really," said Thumbelina, "but I can sing."

"Very well," said Field Mouse "Mole's sight is poor, so a song will be welcomed."

The next day Mole arrived and Thumbelina sang to him about the ladybird flying away and the bees collecting pollen. Mole was quite taken with the small child.

"I want you to come live with me," he said. "I am richer than Field Mouse and you can sing more songs about what you have seen. It will be a wonderful way to pass the cold winter."

Thumbelina was unsure about living under-ground in the dark with Mole. She dreaded the thought of not seeing daylight again. However, she had little choice, and decided that being warm and dry was the most she could hope for. So Thumbelina set off with Mole to his underground house.

As Thumbelina followed Mole through the winding tunnels to his house, Mole stopped abruptly. There, blocking the path, was a bird lying very still. Thumbelina felt tears welling up in her eyes. How sad, she thought: it must have got trapped underground and couldn't find its way out. She had seen birds like this one swooping gracefully in the sky and knew it was a swallow. She noticed how the bird's glossy blue-black feathers were dirty and its eyes were closed.

"Is there something we can do?" she asked Mole.

"The bird is dead; there's nothing else we can do but leave him. I will make a hole up to the surface so that when the body rots, the smell doesn't overwhelm us." Then he proceeded to use his heavy claws to scrape a tunnel up to the surface, allowing some sunlight to creep into the underground cavern. He then reappeared and carried on ahead of Thumbelina. She turned back to give the bird one last look and noticed that its red throat twitched slightly. She gasped, calling out to Mole, "Stop! The bird is still alive – we should help him!' But Mole shrugged. "It will soon be dead. Birds are always trouble," he muttered crossly and carried on with his journey. Thumbelina felt dreadful that she must leave the bird untended, but she had no choice but to follow the mole to his home.

Days went by in Mole's home and Thumbelina felt restless. Mole was kind to Thumbelina, enjoying her songs and her chatter, but he was dull company. While Thumbelina pretended to be happy, part of her couldn't forget the swallow that she had seen trapped in the tunnels. Scraping her courage together, she decided she had to act.

"May I go out for a while?" she asked.

"Don't be too long, will you?" the mole replied. "I like to have you close by."

Quickly, Thumbelina rushed along the dark tunnels and came across the bird still lying on its side. Again, she thought she saw the bird move slightly.

"Are you alive, my friend?" she whispered. She placed her head on the chest of the bird and sure enough, she heard the *thump*, *thump* of its heart. It was alive! She vowed to help the poor creature, and crept along the tunnels until she found some warm moss to cover him and some water from a curled-up leaf for him to drink.

"Thank you for helping me," the swallow whispered. "My wing got caught on some wire and I managed to squeeze myself into this burrow before the snow fell. But my fellow swallows flew off to warmer countries and the mole who lives here does not like birds, so I could not ask him for help."

"I'm so sorry you have been all alone out here. How you must miss your friends," Thumbelina cried. "Just like I miss my mother."

From that day onwards, once Thumbelina had sung to the mole, she came to visit her new friend. The swallow was gaining strength as she nursed him back to health, sneaking him titbits from her dinner and making sure he always had soft, fresh moss for his bed. She didn't tell Mole what she was doing as she knew he wouldn't like it – he wanted Thumbelina all for himself and often said that he didn't know what he would do without her when the spring came.

A week or two passed by and the swallow was making good progress in his recovery with the help of Thumbelina. As the snow began to melt with the warmth of the springtime sun, Thumbelina knew that the swallow would soon be strong enough to leave the underground tunnel. She thought wistfully of the swallow swooping through the air – she, too, longed to be free of the gloomy dirt cavern and wished she could somehow find her way back home to her mother.

The mole also knew that spring was approaching and, reluctant to lose Thumbelina, kept her so busy that she didn't have a moment to herself. This was too much for Thumbelina to bear. While the mole was distracted with his lunch, she fled from his house, calling out to her swallow friend who was stretching his wings in the cramped tunnel. "I am ready to leave this place, dear Thumbelina," the swallow said. "Thanks to you, my wing has healed and I can fly again."

"Please take me with you!" Thumbelina begged.

Just then she heard a sound. It was Mole rushing through the tunnels looking for her.

"Where are you, child? Come back this instant. I want you to tell me a story or sing me a song. You owe me that much for feeding and housing you. Where are you?"

The bird looked at Thumbelina and knew he must help her as she had helped him.

"Come, get on to my back!" he said. And just as the mole turned the corner, the swallow soared high out of the hole in the tunnel above his head. Thumbelina laughed as the swallow flew higher and higher. She couldn't believe she was finally flying like a bird as she had dreamt of so long ago.

"Where would you like to go?" the swallow asked her.

"Home," she said "The toad took me to a dirty pond past a forest; it can't be far from the cottage where I was taken from."

The swallow knew where there was such a pond and began the long journey towards it. Over the forest and round the pond he flew until he spied a cottage nearby.

The window was open and they flew in. Thumbelina's mother was sitting, sad and alone by the fire. She looked up as Thumbelina called her name, wiping her eyes. Her daughter had returned. Weeping joyfully, she hugged her little child and thanked the swallow for bringing her back.

"It is the least I could do for Thumbelina's kindness," he said. "How could I leave her all alone in the dark when she lit up my loneliest, darkest moments?" Enclosing his wings around Thumbelina in a hug, he bid farewell and promised to return when he could.

Overjoyed to be reunited, Thumbelina sat in her mother's palm and told her about her adventures, and the two were never parted again.

Little Red Riding Hood

FRANCE

One of the earliest printed versions of this famous story is by French folklorist Charles Perrault, called Le Petit Chaperon Rouge. *The story was included in his Mother Goose Collection in 1697. It was in Perrault's version that the red riding hood was given centre stage. Later, the Brothers Grimm adapted the story in their famous collection of tales,* Children and Household Tales, *now known as* Grimms' Fairy Tales.

Once upon a time in a small village, a little girl lived with her mother. She was known throughout the village as Little Red Riding Hood for the red cap and cloak she constantly wore, which had been made by her favourite grandmother. The material was a rich crimson and made of lush velvet. Red Riding Hood was a kind girl and was happiest when she was helping around the house and garden. She especially enjoyed picking fruit from the nearby orchard to make pies and crumbles with her mother.

After one baking session, Red Riding Hood's mother asked her to take some freshly baked cakes and fruit cordial to her grandmother, who lived in a small cottage on the other side of the wood.

"Grandmother has been unwell these last few days and these treats will be the perfect way to help her recover her strength," her mother said.

"Of course, mother, I shall go to her straight away," Red Riding Hood replied, gathering up the cakes and bottles and placing them carefully into her basket.

"Mind you stay on the path and don't talk to any strangers," her mother warned her. "Make haste now, I want you home before sunset."

Little Red Riding Hood set off happily along the path, humming a tune as she went. The sun shone brightly, and colourful butterflies of orange, black and gold flew around the wild flowers that grew beside the path. A large butterfly landed on a bluebell and Red Riding Hood was entranced by the beautiful pattern on its wings. Wanting a closer look, she followed the fluttering butterfly into the long grass, completely forgetting her mother's warning that she must stay on the path.

Not long after Little Red Riding Hood left the path, a huge wolf spied her from where he was napping in the long grass. "What a juicy morsel!" he thought, licking his chops at the thought of gobbling her up. Crouching down, he gathered himself to spring at the little girl. Just before he pounced he suddenly remembered the huntsman who lived nearby in the woods. The wolf knew that if he leapt on Little Red Riding Hood straight away, the huntsman would hear her cry and rescue her. *This requires a cunning plan*, he thought. Thinking hard, a sly grin spread across his face. He had just the right idea.

"Good day, young lady!" the wolf cried, stepping out from behind a tree and smiling his friendliest smile. "What are you doing in the woods on a fine day like this?" Red Riding Hood completely forgot what her mother had said about talking to strangers in the face of such a charming creature and smiled back happily at the wolf.

"Why, I'm going to see my grandmother who lives on the other side of the woods. We made her some cake and fruit cordial. I picked the fruit myself," Red Riding Hood said proudly.

"Marvellous!" said the wolf. His ears pricked up greedily, thinking of how he might even have two meals instead of one, if he played his cards right. "Tell me, where exactly does your grandmother live?"

"Through the woods, next to the stream, and not far from the old windmill."

"Ah, I know the place," the wolf replied kindly. "You are such a considerate granddaughter. I am sure that your grandmother will be even happier with your visit if you pick her a bunch of these beautiful wild flowers. Look! They are growing all around us."

"Yes, you are right!" said Red Riding Hood excitedly, knowing her grandmother would love such a thing. Eagerly, she began to gather as many flowers as she could. The wolf, still smiling to himself, bid her goodbye and raced down the path towards the cottage Little Red Riding Hood had described. He knocked on the door.

Knock! Knock!

"Yes? Who is it?" a frail voice called out.

"It's me, your granddaughter Red Riding Hood. I have some cake and fruit cordial for you," said the wolf in a high-pitched voice, mimicking Little Red Riding Hood as closely as he could.

"Lift up the latch, my dear, and come in. I'm so happy you have come to see me." Bounding inside, the wolf swept into the room and gobbled up Red Riding Hood's grandmother in one big gulp. He licked his lips, enjoying his meal with a toothy smile. But remembering Little Red Riding Hood, his mouth started to water again. He had not eaten for days and he definitely had room for dessert. Thinking quickly, the wolf wriggled into the night clothes that were folded at the end of the bed. Next, he placed a frilly cap low on his head and round glasses over his eyes. He hopped into the large springy double bed and pulled the woolly blankets up to hide his furry body. Now he looked just like Red Riding Hood's grandma. All he had to do was wait for the little girl to come knocking and she would be his. His tummy rumbled in anticipation.

He didn't have to wait long. Soon, Red Riding Hood arrived and knocked on the door.

"Yes, who is it?" the wolf called out in his best elderly voice.

"Grandmother! It's me, Red Riding Hood," she said, proud of herself for arranging the flowers into a neat bunch.

"Come in, my child!" the wolf replied in a high sing-song voice, trying his best to sound like a little old lady. Through the heavy door, Little Red Riding Hood didn't notice any difference to her grandmother's usual voice. The room was dark when Red Riding Hood stepped inside, the heavy curtains firmly closed so she didn't spot that the wolf was a different shape to her grandmother tucked up in bed. Squinting a little, she took out the cake and cordial and placed them on to the wooden table. Then she carefully arranged the flowers in an empty jug she found in the kitchen, and placed them on her grandmother's bedside table. All seemed well until Little Red Riding Hood suddenly noticed something slightly odd about her grandmother.

She looked a little more closely. Her grandmother didn't look herself at all. *She must be really ill*, thought Red Riding Hood.

"Grandmother, what big eyes you have."

"All the better to see you with, my child," the wolf replied.

"And your ears, they have become all large and..." Red Riding Hood didn't want to upset her grandmother by insulting her hairy ears. But they really had become very hairy.

"All the better to hear you with, my dear," the wolf replied, wondering when he should pounce on his second meal of the day.

"And your teeth! Your teeth... They are so ... so sharp," said Red Riding Hood, taking a step back, her hands trembling at the sight in front of her.

"All the better to EAT you with!" The wolf leapt out of the bed, still wearing grandmother's night dress. He tried to grab Red Riding Hood but his huge belly was too full and heavy after his recent meal for him to move very quickly. Red Riding Hood seized the jug of flowers from beside the bed and threw it at him with all her might. It smashed into hundreds of pieces, making an enormous crash.

Luckily for Little Red Riding Hood, the huntsman that the wolf had been so keen to avoid was walking outside the cottage just at that moment. Hearing the commotion, he ran to the door of the cottage and saw the wolf crouching over Little Red Riding Hood with his mouth open wide, ready to take a big bite. The huntsman acted immediately and swept into the room, raising his axe and giving the wolf a mighty blow to the head, felling him cold to the floor. Red Riding Hood couldn't believe how close she had been to being eaten up. Horrified, she ran around the cottage looking for her grandmother, but she was nowhere to be seen. Little Red Riding Hood gulped, looking at the wolf's big belly.

"Don't worry, Little Red Riding Hood, I think I know where she is," said the huntsman, and using a sharp hunting knife, he opened up the wolf from top to tail. With a huge heave, he pulled out Little Red Riding Hood's grandmother, who was shaking with fright. The wolf had been in such a hurry for his meal that he had swallowed her whole without taking a single bite!

"Thank you!" she exclaimed. "I'm so glad you found me! I thought for sure I would suffocate in there. You are my heroes." She hugged Red Riding Hood tightly, clutching her.

As the huntsman turned to leave, slinging the wolf over his shoulder, Red Riding Hood thanked him over and over again for coming to their rescue. She packed a piece of cake and a flask of cordial and gave it to him to have on his journey.

Grandmother and Red Riding Hood ate the rest of the cake for tea and Little Red Riding Hood resolved that she would never again be taken in by a smiling stranger.

Maui: The Demigod and Trickster

POLYNESIA

Of all of the myths of the Polynesian Islands (which include Hawaii, Samoa, New Zealand as well as many others) none are more famous than the ones about the demigod Maui. Every island has its own versions of the stories. Even though some of the islands are thousands of miles apart, it is thought voyagers carried Maui's story with them when they settled across the seas, spreading his legend to the new islands they settled on. Maui is often seen as a clever but mischievous demigod and often is referred to as The Trickster.

Maui Hooks the Islands

It was said that Maui was raised by the gods because his mother already had four sons to look after. The gods took pity on him, knowing he wouldn't get much attention with all those older brothers, and raised him in the heavens – giving him magical powers. Maui had the ability to transform into animals, his favourite being a bird. But when he was a teenager, Maui grew bored of being around gods all day and night. He wanted to be on earth with his family.

"Let me go find my mother and my brothers," he begged the gods. "I want to be down there, not up here!"

The gods granted his wish, and he made the journey to earth, arriving at the hut of his mother, Hina.

"Who are you?" Hina asked, spying a young stranger with long black wavy hair and a strong body covered in tattoos of black ink. The strange boy ran towards her with his arms outstretched.

"I am your son, Maui," he said, suddenly coming

to a stop in front of her, feeling shy. He wanted to tell her how much he had missed having a mother around.

"Maui?" she exclaimed. "It cannot be!" She was shocked but happy to see her youngest son again. However, his brothers were not happy to meet him. They had heard of Maui the demigod with the power to transform, and they were jealous of his powers.

Maui moved in with his family, much to the annoyance of his brothers. He spent a lot of time with Hina, and this made his brothers even more jealous, for he was clearly her favourite son.

Hina knew that her sons were unhappy and tried to think of how Maui could fit in with the group a little better. One day, when her four eldest sons were out fishing, she called Maui to her. On her knee rested a gleaming white jawbone, larger than any Maui had seen before.

"What do you have there?" he asked.

"It is a gift for you. It is a magic jawbone that belonged to your grandmother. Make a fish hook from this and it will give you even more power than you already have. But I give this to you on the condition that you will make more effort with your brothers. They resent you because you don't try to befriend them. They don't know you like I do. Show them what a great man you are." Hina made Maui promise that he would go fishing with his brothers from that day onwards and work hard alongside them. Since Maui had arrived, the brothers had been out every day, and not once had Maui been out to help them.

Maui's brothers suspected he was only going because their mother had asked him to do so. As soon as he stepped on to their boat, they began teasing him.

"Maui, you have such great powers, but you are a terrible fisherman. We know you can change your shape into birds and other beasts, but what other things can you do? Your gifts are not that useful for putting food on the table and keeping our family safe."

Maui laughed. "I'll prove you wrong. Just you wait and see," he replied.

"We bring food back to our mother and you sit in the end of our boat watching the waves skim past. Why do you bother coming at all? Sit at home and play with the babies," said another brother with a laugh.

"I will show you what I can do, dear brothers, and

it will amaze you!" Maui stood up in the large canoe, and because his brothers would not give him any of their fishing bait, he made his own finger bleed and smeared the end of the magic fishing hook with it. Then he threw his fish hook into the ocean. His brothers watched on with delight as nothing seemed to happen. Maui sat back and looked relaxed. He didn't seem worried that no fish had been caught yet.

But just then. . .

The line started to tighten.

"I've got something. I told you I'd show you!" he bragged. The bottom of the canoe started to rock and shudder with the weight fighting against the line. Bigger and bigger waves formed in the ocean, and the canoe whipped from side to side like a leaf in a hurricane.

The brothers were all afraid and started to shout at Maui to stop his tricks.

Maui continued to pull the fishing line. Pulling with all his might, he yanked so hard the end of his fish hook scraped the seabed and brought up an enormous chunk of rock from the bottom of the ocean. As it came bobbing up to the surface, it transformed into a lush green island, looming behind the boat as if it had always existed. Maui laughed as he unhooked his fish hook and then lassoed it back into the ocean. Once again, he pulled up a brand new island as if it were a fish. His hands a blur, he continued to pull up island after island.

Each time a different island ascended from the ocean floor, the shape and vegetation was completely unique. Some were large and some were very small. But Maui was proud of them all.

Maui shouted out, turning to his brothers, "These are the fish I came to catch today, not little tiddler ones! Whole islands! Look how powerful I am! Now let me hear you say that I am of no use!"

Maui's brothers were indeed impressed. They sat in the boat looking out at the wonderful islands that had appeared from nowhere. Each brother wished that he had been given the power to create such magnificent islands where people could live and nature could thrive. Maui knew what they were thinking and smiled, his islands standing proudly in the ocean behind him.

MAUI'S QUEST FOR FIRE

Hina, Maui's mother, was fed up of eating raw fish.

"It's always the same – so slimy!" she complained. The family had been without fire for a long time because the volcano Hale-aka-la, once the source of all their fire, had become extinct. Without it they had lost the ability to cook, eating fruit and uncooked roots, shellfish broken from the reef and raw fish from the ocean. Maui, sick of his mother's moaning, promised to find her some fire to cook with. "I will find you fire to light the volcano again," he boasted as his brothers laughed.

One morning soon afterwards, Maui saw the water was calm and the fishing grounds could be reached. He woke his brothers, and together they paddled out to sea. When they had reached far enough from the shore they began to fish. After some time had passed, Maui looked back to the land and cried out. There was a fire on the mountainside.

"Look!" he said. "Fire is burning up there on the mountain – who does it belong to?"

"We don't know who it belongs to," said his brothers.

"We need to hurry to shore and cook our food on that fire," said another brother. Agreeing, Maui and his brothers headed for shore as quickly as they could. Bounding ahead of his brothers, Maui raced up the mountain. Higher and higher he ran until he was sure he had reached the right ridge. Maui rushed up towards the cloudy pillar of smoke – but there was no fire, and instead he saw a family of mud hens scratching the fire out. They flew away just as he reached them. Puzzled, Maui looked around. There was no one else to be seen – the birds must have made the fire themselves. Shaking his head, he resolved to watch the mud hens until he found out the secret of how they made fire.

The next morning, Maui sent his brothers fishing and he stayed behind, hiding near the place where he had found the birds. But the birds were too clever.

"There are only four brothers in the boat and the other one is missing. Maui wants to steal our secret," they exclaimed. "We will not make fire today."

For days Maui tried to follow the birds, but each day they scratched in the dirt and gave no sign of making fire. Just when Maui was about to give up, an idea came to him.

The next day, the birds counted all five brothers in the boat. "Maui must have given up," they cackled, laughing at their cleverness. However, they did not know that Maui had been clever too. He wasn't called *the trickster* for nothing. He had used some of the tapa cloth that his mother wove and rolled it up to look like a man and placed it in the boat.

Whilst his brothers were out fishing with the fake Maui, he crept near to where the mud hens were making fire. Just as the mud hens were collecting sticks to make fire, Maui pounced. As he grabbed the biggest bird, she squawked. "If you kill me, the secret of fire will perish with me!"

Maui had no intention of killing the bird, but needing her help, he promised to spare her if she would tell him what to do.

Not satisfied with giving up her secret so easily, the bird tried to outwit Maui.

"All you have to do is rub the stalks of water plants from the sea together," she said. But when Maui tried it, water ran out of the bottom instead of fire.

Then she told him to "rub reeds together" but they bent and broke and made no fire.

Frustrated, Maui grabbed the bird.

"You lied to me and now you will pay the price!" he growled, hoping he could frighten the bird into telling him the truth. And sure enough, the mud hen was afraid and quailed,

"No, please. I will tell you the secret. All you have to do is to rub two dry twigs together as fast as you can, and fire will spark between them."

Maui followed the mud hen to the tree where the twigs fell. Picking two sticks up, he rubbed them furiously together, his hands a blur as he worked. Before long a tiny plume of smoke curled from between the sticks and a flicker of flame lit the dark sky. Maui had created fire!

Whooping and laughing, he set a large branch in the ground and lit a beacon for all to see. Then he turned to the mud hen, who was blinking before the brightness of the flame, and he dragged a small flame over the feathers at the top of its head, singeing them until the bald head of the bird poked through. "This will teach you to try to outwit the great Maui," Maui boomed. And to this very day the mud hen and her offspring have bald heads as a reminder of how the Hawaiians found fire.

MAUI CATCHES THE SUN

Maui watched his mother Hina making *tapa,* a cloth from natural fibres. The wet tapa was pounded into shape using wooden mallets but, before she could finish her work, the daylight was already almost over. Working in darkness, his poor mother's eyes always hurt and her head ached. The sun seemed to move too fast in the sky for anyone to get any chores finished.

Maui wondered if there was something that he could do to stop the sun from zooming away so fast during the day. He wanted to help his mother and everyone else who was affected by the sun's quick ascent – the fishermen who couldn't catch enough fish, the farmers who couldn't work their fields and the children who just wanted to play. He decided it was his job to catch the sun and make it slow down so that the days were longer. Striding up the hill Hele-a-ka-la, which means "journey of the sun", Maui watched and waited. Soon the sun began to rise, stretching out one of its rays like a leg.

Maui wove long coconut fibres into a rope and tied it to his magic fish hook enchanted by his ancient grandmother. He stretched up and when the sun began to rise, he whirled the rope in a lasso around his head. Flinging his hook at the sun, he caught the first ray of sunlight.

"You, Sun!" he called. "You are a mischief-maker and I, Maui, son of Hina, will make you submit to my will. You are going too fast!"

At first the sun thought he would find it easy to

get out of the trap so, taking no heed of the fish hook, he tried to pull away. But the sun was caught fast, unable to move a centimetre.

"I hear you, little brother Maui. And I promise, I will change my ways. For you, I will go slowly for six months of the year and faster during the other six months."

"Hooray!" shouted Maui triumphantly. Now the sun had given its promise, he untied his fish hook, agreeing to let the sun continue on its journey across the sky.

Sure enough, the sun kept its promise to Maui. And for six months of the year, Maui's mother was able to make her cloth, bathed in sunlight, and the farmers could take care of their crops without hurrying. The people of the island renamed the hill where Maui struck his bargain the "Journey of the Sun", and it still stands today.

Sinbad the Sailor

The story of Sinbad is featured in the folk tale collection One Thousand and One Nights (often known in English as Tales of the Arabian Nights). Traditionally, Arabic folk tales were told as oral tales passing from generation to generation for thousands of years. They are rooted in ancient cultures and civilizations, including those from Persian, Egyptian, Mesopotamian and Indian influences. The collection One Thousand and One Nights was compiled during the Islamic Golden Age and written down in the fourteenth century.

Sinbad, the son of a wealthy merchant, had never been outside of Baghdad, the city he had grown up in. Baghdad was beautiful, but he longed to see more of the world. One day, Sinbad decided to act. He sold his possessions and gained passage on board a merchant ship bound for foreign lands. He was determined to learn to be a sailor, seeing new and strange lands and meeting people from around the world. He had lived a life of comfort and now wanted to find out what it took to be a real sailor.

Life aboard the ship was full of fun and excitement for Sinbad. He learnt new skills from the ship's crew, feeling useful for the first time in his life. Never before had he worked so hard, manning the sail, sweeping the deck, and feeling part of a team. The ocean was vast and Sinbad felt he had found a place he belonged. Each day he watched shoals of colourful fish swim past, he ate foods that were uncommon to his homeland, and he met all kinds of people, many of whom were different from him and spoke in unfamiliar languages. But with many smiles, he found they could communicate no matter where they were from. He was filled with happiness.

After many weeks at sea without a break, the captain of the ship spied a small island on the starboard bow side. The captain called out, "Ahoy! Let us rest our sea legs on that island. Chef can cook up a feast for us. Anchors away! We shall stop here, stretch and relax." Many of the crew were keen to get on to land once again and greeted the news with cheers.

The tiny island appeared flat and green, and Sinbad was looking forward to feeling solid ground beneath his feet. He had become used to the sway of the ship for the most part, but occasionally seasickness reared its ugly head in rough seas.

"This island isn't much bigger than our entire ship!" teased the chef as he passed Sinbad, who was tasked with carrying food down below to the area earmarked for their picnic.

"But it isn't swaying, my friend. That's a relief!" laughed Sinbad.

Sinbad walked down the gangway, his basket filled with fruit and vegetables. A few men followed carrying jugs of water. The chef arrived where Sinbad had begun to unload his basket and began to arrange firewood in a heap.

"Here, let me light the fire," said the chef, who

proceeded to rub a stick between his hands very fast, the tip causing sparks to flash left and right. Soon an impressive fire was burning.

Sinbad sniffed eagerly at the air, his mouth watering at the delicious scent of fish frying on the fire. But before he could taste the delicious fish, something strange happened. The ground beneath Sinbad's feet began to rock from side to side.

"What's happening?" cried Sinbad in panic, falling to the ground. He heard a loud bellow sounding from the depths of the island. Suddenly the ground began to lift – higher and higher into the air! The chef turned tail and ran away as fast as he could, but Sinbad couldn't find his balance. With nothing to hold on to, he could only watch as his shipmates scrambled towards the ship, leaving him stranded, clinging to a rock on the ground.

"It's not an island! It's a giant whale!" Sinbad heard the captain cry out with horror as the ship's anchor was hauled up. Without waiting for the men to return, the ship set out into the ocean, leaving Sinbad stranded on the back of the giant whale. It dipped below the water to quench the fire that had burnt its back. Terrified, Sinbad held his breath for what seemed like hours, but was only minutes. Expecting to be drowned at any moment, Sinbad was relieved when, on surfacing, the whale was peaceful once more, no longer burning with pain from the fire.

Luckily for Sinbad, the whale did not dive again for many miles. It neared a land surrounded by tropical beaches and palm trees. When Sinbad was close enough, he slid off the whale's side into the water and swam as fast as his arms and legs would take him to the sandy shore.

Exhausted, he lay on the beach and looked up to the sky. Not a cloud was to be seen. The sun burnt down on him, drying out his once-soaked clothes. He crawled to a nearby spot shaded by shrubs, and fell fast asleep.

When he woke and blinked his eyes he was sure it had all been a dream. An island that was a whale – how silly! But then he sat up and saw the sparkle of the ocean, felt the sand beneath his body, and he realized that it was not a dream as he had hoped but he was in fact stranded on a desert island. His ship was nowhere to be seen.

Sinbad thought hard about what he should do next. Sailing had not been the only thing he had learnt so far on his voyage. He has learnt to tie complicated knots, to make fire and to use his bare hands to make weapons from sticks and pieces of flint. He would not give up and was determined to find a way off the deserted island.

He knew his best chance of being rescued was to attract the attention of another ship, so he walked inland looking for higher ground. He soon spotted a hill in the middle of the island. "Aha!" he thought, "the perfect spot to begin a fire in the hope that a passing ship will see the smoke."

After marching through the thick greenery, Sinbad finally arrived at the base of the hill.

Step after step, he climbed up the hillside towards the top, the wind whistling around his ears the higher he climbed. Once he was at the peak of the hill he stopped and looked around for somewhere to rest. Just ahead some large trees were growing together in a shaded grove. He thought they would be a good place to make a shelter for the night, away from the ground and any creatures that lurked there. Lassoing some loose vines over a branch, he tied a knot and climbed up, using his feet against the tree trunk.

However, as soon as he had reached the top, something strange caught his eye. Puzzled, he looked closer, finally realizing what it was. It was a huge nest made of twigs and branches, holding gigantic eggs larger than Sinbad himself. "What kind of creature has eggs as large as these?" he wondered. Then, as a large shadow flew overhead, the answer became crystal clear. The eggs belonged to the roc bird, a bird of giant size that Sinbad had only ever heard stories of and hadn't believed existed until right this moment. Legend said that they could devour elephants in one go and now, face to face with the eggs of such a bird, he could believe it. Heart hammering, Sinbad looked up, hoping to shimmy down the tree before the mother roc noticed him.

But as he moved, the eggs began to wobble, sharp cracking noises coming from the largest egg in the centre of the nest. They were going to hatch! The huge shadow of the roc loomed closer, wings outstretched, her claws ready to grab the invader from the nest. It was too late to escape! Landing in a whirlwind of white feathers, the mother roc began to peck at him using its large, sharp beak. Sinbad rolled and dodged out of the way, hiding behind three of the shiny eggs. The roc mother, satisfied she had chased Sinbad from her nest, settled down comfortably on her eggs. Sinbad was crouched beneath her large feathery rear, with only the eggs keeping him from being squashed to death. He knew it would not take long for her to discover that he was hiding below and so he thought quickly, trying to come up with a plan to escape.

As quietly as he could, Sinbad undid his belt, winding it gently around the leg of the massive bird. Then he waited. It wasn't long before the roc needed to hunt again. It lifted its great wings and took off into the sky with Sinbad dangling below, gripping on to his belt for dear life. He looked below and saw the hill and trees he had climbed getting smaller and smaller beneath him. Sinbad was feeling happy with himself, smug even. Until he realized where the roc was headed.

As the roc swooped closer and closer to the ground, Sinbad saw that they were headed for a large channel deep in the rock. But something was strange about the channel – the floor of it seemed to be wriggling. Finally, Sinbad realized that the small valley was filled to the brim with snakes. Deadly, slithering snakes. The roc was going to dive down to catch some. Sinbad knew that being flung into a pit of snakes would surely be the end of him. He tried to be ready to drop down before she reached the pit. ONE. TWO. THREE!

He let go of his belt and tumbled on to the hard,

grey ground a few feet from the pit of snakes. It was the size of a small pond. The snakes started to scatter as the roc clawed at them. She caught many in her beak and even more in her claws. Sinbad stayed low and watched on the opposite edge of the pit. Something sparkled as the snakes scattered to all sides of the pit, trying to escape the roc, and Sinbad saw masses of diamonds sparkling in the sunlight. Curiosity sparked, he peered closer – the pit of snakes was guarding a treasure trove of jewels and gold coins!

Looking around wildly, Sinbad caught sight of some dry branches and driftwood scattered near the pit, which he grabbed and used to build a fire. When sparks flew, he seized one of the big branches and brandished it like a torch, before charging towards the snakes, shifting the burning branch from side to side. The snakes were quick to move out of his way, afraid of the hot fire. Sinbad slid down the side of the pit feet first. He fell on to a patch of ground covered in diamonds, the snakes kept at bay by the bright torch. He filled his pockets and then tried to climb back up, but he could not hold the fire and climb as he needed both of his hands.

"This may be the silliest decision I've ever made!" he said. He let go of the lit branch and began to climb up the side of the pit. The flame fizzled out and the snakes that were back in the pit began to slither towards him, no longer afraid. He reached the top of the pit with the snakes close behind. He ran with all of his might as the snakes chased him and, without thinking, he flung himself forward over the cliff edge and into the sea!

He bobbed in the water for a few moments, savouring the feeling of being alive. Then he began to swim strongly for shore. But before long, he heard the splashing of oars. He began to tread water, looking around frantically for the source of the sound. A small row boat was nearby and a friendly face smiled up at him – it was Chef.

Sinbad waved and swam towards his friend. He was so glad to see him.

"You're alive!" Chef said as he hauled Sinbad over the side of the boat.

"Barely!" Sinbad replied. "I have seen creatures that I didn't believe existed. This voyage has surely opened my eyes to the wonders of this world."

Chef opened a handkerchief and gave Sinbad some biscuits. Sinbad wolfed them down, hungrier than he had ever been in his life.

"And I have something for you, dear friend and

rescuer!" said Sinbad through a mouthful of crumbs. He reached into his pockets and pulled out a fist full of diamonds.

He shared them with Chef, the only person who came back for him.

Despite his brush with death and his crazy adventure, Sinbad was not put off his travels., and after being reunited with the ship, he set off for many more voyages. Life was never boring again.

Puss in Boots

ITALY

Despite the famous image of a sword-wielding cat in popular animated films, the cat in the "Puss in Boots" original fairy tale used his wits rather than his fighting prowess to make life comfortable for himself and his master. The tale originated in Italy around 1550 as "Costantino Fortunato" and then later as "Il gatto con gli stivali" ("The Cat with the Boots") by Giovanni Francesco Straparola, who was one of the first European authors to have written down fairy tales.

$\mathcal{M}$any years ago in a small town, a man worked hard making flour in his mill. To assist him, he had three sons, a donkey to carry flour to market, and a cat to rid him of any mice. Sadly, after many years of hard work, the miller became ill and, on his deathbed, he called for his three sons.

"To you, my eldest son," he croaked, "I bequeath my mill. As for my middle son, I will give you the donkey. And for my youngest son, you can keep the family cat."

Now, the youngest son loved his father, but was at a loss as to what he might do with a simple cat.

"My brothers can grind flour, or ride the donkey, but I can do nothing with this little creature. Perhaps I can make some gloves with his fur to warm my hands in the winter?"

"That would not be a wise thing to do," said the cat, who understood that his new master was none too pleased to have received him as a gift. "If you have just a little faith in me, I will change your fortune. All I ask is that you grant me a pair of leather boots." This certainly was no ordinary cat, thought the youngest son, who was astonished by the cat's ability to talk and by the strange request for boots. *Perhaps my father did leave me something special after all*, he mused. *I will do as the cat asks and see what happens.*

So the son did as he was bid and asked the local cobbler to make some fine black boots for his cat. The cat pulled on his new boots and, with a satisfied look, stood up on his hind legs and began to walk – just like a human! The townspeople were speechless to see such a sight. The young man watched as his cat picked up a sack of grain, slung it over his shoulder and proclaimed, "I shall be back, and when I return, opportunity will surely knock. Be ready!" The miller's son had no idea what the cat was talking about but continued to trust that his father had known what he was doing when he left him the cat in his will. He waved goodbye to the cat and continued about his everyday life.

Now, the cat had a plan to bring back a fortune to his new owner. He knew that the king of the land loved to eat roasted partridges, but he also knew that they hid so well in the woods that no one was able to catch them. So the cat built a cunning trap. Using the sack of grain he had taken from the miller's son, he scattered a bit of grain outside of the sack to lure the partridges inside, waiting behind a bush with the string that shut the sack resting in his hand. He watched and waited, watched and waited.

The hungry partridges finally flew by and began pecking at the grain. They followed the trail into the sack and, with one mighty pull, Puss in Boots had caught his prey! Now he was ready to show the king that he was the only one who could catch not just one partridge, but many of them. He was sure to gain a fortune from the king, who would be delighted to find such a great hunter. Marching up to the gates of the castle, Puss in Boots asked to see the king.

"Halt! What is your business here?" a guard asked, eyeing up the strange cat.

"I have come to see the king," the cat replied.

"You must be mad!" the guard replied. "A cat seeing the king – that is unheard of!"

"Perhaps he will be fun for the king to play with," said another guard. "The king has been mightily bored lately, so maybe this cat will bring him some distraction?"

The first guard thought for a moment and decided that the other guard was right. The king had been quite out of sorts since the hunters had failed to catch his favourite meal. Opening the gates, they gestured for the cat to make his way inside.

The cat walked confidently into the main hall and bowed before the king.

"Your Royal Highness, I come bearing gifts from Count Carabas." Puss was pleased with the name he had made up for his master, the miller's youngest son.

When the king saw there were partridges in the sack, he almost jumped off his throne with joy.

"How marvellous! I thank your count for his generous gift. Guards! Take these to the cook immediately, for I shall eat well tonight." He looked over his furry guest and said, "You are an unusual type of cat, are you not?"

"I am not your average cat, your Majesty," Puss in Boots replied with a slight sparkle in his eye. The king laughed and patted his thigh.

"I am most pleased with your visit today. Go with my guard to the treasury and fill your sack with gold. Thank Count Carabas for his kind gift."

Puss did as he was told and was shown to a room full of gold. As instructed, he filled his sack until it was heavy and headed off back to see the miller's son, pushing the loaded sack on a cart the king's men had given him.

Back at the mill, the miller's youngest son was feeling foolish. Surely he shouldn't have used the last of his money to buy a pair of boots for a cat, a cat he now thought would never return. What a joke had been played on him! But, hearing the trundling of wheels outside, the miller's son rushed to the window, flabbergasted to see the cat strolling into the yard, pushing the sack on a wooden cart. The cat untied the string at the mouth of the sack and let the contents fall on to the floor in front of the young son's feet. The gold shone bright as the miller's son's eyes lit up. The cat laughed. "It is real, master – you are not dreaming. This gold is a gift to you from the king. He sends his kind regards for the partridges that you sent."

"Partridges?" the young miller's son replied, completely bewildered. "I don't understand how you did all of this. I sent you away with a sack of grain and you have come back with riches beyond my wildest dreams."

The cat took off his boots and gave his feet a lick. Then he sat and explained what he had done. "I told the king you were a count so he would reward you handsomely. I shall return to the woods next week and catch more partridges for the king, and I'm certain he will reward you with even more gold and jewels." The miller's son was overjoyed by his wealth and his clever cat.

The following week, Puss caught more partridges and even some rabbits from the warren; they were particularly difficult to catch for most people, but with a little ingenuity, the cat was able to bag a great many of them. The king was delighted with the gifts of his favourite food and continued to allow the cat to fill his sack with gold for the mysterious Count Carabas. The king enjoyed Puss in Boots' company so much that he allowed the cat free reign of his castle and said he could come and go as he pleased.

One day when prowling around the castle, Puss in Boots heard the king's coachman complaining that he had to drive the king to the lake, when all he wanted to do was play cards with his friends. On hearing this, Puss quickly ran back to his master's home at the mill.

"Quickly, if you want more wealth then you have ever dreamt, you must go to the lake and take all of your clothes off. Give them to me and swim in the water. Hurry, hurry, for we do not have much time!"

The youngest son did as he was told and scurried down to the lake, stripped off his clothes, giving them to Puss in Boots to hide, and jumped into the lake. It wasn't a moment too soon as, seconds later, Puss heard the rumbling of the king's carriage approaching.

Puss in Boots stood in the road with his paws waving around. Frantically, he uttered:

"Oh, my king! What a wonder that you are here. My poor master, the Count of Carabas, was robbed by a band of thieves. They stole his clothes, and carriage, and threw him into the river! He will surely die of the cold if he does not get help immediately." The king looked out of his carriage and saw a bedraggled figure shivering in the lake.

"Of course we must help him. Guards, see to the count!" And with that, the guards helped the so-called count out of the lake and wrapped him in a warm blanket. One of them went back to the castle for some fresh clothes made by the king's own tailor. When they returned, the miller's son was warm and dry, wrapped in a blanket by a crackling fire, chatting merrily to the king and his family. With Puss's help, he put on the fine clothes made of the best fabric in the kingdom. Now no one would suspect that he was only a humble miller's son.

"Come sit in our carriage, Count Carabas, and we shall take you back to your abode," said the king, beckoning him into the carriage beside the eldest princess. On hearing this, the miller's son began to go red, for he would surely be found out as the lowly miller's son as soon as the king saw that he did not own a house fit for a count. But once again, Puss in Boots had an idea. He knew he had to find a house fit for his master in moments, otherwise the game would be up.

Running ahead of the carriage, he saw a field where many farmhands were gathering hay.

"Whose field is this?" he asked.

"It belongs to a wicked wizard who lives beyond the fields of wheat," one said.

"When the king passes by, you must say it belongs to Count Carabas. If you do, then you shall be rewarded finely; if you do not then curses shall befall you." The farmhands were taken aback but were fearful of the strange, talking cat standing upright in boots, and vowed to do as he asked.

Next, the cat came upon a field of wheat which was so large that he couldn't see where it ended.

"Whose grain is this?" he asked the hundreds of

workers pulling the grains from the husks.

"It belongs to the wicked wizard who lives beyond the forest," they replied. Again, Puss instructed them to say it belonged to the count and, scared of the odd talking cat, they agreed to do as he asked. With his next bound, Puss came upon a lush, green forest. A crew of woodcutters were cutting down trees and making logs and kindling for the wizard to fuel his fireplace; he worked them hard and gave them little payment. Once more, Puss demanded that they told the king that the land belonged to Count Carabas, offering them riches as a reward. When they hastily agreed, Puss ran onwards.

After the forest, Puss saw the most magnificent mansion emerging from the trees. It was even more beautiful than the king's castle. In the garden was a huge fountain, and flowers of every colour grew along the path that led to the mighty oak door.

Puss in Boots did not hesitate, and he knocked on the door loudly. After a few moments, the wizard answered, taken aback at seeing an odd cat in boots at his door.

"What do you want?" the wizard asked,

"I hear you are a great wizard. If you are, I challenge you to turn yourself into an elephant, for I don't believe the stories are true. Perhaps I could believe it if the rumours said you could transform into a dog, or even a cat like me, but an elephant? You could never do that," the cat spoke quickly, confusing the wizard.

"Pah! Of course I can, you feeble-minded beast." And with a flick of his wand, the wizard transformed himself into a fine elephant with two flapping ears and a long trunk. Now, inwardly, Puss in Boots was very impressed, but he stuck to his plan, for he knew that this was the only hope his master had of appearing wealthy in front of the king.

The wizard transformed back into a man again, raising his eyebrows and awaiting Puss's praise.

"Yes, that is surely excellent, and I must apologize for questioning your power. But I am sure it is easy to turn yourself into something so big – a harder challenge would be to make yourself into a very small creature, for example a mouse? Yes, you would never be able to achieve such a feat."

The wizard was getting fed up with being tested by the cat, but his proud nature wouldn't allow him to ignore the challenge, so with a flick of his wand, he changed into a tiny dormouse the colour of sand. At once, Puss in Boots pounced and swallowed the mouse in one mighty gulp! The wizard was no more, and his huge house was free for the miller's son to use. Running into the grand hallway, the cat declared loudly that the wizard had given the house to the Count of Carabas and that he was on his way with the king to view his new property. The servants quickly prepared themselves for the royal visit with excitement, delighted that the wicked wizard was no more.

Meanwhile, the king and his family were approaching the field in his carriage. Looking out at the bountiful fields, he stopped the carriage and asked the field hands to tell him who owned the field. Of course, the reply came that Count Carabas was the owner. The miller's son nodded in agreement, hoping against hope that Puss in Boots would make everything right as he had so many times before. Next they came upon the field of grain. The king again stopped the carriage to ask who owned such rich farmland and again, the workers replied Count Carabas. The same happened with the beautiful forest. The king and princess were completely taken in by the cat's plan and were enchanted by the beauty of the fine country house when they rode up to the mansion. The miller's son sat speechless in the carriage, astonished at what the cat had managed to achieve.

"You are certainly a fine young man," said the king. "Your land and home are a match even for my own castle." The princess agreed wholeheartedly, smiling at the miller's son.

"Welcome to the house of my fine master, the Count of Carabas!" Puss in Boots declared, sweeping down the steps to greet the carriage. The "count" led the princess and the king to the main hall where a great feast was prepared which, of course, included the king's favourite meal – partridges. The king and the count became fast friends over a wonderful supper and spent many evenings together, their blossoming friendship almost matching that of the new count and his cat, to whom the miller's son was eternally indebted.

After a few months, the count requested the princess's hand in marriage and, delighted, the king gave his blessing to the joyful pair. Years later, when the count became king, his first decree was to make Puss in Boots the prime minister, for he knew the cat was the smartest creature in the land. Under his wise guidance, the country became prosperous and every citizen rejoiced and was happy.

Tokutaro and the Nine-Tailed Fox

JAPAN

By the fourteenth century in Japan, the myth of the kitsune, foxes with magical powers, had become familiar in stories. The more tails a fox had, the stronger its magic and the older it was said to be. This tale of a particularly powerful kitsune was first told in Tales of Old Japan *by Baron A. B Freeman-Mitford (Macmillan 1871).*

In ancient Japan, it was common to hear the warning "Watch out for the kitsune!" when someone was hurrying outside in the dark. In particular, rumours had spread through Kyoto of a shapeshifting nine-tailed fox of such power that it was said she could bewitch a man with a single blink of her eyes, making them her servant for ever.

Tokutaro, the wine merchant's son, didn't believe a word of this rumour and scoffed at his friends as they spoke in hushed tones of the magical fox.

"It is true what they say – the nine-tailed kitsune is real. She is so cunning that she has taken five men already," said a friend, taking a slurp of his rice wine. "The only way they can be defeated is if they are touched by fire."

"What rubbish!" Tokutaro replied. "Kitsune don't exist, and even if they did I would never be fooled by one. I am far too smart!" declared Tokutaro, whose long hair was tied into a topknot on the top of his head. He was a vain young man and he had spent many hours oiling and combing his hair until it shone as black as night.

"Too smart?" said his friend with a laugh. "They have magical powers, Tokutaro, and you have none. You would be lost in seconds."

"Every man who is afraid of being bewitched by a fox must be scared of their own shadows and ordinary shapes in the dark. They aren't real! Stop talking about this nonsense at once and let's enjoy the rest of the night without foolish tales." But his friend wouldn't let the matter drop.

"You know little of the world, Tokutaro. Many people we know have been tricked on the Maki Moors alone and I'm sure you would be no exception if you were to go that way."

Becoming cross that his friends had so little faith in him, Tokutaro set down his cup. Steel lacing his words, he spoke firmly: "To prove that there is no such thing as kitsune, I shall go tonight to Maki Moor, and when I come back you will pay for all of my drinks."

"You are on!" said his friends in unison, laughing at how angry Tokutaro had become.

"You shall see; nobody can make a fool out of Tokutaro!" and with that, Tokutaro marched off into the night, confident that any beasts he should encounter would be more likely to be a mouse or a bird than a magical nine-tailed fox. He strode onwards into the forest as dusk fell, muttering to himself at the stupidity of his friends.

On he trudged, his tummy beginning to grumble with hunger, when suddenly out of the corner of his eye, he spied something rustling among the shrubs. He heard the noise again, and then he blinked, wondering if his eyes had deceived him. He thought he had seen a red bushy tail disappear into the shadows. But he must have been mistaken. The rustling had stopped and there were no creatures to be seen. His mind was playing tricks on him after all of the tall tales his friends had shared. Shaking his head, Tokutaro walked on, only to be stopped dead by the sight of a young woman with skin as pale as moonlight stepping out from behind a tree trunk. Her robe was silver and her eyes were bright as stars. Tokutaro gulped. This was the most beautiful woman he had ever seen. Thinking of the rumours of the kitsune being able to shapeshift, he stepped forward cautiously.

"Hello, traveller. You must be weary. Come to my house over the moor and you can rest a while," the young woman said, gazing into his eyes.

Tokutaro felt uncertain. He thought again about

all of the stories his friends had told him, and he looked at the beautiful lady in front of him. His mind racing, he remembered the disappearing tail he was sure he had seen in the bushes, and gulped rapidly. *She is a kitsune!* he thought. *My friends were right.*

"Do you think I am so brainless that I would go with you? I know what you are – you are a kitsune," he gabbled, his words falling over each other in his haste to deny her.

"I am sorry you are offended by my offer of shelter and food. But I assure you that I am no such thing. Be well and I bid you farewell." The girl smiled and skipped off down the path and out of sight.

Feeling even more foolish, Tokutaro was left alone on the path. Trying to think clearly, he wondered if he had been wrong, but his heart was still racing and he was sure that there was something mysterious about the young girl.

I must warn whoever lives nearby that something strange is afoot, he thought. *And sitting by a warm fire and sharing my story will steady me, too.*

So he ran through the forest over the moors, looking for others to tell. He happened upon a wooden farmhouse, smoke swirling from the chimney, and he knocked urgently on the door.

An older man opened the door. "Yes?" he asked, looking at the bedraggled young man with surprise at his ragged state. "How can I help you?"

"It is I who have come to help you!" Tokutaro replied. "I have just encountered the most terrible kitsune, a magical young girl; she is roaming around this area looking for humans to trick."

"Come in, come in," the man replied. Tokutaro stepped into the warm room and was greeted by an older woman tending to the fire. His heart gave a jolt as he realized that sitting in the corner was the young girl who he had just met in the forest. For an instant he froze, not knowing what to do. Then before he could decide, he blurted out,

"She is the kitsune! She appeared from nowhere in the forest and invited me to her home," Tokutaro declared.

The man, the woman and the girl all laughed.

"Don't be ridiculous; she is our daughter," the old woman replied. She is no more a kitsune than you are the Emperor!" Tokutaro was blushing furiously, his certainty that this was the kitsune becoming stronger. He looked at the girl, who was smiling at him in an amused manner.

"I shall prove that she is a kitsune!" he declared.

And with that, he ran over to her, grabbed her hand and tried to drag her close to the open fire, remembering his friends' words: "They can only be defeated by fire." As he brought the girl close to the fire's blazing heat, a spark leapt from the grate and landed on her hand. The girl screamed. Her mother quickly doused cold water from a pot on to her daughter's hand, but it was flaming red from the heat. The old man pushed Tokutaro away from his daughter.

"Are you mad?" he shouted.

Tokutaro stood back in shame, seeing that the girl was made of ordinary flesh, just like him. "I am so sorry! Please let me make it up to you. I can't believe I acted like this – I became so scared in the woods and my mind must have been playing tricks on me. Please ask anything of me and you shall have it. I am a wealthy man; can I give you money?"

The man and his wife hugged their daughter, their faces angry and accusing.

"We do not want your money," the daughter replied.

"We do not want your apologies," the mother snapped.

"We want you to see the head monk – he will know what to do," the father added.

And so Tokutaro waited, shamefaced, as the man left the house to fetch the town's head monk. He watched as the mother held her daughter's burnt hand in a bucket of cold water and then bandaged it carefully in white gauze. It wasn't long before the girl's father returned with the head monk.

Tokutaro explained his story, thinking it sounded completely mad as he told it out loud. How could he ever have believed this ordinary girl was a kitsune? He, who had never believed in the kitsune in the first place! The monk looked at the family and shook his head.

"This is a very grave situation. I think the best course of action is for me to shave your head and for you to join my order of monks until you have really repented and changed your ways."

Tokutaro's heart sank at the thought of parting with his long beautiful hair and joining the solitary monks. It would be the worst punishment he could have. But he knew he deserved it. "I will do anything you ask; I will be the best disciple you have ever had," Tokutaro said, bowing down to the monk. He knelt before him and the head monk began shaving off all of his long black hair. Tokutaro watched it fall clump by clump. He began to weep silent tears at the sight of his hair being thrown onto the floor. What a fool he had been.

At that moment, a cackle of laughter burst out above his head. The old man, his wife and the girl were suddenly standing up, surrounding him. Confused, he tried to rise, but the girl pushed him down. Laughing at his surprised face, she said, "We heard there was a young man who thought he was cleverer than the kitsune. Do you feel clever now, Tokutaro?" She picked up a clump of his dark hair from the floor and threw it high into the air, cackling wildly. As the hair descended, the house and all of the people in the room vanished in the blink of an eye. Feeling dizzy, Tokutaro found the ground coming to meet him and closed his eyes.

When he came to, daybreak had arrived. The first rays of the suns shone on Tokutaro's face where he lay on the forest path, exactly where he had started his walk yesterday evening. Rubbing his eyes, he wondered whether he had imagined the whole thing; but then, in the distance, he saw four foxes dashing through the undergrowth. One of them turned back to look at him – she had nine tails, one of which was singed black at the tip. The fox smiled at him, then turned and sprinted away.

Tokutaro returned to the village and found that not everything had changed back to normal along with the daybreak – his long, dark hair was gone, and he was left with his shiny bald head for the rest of his days. Shamefaced, Tokutaro vowed to live a humble life from that moment onwards.

Princess Ana and the Charmed Rabbit

PORTUGAL

This is retelling of the Portuguese fairy tale "The Rabbit" by Consiglieri Pedroso, published in Portuguese Folk-Tales (1882). In Pedroso's version the rabbit stole a handkerchief, a garter and locket with a picture of the king.

$\mathcal{L}$ong ago in southern Portugal lived a kind, happy princess called Ana who loved to play and collect pretty things. She was often found rummaging in her mother's jewellery box and dressing up in her mother's elegant robes.

Her father, the king, doted on his only child. He loved to spoil her with trinkets and little presents whenever he could. On the occasion of her eleventh birthday, he gave her a very special gift that he had his servant buy from a special store in Italy: a golden charm bracelet with one charm dangling from it – a small heart-shaped diamond.

"With each year that you grow so too will your collections of charms," the king said. Ana was delighted, and the king was so pleased with her happiness that he promised he would give her a new charm on her birthday every year up until her sixteenth birthday. She received a ruby, a sapphire, an emerald, a pearl, and the final charm was made of amethyst.

"I shall wear a different one each day, Papa. Thank you." She kept them in a wooden box and each day chose one to wear around her wrist.

While Ana loved her birthday gifts, she was also lonely. All of her beautiful possessions didn't quite make up for having no one to talk to or play with. Because of her royal status, she wasn't allowed to play with the servants' children who romped around in the forest below. Sometimes she would look at the gold bracelet and the charms laid out in her jewellery box and secretly wish she could exchange them all for someone to talk to.

One day, Ana was looking out of her window at the forest beyond the palace when a white rabbit appeared. It squirmed through a hole in the palace wall and crept up to her private garden. Smiling with delight, Ana ran outside to greet it, its white coat shining brightly in the sunlight. She called out for the soft furry animal to come and play with her on the patio outside of her room. Long hours passed while Ana played with the creature, stroking its soft fur and chatting away to her new friend.

When it was supper time, Ana told the rabbit, "I must go down to the banquet hall to eat my dinner, but I am so happy you have become my friend.

Please come back to play with me tomorrow." And with one more stroke of the rabbit's fur, she proceeded to unfasten the charm she was wearing that day, the diamond charm, to lather and wash her hands in preparation for dinner. She did not want the precious stone to get chipped by knocking the side of the china bowl. When she had dried her hands on the soft towel her maid had placed beside the bowl, she noticed that her beloved charm was no longer where she had put it. It had gone, and so had the rabbit. Thinking that she would find it later, she went off to dinner.

But on her return, despite turning her room upside down looking for the charm, it was nowhere to be seen. Of course, Ana was sad that the diamond charm was lost, but the thought of her new playmate made the loss less painful as she looked forward to playing with him again the next day.

As before, the next morning the white rabbit appeared from the forest and hopped up to the Ana's private garden to play with her. The day passed in a whirlwind once more, the rabbit thumping his feet as Ana tickled him behind the ear, and sitting still to listen whilst she sang to him.

Again, when it was time for dinner, the maid

brought the bowl filled with hot water and soap for the Ana to wash her hands. Just like the day before, she took off her jewelled charm and placed it next to the bowl. "Dinner time again, dear friend," she said. "You haven't seen my diamond charm from yesterday have you?"

The rabbit simply stared at her with his big dark eyes. "Of course you haven't; you're a rabbit! What would a rabbit do with a precious stone?" She laughed at the silly thought. But, to the princess's horror, once again, after she dried her hands and went to put on her ruby charm, it was gone. And so was the white rabbit.

Something very strange was happening, thought Ana, but she tried hard not to think that the disappearance of her charms might have something to do with the appearance of her new friend. Since the rabbit had come into her life, she had been happier by far than ever before.

However, the pattern went on for the rest of the week. The white rabbit would appear, play with Ana, and then when she had finished washing her hands, she found that her precious charm and the rabbit were gone. That week the princess lost each of her six precious charms – only the plain gold band remained. Horrified and ashamed that she could have been so careless, the princess vowed to watch the rabbit closely the next day when she washed her hands. When the following day arrived, there was no sign of her new friend. The days afterwards were quiet and sad as the princess gazed out of the window, hoping to catch a glimpse of white fur as the rabbit hopped to her garden. But there wasn't a sight of hide nor hair of the white rabbit. Not wanting to tell the king that she had lost the gifts he had given her, and missing her friend's companionship, the princess became silent and withdrawn. She sat in the throne room which overlooked the ocean and thought about how much she wished her white rabbit would return with the charms he must have taken.

"Something is wrong, our happy daughter has not been out to play for days," the king told his wife, looking worriedly at where the princess sat listlessly in the corner.

"Perhaps she is lonely or needs entertaining," the queen suggested. "Let us bring all the best storytellers to the palace and see if any of their tales can help to bring our daughter back to her usual cheerful self!" she declared to the court. The king agreed that this was the best thing to do for their daughter. Many storytellers came and went, but none of their jokes or stories made any difference at all, and Princess Ana was as glum as glum could be. The white rabbit had not returned, she had no precious stones, only the gold bracelet, and she was forced to listen to happy stories told by people she didn't like. It didn't help at all!

As a last resort, the king and queen summoned the queen's old nursemaid, a jolly round woman with rosy cheeks who had once been the finest storyteller in all the land.

Older and slower than she had been in her youth, the nursemaid made her way through the thick depths of the forest to the palace when she started to chatter to herself about what stories she might tell the princess to help her out of her slump.

"Youth has flown from me, and my memory is like sieve. What goes in just falls out again." The old nursemaid sat on a tree stump to rest her weary legs. "I can't for the life of me remember any stories. The queen will be wholly disappointed in me."

To her surprise, from her tree stump seat, she laid eyes upon the strangest sight she had ever seen. A little fluffy white rabbit was riding on top of a strange-looking donkey. The donkey had many stripes all over its body and instead of a hee-haw, the noise it made resembled the crowing of a rooster. "Why, I do believe if I follow that rabbit upon the back of that donkey, I shall find a most interesting story." So the old nursemaid crept along behind the donkey and the rabbit until she came to a little cottage. The donkey bent down and the little rabbit went inside. The donkey just stood outside the door nodding its head and swishing its tail.

A wonderful aroma of soup floated out of the window.

"I wonder if whoever is cooking would mind sharing with me – I am very hungry." she said, tip-toeing towards the cottage entrance. However, with a few steps to go, the donkey bolted its head upright and looked her in the eye.

"Do not come any closer!" the donkey cried. The old woman scurried behind a nearby bush.

"A talking donkey! Something is afoot. I shall investigate further around the back of the cottage." And with that, and feeling brave once again, she crept around towards the rear of the cottage and peeked in through the back window. Inside, she couldn't spot any humans, but instead saw the little white rabbit opening a wooden box. He took a diamond heart-shaped charm, then a ruby one and so forth, until he has six sparkling precious charms laid out in front of him.

The old nursemaid would soon find out that the donkey was not the only talking animal she would encounter that day.

The rabbit lifted each charm up in turn and said in a sing-song voice, "When six charms are worn together, with friendship true I'll be free for ever."

And just like that, he was transformed into a young man with a handsome face. The rabbit skin had fallen to the floor. "If friendship is valued over these precious charms, then I will truly be free," he said sadly.

The old women let out a gasp! Then clamped her hand over her mouth. When she had taken some deep breaths, she quickly scurried away from the house.

"Well, if that isn't the best story I can tell the princess then I don't know what is!"
The old maid rushed off, fast as her old legs would go, towards the palace. She was given an audience with the princess, who sat with her head resting on her hands.

The queen shook her arm gently. "Dearest, here my old nursemaid who told me the best bedtime stories as a child. I am sure she will brighten your day. Just listen to what she has to say."

"But, mother, I am weary of listening to all of the storytellers you have bought here. Please, can you just leave me alone?"

The king sighed and said, "This will be the last one. Just give her a chance and if she does not help, then yes, we will leave you to your thoughts."
The old nursemaid stood before the princess.

"Today's tale begins in the deep dark forest … where wild beasts roam, and the air is filled with magic…"

The princess was already beginning to get bored, when…

"Suddenly, I encountered a small, fluffy white rabbit, sitting on top of a strange striped donkey that made the noise of a rooster."

Ana sat upright. She was sure this was her very own white rabbit.

"Go on, tell me more!" she urged.

The woman told her of the cottage and the white rabbit taking out six sparkling charms.

"You must take me there immediately!" Ana cried out in delight. The thought of seeing her rabbit friend and finding out why he had stolen her charms put a spark back in her eyes that hadn't been there since the rabbit vanished for the last time.

"But it's just a story, my dear," said the king.

"Well, your highness," said the old woman hesitantly, "I actually did see those creatures and the cottage on my way here."

The king and queen couldn't believe their ears, and they stared in puzzlement at the nursemaid. But Ana bounced out of her chair and marched towards the entrance of the palace.

"Come, we shall take the royal carriage. Show me the way," she demanded. With that, the whole of the royal family followed. The woman guided the royal party through the forest until they came upon the little clearing with the cottage. The old nursemaid told her to look into the back window first.

Ana went to the window and looked through. Within, she saw her little rabbit friend, and her heart gave a giant leap at the sight in front of her. There were her charms, too! She watched as the rabbit carefully placed them in front of him. Then he said wistfully, "When six charms are worn together, with friendship true, I'll be free for ever."

And just as the nursemaid had told her, the rabbit skin dropped to the floor and in its place a handsome prince appeared. Ana took off her plain gold bracelet and, holding it out in her hand, she realized that to completely break the spell for good, the gold bracelet must be given up too. The donkey simply looked at her and said, "Go forth."

Ana rushed in through the front door, the gold bracelet in her hand.

"You are my true friend! If that is what is needed to break this curse, I do not need those charms any more! Here, put the six charms on to this bracelet," exclaimed Ana. The prince moved towards her, a large smile on his face and proceeded to loop each charm on to the gold chain.

"Thank you, thank you! I can't believe you found me! I am the Prince of Naples. I have been forced to live out this life in the forest for many years."
"But how did this all happen?" Ana asked.

"I was forced by an evil enchantress to live as a rabbit until the owner of the charm bracelet came to my door and forfeited them for friendship. I'm so sorry for taking your beautiful charms, but it was the only way I could think of to bring you to me."
The princess hugged her friend. "Dear friend, I can't tell you how pleased I am to see you. Whilst I felt dreadful that I had lost the charms my father had

given me, I was much more upset to think I would never see you again. A friend is much more valuable than a few trinkets."

Ana turned to introduce the prince to her family, who stood outside, mouths open wide in surprise at what had just happened. Once they heard the full story of the little rabbit and how happy he had made the princess, the king and queen welcomed the prince with open arms. The strange donkey transformed into the prince's butler and the cottage vanished, and in its place a magnificent castle appeared out of nowhere. The whole party gasped out loud.

Princess Ana and the prince remained good friends all their lives, happily spending time together and keeping each other company until their dying day.

The old storyteller eventually forgot the story of the princess who had lost her charms – but not before they had told it to the crowd of children at the palace, who passed the story on to their children and to their children.

How the Jackal Got Her Stripes

SOUTH AFRICA

This folktale was told by South African Outa Karel in the 1900s. Like many other stories of the oral tradition, this one would have been passed down from generation to generation around the campfire. Storytelling was a way to make sense of the natural order and the ways in which the animal and human worlds often collided. At the heart of the stories was a sense of cooperation, and the knowledge that the landscape could often be harsh for both animals and humans alike.

$\mathcal{A}$ long, long time ago, some hunters were roaming the plains looking for food when they heard a strange cry. It was not a springbok, nor an ostrich, nor a hyena. The sound was different – humanlike – and they knew they had to find its source.

"Wahhhh!" it cried. "Wahhhh!"

"It sounds like a baby," one hunter exclaimed.

They searched the undergrowth, being careful not to disturb any snakes that might be lurking nearby.

The hunters searched high and low, under bushes, and through the tall grass. Finally, one of the hunters pushed back a dusty bush to reveal a strange-looking baby with smooth skin that shone in the sunlight. With no parents to look after it, it called out to all who would listen.

"Dada," it gurgled. The baby pointed to the sun in the sky.

The hunter could not believe it. A child of the sun was here on earth. The baby was lying on his back looking all around with its big brown eyes. It was unlike any other baby the hunters had ever seen. Whilst it may have had the same shape as an ordinary baby, it did something no baby ever could – it glowed! The glow was magnetic, rays of light shining from the baby's eyes and an aura of radiance emanating from its skin. It was a child from out of this world.

The sun baby cried out again. "Wahhh!"

One of the hunters bent down to inspect the baby. "We must take care of this strange creature – it has been left here all alone."

The baby replied with a coo.

The hunters felt sorry for the small child, and pushing any reservations aside, they decided to bring the baby home with them. But as the baby glowed like the sun, it also gave out heat like the sun, and when one of the hunters went to pick up the child, he cried out in pain, sucking his fingers. "The child is as hot as the sun," he exclaimed, backing away hurriedly. The heat from the baby was too much. "I cannot take him! I will burn if I do," he told the other hunters, who looked worried.

Another brave hunter came forward to try.

"I can carry him – let me through!" But again the heat coming from the sun baby beat even the most courageous of the hunters back. He too moved away.

Finally, a third hunter approached. He was sure

that he could use the animal skin around his shoulder to carry the baby. But as he tried to wrap the material around the baby, he found he too could not lift up the special child. Even wrapped inside another skin, the intensity of the heat was too much for his human skin.

"I am burning! The child is burning me!" he said, unwinding the animal skin from the overheated child. Everyone was confused by what was happening. How could such a beautiful child create so much heat?

The hunters all stepped back and stared, unsure of what to do. Without warning, the strange baby turned on the ground. Beams of light shot out from its skin in all directions, some dazzling the hunters, who ran away screaming with fear. They ran and ran towards the village, where a group of woman were tending to their babies. As the men ran past, they shouted:

"Run! The sun's child is here on earth! It will burn us all." The men rushed onwards and the women and children followed close by. Very soon, there wasn't a single human within a mile of the sun baby and his incredible heat.

A creature known for its mischief and

untrustworthiness was watching all of this intently. The humans had left a baby on its own, one that looked juicy and very tasty, she thought. Softly, she padded through the undergrowth to get a closer look. She was a jackal, a hungry beast, usually feeding off scraps and scavenging whatever food she could find.

The sun child could sense there was someone nearby.

"Dada?"

The jackal replied, "I can take you to your father sun. I do not have a skin to wrap you in, but if you want to climb upon my back I will carry you."

The jackal crouched low so that the baby could crawl upon its back. The sun child pulled itself up and held on to the hairs on the jackal's back.

The sun child giggled with delight.

"Where do you wish for me to take you?" asked the jackal, her eyes darting around for any signs of other predators who might steal her meal. With no other creature in sight, she rejoiced, knowing that the baby would be jackal food and jackal food only. The baby now rested on the her back, his head turned to the side near the jackal's neck.

"Dada sun," the baby said sleepily, pointing to the mountain some way off. The jackal immediately began trotting through the sparse terrain, and the baby on its back began to snore gently. Teeth bared, eyes bright with malice, the jackal did not make a path to the mountain; instead, she hurried toward her lair where all of the rest of the jackals lived in a pack. The barks of glee would be loud when they knew she had bought a tasty treat for dinner. Juicy babies were as good to eat as dead antelope, the jackal thought to herself.

But something was wrong. The jackal began to feel uncomfortable as she neared her home. There was a burning sensation near her head where the baby lay sleeping. Wriggling her shoulders, she hissed, "Wake up, baby! Slide down a little as my head and neck are burning. Wake up, I tell you!"

The sun baby groggily opened his eyes and did as the jackal was asking. He nudged himself on to the jackal's shoulders. This seemed fine for a short while as the jackal trotted on, but then the same sensation began to hurt the jackal's shoulders.

"Wake up, baby!" the jackal called out again. "Slide down some more on to my hips, for you are making me too hot again." The baby was tired but did not want to appear to be impolite, and so did as the jackal asked, sliding down the jackal's back towards her hips. The baby was about to go back to sleep when the jackal cried out once more.

"Ouch! Go even further down my back, baby."

But as the jackal walked on, the sun baby began to slip further and further down her side, with one hand holding on to the jackal's tail and the other on to the hairs of the jackal's back. With each pace forward, the baby's heat singed and burnt the jackal. However, the jackal gritted her teeth, desperately wanting to keep her supper. She refused to think of flinging off the baby, for she knew her belly would stay empty if she did.

At last, the baby was so far down the jackal's back that it was only holding on to the jackal's tail. The tail was burning to a crisp, and it was black as could be with the child's hands clutching tightly to it. When the jackal could take the pain no more, she turned, and with her sharp teeth gleaming, she whipped her tail into the air to try and rid herself of the burning pain.

"Help! Help! You are too hot for me. I shall punish you for being such a terrible child and gobble you up right now. I will not wait a moment longer!" The whipping of her tail meant that the baby was flung into the air and landed nearby on the ground. But when the jackal looked again, the baby's eyes shot out streaks of yellow fire, its body wrapped in bright light and heat that only a child of the sun could give. The jackal cowered and covered its eyes with fear! Now she understood that this was no ordinary baby.

"Wahhh! Gobble me?" screamed the baby. The sun in the sky began to beat down rays hotter than the jackal had ever felt. This had all been a very bad idea.

"No, no, you misunderstand," begged the jackal, now afraid for its life.

"Take back!" added the baby.

"I would never eat you! I was joking!" replied the jackal, shielding her eyes from the brightness that blazed throughout the sky. It scooped the baby up on to its back again and ran as fast as it could up the side of the mountain. If the sun was going to reunite with its child it needed to be at the peak of the mountain. The jackal knew that she would not be able to eat this baby and getting it back to its father was the only thing that would save her.

Once at the peak of the mountain, the baby crawled down from the animal's back. The jackal tried to lick her burnt body. The sun rose high in the sky, its rays stretching down to the top of the mountain. It longed to reach its child. The baby shone even brighter and brighter. Soon, not even a baby shape could be made out, just a mass of golden light, and the jackal could no longer look at the baby at all. Her eyelids half-closed to black out the piercing rays, the jackal scrunched her face and bent her head, trying to get away from the searing brightness. Then, the baby was gone.

The jackal scrambled down the mountainside, happy to be away from the sun's baby.

Out from behind a bush, one of the huntsmen appeared.

He had seen what had happened to the jackal and the sun's child. He knew that the jackal had intended to eat the child, but it had changed its mind because the sun was too powerful and wanted its child back.

"Be warned, Jackal. You and your kind shall never be able to look at the sun with those greedy eyes of yours."

That is how the jackal and her descendants gained the stripes on their back and why they only come out at night. For all of the jackal family know that they can never face the sun again.

Aladdin

SYRIA

Antun Yusuf Hanna Diyab was a Syrian storyteller and writer. He was born in Aleppo, and whilst working for a French merchant company, he learnt many languages including French and Italian. Much of what is known about him comes from his autobiography and French folklorist Antoine Galland's diaries. The story of Aladdin was passed to Galland from Diyab, and it was published in 1709 as part of Galland's translation of One Thousand and One Nights (Les Mille et Une Nuits).

$\mathcal{A}$ long, long time ago in the Middle East, there lived a wicked sorcerer. The sorcerer was able to command great magic, but he craved even more power. Hearing tales of magical beings called genies who could grant their master's wishes, the sorcerer was consumed with the idea of owning one of these genies. He knew that with a genie by his side, he would never be defeated and could rule the entire world from the comfort of his palace.

The sorcerer spent many years tracking down rumours of these magical beings until he had located the most powerful genie in the world. However, the sorcerer had a problem. The genie had fallen foul of a spell and was trapped in a magical prison – a tiny lamp buried in the midst of a cavern of treasure, deep underground. The cavern allowed no one with magical ability inside; instead, only an innocent could enter the cave. Indeed, even if anyone did gain entry, an avalanche of stone would be triggered immediately and there would only be a short time before the entrance was buried deep underground.

After many months of trying all his spells in

order to get inside, the sorcerer had to admit defeat, and instead he began hatching a plan to find an unsuspecting boy to do his bidding. He used his magic fountain to scry for a likely lad, and began to watch the local marketplace, seeking one who would be able to retrieve the magical lamp. The cave entrance was only a small hole, and inside there were many dangerous spaces. A person would have shimmy down tight, narrow tunnels, to jump from ledge to ledge, find the room where the treasure was kept and climb back up and squeeze through the small hole again – the sorcerer knew he had to find someone quick and agile, and he spent weeks narrowing down his search until he found the perfect candidate: a young man called Aladdin.

Completely unaware of the sorcerer's plan, Aladdin was browsing the market near where he lived. Poor Aladdin had to scrape together money to eat from begging in the marketplace and doing any odd jobs he could find. But Aladdin was a happy fellow, always joking and smiling no matter how little money he had. Despite this, the sorcerer knew the young man would leap at the chance to earn some money. Carefully, he approached Aladdin, who was feeling sorry for himself after a long day of trying to find a job with no success. He was desperate to work, and his face lit up when he heard the sorcerer's words.

"Young man, come with me. I have a job for you. Come, let us eat together and I shall tell you my plan." Aladdin had not had a proper meal for months. He listened to the sorcerer's deal, stuffing his mouth full of delicious stew.

"The job is an easy one," the sorcerer said. "I know of a cave full of treasure. I want you to go in there, fill your pockets with as many jewels as you can carry – all for you to keep. BUT, you must bring me back a lamp. It is of upmost importance to me. That is the only thing I require. Everything else can be yours." The sorcerer smiled down at Aladdin's open-mouthed disbelief. "Will you do it? I will give you five gold coins now to show you that you can trust me."

Aladdin had nothing but empty pockets. His eyes grew round at the thought of so much treasure, so he agreed without a second's hesitation, and the pair set off over the sand dunes outside the village and headed east until they arrived at the cave entrance.

The sorcerer showed Aladdin where a small channel opened up in the rock and reminded him of his promise. "All you have to do is find the lamp. Everything else is yours. Now go, and bring it to me."

Down into the depths of the cave, Aladdin crawled through dark tunnels of heavy rock. After a while, he came upon a mighty room filled from the floor to ceiling with gold, diamonds, sapphires, rubies and more.

"I can't believe it!" he gasped. "I am going to be rich!" He began to stuff his pockets with diamonds and sapphires as big as his fists, shovelling gold coins down his tunic so that he could carry as much as possible. Laden down heavily with all the treasure he could manage, Aladdin suddenly remembered his promise – he must not forget the lamp. Searching through the gleaming mounds, he finally saw a small, dull lamp sitting on a shelf. Its grubby exterior was tarnished and unimpressive. Shrugging at the oddity of the man wanting such a seemingly unimportant item in amongst such riches, he tied the lamp to his belt and began his return to the surface. Up through the tunnels and passageways he went, excited by the new life of luxury that awaited him. But as he crawled upwards, a rumble shook the tunnels. Frightened, Aladdin scrambled quickly over sharp ledges, losing some of his jewels as he went. The cave shook and rubble began to fall from the roof of the tunnels. Aladdin rushed upwards as fast as he could, towards the hole where had entered. Rocks crashed behind him. He could feel the cave moaning and falling in on itself. He knew something was dreadfully wrong.

As he clawed his way back up the narrow tunnel, he saw the man was waiting with arms outstretched and felt a surge of relief. Aladdin held his arms up for help.

"Ahh. My fine lad, first pass me the lamp!" the sorcerer said, his eyes full of menace. He had no intention of allowing Aladdin to leave the cave alive.

"Help me up first, then you shall have it!" Aladdin panted.

"The cave will not remain open long. Pass me the lamp now!" Small rocks began to fall in front of them.

Aladdin began to panic. "Help me!"

"No! Give me the lamp now!" the sorcerer's pretence was at its end, as the anticipation of getting his hands on the lamp was too much. His real self showing through, he bent down, pushing past Aladdin and reaching for the lamp at his belt.

Aladdin realized that the man meant to trap him after giving him the lamp, and pushed the sorcerer back, holding firmly on to the lamp. Time had run out. The last gaps of daylight were being filled by rocks.

"If you shall not give me the lamp then you will die in there with it!" the sorcerer hissed, and with that he backed away as the rocks poured over the entrance, trapping poor Aladdin alone in the dark.

Aladdin sat, shaking with fear, terrified at being left alone in such a dreadful place.

He slumped down. How had this happened, he wondered? His pockets were empty and he had no way of lighting his path. He was well and truly trapped. Unsure what else to do, he slowly made his way back down to the treasure room, crawling over the rockfalls that blocked his route.

"What use is treasure when I shall perish in this cave?" Aladdin said to himself, as he stumbled over a pile of gold and jewels. Trying to think of a way to light his path, he suddenly remembered the lamp. He unhooked it from his belt and looked around for some oil. As he searched, his hand brushed the side of the lamp, rubbing away some of the dirt that covered the surface.

With a mighty whoosh, the lamp began to shake. From out of its spout, a plume of smoke erupted, and a giant genie emerged into the air, his magical glow shining brightly around the cavern. He was the size of two men and the colour of the sea. Aladdin fell back, stunned at the apparition in front of him.

"What is it you wish, oh master of the lamp?" the genie asked, looking down at the scared boy whose eyes were wide as plates.

"Wish?" said Aladdin, hoping this great mystical being would not devour him.

"You rubbed the lamp, which means I am beholden to fulfill your wishes. I am a genie of the lamp, here to serve you," the genie said, bowing to its new master.

Aladdin didn't know whether the towering being was telling the truth or not, but he wished desperately to get out of the cave. "Take me home!" he commanded. And with a flash of light, Aladdin was magically transported back to his bustling city. Dazed, Aladdin looked around, wondering if his awful adventure had been a dream. But no, in his hand was the lamp – the genie now back inside. Aladdin hastily stuffed it down his tunic for safe keeping and hurried towards his house, keen to examine the lamp further.

As he raced through the streets, a royal guard yelled loudly for him to get out of the way. In his hurry to get home, Aladdin realized he had accidentally joined a parade heading into the city. As he scuttled to one side, Aladdin glanced up and caught sight of the most beautiful girl he'd ever seen, perched high upon an elephant draped in pink and gold. Her hair was black as the night sky and her face was framed by the most exquisite scarves. Aladdin felt his heart flutter. It was love at first sight.

"Make way for the princess!" the guards hollered at the crowd.

As she passed by, Aladdin stood still, filled with a longing such as he had never felt before. He had never cared that he was poor, but now he looked down at his ragged clothing in shame. A princess would never look at a poor beggar boy like him, he thought. But just then, his hand brushed against something at his belt. *The lamp!* he thought with a jolt of excitement. Perhaps the genie could help him transform into someone the princess may be interested in! Running as fast as he could, he found a quiet spot and rubbed the lamp once more. To his delight, with a whoosh of smoke, the genie appeared.

"Genie, you obeyed my wish once before. I beg you, please help me once again. Transform me into a prince!"

"Your wish is my command, master," replied the genie and he snapped his fingers. Instantly, Aladdin was dressed in robes of silk and sitting in the centre of a palace draped with rich tapestries and expensive rugs. He had the finest food and everything a prince could desire. Aladdin was overwhelmed. How could the princess think he was anything other than a prince! As he looked out of his bedroom window, Aladdin realized that his new palace bordered the princess's, and so he rushed over to introduce himself, stopping only to thank the genie for making all of his wishes come true.

The princess instantly liked her new neighbour. He was charming and witty, and not at all like the dull courtiers and advisors in her palace. The sultan, the princess's father, was happy his daughter had such a wealthy and fine friend too. The pair started spending a lot of time together, having picnics and long walks. Soon, Aladdin scraped up the courage to ask for the princess's hand in marriage. The delighted sultan promised to throw them a huge engagement party, and the city rejoiced in the happiness of their young prince and princess.

Aladdin was so swept up in his joyful romance with the princess that he had completely forgotten about the sorcerer. The sorcerer, however, hadn't forgotten Aladdin, and one day, he looked in his magic fountain to find the boy – expecting to see him still trapped in the cave, hungry and alone. But instead, when he peered into the water of his magic fountain, Aladdin's smiling face appeared; he was laughing with the princess, surrounded by the rich trappings of the palace. Consumed by fury that a poor street boy had managed to escape the prison he had sent him to, the sorcerer swore to have his revenge. He knew that Aladdin must have used the lamp to escape, and so the sorcerer hatched a plan to steal it.

Disguising himself as a street seller loaded with many new lamps, the sorcerer muttered a magic spell and was transported immediately outside Aladdin's palace. He went around to the servant's entrance, calling out as he went. "New lamps for old lamps," he cried. One of Aladdin's maids heard the cries of the sorcerer and went to the door.

My master has an old lamp by his bedside, but I am

sure he will be pleased with a shiny new one, she thought and, scurrying into her master's bedchamber, she snatched the lamp from beside the bed and brought it to the lamp seller outside. Immediately, the sorcerer shook off his disguise, crying gleefully that the magic lamp was now his. With shaking hands, he rubbed its grubby side and the genie appeared, towering over the palace behind. With no choice over who his new master was, the genie was bound to do the sorcerer's wishes, and he bowed low to the sorcerer. The sorcerer let out an evil cackle as he demanded that Aladdin be unmasked for the poor street boy he was. Then, with his next wish, the sorcerer wished for the princess to be brought to him. He knew that being exposed as a fraud would hurt Aladdin, but knowing the one he loved was held captive by the sorcerer would be the best revenge he could think of.

He was right.

On discovering that Aladdin was only a poor street boy, and blaming him for the disappearance of his beloved daughter, the sultan had Aladdin thrown in his deepest, darkest dungeon. Aladdin begged the sultan for forgiveness, trying to explain that a wicked sorcerer had kidnapped the princess, but the sultan refused to believe a word that the poor street boy uttered. Aladdin was trapped, tormented by the thought of his beautiful princess in the hands of the wicked sorcerer.

Far away, the princess awoke to find herself in a strange land with the sorcerer. Now, the princess was a very clever woman and, although she was scared, she thought quickly, trying to think of a plan to escape her captor.

"What wondrous magic, oh great sorcerer... I cannot believe that one man can do such great deeds," she flattered. "How did you get your power?" she asked him.

Puffed up by the princess's pretty words, the sorcerer boasted, "Why, it's simple. All I have to do is rub this lamp and the genie inside does all the work for me. It's no effort at all." And with that, he put the lamp up high upon a shelf. The princess continued to flatter and spoil the sorcerer for the rest of the day, waiting until he was deeply asleep to take her chance. Whilst the sorcerer slept, she crept into his room and, with shaking hands, stole the lamp down from the shelf. She rubbed it carefully with her hand.

"What is your wish?" the genie asked of her, exploding from the lamp in a torrent of smoke.

"Send this vile sorcerer to the deepest darkest place you can find, forever to be imprisoned there!" With a whirl and a smile, the genie did as the princess had asked, and the sorcerer vanished from his bed in a puff of smoke.

"What is your wish?" he asked once again when she rubbed the lamp a second time.

"Please, take me back to my beloved." Without a moment's pause, the princess was transported to the dungeon where Aladdin was imprisoned. Weeping with joy, Aladdin hugged the princess tightly. "How on earth did you escape, my darling?" he asked through his tears.

"Oh, a little rub of a dirty old lamp did the trick," the princess said, her eyes twinkling. "That sorcerer won't be bothering us ever again!"

Rubbing the lamp again, the princess wished for the pair to be taken to her father. In an instant, they were standing back inside the palace, and the amazed sultan was overwhelmed to see his daughter back where she belonged. Turning to Aladdin, he thanked him over and over for helping to return his daughter to him, and he apologized for suspecting him of kidnapping the princess. But Aladdin was quiet. After the sultan was finished, Aladdin turned to the princess in shame. "I must confess to you – I'm not all I said I was. I've never been a prince. It was all just a pretence to be able to meet you. The genie helped me transform into a prince, but I'm really just a poor street boy."

Aladdin turned red with embarrassment. "I'm sorry," he said. "I understand if you no longer want to marry me." He looked down at his feet, dreading the princess's next words.

"I like you for who you are, not for what you have. I don't care if you're a street boy or a prince; I have money enough for both of us!" the princess exclaimed, hugging Aladdin tightly.

"Come. Let's get rid of this lamp once and for all. We have enough wealth between us to last lifetimes. We don't need any more."

"You will marry me even without the lamp?"

"Of course," the princess replied.

"In that case..." Aladdin rubbed the lamp for one last time, and the genie appeared once more. "Genie, thank you for all you have done for me. You have made my dreams come true and now I would set you free," he said. With that, he flung the lamp into the fireplace. The flames licked the sides until it began to melt, and the genie gave a great bellow of laughter, flying into the sky and vanishing. Its days of servitude were finally over.

Aladdin and the princess lived happily ever after, never to be disturbed by the sorcerer again.

The Fairies
of Caragonan

WALES

Fairies are a popular theme in Welsh mythology, occur-ring in many traditional tales. A famous collector of such tales was P.H Emerson, who wrote down many of the fairy stories that he heard whilst on holiday in Anglesey, an island off the coast of Wales. He compiled the book Welsh Fairy-Tales and Other Stories in 1894, which included a version of this tale.

$\mathcal{M}$any years ago on an island called Mona, lived the Fairies of Caragonan, led by their splendid queen. The queen had ruled for many years and knew that one day soon she would pass her role to her daughter, a beautiful and wise fairy who was on the verge of coming of age. Whilst the queen was ready to pass on the mantle of leadership, she needed to ensure that her daughter was prepared for the great responsibility of leading their people. Aside from ruling fairly and wisely, the fairy queen also had the grave duty of protecting the humans on the island from the sinister witch Morgana.

Morgana was feared by many humans, and that fear only increased her power. The fairies had tried to use their magic to cast her away but her power was too great and the fairies lived in her shadow, unable to protect the humans of the island from her wickedness. Morgana took delight in creating chaos on the island, spreading illness amongst humans and animals, and now even the trees in the fairy glen were starting to die as a perpetual grey cloud hung over the island, blocking out the full rays of the sun. The fairies needed to act soon to stop their natural home being destroyed for ever.

It had long been foretold that only a human of pure heart and of infinite courage would be able to defeat Morgana. But though the fairies had searched for many years, they hadn't yet found the promised human, and they were beginning to despair.

Knowing that her daughter would soon be taking on the responsibility of protecting the land from Morgana, the queen decided to send her out into the human world to search for the promised human once more.

"Go forth, my daughter, and seek out the human who will help us rid the land of Morgana. Find those who have been afflicted by Morgana's magic, and I am sure that you will discover this human amongst them. Once we have found them, I have a plan that will see us free from Morgana once and for all."

Arwyn, the queen's daughter, was one of many shapeshifters among the fairies, able to flit from fairy to bird form and back again. When she heard of the task her mother had set her, she swiftly changed into her bird form and set off on her flight across the woods to the village near the cliffs. Not long after she left her fairy home, Arwyn came upon a fine stone house on the edge of the village. But there was something strange about the house – to Arwyn's fairy sense, a creeping black shadow was visible all around it, and she knew that this was just what her mother had asked her to look out for. As she hovered near the open window, she spied a man lying in bed, his face red and wet with sweat. He was mumbling feverishly in his sleep. Knowing that there was more to this than a fever, Arwyn entered the man's house through the window and took fairy form once again so she could speak with him.

"Sir, what ails you?" she asked, wondering how she or her mother could possibly help this poor fellow. As she suspected, he answered, telling her of a curse that had been placed upon him.

"Morgana the witch came here and demanded that I give her my land. When I refused, she cast a spell on me, and now my body hurts all over. I can't eat a thing and it's getting worse and worse by the hour." Arwyn knew immediately that she must send for her mother the queen. She promised the man she would return shortly, then bade him farewell and flew for home as quickly as she could.

When the queen of the fairies heard the news, she leapt into action. Assembling her most experienced healers, she flew back to the man's house with her daughter.

The man's colour was even worse than when Arwyn had left him. He was pale and had lost so much weight Arwyn could see the bones standing out on his chest. Without delay, the fairy queen placed a blue pot on the table and lit the magical incense inside. A pleasant earthy smell filled the room. The queen ushered her fellow healer fairies to follow her in an ethereal procession to circle the room. They chanted words of magical power as they walked.

The third time around, the queen of the fairies touched her wand upon the blue pot, and then on top of the man's head. In an instant, the man was out of bed and on his feet, his body free of pain. Astonished and grateful, he bowed his head towards the fairies who had saved his life. Arywn was bursting with pride – what wonderful magic her mother knew and how kind she was to help this man. She vowed to be as good and kind as her mother when she in turn was queen. The now bright and healthy man was overjoyed at his good fortune. "How can I ever repay you, dear fairies?"

The queen looked at him, thinking of the

foretelling, and wondered whether he might be the one to help the fairies rid the land of Morgana. She decided to test him. "Good sir, would you stand with us against the evil witch Morgana who placed this curse upon you?"

But the farmer grew pale and shivered. "Anything but that," he stammered, shaking at the thought. The fairy queen smiled graciously, knowing that he did not have the courage she sought.

"Never fear. All I ask is that you lend me a piece of your land next to the sea above the cliffs. Build a sacred stone circle there and you will be rewarded in time," the fairy queen said.

"It will be done!" the man replied, confused but happy to accommodate the fairies who had helped him fight Morgana's curse.

Arwyn was also puzzled at what seemed like a greedy request from her mother. Later, she asked her mother why she wanted that plot of land from the farmer.

"Did I not tell you I had a plan to get rid of the evil queen Morgana? I do not want the land for ourselves, but to use as a tool in defeating the witch," the queen said. "Now, fly, my lovely daughter, and see if there are any others in need of our help."

Arwyn once more turned into a bird and darted about the countryside of Mona looking for any other calls for help. She had not been looking long when she came upon a farm which appeared to have a shadow all around it. Flying within the shadow, a young farmer was tending to a cow that was lying down on its side. Arwyn transformed back into her fairy self, her wings neatly tucked into her back so as to not alarm the young man.

The young man looked up as she approached, and she saw that he had tears in his eyes.

"The cows, the cows are all ill and dying. They haven't given any milk since yesterday. They are all lying down and calling in pain, just like this one," the farmer said, frantically pointing to the cow he was tending. "We will be ruined if all of the cows die. What can we do?"

Arwyn's heart sank. She knew it must be the work of Morgana the witch once more.

"Wait here – I will fetch my mother and we will help you." With that she turned into a bird and flew away. The farmer was too busy caring for his cows to notice.

When Arywn told her mother what she had seen, the queen's eyes lit up. She hoped that this was the human, the one of infinite courage, the one she was waiting for to help her get rid of the witch once and for all. "Take me to him," she said.

The two fairies arrived at the farm and saw for themselves that all of the cows were lying down in the field, close to death.

"Would you like me to cure your cows?" the queen asked the young man.

"Please, if you can!" he exclaimed hopefully.

"If I do so, I will ask a favour of you – are you prepared to help me?" the queen asked sternly. The farmer replied fervently, "I would do anything. Just please help my cows!" A smile spread across the queen's face; the boy hadn't hesitated before offering his assistance. She was sure this was the human that had been foretold many years ago. Together, they could rid the world of Morgana.

Like before, the queen placed the blue pot of incense in the middle of the field and the fairies lined up behind her as they walked three times around the edge of the field. Again they chanted softly as they walked.

The queen tapped the pot and then flew around the field, touching each cow on the head with her magic wand. Once each cow in the field had been marked, every one of them stood up on legs that were no longer wobbly but strong and fresh. They began to eat the green grass and gently swish their tails as if nothing had ever happened. The farmer could not believe his eyes. He was filled with admiration and delight for what the fairies had done for him and the farm, for if the cows had died then the farm would surely have been lost.

"Please tell me what you would have me do," the farmer said. "Whatever it is, it will be worth the price."

"Money is no use to me. All I need from you is your help in ridding our island of the vile witch Morgana, she who put this curse on your cows. Are you brave enough to take the challenge?"

"I am," said the farmer.

"Meet us on top of the cliff tomorrow by the sea. Make your way to where a stone circle awaits."

And with that, the fairies flew away.

The next day, Arwyn, her mother and the rest of the fairies gathered at the newly built stone circle. They saw the farmer was waiting there for them. When the procession of fairies arrived, the queen told the farmer to walk around the fairy circle holding a simple hand mirror.

"Arwyn, you will ask him what he sees on each

turn around the circle," her mother told her.

The farmer walked once around. The fairies chanted:

> Round and round three times three
> Tell me now, what do you see?

Then Arwyn asked him, "Lift the mirror up and tell us what you see."

The farmer did as he was bid and replied excitedly, "I see the witch! I can see her in the mirror!"

The second time the farmer walked around the circle, the fairies chanted their chant and Arwyn asked him again what he saw. This time, the young man was nonplussed, replying, "I cannot see the witch any more. Instead, all I see is a brown hare."

But the fairies weren't disappointed in the least. They knew that this was Morgana revealing her true, animal form. With mounting excitement they chanted their chant again, urging the young farmer around the fairy fort once more.

The third time, the boy responded with a faraway look in his eyes, "I see a mill. The hare is bounding towards a mill in the distance."

And with that information the queen nodded and

took the mirror from the farmer. With a deep breath, she turned to her daughter.

"This is our moment, dear daughter. Now we have seen the true form of the witch, we know we can rid the island of her torment once and for all. With the help of this young man, we shall soon be free of her." Bidding Arwyn to go with the young farmer, she gave her daughter the blue pot full of incense, a slingshot and a smooth stone.

"When the time is right, burn the incense as you have seen me do it, wave the stone over the top three times and then give the slingshot to the boy. He can kill the hare with the stone. Then the witch will be gone for good!" said the queen. "Do not be fearful – I know I can trust you with this task. After all, you will soon be queen of the fairies and you are my daughter. " The queen kissed Arwyn on both cheeks and sent her forth with a smile.

Nervously, Arwyn and the farmer left the fairy circle and began the short walk to the mill.

When they arrived, the pair ducked down behind a small grey stone wall and Arwyn did as her mother had instructed, lighting the incense in the blue pot and waving the stone over the container. The stone began to glow, becoming brighter and brighter in

Arwyn's hand as the magic of the fairies seeped into it. Arwyn and the farmer gazed at the bright stone, knowing it was no longer an ordinary stone but one filled with magic, sure to seek its target without fail.

Arwyn gave the slingshot and the stone to the farmer. He took it but his hands were shaking with fear at the thought of taking on Morgana, who had so long terrorized the village. Arwyn knew that his fear could mean failure. She held his hand.

"You can do this," Arwyn whispered to him. "Only a human can do this part, one with a pure heart and infinite courage. As long as you are brave and try, you cannot fail. Aim at the hare's head. You have one shot." The farmer took a deep breath and stood up. He outstretched one arm, whilst pulling back with the stone in the sling with the other. He closed one eye.

Arwyn could feel excitement and hope coursing through her body.

The farmer stood tall and breathed out, focusing on the hare and pushing away any feelings of fear. The stone flew straight and true. It hit its target straight between the eyes. The hare disappeared and in its place lying still on the floor was the witch. She did not move. Just then, the clouds in the sky above opened up to reveal the full rays of the sun that had been absent for so long. Instantly, the trees stood taller, green and strong. Even the blades of grass saluted the sky. Birds flew through the sky in unison. The curse on the island was lifted!

Arywn hugged the farmer. "You did it!" she sang out. The farmer had a look of relief on his face.

The fairies and villagers celebrated the banishment of the witch at the stone circle overlooking the sea. The queen looked fondly at her daughter dancing with the villagers and knew that she would one day make a fine queen.

And the witch Morgana never troubled anyone ever again.

Here is a sneak peek into another selection of enchanted tales...

Irish Fairy Tales, Myths & Legends

The King's Secret

This is a story about Labhraidh Loingseach (pronounced Lowry Lynshock). As a child, he stopped speaking, after witnessing the murder of his father and grandfather. For a long time he remained dumb, until he got hit on the shin during a game of hurling and cried out, "I'm hurt!" From then on he was called "Labhraidh" which means "he speaks" in Irish.

There once was a king of Ireland called Labhraidh Loingseach. He had unusually long hair which flowed around his shoulders in dark curls. He also wore an unusually high crown which made him appear taller than he was. The long hair and big crown were not fashion statements, but were there to hide a terrible secret, that if discovered, could end his reign as king.

You see, the king had been born with horse's ears instead of ordinary human ones. They hung on each side of his head but pricked to attention when he was straining to listen. The long hair was to hide the ears when they were hanging down, and the crown was to hide them when they were standing up.

When Labhraidh went to war, he wore a bronze helmet with two horns on top to hide his ears. When he went swimming, he wore a cloth cap in which he stuffed his hair and ears. People thought his head-gear was unusual but nobody said anything – kings were allowed to be a bit eccentric.

Once a year, the king had his hair cut in a private room by a barber, often invited from far away. The barbers were always honoured to be invited to the royal court to cut the king's hair, but if they could have known what was going to happen to them, they most certainly would have refused.

Because, while cutting the king's hair, the barber would discover the king's secret, and while shocked by the discovery, the barber was even more shocked that the king never swore him to secrecy.

The reason the king wasn't worried about his secret getting out was because he made sure each barber was killed after cutting his hair. Many barbers went in through the king's front door, but none ever came out.

After many years, word got out that anybody who cut the king's hair never lived to tell the tale. Barbers abandoned their jobs or worked in secret, for fear of being summoned to Labhraidh Loingseach's royal fort to cut his hair.

It became so difficult to find a barber in Ireland that people had to let their hair grow so long that they tripped over it.

Every year, the king found it more and more of a challenge to find a barber. When his royal servants did find one, the barber never wanted the job and would plead to be excused. The servants, however, were under orders not to return to Labhraidh Loingseach's fort empty-handed, so they drew their weapons and escorted reluctant barbers to their last ever job.

One such barber who was summoned went by the name of Marcán. When his mother, a widow, heard that her only son had been brought to cut Labraidhh Loingseach's hair, she was distraught and followed the cavalcade to the royal fort. She pleaded with the guards to let her in, where she found Marcán, scissors in hand, about to cut the king's hair.

"Your Majesty," she said, bowing down before the king. "Please ensure that no harm comes to my boy. He is all I have left in the world, and if he were to die, I think I would too."

"I don't know what you're talking about, woman," replied the king. "Your son has only been brought here to cut my hair."

"No offence intended, Your Majesty, but the whole world and its mother knows that any barber that enters this place never leaves."

The king bowed his head in shame, for he didn't know that this was public knowledge. His servants had kept that from him as well as the fact that barbers were in short supply.

"Can your son keep a secret?" asked Labhraidh.

"Of course," said the widow, looking at Marcán.

He nodded nervously.

"I give you my word," said the king, "that no harm will come to your son, if he promises to keep secret all he sees here."

"I promise," said Marcán.

"Good enough," said Labhraidh, removing his crown. "Now, leave us, woman. I want to get my hair cut in peace."

Tears of joy made the widow's eyes glassy as she bowed with gratitude and left her son to do his job.

Marcán removed his scissors and sharpened the blades on a whetstone. Then, he began cutting the king's hair.

As the dark curls fell to the floor, the boy spied something in the hair on each side of the king's head.

"Your Majesty..." mumbled the barber.

"Speak up, boy," said the king, whose ears, straining to hear, stood erect on his head.

Marcán gasped and stumbled backwards, dropping his scissors to the floor.

"Now you know the king's secret," said Labhraidh. "And for that, you should be put to death, but I vowed to your mother that no harm would come to you, and I'll keep my promise if you keep yours."

"I promise I won't tell a living person what I've seen here," said Marcán.

The barber finished cutting the king's hair, and Labhraidh, happy with the job, said, "I appoint you Royal Barber, to return once a year to cut my hair."

Marcán nodded.

"Just remember your promise, boy."

Marcán bowed and left, not only with a handsome reward for his services, but with his life, relieved and grateful.

The people of Marcán's village were gobsmacked to see him return home for they were sure he was a dead man.

"He must be a mighty fine barber," they said.

The next morning there was a queue of people outside Marcán's house waiting to have their hair cut, though many of them didn't need it. Some of them were even bald!

As Marcán snipped and trimmed, the customers plagued him with questions about the eccentric king, but Marcán's lips were sealed.

Over time, his fame grew far and wide. There was a constant queue outside his door. Everybody wanted to have their hair cut by the Royal Barber.

Marcán became a wealthy man, but he was not happy. The king's secret weighed heavily upon him, keeping him awake at night and putting him off his food. He would have no peace until he shared the secret. You know what they say: a burden shared is a burden halved.

He went to a local druid for advice.

"A secret will burn a hole in your heart," said the holy man. "The only cure is to share it."

"But I promised the king."

"What exactly did you promise him?"

Marcán squinted his eyes, trying to remember the exact words. "I promised not to tell a living person what I saw."

"A living person," repeated the druid. "That doesn't mean you can't tell a rock, a tree, a river or animal. Go into the forest and find something to share your secret with. The very act of saying the words out loud will ease your burden."

Marcán did as the druid instructed, and went deep into the forest until he was sure he was alone.

Then, leaning into a walnut tree, he whispered his secret into its bark. "The king has horse's ears."

Immediately, he felt better, as if a crushing boulder had been lifted from his back. He whispered it again. "The king has horse's ears. The king has horse's ears."

Each time he said it, he felt a little better. He kept saying it until he felt like a new man, released from prison. He skipped and sang the whole way home.

Not long after this, one of Ireland's most renowned harpists, Craiftine, happened to be in the very same forest sourcing wood to make a new harp. As soon as he saw the handsome walnut tree he knew it would be perfect for his new instrument. He cut it down and carved the wood into a beautiful harp. When it was polished, the grain gleamed like golden veins.

He had just finished decorating the harp's pillar with carved Celtic knot-work and inset gemstones, when he received an invitation to play for none other than the king himself, Labhraidh Loingseach. Craiftine felt honoured to be invited.

A perfect opportunity to showcase my new harp, he thought, packing it carefully into a leather bag.

The harpist arrived at Labhraidh Loingseach's fort, marvelling at the splendour of the feast. Long tables were laden with succulent roast meats, fruit and vegetables. Mead and the finest of imported wine flowed from intricately carved goblets, and the sound of laughter and conversation filled the air. The king's great hunting dogs prowled between the tables looking for scraps, while jugglers and acrobats entertained the guests.

After the feasting was over, the king clapped his hands, calling for music. Craiftine took his place on a low stool at the top of the hall and removed his magnificent new harp from its bag. He took a deep breath and placed his fingers on the strings.

When he plucked them, however, he didn't hear the usual melodic harp notes, but a high-pitched voice.

"The king has horse's ears. The king has horse's ears," sang the harp.

The guests gasped and then fell silent.

Craiftine removed his fingers from the strings but the harp continued to sing, "The king has horse's ears. The king has horse's ears."

Labhraidh Loingseach was so stunned that he shot to his feet, sending his crown flying and revealing his two tall horse's ears standing up on his head, listening to the harp.

He expected everybody to laugh, point and mock, but nobody did, for now they all knew the reason for Labhraidh's unconventional headgear and long hair. Many felt sorry that their king had such a burden to bear. This was the moment Labhraidh had dreaded all his life, but now that his secret was known, he felt free. Just as the barber had experienced, it was a relief to have it out in the open.

From that day on, the king wore his horse's ears with pride. He was happy, which meant his subjects were happy, especially the barbers who crawled out of hiding to give the people of Ireland much-needed haircuts.

Do chickens have lips? said Jake. Okay, here's what I dream about. I dream about your bum, a hundred times life-size, floating in the sky, covered with neon lights and flashing on and off. How's that?

Don't put me down, said Rennie.

I like you down, said Jake. Flat on your back. He rolled over on top of her and started biting her neck. I'm uncontrollable, he said. I'm an animal in the dark.

Which one? said Rennie. A chipmunk?

Watch it, pussycat, said Jake. Remember your place. He got hold of her two hands, held her wrists together, shoved himself in between her thighs, squeezing her breast harder than he needed to. Feel that, he said. That's what you do to me, the fastest erection in the West. Pretend I just came through the window. Pretend you're being raped.

What's pretend about it? said Rennie. Stop pinching.

Admit it turns you on, said Jake. Admit you love it. Ask for it. Say please.

Fuck off, said Rennie. She kicked him on the backs of his legs with her heels, laughing.

Jake laughed too. He liked it when she swore; he said she was the only woman he knew who still pronounced the *g* in "fucking." This was true enough: swearing was one of the social graces Rennie hadn't learned early in life, she'd had to teach herself.

You have a dirty mouth, Jake said. It needs to be washed out with a tongue.

What do you dream about? Rennie asked Daniel.

I don't know, said Daniel. I can never remember.

●

Last night Rennie set her alarm for seven. She lies in bed, waiting for it to be seven. When the alarm goes off she claws her way through the mosquito netting and pushes the OFF button.

If it weren't for Lora and the grandmother and the bad heart, she wouldn't have to get up at all. She considers staying in bed, she could always say she slept in. But Griswold is ingrained in her. If you can't keep your word, don't give it. Do unto others. She struggles out through the cocoon of mouldy-smelling gauze, feeling not virtuous but resentful.

She wants to have breakfast before taking a taxi to the airport, but the Englishwoman says breakfast isn't ready yet, it won't be for another hour. Rennie can't wait. She decides to have a coffee and a doughnut at the airport. She asks the Englishwoman to call for a taxi for her and the Englishwoman points to the phone. "You don't need to call for one," she says, "they're always hanging around down there." But Rennie calls anyway.

The car's interior is upholstered in mauve shag, the kind they use for bedroom slippers and toilet seat covers. A St. Christopher doll and a pair of rubber dice swing from the mirror. The driver is wearing purple shorts and a T-shirt with the sleeves ripped off, and a gold cross on a chain around his neck. He's young, he turns the music up as loud as it can go. It's a noxious capon-like rendering of "I Saw Mommy Kissing Santa Claus," and Rennie wonders what month they're in; already she's lost track. She's far too cowardly to ask him to turn it down, and she clenches her teeth against the adenoidal soprano as they drive into town, much too fast, he's doing it on purpose. They pass a clump of people, gathered outside a store for no discernible purpose, and he honks the horn, a long drawn-out blare, drawing attention to them as if it's a wedding.

At the airport Rennie wrestles with the door, gets it open and climbs out. The driver makes no move, so she goes around to his side.

"How much?" she says.

"You leavin' us?" he says.

"No, I'm just picking up a package," says Rennie, and realizes immediately that she's made a mistake, because he says, "I wait for you here."

"That's all right," says Rennie. "I may be a while."

"Nothin' else to do," he says cheerfully.

The airport is almost empty. Rennie looks around for the snack bar and finds it, but it's closed. The customs window is closed too. There's a large poster Scotch-taped to the glass: ELLIS IS KING.

It's quarter to eight. Rennie sits down on a bench to wait. She hunts through her purse, looking for Lifesavers, cough drops, anything she could eat, but there's nothing. Beside the bench is a photo machine, a booth with a curtain and a slot for the coins. Rennie considers this, but it takes only American quarters. She stares across at the poster, the one with the rooster on it. THE BIONIC COCK. IT GIVES YOU SPURS. *Prince of Peace*, someone has scrawled across it.

At eight-thirty the window slides up, there's someone behind it. Rennie digs the crumpled customs form out of her purse and goes over.

"I'm looking for Harold," she says, feeling very silly, but the man behind the counter isn't surprised.

"Yeah," he says. He disappears into a back room. Rennie thinks he's gone to find Harold, but he returns with a large oblong box.

"Are you Harold?" she says.

He regards this as a stupid question and doesn't answer it.

"That must be one fat old lady," he says. "She get six parcel this month. From New York. Food, it say. What she needin' all this food for?"

He looks at her slyly, smiling as if he's told a joke. The box is too big to go through the window, so he unlocks the door at the side.

Rennie was expecting something more like a package. "Isn't

119

that the wrong box?" she says. "I'm looking for a smaller one. It's just some medicine."

"That in here too," he says airily, as if he's been through the contents himself. "This the one, ain't no other box I see."

Rennie is dubious. She reads the label, which indeed has the right name on it. "You forgot this," she says, handing him the customs form. He glances at it with contempt, then tears it in two.

"Shouldn't I sign something?" says Rennie, whose sense of correct procedure is being violated. He scowls at her.

"You tryin' to get me in trouble?" he says. "You take that and go on out of here." He locks himself in his cubicle and turns his back on her.

The box weighs a ton. Rennie has to drag it. It occurs to her that she has no idea where Lora lives or where the grandmother lives, or how she's supposed to deliver the box to either of them. The address is typed clearly enough, but all it says is ELVA, *Ste. Agathe.* There isn't any last name. What next? She feels she has been either duped or used, but she isn't sure which or how. She makes it through the front door and looks for her taxi. It's nowhere in sight and there isn't another; probably they come to the airport only when there's a plane. There's a single car parked across the street but it isn't a taxi, it's a jeep. There's a policeman sitting in it, smoking a cigarette and talking with the driver, and Rennie realizes with a small shock that the driver is Paul. He doesn't see her, he's facing straight ahead, listening to the policeman. Rennie thinks of asking him for a lift; he could carry the box up those stairs for her and then they could have breakfast together. But she's embarrassed, she can't ask him to do that. After the way she's behaved. Chickening out on friendly sex with no explanation at all is socially gauche, inexcusable really: she treated him as if she though he had genital wens. He'd be right to be angry.

She'll have to lug the box back into the terminal building and phone for another taxi; then she'll have to wait for it to arrive. While she's sifting through her purse for pay-phone change, a taxi pulls up, the original. The driver is eating a huge roti; filling drips down his wrist, meat sauce. The smell reminds Rennie that she's nearly faint with hunger, but she can hardly ask for a bite. That would be borderline familiar.

The box is too big to fit into the trunk. The driver tosses the remains of his roti on the sidewalk, wipes his hands carefully on his shorts so as not to damage his mauve upholstery, and helps Rennie slide the box into the back seat. Rennie sits beside him in the front. This time the music is Nat King Cole, singing "I'm Dreaming of a White Christmas," which is better.

"How much?" Rennie asks again, outside the hotel.

"Twenty E.C.s," he says promptly. Rennie knows this is outrageous.

"It's only seven one-way from the airport," she says.

"The extra for waitin'," he says, grinning at her.

Before, on a trip like this, Rennie would have haggled; once she prided herself on haggling. Now she doesn't have the energy, and he knows it, they all know it, they can smell it on her. She gives him twenty-three and goes around to haul out the box.

To her surprise, the driver gets out of the car, though he doesn't help her, he just watches.

"You a friend of Miss Lora's?" he says. "I see you with her. Everyone know Miss Lora."

"Yes," says Rennie, to avoid explanations. She's grappling with the box; the end slides off the back seat and hits the street.

"She a nice lady," he says softly. "You a nice lady too, like her?" Two other men, also with sleeveless T-shirts, have stopped and are leaning against the wall.

Rennie decides to ignore this. There's an innuendo but she can't interpret it. She smiles, politely she hopes, and retreats toward the inner courtyard, dragging the box with what she hopes is dignity. Laughter trails her in.

At the foot of the stairs the deaf and dumb man is curled, asleep and snoring, drunk most likely. His fly is open, revealing torn cloth, grey; there's a recent cut across his cheek, the white stubble on his face is now half an inch long. Rennie can't get the box up the stairs without moving his legs, so she moves them. When she's setting down his feet, bare and crusted with drying mud, he opens his eyes and smiles at her, a smile that would be innocent, blissful even, if it weren't for the missing teeth. She's afraid he will want to shake her hand again, but he doesn't. Maybe he thinks she has enough good luck already.

Rennie negotiates the stairs, hugging the box, lifting it one stair at a time. It's too hot to be doing this; she's an idiot for getting herself into it, for saying she would.

When she reaches the front desk the Englishwoman informs her that it's now too late for breakfast.

"What can I have then?" says Rennie.

"Tea and biscuits," says the Englishwoman crisply.

"Can't I have some toast?" says Rennie, trying not to whine.

The Englishwoman gives her a contemptuous look. "You might find something else," she says, "out there." Her tone implies that anything eaten out there will result in cholera or worse.

Rennie orders the tea and biscuits and pulls the box along the hall to her room. By now it's almost like another person, a body, a dancing partner who's passed out cold. There's no place to put it, it won't fit into the bureau and there's no closet. Rennie slides it under the bed, and she's still on her knees when one of the waitresses brings the tea and biscuits, on a plastic tray with a picture of Windsor Castle on it.

Rennie clears the Bible and her clock off the night table so the waitress can set the tray down. The bed hasn't been made. When the waitress has gone Rennie bundles the mosquito netting into a loose knot and sits down on the twisted sheets.

The tea is made with a Tetley's teabag, and water that was obviously not boiling. The biscuits are arrogantly English, flat beige ovals with the edges stamped into a Victorian-ceiling design and the centres dabbed with putty-like red jam. They look like enlarged corn plasters. Rennie bites into one. It's uncompromisingly stale, it tastes like a winter foot, like a cellar, like damp wood. Rennie wants to go home.

●

Rennie sits by the window, staring at her notebook, in which she's managed to write four words: *Fun in the Sunspots*. But why worry? The editors always change her titles anyway.

There's a knock at the door. A man, says the maid, is waiting for her at the front desk. Rennie thinks it must be Paul; she checks her face in the small mirror. Now she will have to explain.

But it's Dr. Minnow, in a khaki shirt and immaculate white shorts, looking even neater than he did on the plane.

"You are enjoying your stay?" he asks, smiling his crooked smile. "You are learning about local customs?"

"Yes," says Rennie, wondering what he wants.

"I have come to take you to the Botanic Gardens," he says. "As we arranged."

Rennie can't remember having arranged any such thing, but perhaps arrangements are more casual here. She also can't remember having told him where she's staying. The Englishwoman is looking at her from behind the desk. "Of course," says Rennie. "That would be very nice."

She collects her camera, just in case, and Dr. Minnow ushers her to his car. It's a maroon Fiat with an ominous dent in the left fender. When Rennie is strapped in, Dr. Minnow turns to her with a grin that verges on slyness. "There are things more useful for you to see," he says. "We will go there first."

They drive, alarmingly fast, along the main street, away from the bankers' end. The road ceases to be mostly paved and becomes mostly unpaved; now they're in the market. The signs are still up here and there but the orange-crate platforms are gone.

Dr. Minnow hasn't slowed down as much as Rennie thinks he ought to. People stare at them, some smile. Dr. Minnow has rolled down his window and is waving. Voices call to him, he answers, everyone seems to know who he is.

Palms press flat against the windshield. "We for you," someone shouts. "The fish live!"

Rennie's beginning to be worried. The crowd around the car is too thick, it's blocking the car, not all of these people are smiling. Dr. Minnow honks his horn and revs the engine and they move forward.

"You didn't tell me you were still in politics," Rennie says.

"Everyone is in politics here, my friend," says Dr. Minnow. "All the time. Not like the sweet Canadians."

They turn uphill, away from the centre of the town. Rennie grips the edge of the seat, her hands sweating, as they careen along the road, barely two lanes and switchbacked up a steep hill. She looks at the ocean, which is below them now, too far below. The view is spectacular.

They bump at a forty-five degree angle through an arched stone gateway. "Fort Industry," says Dr. Minnow. "Very historical, built by the English. You will want to take some pictures." There's a field of sorts, rutted partially dried mud with a little grass growing on it, and a number of tents, not tents really, pieces of canvas held up by poles. Dr. Minnow parks the car on the near side of the tents and gets out, so Rennie gets out too.

Even outside there's a smell of bodies, of latrines and lime and decaying food. There are mattresses under the canvas roofs, most without sheets. Clothing is piled on the beds and hangs from ropes running from pole to pole. Between the tents are cooking fires; the ground around them is littered with utensils, pots, tin plates, pans. The people here are mostly women and young children. The children play in the mud around the tents, the women sit in the shade in their cotton dresses, talking together and paring vegetables.

"They from the hurricane," says Dr. Minnow softly. "The government have the money to rebuild their houses, the sweet Canadians send it to them. Only it has not yet happened, you understand."

An old man comes over to Dr. Minnow, an older woman, several younger ones. The man touches his arm. "We for you," he says gently. They look sideways at Rennie. She stands awkwardly, wondering what she's supposed to do or say.

Across the field, walking away from them, there's a small group of people, white, well dressed. Rennie thinks she recognizes the two German women from the hotel, the old couple from the reef boat, binoculars pointed. That's what she herself must look like: a tourist. A spectator, a voyeur.

Near her, on a mattress that's been dragged out into the sun, a young girl lies nursing a baby.

"That's a beautiful baby," Rennie says. In fact it isn't, it's pleated, shrivelled, like a hand too long in water. The girl says nothing. She stares woodenly up at Rennie, as if she's been looked at many times before.

Should we have a baby? Rennie said to Jake, only once.

You don't want to limit your options too soon, said Jake, as if it was only her options that would be limited, it had nothing to do with him. Maybe you should postpone it for a while. You want to get the timing right.

Which was true enough. What about you? said Rennie.

If you don't like the road, don't go, said Jake, smiling at her. I'm not too good at lifetime goals. Right now I like the road.

Can I have a baby? Rennie said to Daniel, also only once.

Little boys say *Can I*, said her grandmother. Little girls are more polite. They say *May I*.

Do you mean right now? said Daniel.

I mean ever, said Rennie.

Ever, said Daniel. *Ever* is a pretty big word.

I know. Big words get you in trouble, said Rennie. They told me that at school.

It's not a question of whether you can or not, said Daniel. Of course you can, there's nothing physical that would stop you. You could probably have a perfectly normal, healthy baby.

But? said Rennie.

Maybe you should give yourself some time, said Daniel. Just to adjust to things and consider your priorities. You should be aware that there are hormonal changes that seem to affect the recurrence rate, though we don't really know. It's a risk.

God forbid I should take a risk, said Rennie.

The girl pulls the baby off her breast and switches it to the other side. Rennie wonders if she should give her some money. Would that be insulting? Her hand moves towards her purse, but now she's surrounded by a mob of children, seven or eight of them, jumping excitedly around her and all talking at once.

"They want you to take their pictures," says Dr. Minnow, so Rennie does, but this doesn't seem to satisfy them. Now they want to see the picture.

"This isn't a Polaroid," says Rennie to Dr. Minnow. "It doesn't come out," she says to the children. It's hard to make them understand.

●

It's noon. Rennie stands under the violent sun, rubbing lotion on her face and wishing she had brought her hat. Dr. Minnow seems to know everything there is to know about this fort, and he's going to tell it all to her, brick by brick, while she dehydrates and wonders when she'll faint or break out in spots. What does he want from her? It must be something. "You shouldn't take the time," she's protested, twice already. But he's taking it.

The number of things Rennie thinks ought to happen to her in foreign countries is limited, but the number of things she fears may happen is much larger. She's not a courageous traveller, though she's always argued that this makes her a good travel writer. Other people will want to know which restaurant is likely to give you the bends, which hotel has the cockroaches, she's not the only one. Someday, if she keeps it up, she'll find herself beside a cauldron with an important local person offering her a sheep's eye or the boiled hand of a monkey, and she'll be unable to refuse. The situation has not reached that point. Nevertheless she's a captive; though if worst comes to worst she can always get a lift back with the other tourists.

Now Dr. Minnow is speculating on the methods of sanitation used by the British. It's almost as if they're extinct, a vanished tribe, and he's digging them up, unearthing their broken Queen Anne teacups, exhuming their garbage dumps, exclaiming with wonder and archaeological delight over their curious customs.

The fort itself is standard Georgian brickwork, falling into decay. Although it's listed in the brochure as one of the chief attractions, nothing has been done to improve it or even to keep it in repair. Below is the muddy open space cluttered with tents, and beyond that a public toilet that's ancient and wooden and looks temporary. The only new structure is a glassed-in cubicle with an antenna of some sort on top.

"They have a high-power telescope in there," Dr. Minnow tells her. "They can see everything that comes off the boats. When it is not so hazy you can see Grenada." Beside the cubicle is a square hut that Dr. Minnow says is the prison bakery, since the fort is used as a prison. A goat is tethered beside the toilet.

Dr. Minnow has scrambled up the parapet. He's remarkably active for a man of his age. He seems to expect Rennie to climb up there too, but it's a sheer drop, hundreds of feet to the sea. She stands on tiptoe and looks over instead. In the distance, there's a blue shape, long and hazy, an island.

Dr. Minnow jumps down and stands beside her.

"Is that Grenada?" says Rennie.

"No," says Dr. Minnow. "Ste. Agathe. There, they are all sailors."

"What are they here?" says Rennie.

"Idiots," says Dr. Minnow. "But then, I am from Ste. Agathe. The British make a big mistake in the nineteenth century, they put us all together in one country. Ever since then we have trouble, and now the British have got rid of us so they can have their cheap bananas without the bother of governing us, and we have more trouble."

He's watching something below them now, his head with its high-bridged nose cocked to one side like a bird's. Rennie follows his gaze. There's a man moving among the refugees, from group to group, children following him. He's handing something out, papers, Rennie can see the white. He's wearing boots, with raised heels, cowboy boots: when he pauses before a trio of women squatting around their cooking fire, a small child runs its hands up and down the leather.

Dr. Minnow is grinning. "There is Marsdon," he says. "That boy always busy, he's working for the Prince of Peace. They're making the leaflets in the People's Church, there is a machine. They think they have the one true religion and you go to hell if you don't believe, they be glad to send you. But with these people they will not get far. You know why, my friend?"

"Why?" says Rennie, humouring him. She's tuning out, it's too much like small-town politics, the tiny feuds in Griswold, the grudges, the stupid rivalries. Who cares?

"Always they hand out papers," says Dr. Minnow. "They say it explain everything, why the sun shine, whose arse it shine out, not mine I can assure you of that." He chuckles, delighted with his own joke. "But they forget that few can read."

The children caper in Marsdon's wake, holding the squares of paper up in the air by their corners, waving them, white kites.

Another car drives into the muddy space and parks in front of the bakery; there are two men in it but they don't get out. Rennie can see their upturned faces, the blank eyes of their sunglasses.

"Now we have the whole family," says Dr. Minnow. "This kind does not hand out papers."

"Who are they?" says Rennie. His tone of voice is making her jumpy.

"My friends," he says softly. "They follow me everywhere. They want to make sure I am safe." He smiles and puts his hand on her arm. "Come," he says. "There is more to see."

He steers her down some steps to a stone corridor, where at least it's cooler. He shows her the officers' quarters, plain square rooms with the plaster falling away from the walls in patches.

"We wanted to have a display here," he says. "Maps, the wars between the French and the English. And a gift shop, for the local arts and culture. But the Minister for Culture is not interested. He say, 'You can't eat culture'." Rennie wants to ask what the local arts and culture are, but decides to wait. It's one of those questions to which she's already supposed to know the answer.

They go down more stone stairs. At the bottom there's a line of fresh washing, sheets and flowered pillowcases hung out to dry in the sun. Two women sit on plastic-webbed chairs; they smile at Dr. Minnow. One of them is making what looks like a wallhanging from shreds of material in pastel underwear colours, peach, baby-blue, pink; the other is crocheting, something white. Perhaps these are the local arts and culture.

A third woman, in a brown dress and a black knitted hat, comes from a doorway.

"How much?" Dr. Minnow says to the woman who's crocheting, and Rennie can see that she's expected to buy one of the white objects. So she does.

"How long did it take you to make it?" Rennie asks her.

"Three days," she says. She has a full face, a pleasant direct smile.

"That if your boyfriend not around," says Dr. Minnow, and everyone laughs.

"We here to see the barracks," Dr. Minnow says to the woman in brown. "This lady is from Canada, she is writing about the history here." He's misunderstood her, that's why he's showing her all this. Rennie doesn't have the heart to correct him.

The woman unlocks the door and ushers them through. She has a badge pinned to her shoulder, Rennie sees now. MATRON.

"Do those women live here?" she asks.

"They are our women prisoners," Dr. Minnow says. "The one you buy the thing from, she chop up another woman. The other one, I don't know." Behind her the matron stands beside the open door, laughing with the two women. It all seems so casual.

They're in a corridor, with a row of doors on one side, a line of slatted windows on the other, overlooking a sheer drop to the sea. They go through a doorway; it leads to another corridor with small rooms opening off from it.

The rooms smell of neglect; bats hang upside down in them, there are hornets' nests on the walls, debris rotting in the corners. DOWN WITH BABYLON, someone has scrawled across one wall. LOVE TO ALL. The rooms farthest from the sea are damp and dark, it's too much like a cellar for Rennie.

They go back to the main corridor, which is surprisingly cool, and walk towards the far end. Dr. Minnow says she should try to imagine what this place was like with five hundred men in it. Crowded, thinks Rennie. She asks if this is the original wood.

Dr. Minnow opens the door at the end, and they're looking at a small, partly paved courtyard surrounded by a wall. The courtyard is overgrown with weeds; in a corner of it three large pigs are rooting.

In the other corner there's an odd structure, made of boards nailed not too carefully together. It has steps up to a platform, four supports but no walls, a couple of cross-beams. It's recent but dilapidated; Rennie thinks it's a child's playhouse which has been left unfinished and wonders what it's doing here.

"This is what the curious always like to see," Dr. Minnow murmurs.

Now Rennie understands what she's being shown. It's a gallows.

"You must photograph it, for your article," says Dr. Minnow. "For the sweet Canadians."

Rennie looks at him. He isn't smiling.

●

Dr. Minnow is discoursing on the Carib Indians.

"Some of the earlier groups made nose cups," he says, "which they used for taking liquid narcotics. That is what interests our visitors the most. And they took drugs also from behind. For religious purposes, you understand."

"From behind?" says Rennie.

Dr. Minnow laughs. "A ritual enema," he says. "You should put this in your article."

Rennie wonders whether he's telling the truth, but it's too

131

grotesque not to be true. She's not sure the readers of *Visor* will want to hear about this, but you never know. Maybe it will catch on; for those who cough when smoking.

Dr. Minnow has insisted on taking her to lunch, and Rennie, hungry enough to eat an arm, has not protested. They're in a Chinese restaurant, which is small, dark, and hotter than the outside sunlight. Two ceiling fans stir the damp air but do not cool it; Rennie feels sweat already wetting her underarms and trickling down her chest. The table is red formica, spotted with purplish brown sauce.

Dr. Minnow smiles across at her, kindly, avuncular, his bottom teeth clasped over the top ones like folded hands. "There is always a Chinese restaurant," he says. "Everywhere in the world. They are indefatigable, they are like the Scots, you kick them out in one place, they turn up in another. I myself am part Scottish, I have often considered going to the Gathering of the Clans. My wife says this is what makes me so pig-headed." Rennie is somewhat relieved to hear that he has a wife. He's been too attentive, there must be a catch.

A waiter comes and Rennie lets Dr. Minnow order for her. "Sometimes I think I should have remained in Canada," he says. "I could live in an apartment, or a split-level bungalow, like all the sweet Canadians, and be a doctor of sheep. I even enjoy the snow. The first time it snowed, I ran out into it in my socks, without a coat; I danced, it made me so happy. But instead I come back here."

The green tea arrives and Rennie pours it. Dr. Minnow takes his cup, turns it around, sighs. "The love of your own country is a terrible curse, my friend," he says. "Especially a country like this one. It is much easier to live in someone else's country. Then you are not tempted."

"Tempted?" says Rennie.

"To change things," he says.

Rennie feels they're heading straight towards a conversation she doesn't really want to have. She tries to think of another topic. At home there's always the weather, but that won't do here, since there is no weather.

Dr. Minnow leans across the table towards her. "I will be honest with you, my friend," he says. "There is something I wish you to do."

Rennie isn't surprised. Here it comes, whatever it is. "What's that?" she says warily.

"Allow me to explain," says Dr. Minnow. "This is our first election since the departure of the British. Perhaps it will be the last, since it is my own belief that the British parliamentary system will no longer work in this place. It works in Britain only because they have a tradition, there are still things that are inconceivable. Here, nothing is inconceivable." He pauses, sips at his tea. "I wish you to write about it."

Whatever Rennie's been expecting, it isn't this. But why not? People are always coming on to her about their favourite hot topic. She feels her eyes glaze over. *Great*, she should say. *Good idea*. Then they're satisfied. Instead she says, "What on earth could I write about it?"

"What you see," says Dr. Minnow, choosing not to pick up on her exasperation. "All I ask you to do is look. We will call you an observer, like our friends at the United Nations." He gives a small laugh. "Look with your eyes open and you will see the truth of the matter. Since you are a reporter, it is your duty to report."

Rennie reacts badly to the word *duty*. Duty was big in Griswold. "I'm not that kind of reporter," she says.

"I understand, my friend," says Dr. Minnow. "You are a travel writer, it is an accident you are here, but you are all we can turn to at the moment. There is no one else. If you were a political journalist the government would not have been happy to see you, they would have delayed your entry or expelled you. In any case, we are too small to attract the attention of anyone from the outside, and by the time they are interested it will be too late. They always wait for the blood."

"Blood?" says Rennie.

"News," says Dr. Minnow.

The waiter brings the platter of tiny corncobs and some things that look like steamed erasers, and another of greens and squid. Rennie picks up her chopsticks. A minute ago she was hungry.

"We have seventy-percent unemployment," says Dr. Minnow. "Sixty percent of our population is under twenty. Trouble happens when the people have nothing left to lose. Ellis knows this. He is using the foreign aid money from the hurricane to bribe the people. The hurricane was an act of God, and Ellis thinks that too. He hold out his hands to heaven and pray for someone up there to save his ass for him, and bang, all that money from the sweet Canadians. This is not all. He is using threats now, he says he will take away the jobs and maybe burn down the houses of those who do not vote for him."

"He's doing this openly?" says Rennie.

"On the radio, my friend," says Dr. Minnow. "As for the people, many are afraid of him and the rest admire him, not for his behaviour, you understand, but because he can get away with it. They see this as power and they admire a big man here. He spends their money on new cars and so forth for himself and friends, they applaud that. They look at me, they say, 'What you can do for us?' If you have nothing you are nothing here. It's the old story, my friend. We will have a Papa Doc and after that a revolution or so. Then the Americans will wonder why people are getting killed. They should tell the sweet Canadians to stop giving money to this man."

Rennie knows she's supposed to feel outrage. She remembers the early seventies, she remembers all that outrage you were supposed to feel. Not to feel it then was very unfashionable. At the moment though all she feels is imposed upon. Outrage is out of date.

"What good would it do, even if I wrote it?" says Rennie. "I couldn't get it published here, I don't know anyone."

Dr. Minnow laughs. "Not here," he says. "Here there is one paper only and Ellis has bought the editor. In any case, few read. No, you should publish it there. This will be of help, they pay attention to the outside, they are sensitive about their foreign aid. They would know they are being watched, that someone knows what they are doing. This would stop excesses."

Rennie wonders what an excess is. "I'm sorry," she says, "but I can't think of anyone who would touch it. It isn't even a story yet, nothing's happened. It's hardly of general interest."

"There is no longer any place that is not of general interest," says Dr. Minnow. "The sweet Canadians have not learned this yet. The Cubans are building a large airport in Grenada. The CIA is here, they wish to nip history in the bud, and the Russian agents. It is of general interest to them."

Rennie almost laughs. The CIA has been done to death; surely by now it's a joke, he can't be serious. "I suppose they're after your natural resources," she says.

Dr. Minnow stares across at Rennie, smiling his cramped smile, no longer entirely kind and friendly. "As you know, we have a lot of sand and not much more. But look at the map, my friend." He's no longer pleading, he's lecturing. "South of St. Antoine is Ste. Agathe, south of Ste. Agathe is Grenada, south of Grenada is Venezuela with the oil, a third of U.S. imports. North of us there is Cuba. We are a gap in the chain. Whoever controls us controls the transport of oil to the United States. The boats go from Guyana to Cuba with rice, from Cuba to Granada with guns. Nobody is playing."

Rennie puts down her chopsticks. It's too hot to eat. She feels as if she's stumbled into some tatty left-liberal journal with a two-colour cover because they can't afford three colours. She's allowed this conversation to go on too long, a minute more and she'll be hooked. "It's not my thing," she says. "I just don't do that kind of thing. I do lifestyles."

"Lifestyles?" says Dr. Minnow. He's puzzled.

"You know, what people wear, what they eat, where they go for their vacations, what they've got in their livingrooms, things like that," says Rennie, as lightly as she can.

Dr. Minnow considers this for a moment. Then he gives her an angelic smile. "You might say that I also am concerned with lifestyles," he says. "It is our duty, to be concerned with lifestyles. What the people eat, what they wear, this is what I want you to write about."

He's got her. "Well, I'll think about it," she says limply.

"Good," says Dr. Minnow, beaming. "This is all I wish." He picks up his chopsticks again and scrapes the rest of the squid into his bowl. "Now I will give you a good piece of advice. You should be careful of the American."

"What American?" says Rennie.

"The man," says Dr. Minnow. "He is a salesman."

He must mean Paul. "What does he sell?" says Rennie, amused. This is the first she's heard of it.

"My friend," says Dr. Minnow. "You are so very sweet,"

●

There's a small stationery shop across the street from the hotel, and Rennie goes into it. She passes over the historical romances, imported from England, and buys a local paper, *The Queenstown Times*, which is what she's come to the shop for. Guilt impels her: she owes at least this much to Dr. Minnow.

Though it's becoming clear to her that she has no intention of doing what he wants her to do. Even if she wanted to, she could hardly run all over the place, talking to men in the street; they don't understand the convention, they'd think she was trying to pick them up. She can't do proper research, there are no books in the library here; there's no library. She's a hypocrite, but what else is new? It's a Griswold solution: if you can't say anything nice, don't say anything at all. I'm dying, she should have told him. Don't count on me.

She orders tea and biscuits and takes the paper in to the leatherette lounge. What she really wants is to lie down and sleep, and if she goes back to her room she knows she will. She's trying to resist that; it would be so easy here to do nothing but eat and sleep.

The Englishwoman brings the tea tray herself and slams it down in front of Rennie. "I don't know where *they've* gone to," she says.

Rennie expects her to go away, but instead she hovers. "There's no water," she says. "They should have it fixed in a few hours." Still she lingers.

"May I offer you some advice?" she says at last. "Don't have anything to do with that man."

"What man?" says Rennie. The Englishwoman's voice suggests some violation of sexual morality, and Rennie wonders what she's done to deserve this.

"That man," says the Englishwoman. "Calls himself a doctor."

"He just wanted to show me the Botanic Gardens," says Rennie, conscious of a slight lie. She waits for the woman to tell her that Dr. Minnow is really a notorious sexual molester, but instead she says, "The trees have signs on them. You can read them yourself, if that's what you want."

"What's the matter with him?" says Rennie. Now she expects racial prejudice.

"He stirs people up for nothing," says the Englishwoman.

This time the biscuits are white and sprinkled with sand. The tea is lukewarm. Rennie fishes the teabag out by its string. She doesn't want to leave it on her saucer, it's too much like a dead mouse, so after some thought she conceals it in the earth around the mottled plant.

The editorial is about the election. Dr. Minnow, it seems, is almost as bad as Castro, and Prince Macpherson is worse. If anyone at all votes for either of them, they are likely to combine forces and form a coalition, and that will be the end of the democratic traditions that St. Antoine has cherished and protected for so long, says the editor.

On the front page there's a story about the new sugar factory Prime Minister Ellis is planning, and an article about road repairs. There's a picture of Ellis, the same picture that's everywhere on the posters. The Canadian High Commissioner has recently paid a visit from his base in Barbados, and a reception was given for him at Government House. Canada is sponsoring a diver training program for lobster fishermen on Ste. Agathe, where most of the fishermen live. The inhabitants of Songeville will be pleased to learn that the United States has contributed an extra five hundred thousand dollars to the hurricane relief fund, which will be used to repair roofs and fix the schoolhouse. Those still living in temporary camps and in churches will soon be able to return to their homes.

The Englishwoman comes back in, white-faced, tight-lipped, dragging an aluminum step ladder which screeches on the wooden floor. "If you want it done, do it yourself," she announces to Rennie. She sets the ladder up, climbs it, and starts taking down the tinsel festoons, her solid white-marbled calves two feet from Rennie's head. There's a strong smell of women's washrooms: tepid flesh, face powder, ammonia. Rennie tries to read a story about the sudden increase in petty thievery, but the Englishwoman is making her feel lazy and selfish. In a minute she'll offer to help and then she'll be stuck, catching those fuzzy fake poinsettias as the Englishwoman tosses them down and putting them away in that tatty cardboard box. She folds up her newspaper and retreats to her room, carrying her cup of cold tea.

"WHAT TO DO IF THE THIEF VISITS YOU," she reads. 1. Have a flashlight by your bed. 2. Have a large can of Baygon or other insect spray. 3. Shine the flashlight into his face. 4. Spray the Baygon into his face. 5. Go to the police, make a statement." Rennie wonders what the thief is supposed to do while you're spraying the Baygon into his face, but doesn't pursue this further. Like everything else she's been reading, the instructions are both transparent and impenetrable.

She skips the column entitled "Spiritual Perspectives," toys with the idea of doing the crossword puzzle but discards it; the answers are on page 10 and she knows she'll cheat. The Housewives' Corner has nothing in it but a recipe for corn fritters. The Problem Corner is by Madame Marvellous.

Dear Madame Marvellous:

I am in love with a boy. Both of us are Christians. Sometimes he asks me for a kiss, but I have read that kissing before marriage is not right because it arouses passions that lead to sex. But he does not believe that sex before marriage is wrong. The Bible says that fornication is wrong, but he says fornication is not sex. Please explain this in a clear way.

Worried.

Dear Worried:

My dear, love is the full expression of oneself. As long as you remember this you will not go wrong. I do hope I have helped you.

Madame Marvellous.

Rennie closes her eyes and pulls the sheet up over her head. She doesn't have the strength to untangle the mosquito netting.

Oh please.

●

Rennie lies in bed and thinks about Daniel. Which is hopeless, but wasn't it always? The sooner she stops the better. Still, she keeps on.

It would be easier if Daniel were a pig, a prick, stupid or pompous or even fat; especially fat. Fat would be a big advantage. Unfortunately Daniel is thin. Also he loves Rennie, or so he said, which is no help at all. (Though what did it amount to? Not much, as far as Rennie could see. She isn't even sure what it meant, this love of his, or what he thought it meant; which may not be the same thing.)

Rennie once spent a lot of time trying to figure out what Daniel meant. Which was difficult, because he wasn't like any of the people she knew. The people she knew spoke of themselves as bottoming out and going through changes and getting it together. The first time she'd used these phrases with Daniel, she'd had to translate. Daniel had never bottomed out, as far as she could tell, and apparently he'd never felt the need to get it together. He didn't think of himself as having gone through changes. In fact he didn't seem to think of himself much in any way at all. This was the difference between Daniel and the people she knew: Daniel didn't think of himself.

This sometimes made it hard for Rennie to talk to him, since when she asked him questions about himself he didn't know the answers. Instead he acted as if he'd never even heard the questions. Where have you been for the past twenty years? she wanted to ask him. Etobicoke? It was more like Don Mills, but Daniel didn't seem to care where he lived. He didn't care what he ate, he didn't care what he wore: his clothes looked as if they'd been picked out by his wife, which they probably had been. He was a specialist, he'd been immersed, he knew only one thing.

He thought Rennie knew thing she didn't know but ought to; he thought she lived in the real world. It pleased him to believe this, and Rennie wanted him to be pleased, she liked to amuse him, though she was afraid that sooner or later he would decide that the things she knew weren't really worth knowing. Meanwhile he was like a Patagonian in Woolworth's, he was enthralled by trivia. Maybe he's having a mid-life crisis, thought Rennie. He was about that age. Maybe he's slumming.

Sometimes they had lunch together, but not very often because most of Daniel's life was spoken for. At lunch Rennie did tricks, which was easy enough with Daniel: he could still be surprised by things that no longer surprised anyone else. She deduced the customers from their clothes, she did them over for him at front of his very eyes. This one, she said. A receptionist at, let's see, Bloor and Yonge, but she'd like you to think she's more. Overdid it on the eyeshadow. The man with her though, he's a lawyer. At the next table, middle management, probably in a bank. I'd redo the cuffs on the pants, the lawyer's, not the other one. On the other one, I'd redo the hair.

I don't see anything wrong with his hair, said Daniel.

You don't understand, Rennie said. People love being redone. I mean, you don't think you're finished, do you? Don't you want to change and grow? Don't you think there's more? Don't you want me to redo you? It was one of Rennie's jokes that the perfect magazine title would be "Sexual Makeovers." People thought of their lives as examinations they could fail or pass, you got points for the right answers. Tell them what was wrong, preferably with them, then suggest how to improve it. It gave them hope: Daniel should approve of that.

Who would you redo me? said Daniel, laughing.

If I could get my hands on you? said Rennie. I wouldn't, you're perfect the way you are. See how good I'd be for your ego, if you had one?

Daniel said that he did have one, that he was quite selfish in fact, but Rennie didn't believe him. He didn't have time for an ego. During lunch he looked at his watch a lot, furtively but still a lot. "Romance Makes a Comeback," thought

141

Rennie. She kept hoping she'd see enough of him so she'd begin to find him boring; talking with Daniel was a good deal like waltzing with a wall, even she knew that. But this failed to happen, partly because there wasn't a whole lot of him to see. When he wasn't at the hospital he had family obligations, as he put it. He had a wife, he had children, he had parents. Rennie had trouble picturing any of them, except the parents, whom she saw as replicas of American Gothic; only Finnish, which was what they were. They didn't have a lot of money and they were very proud of Daniel, who wasn't any more Finnish than she was except for the cheekbones. Sundays the parents got him; Saturday's were for the kids, evenings for the wife. Daniel was a dutiful husband, a dutiful parent, a dutiful son, and Rennie, who felt she had given up being dutiful some time ago, found it hard not to sneer and hard not to despise herself for wanting to.

She wasn't jealous of his wife, though. Only of his other patients. Maybe I'm not the only one, thought Rennie. Maybe there's a whole line-up of them, dozens and dozens of women, each with a bite taken out of them, one breast or the other. He's saved all our lives, he has lunch with us all in turn, he tells us all he loves us. He thinks it's his duty, it gives us something to hold on to. Anyway he gets off on it, it's like a harem. As for us, we can't help it, he's the only man in the world who knows the truth, he's looked into each one of us and seen death. He knows we've been resurrected, he knows we're not all that well glued together, any minute we'll vaporize. These bodies are only provisional.

At the beginning, when she still believed she could return to normal, Rennie thought that they would see each other a certain number of times and then they would have an affair; naturally; that's what people did. But this also failed to happen. Instead, Daniel spent one whole lunch explaining, earnestly and unhappily, why he couldn't go to bed with her.

It would be unethical, he said. I'd be taking advantage of you. You're in an emotional state.

What is this, thought Rennie, Rex Morgan, M.D.? People she knew prided themselves on taking emotional risks. She couldn't decide whether Daniel was being wise, principled or just a coward.

Why is it such a big deal? she said. Once wouldn't kill you. Behind a bush, it would only take five minutes.

It wouldn't be once, he said.

Rennie felt suspended; she was waiting all the time, for something to happen. Maybe I'm an event freak, she thought. The people she knew, Jocasta for instance, would have regarded it all as an experience. Experiences were like other collectables, you kept adding them to your set. Then you traded them with your friends. Show and tell. But Rennie had trouble thinking of Daniel as just an experience; besides, what was there to tell?

What do you get out of this? she said. What do you want?

Does there have to be something? he said. I just want it to go on the way it is.

But what *is* it? she said. It isn't anything. There's nothing to it.

He looked hurt and she was ashamed of herself. What he probably wanted was escape, like everyone else; a little but not too much, a window but not a door.

I could ask you the same thing, he said.

I want you to save my life, thought Rennie. You've done it once, you can do it again. She wanted him to tell her she was fine, she wanted to believe him.

I don't know, she said. She didn't know. Probably she didn't really want him to go to bed with her or even touch her; probably she loved him because he was safe, there was absolutely nothing he could demand.

Sometimes they held hands, discreetly, across the table in

the corners of restaurants; which, in those weeks and then those months, was about as much as she could stand. Afterwards she could feel the shape of his hand for hours.

●

There's someone knocking at the door. The room is dark. Whatever sings at night is singing outside her window, and there is the same music.

The knocking goes on. Perhaps it's the maid, coming far too late, to make up the bed. Rennie pulls off the damp sheet, walks to the door in her bare feet, unlocks it, opens it. Paul is there, one shoulder leaning against the wall, looking not at all like a salesman.

"You shouldn't unlock your door like that," he says. "It could be anyone." He's smiling though.

Rennie feels at a disadvantage without her shoes on. "I'm lucky this time," she says. She's glad to see him: he's the closest facsimile here to someone she knows. Maybe they can just skip yesterday and start again, as if nothing at all has happened. Which is true enough, since nothing has.

"I thought you might like dinner," he says, "some place with real food."

"I'll put my shoes on," says Rennie. She turns on the mermaid lamp. Paul comes into the room, and closes the door, but he doesn't sit down. He just stands, gazing around as if it's an art gallery, while Rennie picks up her sandals and purse and goes into the bathroom to see what she looks like. She brushes her hair and sticks on a little blue eyeliner pencil, not too much. She thinks about changing her dress but decides against it; it might look anxious. When she comes out he's sitting on the edge of her bed.

"I was having a nap," says Rennie, feeling she has to explain the unmade bed.

"I see you got Lora's box for her all right," he says. "Any problems?"

"No," says Rennie, "except it was a little bigger than I thought, and now I don't know what to do with it." It occurs to her that she may be able to fob the box off on Paul, since he knows Lora. "I don't know where this woman lives," she says, as helplessly as she can.

"Elva?" says Paul. "You just take it over to Ste. Agathe, there's a boat every day at noon. Once you get there anyone can tell you." He doesn't offer to take it himself.

Rennie turns off the mermaid lamp and locks the door and they walk out past the front desk and the Englishwoman's laser-beam gaze, and Rennie feels she's sneaking out of the dorm.

"The dinner's part of the plan," says the Englishwoman behind them.

"Pardon?" says Rennie.

"If you don't eat it you pay for it anyway. It's part of the plan."

"I realize that," says Rennie.

"We lock up at twelve," says the Englishwoman.

Rennie's beginning to understand why she dislikes this woman so much. It's the disapproval, automatic and self-righteous, it's the ill-wishing. Rennie knows all about that, it's part of her background. Whatever happens to Rennie the Englishwoman will say she was asking for it; as long as it's bad.

They go down the stone steps and through the damp little courtyard and step out into the musical night. Paul takes hold of Rennie's arm above the elbow, his fingers digging in. "Just keep going," he says. He's steering her.

Now she sees what he's talking about. A little way up the street, in the dim light over by the stationery store, two of the blue-shirted policemen are beating a man up. The man is on his knees in the pot-holed road and they are kicking him, in the stomach, on the back. All Rennie can think of is that the two policemen are wearing shoes and the man isn't. She's never seen anyone being beaten up like this before, only pictures of it. As soon as you take a picture of something it's a picture. Picturesque. This isn't.

Rennie has stopped, though Paul is pushing her, trying to keep her moving. "They don't like you to stare," he says. Rennie's not sure who he means. Does he mean the policemen, or the people they beat up? It would be shaming, to have other people see you so helpless. There are other people on the street, the usual clumps and knots, but they aren't staring, they're looking and then looking away. Some of them are walking, nobody is doing anything, although the walking ones deflect themselves, they go carefully around the man, who is now doubled over.

"Come on," says Paul, and this time Rennie moves. The man is struggling onto his knees; the policemen are standing back, watching him with what seems like mild curiosity, two children watching a beetle they've crippled. Perhaps now they will drop stones on him, thinks Rennie, remembering the schoolyard. To see which way he will crawl. Her own fascination appals her. He lifts his face and there's blood streaming down it, they must have cut his head, he looks directly at Rennie. Rennie can remember drunks on Yonge Street, men so drunk they can't stand up, looking up at her like that. Is it an appeal, a plea for help, is it hatred? She's been seen, she's being seen with utter thoroughness, she won't be forgotten.

It's the old man. He can't be totally mute because there's a sound of some kind coming out of him, a moaning, a stifled reaching out for speech which is worse than plain silence.

They reach the jeep and this time Paul opens the door and helps her in, he wants her in there as fast as possible. He closes the door carefully, tests it to make sure it's really shut.

"Why were they doing that?" Rennie says. She's pressing her hands together, she refuses to shake.

"Doing what?" says Paul. He's a little sharp, a little annoyed. She stalled on him.

"Come on," says Rennie.

Paul shrugs. "He was drunk," he says. "Or maybe they caught him thieving. He was hanging around the hotel when I came in, they don't like people bothering the tourists. It's bad for business."

"That was horrible," says Rennie.

"Up north they lock them up, down here they just beat them up a little. I know which I'd choose," says Paul.

"That wasn't a little," says Rennie.

Paul looks over at her and smiles. "Depends what you think a lot is," he says.

Rennie shuts up. She's led a sheltered life, he's telling her. Now she's annoyed with herself for acting so shocked. Squealing at mice, standing on a chair with your skirts hitched up, that's the category. *Girl.*

Paul drives through the darkness with elaborate slowness, for her benefit. "You can go faster," she says. "I'm not about to throw up." He smiles, but he doesn't.

●

The Driftwood at night is much the same as the Driftwood by day, except that it's floodlit. There's a half-hearted steel band and two couples are dancing to it. The women are wearing shirts made from fake flour sacks; the blonde is taking pictures with a flashcube camera, the brunette is wearing a captain's cap, backwards. One of the men has a green shirt with parrots on it. The other one is shorter, fatter, with the fronts of his legs so badly burned that the skin is peeling off in rags. He's wearing a red T-shirt that says BIONIC COCK. It's the usual bunch, from Wisconsin Rennie decides, dentists and their wives fresh off the plane, their flesh like uncooked Dover sole, flying down to run themselves briefly under the grill. The dentists come

147

here, the dental assistants go to Barbados, that's the difference.

Rennie and Paul sit at a metal table and Rennie orders a ginger ale. She's not going to get sick in the jeep again, once was enough. She's thinking about the man on his knees in the dark road, but what is there to think? Except that she's not hungry. She watches the awkward stiff-legged dancers, the steel-band men, who are supple, double-jointed almost, glancing at them with a contempt that is almost but not quite indifference.

"Dentists from Wisconsin?" she says to Paul.

"Actually they're Swedes," he says. "There's been a rash of Swedes lately. Swedes tell other Swedes, back in Sweden. Then all of a sudden the place is swarming with them."

"How can you tell?" says Rennie, impressed.

Paul smiles at her. "I found out," he says. "It's not hard. Everyone finds out about everyone else around here, they're curious. It's a small place, anything new or out of the ordinary gets you noticed pretty fast. A lot of people are curious about you, for instance."

"I'm not out of the ordinary," says Rennie.

"Here you are," he says. "You're at the wrong hotel, for one thing. It's mostly package tours and little old ladies who stay there. You should be at the Driftwood." He pauses, and Rennie feels she has to supply an answer.

"Pure economics," she says. "It's a cheap magazine."

Paul nods, as if this is acceptable. "They wonder why you aren't with a man," he says. "If you'd come on a boat they'd know why, they'd figure you're just boat-hopping. Girls do that quite a bit here, it's like hitchhiking, in more ways than one. But you don't seem the type. Anyway, they know you came in on the plane." A smile, another pause. It occurs to Rennie that it may not be *they* who want to know these things about her, it may only be Paul. A small prickle goes down her spine.

148

"If they know so much, they must know what I'm doing here," she says, keeping her voice even. "It's business. I'm doing a travel piece. I hardly need a chaperone for that."

Paul smiles. "White women have a bad reputation down here," he says. "For one thing, they're too rich; for another they lower the moral tone."

"Come on," says Rennie.

"I'm just telling you what they think," says Paul. "The women here think they spoil the local men. They don't like the way white women dress, either. You'd never see a local woman wearing shorts or even pants, they think it's degenerate. If they started behaving like that their men would beat the shit out of them. If you tried any of that Women's Lib stuff down here they'd only laugh. They say that's for the white women. Everyone knows white women are naturally lazy and they don't want to do a woman's proper work, and that's why they hire black women to do their work for them." He looks at her with something between a challenge and a smirk, which Rennie finds irritating.

"Is that why you like it here?" she says. "You get your grapes peeled for you?"

"Don't blame it on me," Paul says, with a little shrug. "I didn't invent it."

He's watching her react, so she tries not to. After a minute he goes on. "They also think you aren't only a journalist. They don't believe you're really just writing for a magazine."

"But I am!" says Rennie. "Why wouldn't they believe that?"

"They don't know much about magazines," says Paul. "Anyway, almost nobody here is who they say they are at first. They aren't even who somebody else thinks they are. In this place you get at least three versions of everything, and if you're lucky one of them is true. That's if you're lucky."

"Does all this apply to you?" says Rennie, and Paul laughs.

"Let me put it this way," he says. "For ten thousand dollars you can buy a St. Antoine passport; officially, I mean, unofficially it costs more. That's if you've got the right connections. If you want to, you can open your own private bank. The government even helps you do it, for a cut of the action. Certain kinds of people find it very convenient."

"What are you telling me?" says Rennie, who senses increasingly she's been asked out to dinner for a reason, which is not the same as the reason she had for accepting. She looks into his light-blue eyes, which are too light, too blue. They've seen too much water. Burned out, she thinks.

Paul smiles, a kindly threatening smile. "I like you," he says. "I guess I'm trying to tell you not to get too mixed up in local politics. That is, if you really are writing a travel piece."

"Local *politics*?" says Rennie, taken by surprise.

Paul sighs. "You remind me of a certain kind of girl back home," he says. "The kind who move to New York from the Midwest and get jobs on magazines."

"In what way?" says Rennie, dismayed.

"For one thing you're nice," says Paul. "You'd rather not be, you'd rather be something else, tough or sharp or something like that, but you're nice, you can't help it. Naïve. But you think you have to prove you're not merely nice, so you get into things you shouldn't. You want to know more than other people, am I right?"

"I don't have the faintest idea what you're talking about," says Rennie, who feels seen through. She wonders if he's right. Once he would have been, once there were all kinds of things she wanted to know. Now she's tired of it.

Paul sighs. "Okay," he says. "Just remember, nothing that goes on here has anything to do with you. And I'd stay away from Minnow."

"Dr. Minnow?" says Rennie. "Why?"

"Ellis doesn't like him," says Paul. "Neither do some other people."

"I hardly know him," says Rennie.

"You had lunch with him," says Paul, almost accusingly.

Rennie laughs. "Am I going to get shot, for having *lunch*?"

Paul doesn't think this is funny. "Probably not," he says."They mostly shoot their own. Let's go get something to eat."

Under an open-sided hut with fake thatching there's a buffet laid out, bowls of salad, platters of roast beef, lime pies, chocolate cakes with hibiscus flowers stuck into them. As much as you can eat. There are more people now, piling food high on their plates. To Rennie, they all look Swedish.

She takes her plate back to the table. Paul is silent now and absent. It's almost as if he's in a hurry to get away. Rennie sits across from him, eating shrimp and feeling like a blind date, the comic-book kind with buck teeth and pimples. In situations like this she reverts to trying to please, or is it appease? Maybe he's with the CIA, it would all fit in, the warning and the neo-hippie haircut, camouflage, and the time in Cambodia, and the boats he shouldn't be able to afford. The more she thinks about it the more sense it makes. She's innocent, she doesn't want him to get the wrong impression, he might end up putting some kind of weird drug into her guava jam. Does he think she's a dangerous subversive because she had lunch with Dr. Minnow? She wonders how she can convince him that she is who she is. Would he believe drain-chain jewellery?

Finally she asks him about tennis courts. She wants things to return to normal; she wants the situation to normalize, as they say on the news. "Tennis courts?" Paul says, as if he's never heard of them.

Rennie feels that she's been investigated and dismissed, she's been pronounced negligible, and this is either because Paul believes her or because he doesn't. Which is worse, to be irrelevant or to be dishonest? Whichever it is has erased her as far as he's concerned. As for her, all she can think of is how to recapture his interest, now that it's no longer there. She's almost forgotten there's some of her missing. She realizes she was looking forward, though to what she doesn't know. An event, that's all. Something. She's had enough blank space recently to last her for a long time.

●

Rennie and Jocasta were trying on used fur coats in the Sally Ann at Richmond and Spadina. According to Jocasta this was the best Sally Ann in the city. It was really Jocasta who was trying them on, since Rennie didn't have much interest in used fur coats, she stuck to her classic down-fill from Eddie Bauer's. They were supposed to be shopping for Rennie; Jocasta thought it would make her feel better if she went out and bought something. But she should have known. With Jocasta you always ended up in the Sally Ann.

I won't wear seal though, said Jocasta. I draw the line. Look at this, what do you think it is?

Dyed rabbit, said Rennie. You're safe.

Jocasta turned the pockets inside out. There was a stained handkerchief in one of them. What I'm really looking for, she said, is a black hat with a pheasant feather, you know those curved ones? Gloria Swanson. How's everything?

I'm having a thing with this man, said Rennie, who had resolved many times never to discuss this with anyone, especially Jocasta.

Jocasta looked at her. The pause was just a little too long, and Rennie could hear Jocasta wondering how much of her was gone, chopped away; under all that, you couldn't tell really. A thing with a man. *Bizarre*. Possibly even gross.

That's wizard, said Jocasta, who liked resurrecting outmoded slang. Love or sex?

I'm not sure, said Rennie.

Love, Jocasta said. Lucky you. I can't seem to get it up for love any more. It's such an effort.

She slipped her arms into a late forties lantern-sleeve muskrat, whole Rennie held it for her. A little tatty around the collar, but not bad, said Jocasta. So it's walking-on-air time, a little pitty-pat of the heart, steamy dreams, a little how-you-say purple passion? Spots on the neck, wet pits? Buying your trousseau yet?

Not exactly, said Rennie. He's married.

Before Daniel, Rennie had never paid much attention to married men. The mere fact that they were married ruled them out, not because they were off-limits but because they had demonstrated their banality. Having a married man would be like having a Group of Seven washable silkscreen reproduction in your livingroom. Only banks had those any more, and not the best banks, either.

Lately, though, she'd been seeing it from a different angle. Maybe Daniel wasn't an afterglow from the past; maybe he was the wave of the future. As Jocasta said about her wardrobe, save it up. Never throw anything away, because time is circular and sooner or later it all comes round again. Maybe experiments in living, trying it out first, and infinitely renegotiable relationships were fading fast. Soon Daniel would be *in*, limited options would be *in*. No way out would be *in*. Group of Seven silkscreens were coming back too, among the ultra *nouveau wavé*, but they had to be washable.

Sometimes married is better than not married, Jocasta said. They've got their own lives, they don't need to muck up yours. You can do it in the afternoon, have a nice fuck, hear all about how important you are in their life, listen to their little troubles, their mortgage the way their kid grinds screwed-up caramels into the shag, how they had to get the clutch on the Volvo replaced, and then you can go out with someone fun at night. I used to like stoles, but you know those little shortie jackets they used to wear with formals? With the handkerchief pocket. They're better.

You don't quite see it, said Rennie. He's *really* married. He thinks of himself as married.

You mean he says stuff like his wife doesn't understand him, Jocasta said. That can be boring. Usually their wife understands them backwards, that's the problem. I went through all that ten years ago, when I was still a junior buyer for Creeds. Every time I had to go to New York; it was the goddamn supervisor. He thought I was so *dirty*, you know? *Turkey*ville! I must have been desperate, I hadn't discovered cucumbers then. What they usually mean is that their wives won't go down on them, as far as I can figure out. Kids? Let me guess. Two.

Three and a half, Rennie said.

You mean one's brain-damaged? said Jocasta, looking over her shoulder in the mirror. Waltz length. Remember waltz length?

No, said Rennie. His wife's pregnant again.

And he loves his wife, of course, said Jocasta. And she loves him. Right?

I'm afraid so, said Rennie.

Daniel had not said *I'm afraid so*. He'd said *I think so*.

You mean you don't know? said Rennie.

We don't talk about it, he said. I guess she does. She does.

So sit back and enjoy it, said Jocasta. What do you have to worry about? Except Jake, but he's cool.

Rennie wondered how cool Jake actually was. She hadn't told him about Daniel. Daniel, however, asked about Jake almost every time they saw each other. How's Jake? He would say hopefully, and Rennie would always say, Fine. She knew about bookends, she knew that one wouldn't work without the other. Any damage to Jake and Daniel would be off and running. He wouldn't want to be stuck with the whole package. She might be the icing on his cake but she sure as hell wasn't the cake.

Jake's a grownup, she said. *Open-ended* is one of his favourite words.

Well, there you go, said Jocasta. Nifty. Two's better than one any day, as long as you don't go all soft and grubby and Heartbreak Hotel.

You still don't see it, said Rennie. Nothing's happening.

Nothing? said Jocasta.

Unless you count some pretty frantic hand-holding, said Rennie. She was embarrassed to have to admit this, she knew how abnormal it was, but she wasn't as embarrassed as she would have been once. The fact was that she wasn't sure whether she wanted it or not, an affair with Daniel. It would not be what you would call relaxed, it wouldn't be very much fun. Pulling the plug on all that repression. It would be like going over Niagra Falls in a spin-dryer, you could get inured that way.

Why not? said Jocasta.

I told you, said Rennie. He's too married.

They looked at one another. Nothing, said Jocasta. Weird. She put her hand on Rennie's shoulder. Listen, she said, it could be worse, look at it this way. I mean, an affair's just another affair, what else is new? It's like one chocolate bar after another; you start having these fantasies about being a nun, and you know what, they're enjoyable. But nothing, that's kind of romantic; he must think a lot of you. There's something to be said for nothing.

●

After the chocolate cake they drive back, straight back, no stopping in the woods this time. Rennie sits jolting in the front seat, trying not to feel disappointed. What does she need it for anyway? It's foolishness, as her grandmother would say. Her mother too. They all have the category, it gets passed down like a cedar chest, though they each put different things into it.

When they reach the hotel Paul doesn't touch her, not even a peck on the cheek. He opens his door and gets out, whistling through his teeth. He doesn't take her hand to help her down, he takes her arm, and he doesn't go as far as her room. He waits at the bottom of the stone stairs until she reaches the top, that's all.

Rennie walks down the green wooden corridor, feeling

very tired. What is she supposed to make of all this? Why is she trying to make anything? He asked her for dinner and dinner is what she got. She remembers seeing a film years ago, about the effects of atomic radiation on the courtship instincts of animals: birds ignoring each other or attacking instead of dancing, fish going around in lopsided circles instead of spawning, turtles leaving their eggs to fry in the sun, unfertilized anyway. Maybe this is what accounts for the New Chastity: a few too many deadly rays zapping the pineal gland. The signals are all screwed up and nobody understands any more what they used to mean.

What she remembers most clearly about the evening is not even Paul. It's the deaf and dumb man on his knees in the street, the two men kicking at him, then watching him with that detachment, that almost friendly interest.

A long time ago, about a year ago, Jocasta said, I think it would be a great idea if all the men were turned into women and all the women were turned into men, even just for a day. Then they'd all know exactly how the other ones would like to be treated. When they got changed back, I mean. Don't you think that's a great idea?

It's a great *idea*, said Rennie.

But would you vote for it? said Jocasta.

Probably not, said Rennie.

That's the problem with great ideas, said Jocasta. Nobody votes for them.

Jocasta thinks it would be a great idea if all the men were changed into women and all the women were changed into men for a week. Then they'd each know how to treat the other ones when they got changed back, said Rennie.

Jocasta's full of crap, said Jake. And too bony. Bony women shouldn't wear V-necks.

What's the matter with it? said Rennie. Wouldn't you like to know how women want to be treated? Wouldn't it make you irresistible?

156

Not if everyone else knew it too, said Jake. But first of all, that isn't what would happen. The women would say, Now I've got you, you prick. Now it's my turn. They'd all become rapists. Want to bet?

What would the men say? said Rennie.

Who knows? said Jake. Maybe they'd just say, Oh shit. Maybe they'd say they don't feel like it tonight because they're getting their periods. Maybe they'd want to have babies. Myself, I could do without it. Feh.

That would take more than a week, said Rennie.

Anyway, said Jake, do you really know how you want to be treated? You ever met anyone who does?

You mean any woman, don't you, said Rennie.

Skip the semantics, said Jake. Tell the truth. Tell me how you want to be treated. In twenty-five words or less. You say it, I'll do it.

Rennie began to laugh. All right, she said. Is that a promise?

Later she said, It depends who by.

●

Rennie unlocks the door of her room. The mermaid lamp is on, and for a moment she can't remember whether or not she turned it off when she left. She could swear she did. There's a smell in the room that wasn't there before.

She sees her notebook, laid out on the bed, with the material she's been collecting, maps and brochures, neatly beside it. Someone's been in here. Rennie senses an ambush. She had her purse with her, the camera and lenses are at the front desk, there's nothing anyone would want. Is there? She opens the bureau drawer and hunts for the joints but they're safely in place.

In the bathroom her cosmetic bag has been emptied into the sink: toothbrush, toothpaste, Love deodorant, dental floss, bottle of aspirins, the works. Two of the glass louvres have been slid out of the metal frame that holds them in place. They're nowhere in sight, they must be outside somewhere on a balcony, a fire escape, the ground, who knows what's out there, and there's no way of putting them back. That is how he got in, sliding himself into the bathroom like an anonymous letter. The man in the bathing suit. She thinks of herself standing there with a flashlight and a can of insect spray. God knows what he'd do, she's glad she wasn't here.

But it's only a thief, there are worse things. Whatever he wanted, which was probably only money, he didn't get: nothing is missing. She moves her notebook, *Fun in the Sunspots*, and sits down on the bed. Then she looks under it.

The box is there all right, but it's been opened, the packing tape slit neatly. Styrofoam beads leak out onto the floor. Perhaps he's made off with the heart medicine. She slides the box out, lifts the flap, and thrusts her hand into the fake snow.

At first there's nothing. Then there are two tins of smoked oysters, which Rennie sets on the floor, and after that her hand hits something that is in no way like a tin of anything at all, except that it's hard and metallic. Rennie pulls and it comes towards her, scattering styrofoam beads, this is something else she's only seen pictures of. It's the front end of a small machine gun.

Rennie shoves it back, replaces the smoked oysters and the styrofoam beads, and closes the flap. She wonders if the Englishwoman has any Scotch tape. She pushes the box as far under the bed as it will go and re-arranges the chenille coverlet, spreading it so it hangs to the floor.

This, thinks Rennie, is an exceptionally tacky movie. What next, what now? It's not even a good lunchtime story, since the main point of it would have to be her own stupidity. Dumb, gullible, naïve, to believe people; it came from drinking too much. Now she must try not to panic.

Everything, especially this room, is now unsafe, but it

happens to be the middle of the night and there's no way she can move. She can't report the break-in to the police or even to the Englishwoman: she may be naïve but it's not terminal. No one would believe she didn't know what was in the box when she picked it up at the airport. Lora knows, of course: that's why she sent Rennie instead of picking it up herself. Who else knows? Whoever sent the box. Harold the customs official, maybe. And now another man, possibly in a bathing suit. A faceless stranger. Mr. X, in the bedroom, with a knife.

Rennie goes to the bathroom door, closes it, tries to lock it. She doesn't want anyone else coming in through the bathroom window while she's asleep. The lock is broken. She opens the bureau drawer again, takes out Lora's joints, crumbles them into the toilet and flushes them down. She refolds her mix 'n' match wardrobe and packs it into her bag. She cleans her things out of the bathroom. Then she lies down on the bed in her clothes and turns out the light. She wants somebody to be with her, she wants somebody to be with. A warm body, she doesn't much care whose.

●

IV

VI

In the summer, soon after she'd come out of the hospital, Rennie called up Jocasta and asked if they could have lunch. She wanted some support. *Support* was what the women she knew said to each other, which had once made Rennie think of stretch stockings for varicose veins. Firm support, for life crises or anything else you could mention. Once Rennie had not intended to have life crises and she did not feel in need of support. But now she did. Jocasta was a little too surprised to hear from her, a little too pleased.

Rennie made it to the restaurant in the usual way, one foot in front of the other on a sidewalk that wasn't really there; but it was important to keep your balance, it was important to behave normally. If you did that enough, Daniel said, sooner or later you would begin to feel normal.

Jocasta drank red wine and Perrier and gobbled up her spinach salad in no time flat. Then she started on the bread. She didn't ask Rennie how she was, she didn't ask her anything. Politely, elaborately, she avoided the subject of Rennie. If anyone brought it up it wouldn't be her.

Rennie picked at her quiche, watching Jocasta's angular face with the huge mime's eyes. She wondered whether she herself would be that odd at forty. She wondered whether she would ever be forty. She wanted Jocasta to reach across the table, past the breadbasket and the blue silk rose in the bud vase, and put her hand on top of Rennie's and say that everything was going to be fine. She wanted to tell Jocasta she was dying.

Jocasta had just moved in with someone, or was it out on someone? Go with the flow, said Jocasta. She did a lot of moving. She was talking much too fast, Rennie embarrassed the hell out of her. Rennie concentrated on behaving normally. If she drank just enough but not too much, she could do it.

Who knows what goes on in their heads? said Jocasta. They were well into the second carafe of wine. Not me, I've stopped even trying. It used to be women that were so mysterious, remember? Well, not any more, now it's men. Me, I'm an open book. All I want is a good enough time, no hassle, a few laughs, a little how-you-say romance, I'll take the violins if they're going around, dim lights, roses, fantastic sex, let *them* scrape the pâté off the rug in the morning, is that too much to ask? Are they afraid of my first name or something, is that it? Remember when we all batted our eyes and pretended not to know what dirty jokes meant and crossed our legs a lot and they chased around like pigs after a truffle and God did they complain. Frigid, cock teaser, professional virgin, remember those? Remember panty girdles, remember *falsies*, remember Peter Pan brassieres in the front seat after the formal, with your wires digging into his chest?

Rennie didn't remember these things too well. But she didn't say so, she didn't want to remind Jocasta about her age.

There's probably men still around who don't think a woman's a woman unless she feels like a car grille, or the insides of a toaster, said Jocasta. Not the back seat though, God forbid the word should get around you were an easy out.

Well, so two months ago this man, a nice enough man, nice

shoulders, said why didn't we go out for dinner. I've known him a while, I like him okay, he's fine, nothing wrong with him, not ultra bright but not a nylon stocking murderer either, and I've always felt I wouldn't mind, you know. If the occasion should arise. Well, it looked as if it was arising, pardon the pun, so I tarted myself up, nothing too obvious, I just bought this fabulous black knitted sheath for the store, remember bat wings?

So out we go, he was paying it seems, though I did offer, it's a new place over on Church, not too many of those damn asparagus ferns shedding down your back. I had the quails, which was a mistake, gnawing on those tiny bones and trying to look soignée. But everything was going fine, a lot of eye contact, we talked about his career, he's into real estate, doing up downtown houses. All he has to do is beat off the Marxists, the ones that rent rather than owning. The ones that own don't care, it jacks up their property values.

So I admire him some and he asks me back to his place, and we sit on the broadloom drinking white wine, and he puts on a record, Bartok, which I thought was a little heavy for the occasion but never mind, and he wants to talk about himself some more. Okay, I don't mind listening, but all this time he doesn't touch me. What's the matter, you think I have vaginal warts, I want to ask him, but I'm doing some serious listening, it's all about his two business partners and how they can't express anger. I personally think it's just dandy when people can't express anger, there's enough of it in the world already.

So nothing happens and finally I say, I'm really tired, this certainly has been nice but I've got to get home, and he says, Why don't you stay the night? Funny you should ask, I think, though I don't say it, so we go into the bedroom and I swear to God he turns around so his *back* is to me and he takes off all his clothes. I can't believe it, I stand there with my mouth open, and before you know it he's all tucked into his side of the bed, he was practically wearing striped flanelette pyjamas if you know what I mean. He asks if I want the light on or off, and by this time I'm so freaked I say *off*, so he turns it off and there I am, taking my clothes off all by myself in the dark. If I was smart I'd have left them on and headed fast for the Down elevator, but you know me, Little Mary Sunshine, ever hopeful, so I climb into the bed, expecting to be embraced passionately, maybe he's just afraid of the light, but he says good night and turns over and goes to sleep!

Talk about feeling like an asshole. Now if a girl did that, what would she be called? There I was, horny as hell from looking at his *shoulders* for about five hours, and he's sleeping away like a baby. So I got up and spent the night on his sofa.

So in the morning he waltzes in, all bright and shiny in his brown velour dressing gown with the monogram on the pocket, with two glasses of fresh orange juice, and he says, Where did *you* go last night? When I woke up this morning you weren't there.

He hadn't even noticed, he hadn't noticed all night that I was gone.

I'm sorry, I said, but I think we have a semantic problem. A problem in communications, or maybe it's linguistics. What does *spending the night* usually mean to you? I mean, I'm not knocking the orange juice but I don't have to spend the night on the sofa to get it, I can squeeze it myself, you know what I mean?

Well, it turns out he's having an identity crisis, boy, am I sick of those. Before this he's only made it with younger, dumber chicks, women who're easy to impress, he says, and he's never tried it with someone like me, notice he meant old and wise, like an owl maybe. If you have to be a bird, which would you rather be, a chick or an owl? He's not sure someone like me would think he has anything to offer besides sex, and he wants to be valued for himself, whatever that is. Chin*ese*! He wants a long-term meaningful relationship. I can tell he was a bedwetter as a child. Maybe still is for all I know.

I'm sitting there with my hair not brushed and I really have to pee, but I don't want to interrupt him because he obviously finds this important, and I'm thinking, I've heard this before, only it used to be women saying it to men. I can't believe it! And I'm thinking, do I want a long-term meaningful relationship with this guy? And then I'm thinking, *does* he have anything to offer besides sex?

Well, the answer was no. But that didn't used to matter, did it? How come it matters all of a sudden? Why do we have to start respecting their *minds*? Who keeps changing the rules, them or us? You know how many times that's happened to me since then? Three more times! It's an epidemic! What do they *want*?

My theory is that when sex was such a big deal, above the waist, below the waist, with stages of achievement marked on it like the United Appeal thermometer, they wanted it that way because you could measure it, you could win, scoring, you know? Our team against their team. Getting away with it. One in the teeth for Mummy. So we said, you want it, fine, we want it too, let's get together, and all of a sudden millions of pricks went limp. Nation*wide*! That's my theory. The new scoring is *not* scoring. Just so long as you keep control. They don't want love and understanding and meaningful relationships, they still want sex, but only if they can *take* it. Only if you've got something to lose, only if you struggle a little. It helps if you're eight years old, one way or another. You follow me?

Jocasta paid for Rennie's lunch. That meant she thought Rennie was in terrible shape, on the brink of death in fact, since ordinarily she never paid for anything if she could help it.

I'm hardly dead yet, Rennie wanted to say. But she was touched by this gesture, it was support after all, Jocasta had done what she could. She had paid for the lunch, which was a big thing, and she'd been as amusing as possible, a cheerful bedside visit in the terminal ward. Talk about your own life, life after all goes on, shun morbid subjects. A positive attitude does wonders for out-of-control cell division.

Rennie walked back to the apartment, unsupported, one foot in front of the other, keeping her balance. When she got there Jake was sitting in the livingroom. There were two beer bottles, Carlsberg, on the floor beside the plump pink chair. Ordinarily he never drank from the bottle. He didn't get up.

Once Rennie would have known why he was there, in the middle of the day. But he would not have been sitting in a chair, he would have been hiding behind the door, he'd have grabbed her from behind.

What's wrong? she said.

Jake looked up at her. His eyes were puffy, he hadn't been sleeping well lately. Neither had Rennie, as far as that went, but every time she mentioned it it turned out he'd slept even worse than she had. They were competing for each other's pity, which was too bad because neither of them seemed to have a lot of it lying around, they'd been using it up on themselves.

Rennie went over and kissed Jake on the top of the head. He looked so awful.

He took her hand, held on to it. We should try again, said Jake.

●

If I could do it over again I'd do it a different way, says Lora, God knows. Except maybe I wouldn't, you know? Look before you leap, my mother used to say, not that she ever did, she never had the time. When they're right behind you you don't look, you only leap, you better believe it, because if you don't leap that's fucking it, eh? Just keep moving, is my motto.

The year I turned sixteen my mother got a job selling Avon door to door, so she wasn't there in the afternoons when I got home. I didn't like being there in the cellar with just Bob, he gave me the creeps, so I used to hang out after school with Gary, that's my boyfriend. Sometimes we'd skip after lunch, and we'd have a few beers in his car, he sure loved that car, and then we'd neck afterwards. We never went all the way. Everyone thought it was the girls like me and Marie who went all the way, but mostly it was the nice girls. They figured it was okay if you were going with the guy and you were in love with him. Sometimes they'd get caught, that was before the Pill was a big thing or abortions either, and Marie and me would kill ourselves laughing, because we were the ones always getting accused of it.

At that high school they thought we were the tough girls and I guess we thought that too. We wore this heavy eye makeup and white lipstick, I guess we were something. But I never let myself get too drunk or carried away or anything. When the nice girls got in trouble their parents bought them trips to the States to get fixed up, but I knew what happened to you if you couldn't afford it. Somebody's kitchen table. There was one girl a couple of grades ahead of us at school, she tried it herself with a knitting needle only it didn't work. The teachers told us it was some kind of rare disease but everyone knew the truth, it got around. As for me, I knew Bob would make sure I'd be out on my ass just as soon as he could throw me out, and that would be it.

Gary liked me to stop him, he said he respected me for it. He wasn't the motorcycle type, he had a job too on weekends. It was the other kind you had to look out for, the ones with money. No one at our school was a millionaire or anything but some had more money than others and they thought they were the cat's ass. I never went out with them, they'd never ask me anyway except to somewhere like the back of the field hut. It was all how much money you had. If you had enough you could get away with anything, you know?

Whenever I'd come in late Bob would be there, sitting at

the kitchen table with his cardigan sleeves coming unravelled, and he'd look at me like I was dirt. He didn't slap me around any more though; I was too big for that. I used to get Gary to park right in front of the kitchen window, it was half below street level because we lived in a cellar, and we'd neck away like crazy right where Bob could hear us and maybe see us too if he looked out.

Then I quit school and started working full-time, at the pizza takeout, it was no great hell but it was money. I figured I'd have enough soon to move into my own place, and Gary said, Why don't we get married. That was what I wanted then, I wanted to get married, have kids; only I wanted to do it right, not like my mother.

It was pretty soon after that I let him go all the way, it was okay because we were getting married anyway. It just happened that way, we didn't have a safe or anything. It was in the back seat of his car, right in broad daylight behind this reservoir where we used to go. It was uncomfortable as hell, and I kept thinking someone would come along and look in the window. There wasn't all that much to it, except it hurt, not a lot though, and I couldn't figure out what they were always making so much fuss about. It was like my first cigarette, I was as sick as a dog, though I ended up smoking in a big way.

We didn't have any Kleenex or anything so we had to use this old undershirt he had in the trunk, to polish the car with, he made some joke about running me through the car wash. When he saw the blood though he stopped laughing, he said everything would be okay, he'd take care of me. What he meant was we were still getting married.

I had to go to work that night, I was working three evenings with two afternoons off, so I got Gary to drop me off at the apartment so I could change into my uniform. After I did that I went into the kitchen to make myself some dinner, I could get free pizza at the shop but by that time I couldn't stand the sight of it. You don't like it so much once you know what they put into it. Bob was in there as usual, smoking and finishing off a beer. I guess by that time my mother was supporting him because he didn't seem to be in the television business any more.

His damn cats came over right away and began rubbing on my legs, they must've smelled it, like I was a raw steak or a fish or something. It was the same when I got the curse, when I started using Tampax they'd fish the used ones out of the garbage and go around with the strings hanging out of their mouths, the first time Bob saw that he was so proud, he thought they'd finally caught a mouse and those were the tails. When he found out what it really was he was mad as hell.

I kicked one of the cats away from my legs and he said, Cut that out. I started opening a can of soup, like nothing was happening, Campbell's Chicken Noodle, and I could feel Bob looking at me and all of a sudden I was scared of him again just like when I was little.

Then he stood up and took hold of my arm and pulled me around, he hadn't tried the belt routine for a while, he hadn't put a hand on me for years, so I wasn't expecting it. I slammed into the refrigerator and this bowl on top of it fell off, my mother was keeping the used lightbulbs in it, she had this idea she was going to paint them and make Christmas tree ornaments out of them and sell them but she never did, it was the same as her other ideas. Anyway the lightbulbs broke and the bowl too. I thought he was going to slap me around but he didn't. He just smiled down at me with those grey teeth of his with the fillings showing and the black gums around the edges. If there's anything I can't stand it's bad teeth. Then he put his other hand right on my tit. He said, Your mother won't be home till six, and he was still smiling. I was really scared, because I knew he was still stronger than me.

I thought about screaming, but there was a lot of screaming around there and people had this thing about minding their own business. I reached behind me and picked up the can opener from the kitchen table, it was that kind with the prong, you know? And I shoved it into him as hard as I could, and at the same time I brought my knee up right into his balls. So it wasn't me that screamed. He fell on to the floor, right onto the lightbulbs and the dish of cat food, I heard that sound of glass breaking, and I ran like hell out of there, I didn't care if I'd killed him or not.

I phoned my mother the next day and told her why I wasn't coming back. She was really mad, not at him but at me. It wasn't that she didn't believe me, she did and that was the trouble. You're asking for it, she said, you flaunt it around enough, it's a wonder every man in the city didn't do the same thing a long time ago. Later on I thought maybe I shouldn't of told her. She didn't have that much in life and God knows he wasn't much either but at least she had him. You won't believe this, but I guess she thought I was trying to take him away from her. She wanted me to apologize for sticking the can opener into him, but I wasn't sorry.

●

There's a line between being asleep and being awake which Rennie is finding harder and harder to cross. Now she's up near the ceiling, in the corner of a white room, beside the air-conditioning unit, which is giving out a steady hum. She can see everything, clear and sharp, under glass, her body is down there on the table, covered in green cloth, there are figures around her, in masks, they're in the middle of a performance, a procedure, an incision, but it's not skin-deep, it's the heart they're after, in there somewhere, squeezing away, a fist opening and closing around a ball of blood. Possibly her life is being saved, but who can tell what they're doing, she doesn't trust them, she wants to rejoin her body but she can't get down. She crawls through the grey folds of netting as if through a burrow, sand in her eyes, blinking in the light, disoriented. It's far too early. She takes a shower, which helps a little, and gets dressed. Routines are calming.

The box under her bed is making her very nervous. She doesn't want to let it out of her sight, but she can hardly take it to breakfast with her. She locks it in the room, convinced that once she's around the corner it will hatch and something unpleasant will emerge. All the time she's eating, watery scrambled eggs, she worried about it. She could check out of the hotel and leave it behind in the room, she could try for the next flight out, but that would be risky. The English-woman would be into it before she was down the stairs, and there's no doubt about it, she's the police-phoning type. She'd make sure Rennie got arrested at the airport. The only thing to do with it is to get the box to Elva as quickly as possible and then forget about it.

After breakfast she walks across the street to the stationery store and buys a roll of packing tape. She goes back to her room and tapes the box shut, trying to make it seem as much as possible like the original job. If the box doesn't look opened she can always plead ignorance. She orders tea and biscuits in her room and puts in some time looking at her watch. Then she goes to the front desk and tells the English-woman she'll be over at Ste. Agathe tonight but she wants the room held for her.

"You have to pay for it, you know," the Englishwoman says. "Even if you're not in it."

Rennie says she's aware of this. She considers haggling about the meals, but drops the idea. It's what the English-woman is expecting her to do, she's tapping her pencil on the edge of the desk, waiting for it. Rennie's not up to that gooseberry stare.

She lugs the box out of her room and props it against the

front desk. She goes back for her bags and checks her camera out of the safe; she leaves the passport, it's safer here. Then she goes down the stone stairs to look for a taxi.

There are no taxis, but there's a boy with a wheelbarrow. He looks about eight, though he's probably older, and after hesitating a moment Rennie hires him. She sends him upstairs for the box, which she doesn't want to touch any more than she has to. The boy is shy and doesn't talk much. He loads all her things, even her purse, into the wheelbarrow and sets off along the pockmarked road in his bare feet, almost running.

At first Rennie thinks he's going this fast because he has some notion of making off with her possessions. She hurries behind him, sweating already and feeling not very dignified. But then she notes his thin arms and decides that he's like rickshaw drivers, he had to go this fast to keep up the momentum. He takes her a back way, between two ramshackle wooden buildings, along a rutted path too narrow and muddy for cars, cluttered with discarded cardboard boxes. Then there's a tiny house with a family of chickens scratching around it, then a storage warehouse piled with sacks, and they come out onto the pier.

The boy, who has not looked back once, speeds up on the level ground, heading for the boat, which must be the one at the end. Rennie sees the virtue of arriving at the same time he does. Even if he's honest the others may not be, and there are several of them now, a whole group of young boys, running beside the wheelbarrow, calling out things she can't understand, grinning back at her as she jogs, puffing now, the edges of her straw hat flapping, chasing her own purse as it flees ahead of her down the pier, around piles of wooden crates, parked trucks covered with tarpaulins, small mounds of fruit and unknown vegetables discarded and rotting. Opposite the boat the boy stops and waits for her with a smile she can't interpret, and the other boys draw back into a circle, leaving a gap for her to enter. Is he making fun of her?

"How much?" she says.

"What you wish," he answers. Of course she overpays him, she can tell by his grin and those of the other boys, delighted and mocking. They want to put things on the boat for her, they're grabbing for the purse, the camera bag, but she fends them off, she's had enough of that. She piles her things on the dock and sits down on top of them, feeling like a hen. Now, of course, there's no way she can leave the pile to ask about the fare and the departure time, and the boy has already run off with his wheelbarrow. She sees why he was going so fast: he wants to get in as many trips as possible before the boat leaves.

Rennie catches her breath. Nobody is watching her, she's avoided suspicion. She remembers the time Jake got pulled over for speeding, with some hash in the glove compartment. Act normal, he said to her quickly before rolling down the window, and Rennie had to think about that. Normal for her would be getting out of the car and walking as fast as possible in any direction as long as it was away. But she sat there without saying anything at all, and that was acceptable enough, though she'd felt guilt shining around her like a halo.

As she does now. She decides to act like a journalist, for the benefit of anyone watching but also for her own. If she goes through the motions, takes a few pictures, a few notes, maybe she'll convince herself. It's like making faces: her mother used to say she shouldn't do that or her face would grow that way permanently. Is that what happened to you? she'd said once, when she was thirteen, the backchat age her mother called it. But she said it under her breath.

She looks around her for possible subjects, takes out her camera, fiddles with the lens. There's the boat, for instance, which is tied to the pier with looped ropes thick as a wrist. It was black once but is now mottled with rusty brown where the paint has weathered. The name is fading on the bow: *Memory*. Rennie feels about it much as she felt about the plane she came on: can it really float? But it makes the trip, twice a day, to the blue shape in the distance, there and back.

Surely people would not use it if it weren't safe.

The deck is a jumble of wicker hampers, suitcases and bundles. Several men are tossing cardboard boxes aboard and stowing them through the open hatchway and under the outside benches. Rennie takes a picture of them, shooting into the sun, catching a box in midair with two pairs of outstretched arms framing it, thrower's and catcher's. She hopes the picture will look dramatic, though she knows that when she tries for such effects they usually don't turn out. Overexposure, Jake says. On Ste. Agathe she'll take pictures of the restaurants, if any, and of old women sitting in the sun peeling lobsters, or peeling anything within reason. She knows there will be old women peeling things but she's not dead certain about the lobsters.

There's a hand on her shoulder and Rennie freezes. She's been watched, they know, she's been followed. But then she hears the voice, "Hi there," and it's Lora, in cerise today with blue orchids, smiling away as if she's supposed to be here.

Rennie stands up. "I thought you were over on Ste. Agathe," she says. It will take a moment but very soon she'll be angry.

"Yeah, well, I got held up," says Lora. She's glancing around, down, she's already checked out the box, swiftly and casually. "I missed the boat. Anyway, Elva got better."

Both of them know this is a lie. But what should she do now? One question too many may take her somewhere she definitely doesn't want to go. There's no way she wants Lora to find out that she knows what's in the box, that she knows she's been used. The less she admits to knowing the better. When people play with guns, sooner or later they go off, and she would rather be somewhere else at the time.

Lora's scanning the pier now, noting who's there, who isn't. "I see you got Elva's box okay," she says.

"No problem," says Rennie, amiably, neutrally. "I guess we can just have it put down there in the hold?"

"Keep it with you," says Lora. "Things disappear around

here. Anyway Elva always comes down for her box, she gets impatient if she has to wait around for them to unload all that stuff. She hates standing out in the sun."

Lora doesn't offer to take charge of the box. She does however get it lifted on board and stowed under the seat, Rennie's seat, the wooden bench running along the side. Upwind, says Lora, and outside. That way you don't get wet and it's not so smelly. "Never sit in the cabin," she says. "You just about choke to death. If we're lucky they'll only use the sails."

"Where do we pay?" says Rennie

"They collect once you're on," says Lora. She's looking around the pier again.

Without any signal people begin to board. They wait until the boat rocks towards them, them jump the gap of water where seaweed washes out from underneath the pier, swatches of rubber hair. When it's Rennie's turn, one of the men grabs her purse, wordlessly, then grips her arm to pull her across.

The deck fills with people, most of them brown or black. They sit on the benches, on the crates and canvas-covered baggage, anywhere, and Rennie begins to remember stories about overloaded boats capsizing. The two German women from the hotel appear, looking around for seats. The retired American couple from the reef boat climb on board too, still wearing their baggy wide-legged shorts, but they choose to stand. Already they're peering up into the sky.

"Is it usually this crowded?" Rennie asks.

"This is extra," Lora says. "They're going home to vote. The election's tomorrow."

The men are casting off, there are legs and feet beside Rennie's head, the thick ropes come aboard. A pink-faced fattish man in a greasy white hat and a dark blue jacket has come up through the hatchway, which they're now closing, pulling a tarp over it; he shoves himself among the people, squeezing past legs, climbing over bodies, collecting the money.

Nobody is giving orders, least of all him, though suddenly there are about ten men all undoing knots. The edge of the pier is crowded, everyone's shouting. Water grows between the boat and the shore, a split, a gap.

Behind the line of people a maroon car is driving slowly out onto the pier. It stops, a man gets out, then another; their mirror sunglasses are turned towards the boat. Lora bends down, scratching at her ankle. "Damn fleas," she says. The motor starts and the cabin immediately fills with smoke.

"See what I mean?" says Lora.

●

Ste. Agathe emerges out of the blue hazy sky or sea, rising slowly, sinking slowly, at first only an indistinct smudge, then clearer, a line of harsh vertical cliffs flat-topped and scrubby past the glassy slopes of waves. It looks dry, not like St. Antoine, which from this distance is a moist green, its outline a receding series of softly rounded cones. Queenstown is now just a sprinkling of white. Rennie decides the pale oblong on the hill above it must be Fort Industry. From here the whole place looks like a postcard.

They've turned off the motor and are coasting, the three sails bellying out like old sheets on a line, patched and stained, revealing too many secrets, secrets about nights and sicknesses and the lack of money. They remind Rennie of the lines of washing seen from trains, the trains she used to take for Christmas visits home during university, since no planes go to Griswold. Dryers were invented not because they were easier but because they were private. She thinks about her mother's red knuckles and her phrase for disreputable stories: *dirty laundry*. Something you weren't supposed to hang out in public. Her mother's red knuckles were from hanging the sheets out on the line, even in winter, to get the sun she said, but of course her sheets were always very clean.

Lora says this is a calm day, but Rennie feels queasy anyway; she wishes she'd had the foresight to take something, there must be a pill. The people sitting on the downwind side get the occasional bucketful of spray as the boat creaks and lurches heavily into a trough.

Lora is sitting beside her; she's taken a small loaf of bread out of her purple bag and is breaking pieces off of it and chewing them. At their feet four men are lying on the floor, half on top of the canvas-covered suitcases, passing around a bottle of rum. They're already quite drunk and they're getting drunker, they're laughing a lot. The bottle sails past Rennie's head into the sea, they've already got another one. Lora offers the bread silently to Rennie, who says no thanks.

"It'll help you out," says Lora. "If you're not feeling too good. Don't look down, look out at the horizon."

Right beside them there's a small boat, no bigger than a rowboat it seems to Rennie, with a reddish-pink sail; two men are on it, fishing. The boat rolls and tips, it looks very unsafe.

"It's boats like that they hunt the whales in," Lora says.

"You're joking," says Rennie.

"Nope," says Lora. She tears another piece off the loaf. "They have a lookout, and when they see a whale they get into those boats and row like shit. Sometimes they even catch one, and then there's a big feast." Rennie doesn't want to think about anyone eating anything.

Down by their feet there's more laughter. One of the men, Rennie sees now, is the deaf and dumb man, the man they were beating up. He has a cut on his forehead, but apart from that he doesn't seem any worse off than the others, he's drunk as a skunk and grinning away, no teeth at all now. The old American couple in their wide-legged shorts step carefully over the bodies on their way to the stern. "Careful, Mother," says the man, gripping the thin freckled elbow. Laughter rises around their four white chicken-shank legs. Rennie tugs at her skirt, pulling it down over her knees.

And then Paul comes out of the cabin. He too pushes past the knees, picks his way over the lolling bodies. He nods to Rennie and Lora but keeps on going, he's in no hurry, he wanders back to the stern, ducking under the mainsail boom. Rennie didn't see him get on. He must have been down there all the time, when the boat was tied up at the pier.

Suddenly she's hungry, or at least the rocking emptiness, the absence of a centre of gravity, feels now like hunger. She never liked roller coasters either. "I'll take you up on the bread," she says.

"Have the rest," says Lora handing her the heel of the loaf. "It swells up inside, you know?" She gets out her cigarettes and lights one, tossing the match over the side.

"Can I ask you something?" says Rennie. She's almost finished the bread. It works, already she feels better.

"Sure," says Lora, looking at her with what Rennie is almost sure is amusement. "You want to know if I'm making it with Paul, right? The answer is, Not any more. Help yourself, be my guest."

This is not what Rennie thought she wanted to know, nor does she appreciate Lora's generosity; nor is Paul a buffet casserole or a spare room, Occupied or Vacant as the case may be. "Thanks," she says, "but really I wanted to ask you something quite different. Is he working for the CIA?"

"The CIA?" says Lora. "Him?" She begins to laugh, throwing her head back, showing all her white teeth. "Hey, that's great! Wait'll he hears that! Is that what he told you?"

"Not exactly," says Rennie, who now feels foolish, and annoyed because of it. She turns away, watching the scrubby cliffs as they slide too slowly past the boat.

"Listen, if that's what he told you," says Lora, "who am I? Hey, maybe he thinks it turns you on!" She laughs some more, until Rennie is ready to shake her. Then she stops. "You want to know who the CIA really is around here?" she says. "Look down there." She points to the old American couple standing in the stern, harmless and implausible in their khaki shorts. They're flipping through their bird book now, heads together, like eager children. "They are," says Lora. "Both of them."

"I can't believe that," says Rennie, who can't. Surely these people are the embodiment of midwestern innocence, not at all the kind; though she's no longer sure what the kind is. After all, she was willing to believe Paul was; and if him, why not anyone?

Lora laughs again. She's delighted, as if the whole thing is a joke she's telling. "It's great," she says. "I love it. It's them all right, everyone knows. Prince always knows which one's the CIA. When you're in local politics you have to know."

"Aren't they too old?" says Rennie.

"They don't have much of a budget for down here," says Lora. "Listen, who's complaining? Everyone tells them stuff just to keep them happy; if they didn't have anything to put in their reports someone up there might get the idea they're senile or something and send down somebody heavy. Of course they're supposed to support Ellis, that's the official line, so Ellis loves them, and Prince loves them because they're so dumb; even Minnow doesn't mind them all that much. Sometimes he takes them out to lunch and tells them all this stuff about what the U.S. should be doing to avoid a revolution, and they write it all down and send it off, it keeps them busy. As for them, they haven't had so much fun since they got to go through the wastebaskets in Iceland, that was their last posting. They tell everyone he's a retired bank manager."

Maybe he is, thinks Rennie. Lora is laughing too much. "So who is he really?" she says. Paul, she means, and Lora picks that up too quickly, she's been waiting for it, the shrug and the answer are right there. "A guy with four boats and some money," she says. "Guys with boats and some money are a dime a dozen down here. It's the ones with boats and no money you've got to look out for."

Rennie eats the rest of the bread, slowly, feeling more and more dim-witted. She may not have asked the wrong question, but she's asked the wrong person. She knows she should pretend to believe the answer, that would be clever, but she just can't manage it.

Lora must sense this; she lights another cigarette from the butt of the first and leans forward, resting her elbows on her spread knees. "I didn't mean to laugh," she says, "except it's so funny, when you really know."

The boat is pulling around into the harbour, out of the wind, and they turn on the smelly motor. Around Rennie people are stirring, gathering up small parcels, stretching their legs out. The harbour seems crowded, small fishing boats, a police launch, yachts at anchor, sails furled, bright flags fluttering from their masts. The *Memory* threads through them, trailing grey smoke. Ahead the pier swarms with people, waving, calling.

"They come down for the eggs," Lora says. "And the bread. There's never enough eggs and bread here. You'd think someone would get a bright idea and start a bakery or something."

"When you know what?" says Rennie.

Lora looks at her with that posed smile, then leans over and forward, getting into the right position for the truth, the confidence. "Who he really is," she says. "Really, he's the connection."

●

The *Memory* hits with a soft thud; there's a line of tractor tires nailed along the dock to keep it from scraping. Already there are men roping the boat to the shore. Rennie's caught in the scramble, legs around her head, it's like a football team walking across her. There's a lot of shouting, friendly she thinks. In self-defence she stands up, then feels it will be safer sitting down; but Lora's pulling at her arm and there's a man on his knees in front of her, digging for the box. She stands up again and hands reach for her, she makes the leap, she's been landed.

Right in front of her there's a small woman, not five feet tall. She's wearing a pink cotton skirt with red flamingoes on it and a black jockey cap, and a red T-shirt with PRINCE OF PEACE on it in white. Now Rennie remembers her.

"You got my food?" she says, not to Lora but directly to Rennie herself. She says nothing at all about heart medicine. It's an old face, but her black hair is in pigtails today; they stick out sideways from under the jockey cap.

"It's here," says Lora, and it is, she's holding the box upright, steadying it with one hand.

The woman ignores her. "Good," she says, to Rennie alone. She takes the box by its sides and lifts it on to her head, much more easily than Rennie could have done, balancing it on the woolly jockey cap. She steadies it with one hand and marches off without another word to either of them. Rennie, who's been expecting a cross between Aunt Jemima and a basket case, watches her go. What will happen when she opens the box? Rennie can hardly believe she knows what's in it. But if Rennie can believe the geriatric CIA she can believe anything. Possibly this woman's the local gun runner.

Still, Rennie can't quite imagine her opening the box, unpacking the gun, assembling it if it needs assembling, and then what? Does she sell them, and if so, who's buying? What are they used for, here? But these questions are not ones Rennie needs the answers for. Yesterday she would have asked; today she knows it's safer not to. The box is off her back, which is where it should be: off.

She looks around for Paul but he's gone already; she spots him up on the road, getting into a jeep, with another man and the driver. Elva's on the beach, walking along with the machine-gun box on her head, as if that's the most normal thing in the world.

"She's amazing," Rennie says to Lora. "That's a heavy box.

I thought you said she had a heart condition," she adds. Now that she's safe she can risk it.

"That's the other grandmother," says Lora, lying without much energy.

"And they're both called Elva," says Rennie.

"Yeah," says Lora, "this place is crawling with grandmothers. The old bitch, you see the way she didn't speak to me? She hates it that I'm living with Prince, but she also hates it that we don't have kids. Around here, if you don't have kids you're nothing, that's what she keeps telling me. She wants me to have a son for Prince, so she can have a great-grandson. *For* Prince, that's what she says. 'You too smart to make babies?' she says. At the same time she hates it that I'm white; but she thinks she's practically related to the Royal Family, *my* Princess Margaret, *my* Prince Charles, last time I heard they were all white, eh? You figure it out."

"Maybe she's just old," says Rennie.

"Sure," says Lora. "Why not. Where you staying?"

Rennie hadn't considered this. She's just assumed there would be a hotel.

"But it's the election," says Lora. "They might be full up. I can ask for you, though."

When they step onto the beach Lora takes off her shoes, so Rennie does too. Lora's carrying her camera bag for her. They walk along the packed sand, under the trees, palm trees. The beach is wider than the one on St. Antoine and it's fairly clean. Boats are hauled up on it, turned over. Above the beach the town begins, one main road, a couple of foreign banks, a couple of stores, all two-storey and white; a church, then square houses, white and pastel, scattered up the hillside.

They come to a cliff jutting into the sea and wade around it, hitching up their skirts. Then there's more beach and more palm trees, and finally a stone wall and some steps. There's a sign, sea-shells glued on wood: THE LIME TREE. The hotel's hardly bigger than a house.

"The food's not bad here," Lora says. "Only, Ellis is trying to squeeze them out. He wants to buy it and put in his own people. Funny thing, their electricity keeps going off."

"Why?" says Rennie. "Why would he want to do that?"

"Politics, is what they say," says Lora. "They're for Minnow. What I figure is, he hates anyone making money. Except him, of course."

"If this man is so terrible," says Rennie, "why does he keep getting elected?"

"Search me," says Lora. "I'll see about the room." She walks off towards the main building.

Rennie's standing in a beach bar, surrounded by low wooden tables and chairs with people in them. She sits down and piles her bags on the chair beside her and orders a rum and lime. She drinks it, looking out at the boats in the harbour, the flags: Norway, she thinks, Germany, France for sure, and some others.

The rum is going right into her, smoothing her down from the inside. She can relax now, she's off the hook. One hook at any rate.

At the table beside her there's a young couple, the girl brown-haired, lightly tanned, in a white dress, the man in jogging shorts, his nose peeling. The man is fooling with his camera, expensive enough but jammed. "It's the light meter," he says. They're people like her, transients; like her they can look all they want to, they're under no obligation to see, they can take pictures of anything they wish.

●

There's a small dock in front of the Lime Tree, and on it there's a man, shouting and waving his arms. Rennie watches him for a moment and decides that he's teaching three girls to wind-surf: there they are, out in the harbour. "Upright!" the man shouts, lifting both arms like an orchestra conductor.

185

"Bend the knees!" But it's no use, the sail collapse and the girls topple almost in unison into the sea. In the distance the two German women from the hotel are wading around the cliff, their skirts hitched up, carrying their suitcases. One of their sunhats has blown off into the water.

Rennie wonders where Lora is. She orders a cream cheese and banana bread sandwich from the bar, and another rum and lime. She goes back to her chair and moves it so it's out of the sun.

"May we sit here?" says another voice, a woman's. Rennie looks up. It's the old American couple, in their adventurous shorts, their binoculars hanging like outsized talismans around their necks. Each of them is carrying a glass of ginger ale. "There don't seem to be any other chairs."

"Of course," Rennie says. "I'll move my things for you."

But the old man insists on doing it himself. "My name is Abbott," he says, "and this is Mrs. Abbott." He holds the chair for his wife, who sits down and fixes Rennie with eyes round as a baby's.

"That's very nice of you, dear," she says. "We saw you on the reef boat. Disappointing, we thought. You're Canadian, aren't you? We always find the Canadians so nice, they're almost like members of the family. No crime rates to speak of at all. We always feel quite safe when we go up there. We go to Point Pelee, for the birds. Whenever we can, that is."

"How did you know?" says Rennie.

Mrs. Abbott laughs. "It's a very small place," she says. "You hear things."

"Nice though," says her husband.

"Oh yes. The people are so lovely. So friendly, not like a lot of places." She sips her ginger ale. "So independent," she says. "We have to go back soon, we're getting too old for it. It's a little primitive down here, on Ste. Agathe especially, they don't have many of the conveniences. It's all right for younger people but it's sometimes difficult for us."

"When you can't get toilet paper," says Mr. Abbott.

"Or garbage bags," says his wife. "But we'll be sorry to leave it."

"You don't see many beggars," says Mr. Abbott, who is looking at something in the harbour through his binoculars. "Not like India."

"Do you travel a lot?" says Rennie politely.

"We love to travel," says Mrs Abbott. "It's the birding, but we like the people too. Of course with the exchange rate these days it's not as easy as it used to be."

"You're right about that," says her husband. "The U.S. borrowed too much money. That's the whole problem in a nutshell. We should stop living beyond our means."

"He ought to know," says Mrs. Abbott, proudly and fondly. "He's a retired bank manager." Mr. Abbott now has his head tilted back and is looking straight up.

Rennie decides that Lora must be wrong. Surely two such innocuous, kindly, boring people cannot possibly be CIA agents. The question is, how can she get rid of them? They appear to have settled in for the afternoon. Rennie waits for the pictures of the grandchildren to make their appearance, out of Mrs. Abbott's sensible canvas shoulder bag.

"Do you see that man over there?" says Mrs. Abbott, pointing towards the bar, which is more crowded than when Rennie first arrived. Rennie isn't sure which one, but she nods.

"He's an international parrot smuggler," says Mrs. Abbott, dropping her voice.

"A parrot smuggler?" says Rennie faintly.

"Don't laugh," says Mrs. Abbott. "It's a big business. In Germany you can get thirty-five thousand dollars for a mated pair."

"The Germans have too much money," says Mr. Abbott. "It's coming out of their ears. They don't know what to do with it."

"It's the St. Antoine parrot," says Mrs. Abbott. "They're

very rare, you know. You don't find them anywhere but on St. Antoine."

"It's disgusting," says Mr. Abbott. "They give them drugs. If I ever caught him with one of those little parrots I'd wring his neck."

From the horror in their voices, they could be talking about a white-slave ring. Rennie concentrates on taking this seriously.

"How do they smuggle them?" she says.

"On the yachts," says Mr. Abbott, "like everything else around here. We made it our business to find out about him. He's not from here, he's from Trinidad."

"Then we reported him to the association," says Mrs. Abbott, pleased. "It didn't stop him but it slowed him down. He didn't know it was us, though. Some of them are dangerous and we really aren't equipped to deal with that sort of thing."

"Not at our age," says Mr. Abbott.

"Which association?" says Rennie.

"The International Parrot Association," says Mrs. Abbott. "They're quite good, but they can't be everywhere at once."

Rennie figures she'd better have another drink. If surrealism is taking over the world, she might as well enjoy it. She asks the Abbotts if they would like another ginger ale, but they say they're quite happy. In any case it will soon be dusk.

"Roosting time," says Mr. Abbott happily, as he stands up.

●

This is Rennie's third rum and lime. She's fuzzy, but not too fuzzy. It's occurred to her several times that there's no boat back and she doesn't have a place to stay. She supposes there's always the beach.

It isn't dark yet, but beneath the overhanging porch roof the waitresses are setting the tables for dinner, lighting the candles inside the little red glass chimneys. The tables outside are full now, with yacht people, and the bar is lined with men, brown and black mostly. Some of them look familiar, but maybe they aren't. She spots a pair of boots, that one she knows anyway, the man with the South American moustache. This time he's ignoring her. There are a few white men with the leathery dull skin and the dry albino hair of those who spend constant time in the sun.

While she's walking back from the bar, Dr. Minnow steps onto the patio. He hasn't come along the beach but down through the garden behind the hotel. He's with three other men; two of them are wearing T-shirts that say THE FISH LIVES, with a picture of a whale, and, underneath, VOTE JUSTICE PARTY. The third man is white and thin; he's wearing a safari jacket and tinted glasses. He stays a little behind.

Dr. Minnow spots Rennie and comes over to her at once. The two men head for the bar, but the third hesitates a moment and then comes over too.

"Well, my friend," says Dr. Minnow. "I see you are covering the election after all." He smiles his crooked smile.

Rennie smiles back. She thinks he's treating it as a joke now, and she can handle that. "From the bar," she says. "All good journalists cover elections from bars."

"I'm told it is the best place," says Dr. Minnow. His accent is broader here, he's less controlled. Rennie thinks he's had a few himself. "Everyone is here. For instance, that is our Minister of Justice over there. He is preparing himself for his defeat." He laughs. "You will excuse me for talking sedition," he says to the white man with him. "This is a compatriot of yours, my friend. He is with the Canadian High Commissioner in Barbados; he come here to see why no one attend the diving program sponsored by the sweet Canadians."

Rennie doesn't catch the name, it's something Middle European, she thinks. A multiculturalism functionary. The man shakes her hand.

"I understand you're a journalist," he says. He's nervous.

"I just do food," says Rennie, to make him feel better. "Things like that."

"What could be more important?" he says politely. They both sit down.

"I tell you why, my friend," Dr. Minnow says. "The sweet Canadians wish to teach the fishermen how to dive so they don't get the bends and come up crippled. What do they do? They hire an expert who comes just at the lobster season when the fishermen all have to be out fishing. That's the money they live on. There is no conspiracy, it is all very simple. Tell them next time they should ask first. Ask someone who knows."

The man smiles and takes out a cigarette, a brown one, and screws it into a black holder. Rennie decides this is pretentious. It embarrasses her that her country's representative is wearing a safari jacket. Where does he think he is, Africa? He could at least have chosen a different colour: the beige should not wear beige.

"You know what they're like," he says. "Governments have to deal with governments in power, which does not always produce the most accurate information."

"Are you going to win?" Rennie says to Dr. Minnow.

"Yesterday," Dr. Minnow says conversationally, his eye on the Canadian, "the government offer me a large sum of money to go over to their side. Minister of Tourism, they offer me."

"I take it you didn't accept," says Rennie.

"Why cut your own throat?" says Dr. Minnow, who seems very pleased. "I have not read Machiavelli for nothing. If they offer, it means they are scared, they think they could lose. So I turn them down, and today they are slandering me in a new way. Before it was Castro, now they say I am in the pocket of the Americans and the plantation owners. They should make up their minds, one way or the other. It confuses the people: they may think I am neither, which would be the truth. If we begin to believe the truth here, that would be the end of Ellis, and also of the Prince of Peace, as he calls himself. He think he got the true religion, all right." He stands up.

"Tomorrow I will make a speech on the problems of garbage collection, among other things," he says. "It is one of our most urgent problems on these islands, what to do with the garbage. You should attend, my friend." He bestows one more smile upon Rennie and moves away towards the bar, the neutral-coloured Canadian trailing.

●

As she's coming back from the bar again, Rennie sees the two German women climbing the stone steps. The bottoms of their dresses are dripping wet and their hair has come unglued and is hanging in wisps and strands; their faces are dangerously pink. They seem to have abandoned their suitcases. One of them is supporting the other, who is limping and uttering little shrieks of pain. Both have been crying, but as they enter the bar and the ring of curious faces that quickly surrounds them, they pull themselves together. Someone offers a chair.

"What on earth?" says Rennie, to no one in particular. Everyone in the place is peering at the German woman's foot, plump and white and pink-toed, stuffed-looking, which her friend holds up like a trophy.

"She stepped on a sea urchin," says Lora, who's back again. "They always do it, they should watch where they're going. It hurts at first but it's no big deal."

The woman is lying back with her eyes closed; her foot sticks straight out. After a few minutes Elva comes through the doorway that leads to the kitchen; she no longer has the box, she's wearing a red and white checked apron and carrying a lime and a candle. She kneels in front of the outstretched foot, appropriates it, peers at the toes. Then she begins rubbing with the cut lime. The German woman screams.

"Keep still," says Elva. "It nothin'. This will be gone tomorrow."

"Can you not take them out?" says the other woman. She's anxious, she's almost incoherent. This is not according to schedule.

"They break off and poison you," Elva says. "You got matches?"

There's no doubt who's in charge. Someone from the circle produces a box of matches and Elva lights the candle. She tilts it and drops the hot wax over the toes, rubbing it in. "You should of pee on it," she says to the other woman. "When this happen here, the boy pee on the girl's foot or the girl pee on the boy's. That take away the pain."

The German woman opens her eyes and gazes at Elva. Rennie recognizes the look, it's a look you can give only to a foreigner, a look of hope, a desperate clinging to the illusion that it's all a translation problem and you haven't really heard what you know you've just heard.

Several people laugh, but not Elva. She's got the other foot now, the uninjured one, she's digging her thumbs into it. The German woman gasps and looks around for help: she's been invaded, this is the wrong foot. She has the controlled, appalled expression of a visiting duchess who knows she must not openly disparage the local customs, however painful or revolting.

Elva digs harder. She's smug now, she has an audience, she's enjoying herself. "Your veins block," she says. "I unblock your veins, the blood carry the poison away."

"I wouldn't let her near me," says Lora. "She's got thumbs like hammers. She'll total your back as soon as look at you. She says she can cure just about anything but I'd rather be sick, thank you very much."

There's an audible snapping sound; the tendons, Rennie thinks. The German woman's face is twisted, her eyes are screwed up, she's not going to yell or moan, she's determined to preserve her dignity. "You hear the veins cryin' out?" says

Elva. "That the gas, movin' in them. You feel lighter?"

"There's no rooms," Lora says to Rennie. "It's full up, it's the election."

"Maybe I should phone the other hotels," says Rennie, who is still watching Elva.

"Phone?" says Lora. "Other hotels?" She laughs a little.

"There aren't any other hotels?" says Rennie.

"There used to be," says Lora, "but they're closed down now. There's one for the locals, but I wouldn't stay there. A girl could get seriously misunderstood. I'll try somewhere else for you."

"It in the hands," says Elva to the onlookers. "It a gift, I have it from my grandmother, she give me that when I small. She pass it to me. You feel this lump?"

The German woman nods. She's still wincing, but not as much.

"Your mama give you a blow when you small," Elva says. "You too small that time, you don't remember. The blood lie down, it make a lump. Now it have to move or the poison grow into a cancer." She digs in both thumbs again. "The pain is your youth, risin' up now."

"The old fake," says Lora. "Give her a tourist and she's happy as a pig in shit. Even if they don't believe her they have to act like they do. There's no doctor around here anyway, so they don't have a whole lot of choice; if you sprain your ankle it's her or nothing."

"I think this is maybe enough," says the other woman, who's been hovering around like a concerned parent.

Elva gives her a look of contempt. "I say when I done," she says. The foot cracks, bends in her hands like rubber.

"Now," Elva says, sitting back on her heels. "Walk on it."

Tentatively the German woman puts both feet on the ground. She stands up.

"The pain gone," says Elva, looking around the circle.

The German woman smiles. "It is remarkable," she says.

Rennie, watching, wants to hold out her own foot, even

though there's nothing wrong with it, even though it will hurt. She wants to know what it feels like, she wants to put herself into the care of those magic hands. She wants to be cured, miraculously, of everything, of anything at all.

●

Paul is standing in the kitchen doorway, looking without hurry; Rennie sees him, but decides not to wave. He comes over anyway.

"Taking it easy?" he says to Rennie. "Lora says you don't have a place to stay. I've got space, if you like."

"On a boat?" Rennie says dubiously. She ought to have said thank you first.

"I have a house too," Paul says, smiling. "Two bedrooms. Two beds."

Rennie's not sure what is being offered, but suspects it's not much. There's some room in this world for face value.

"Well," she says. "If you're sure it's all right."

"Why wouldn't it be?" says Paul.

They walk back through the garden. It's full of trees, flowering, overgrown, limes and lemons and something else, odd reddish-orange husks split open to show a white core and three huge black seeds like the eyes of insects. There are a lot of things here that Rennie has no names for.

At the back of the garden there's a five-foot stone wall. Paul lifts her camera bag and her other bag to the top, hoists himself up, and reaches down for her. She takes hold of his hands; she doesn't know where they're going.

●

Rennie and Daniel were sitting in Daniel's car, which was an unusual thing for them to be doing. It was night, which was also unusual, and it was raining, which was par for the course. When they were together it always seemed to be raining.

They'd just had dinner, dinner, not lunch. Rennie wondered whether Daniel was about to do something out of character.

Well, how about it? she said to him. A little reckless hand-holding? Want to roll around on the gear shift?

I know I can't offer you much, he said.

He looked so miserable that she felt she ought to express compassion, she ought to comfort him, she ought to tell him everything was fine. Instead she said, You're right. You can't offer me much.

Daniel looks at his watch, then out the window at the rain. There were cars going by but nobody walking on the street. He took hold of Rennie's shoulders and kissed her gently on the mouth. He ran the ends of his fingers over her lips.

I'm very fond of you, he said.

Flamboyant adjectives will be your downfall, said Rennie, who couldn't resist.

I know I don't express myself very well, Daniel said. Rennie wasn't sure she could take that much sincerity all at once. He kissed her again, quite a lot harder. Rennie put her face against his neck and the collar of his shirt. He smelled like laundry. It was safe enough, he could hardly take off her clothes or his in a parked car on a street with two-way traffic.

She wanted him to though, she wanted to lie down beside him and touch him and be touched by him; at the moment she believed in it, the touch of the hand that could transform you, change everything, magic. She wanted to see him lying with his eyes closed, she wanted to see him and not be seen, she wanted to be trusted. She wanted to make love with him, very slowly, she wanted it to last a long time, she wanted the moment just before coming, helplessness, hours of it, she wanted to open him up. There was such a gap between what she wanted and where she was that she could hardly stand it.

She pulled back. Let's go home, she said.

It's not that I don't want to, he said. You know that.

His face for a moment was like a child's looking up, he was so sweet it hurt, and Rennie felt brutal. He had no right to appeal to her like that, to throw himself on her mercy. She wasn't God, she didn't have to be understanding, which was a good thing because she was rapidly understanding less and less about this and soon she wouldn't understand anything at all. Rennie liked to know the names for things and there was no name for this.

What do you do afterwards, she said, go home and jerk off? Or maybe you go home and stick your hand into the job jar. Don't tell me you haven't got one, I know you do. What else would you do with your spare time?

He put his hand gently on the back of her neck. What would you like to do? he said. If you really want to, we'll check into a hotel somewhere. I can only stay an hour, that's all I've got, and then what? Would that be love? Is that what you want?

No, said Rennie. As usual she wanted everything, which was in short supply.

I'm not good at that sort of thing, Daniel said. I'd resent you for it and I don't want that. I care about you, I care what happens to you. I guess I think I can do more for you as your doctor; I'm better at it. He looked down at his hands, which were on the steering wheel now.

Why not both? said Rennie.

That's the way I am, said Daniel. There are some things I just can't do.

It struck Rennie that Daniel was a lot like Griswold, not as it was but as it would like to be. Ordinary human decency, a fine decent man they would say, with a list of things you just couldn't do. This insight did not fill her with joy. He was normal, that was what she'd fallen in love with, the absolutely ordinary raised to the degree of X. What were you supposed to be. He did make his living cutting parts off other people's bodies and patting their shoulders while they died, he used the same hands for both, but nobody considered that unusual. He was a good man, a mystery, Rennie wanted to know why. Maybe it was habit.

What do you believe in? she said to him. I mean, what keeps you ticking over? What makes you get up in the mornings? How do you know what kinds of things you can do and what kinds you can't do? Don't tell me it's God. Or maybe you've got those things in the job jar, along with the jobs. Saying this, she felt like a troll, but Daniel took it straight.

I don't know, said Daniel. I've never thought that much about it.

Rennie felt cold, she felt she was dying and Daniel knew it, he just hadn't told her about it yet. But making love for an hour in a hotel room with Daniel would not work, she could see that now. They would go in and close the door and take off their damp coats and he would sit down on the edge of the bed. Seeing him with his head bent, dutifully undoing his shoelaces: this would be too much for her, it would be too sad. You don't have to, she would say. She would hold onto his hands and cry and cry.

She no longer expected Daniel to save her life. She no longer expected Daniel. Maybe that was the right way to do it, never to expect anything.

Let's go home, she said.

●

Rennie lay on the bed, their bed, stiff as plaster, waiting for Jake to come out of the shower. They'd talked about it enough. The truth was that she didn't want him to touch her and she didn't know why, and he didn't really want to touch her either but he wouldn't admit it.

You have to try, he said. You won't let me try.

You sound like the little engine that could, she said. I think I can, I know I can.

You really are relentless, he said.

So they were going to try. She'd stood in front of her open closet, wondering what you should wear to try, to a trial. A trial of strength. She wanted to wear something and knew she had to; these days she always wore something to bed. She didn't want to be seen, the way she was, damaged, amputated.

Once he'd given her a purple one-piece number that snapped together at the crotch and they'd got very high on some top-grade Colombian, and at the crucial moment neither of them could get the snaps undone. They'd hugged each other, rolling around and laughing so much they almost fell off the bed. So much for sexy underwear, she'd said.

She decided on black, two pieces, he'd given that to her a while ago. He could leave the top part on if he wanted to. She lit some candles and lay down on the bed, raising one knee, arranging herself. It was no good.

She tried to think about Daniel, lying here beside her instead, hoping that would make her feel better, softer, but she couldn't. She could hardly imagine him without clothes. All she could imagine were his hands, hands with thin fingers and with the marks of a slow dark burning on their backs. In the Middle Ages they'd painted pictures of souls, the souls of the dying leaving their bodies, and for a long time they'd argued about what part of the body the soul inhabited when you were alive. There was no doubt about Daniel at all: his soul was in his hands. Cut them off and he'd be a zombie.

One man I'm not allowed to touch, she thought, and another I won't allow to touch me. I could write a piece on it: "Creative Celibacy." "Sexual Abstinence, the Coming Thing." Except it's been done. What's supposed to come next? Sublimation? Ceramics? Devotion to a good cause?

Jocasta would have advised her to try masturbation. That too was once supposed to be the wave of the future. *Listen, when all else fails let your fingers do the walking.* But masturbation didn't interest her, it would be like talking to yourself or keeping a journal. She'd never been able to understand women who kept journals. She already knew what she would be likely to say. Unlikely things could only be said by other people.

Jake came in from the shower with a blue towel tucked around his waist. He sat down on the bed beside her and kissed her gently on the mouth.

I'd like the candles out, she said.

No, he said, leave them on. I want to see you.

Why? she said.

You turn me on, he said.

She didn't answer. He ran his hand up her right leg, across her belly, down the left thigh, over the bent knee. He did that again, moving the black cloth down. He didn't go above the waist. Upsidedown high school, Rennie thought. He moved his hand between her legs, bent to kiss her navel.

Maybe we should smoke some dope, he said.

To help me relax? she said, watching him from her head, which was up there on the pillow at the other end of her body. She felt her eyes sparkling like those of some small malicious animal, a weasel or a rat. Red, intelligent, in a sharp little face with tiny incisors. Cornered and mean.

That's right, he said. He brought the tea canister in and opened it and rolled a joint and lit it and passed it to her. I love you, he said, but you can't believe it.

What's the difference between a belief and a delusion? she said. Maybe you just think you ought to. Maybe I make you feel guilty. You've always told me guilt was a big thing with Jewish mothers.

You aren't my mother, he said. A good thing, too.

How could I be? she said. I'm not Jewish.

Nobody's perfect, he said. You're my golden *shiksa*. We all have to have at least one, it's obligatory.

So that's what I am, said Rennie. I guess that's it for my

identity crisis. It's nice to know who you are. But I'm hardly golden.

Gilt-edged security, anyway, said Jake.

Is that a pun? said Rennie.

Don't ask me, said Jake, I'm a functional illiterate and proud of it.

But up and coming, said Rennie.

As often as possible, said Jake. You think we could set this to music?

This isn't a forties movie, said Rennie.

You could have fooled me, said Jake.

Rennie felt she was going to cry. What she couldn't bear was the effort he was making to pretend nothing was different, the effort she was making to help him pretend. She wanted to say, I'm dying, but that would be melodrama, and anyway she probably wasn't.

Jake began rubbing her left thigh, slowly up and then down. I feel awkward, he said. I feel you don't want me to be doing this.

She was watching him but she didn't know how to help him. I can't believe, she thought. Why not? The words in her head came one at a time, as if they were being spoken by someone else. She watched them form, rise, burst. It was strong grass.

You don't have to be perfect, he said.

He bent down and kissed her again, supporting himself with his arms so his torso didn't touch her. He's doing this for me, she thought. It's not for him, he doesn't want to.

He lifted her and slid the black satin shorts down and put his mouth on her.

I don't want that, she said. I don't need charity. I want you inside me.

Jake paused. He raised her arms, holding her wrists above her head. Fight me for it, he said. Tell me you want it. This was his ritual, one of them, it had once been hers too and now she could no longer perform it. She didn't move and he let go of her. He put his face down on her shoulder; his body went limp. Shit, he said. He needed to believe she was still closed, she could still fight, play, stand up to him, he could not bear to see her vulnerable like this.

Rennie knew what it was. He was afraid of her, she had the kiss of death on her, you could see the marks. Mortality infested her, she was a carrier, it was catching. She lay there with his face against her neck, thinking of something she'd seen written in a men's washroom once when she was doing a piece on graffiti. *Life is just another sexually transmitted social disease.* She didn't blame him. Why should he be stuck with it? With her.

After a while he raised his head. I'm sorry, he said.

So am I, said Rennie. She waited. You're having a thing with someone else, aren't you?

It's not important, said Jake.

Is that what you say about me? Rennie said. To her?

Look, said Jake, it's either that or a warm wet washcloth. You won't let me touch you.

Touch, said Rennie. Is that all? Does it matter that much? Isn't there any more to it than that?

She stroked the back of his neck and thought of the soul leaving the body in the form of words, on little scrolls like the ones in medieval paintings.

Oh please.

●

They walk inland, uphill. Rennie tries to think of something neutral to say. He's carrying her camera bag and the other bag. It's the minimum, but she shouldn't have brought so much.

It's about five-thirty and although the asphalt road is hot it's not too hot, the trees cast shadows. There are little houses set back from the road, people are sitting out on their porches, the women wear print dresses, some of the older ones have hats on, and Paul nods to them, they nod back, they don't stare but they look, taking note. A group of girls passes, going down the hill, fifteen- or sixteen-year-olds in white dresses, some with bows or flowers in their hair, which is braided and pinned up; they look oddly old-fashioned, costumed. They're singing, three-part harmony, a hymn. Rennie wonders if they're going to church.

"It's up here," Paul says. The house is concrete block like the others and only a little bigger, painted light green and raised on stilts above the rainwater tank. There's a rock garden covering the hill, cactus and rubbery-looking plants. The shrubs at the gateway are dying though, there's a many-stranded yellow vine covering them like a net, like hair.

"See that?" Paul says. "Around here they break pieces of that off and throw it into the gardens of the people they don't like. It grows like crazy, it strangles everything. Love vine, they call it."

"Are there people here who don't like you?" Rennie says.

"Hard to believe, isn't it?" he says, grinning at her.

Inside, the house is neat, almost blank, as if no one is actually living in it. The furniture is noncommittal, wood-frame chairs of the kind Rennie has seen in the beach bars. Beside one of the chairs there's a telescope on a tripod.

"What do you watch through it?" says Rennie.

"The stars," says Paul.

On the wall above the sofa there's a map, on the wall facing it another, island after island, navigational maps with the soundings marked. There are no pictures. The kitchen is an open counter with appliances behind it, a stove, a refrigerator, no clutter. Paul takes ice cubes from the refrigerator and fixes two drinks, rum and lime. Rennie looks at the maps; then she goes out through the double doors, there's a porch with a hammock, and leans on the railing, looking down over the road to the tops of the trees and then the harbour. There's a sunset, as usual.

The bed is expertly made, hospital corners firmly tucked in. Rennie wonders where he learned to do that, or maybe someone comes in to do it for him. Perhaps this is the spare bedroom, it's empty enough. There are two pillows, though nobody lives with him. He untwists the mosquito net, spreads it over the bed. "We can go for dinner, if you like," he says.

Rennie's wearing a white shirt and a wrap skirt, also white. She wonders which she should take off first. What will happen? Maybe there's no point to taking off anything, maybe she should offer to sleep in the other bed. All he said was that he had room.

Nevertheless she's afraid, of failure. Maybe she should be fair, maybe she should warn him. What can she say? I'm not all here? There's part of me missing? She doesn't even have to do that, failure is easy to avoid. All you have to do is walk away.

Then she realizes she doesn't care. She doesn't care what he thinks of her, she never has to see this man again if she doesn't want to. She never has to see anyone again if she doesn't want to. She's been hoping for some dope, he's in the business, he must have some; it would help, she thought, she'd be able to relax. But she doesn't need it; already she feels light, insubstantial, as if she's died and gone to heaven and come back minus a body. There's nothing to worry about, nothing can touch her. She's a tourist. She's exempt.

He's standing in front of her, in the half-light, smiling a little, watching her to see what she'll do.

"I thought you didn't want that," he says.

He doesn't touch her. She undoes the buttons on the blouse, he's watching. He notes the scar, the missing piece, the place where death kissed her lightly, a preliminary kiss.

He doesn't look away or down, he's seen people a lot deader than her.

"I was lucky," she says.

He reaches out his hands and Rennie can't remember ever having been touched before. Nobody lives forever, who said you could? This much will have to do, this much is enough. She's open now, she's been opened, she's being drawn back down, she enters her body again and there's a moment of pain, incarnation, this may be only the body's desperation, a flareup, a last clutch at the world before the long slide into final illness and death; but meanwhile she's solid after all, she's still here on the earth, she's grateful, he's touching her, she can still be touched.

V

J ake liked to pin her hands down, he liked to hold her so she couldn't move. He liked that, he liked thinking of sex as something he could win at. Sometimes he really hurt her, once he put his arm across her throat and she really did stop breathing. Danger turns you on, he said. Admit it. It was a game, they both knew that. He would never do it if it was real, if she really was a beautiful stranger or a slave girl or whatever it was he wanted her to pretend. So she didn't have to be afraid of him.

A month before the operation Rennie had a phone call from *Visor*. Keith, the managing editor, thought it would be sort of fun to do a piece on pornography as an art form. There had already been a number of anti-porn pieces in the more radical women's magazines, but Keith thought they were kind of heavy and humourless. They missed the element of playfulness, he said. He wanted a woman to write it because he thought they'd crack the nuts of any guy who tried to do it. Rennie tried to find out who he meant by "they," but he was vague. Tie it in with women's fantasy lives, if you can, he said. Keep it light. Rennie said she thought the subject might have more to do with men's fantasy lives, but Keith said he wanted the woman's angle.

Keith fixed it up for her to interview an artist who lived and worked in a warehouse down off King Street West and did sculptures using life-sized mannequins. He was making tables and chairs from the mannequins, which were like store mannequins except that the joints had been filled in and plastered over to make them smooth. The women were dressed in half-cup bras and G-string panties, set on their hands and knees for the tables, locked into a sitting position for the chairs. One of the chairs was a woman on her knees, her back arched, her wrists tied to her thighs. The ropes and arms were the arms of the chair, her bum was the seat.

It's a visual pun, said the artist, whose first name was Frank. He had one woman harnessed to a dogsled, with a muzzle on. It was called *Nationalism is Dangerous*. There was another one with a naked mannequin on her knees, chained to a toilet, with a Handy Andy between her teeth like a rose. It was called *Task Sharing*, said Frank.

If a woman did that, said Rennie, they'd call it strident feminism.

That's the breaks, said Frank. Anyway, I don't just do women. He showed her a male figure sitting in a swivel chair with a classic blue pinstripe business suit on. Frank had glued nine or ten plastic dildoes to the top of his head, where they stood out like pigtails or the rays of a halo. *Erogenous Zone Clone Bone*, it was called.

You're going to find this boring, said Rennie, but your work doesn't exactly turn me on.

It's not supposed to turn you *on*, said Frank, not offended. Art is for contemplation. What art does is, it takes what society deals out and makes it visible, right? So you can *see* it. I mean there's the themes and then there's the variations. If they want flower paintings they can go to Eaton's.

Rennie remembered having read these opinions already, in the file on Frank given to her by *Visor*. I guess I see your point, she said.

I mean, said Frank, what's the difference between me and Salvador Dali, when you come right down to it?

I'm not sure, Rennie said.

If you don't like my stuff, you should see the raw material, he said.

That was the other part of Keith's plan, the raw material. The Metro Police had a collection of seized objects, Keith said; it was called Project P., P for pornography, and it was open to the public. Rennie took Jocasta with her, not because she didn't think she could get through it on her own, she felt she was up to almost anything. Still, it didn't seem like the kind of thing you would do by yourself if you could help it. Someone might see you coming out and get the wrong idea. Besides, it was Jocasta's kind of thing. Bizarre. Human ingenuity, that's what you should stress, said Keith. Infinite variety and that.

The collection was housed in two ordinary rooms at the main police building, and this was the first thing that struck Rennie: the ordinariness of the rooms. They were rectangular, featureless, painted government grey; they could have been in a post office. The policeman who showed them around was young, fresh-faced, still eager. He kept saying, Now why do you think anyone would want to do *that*? Now what do you think *that* could be for?

Rennie made it through the whips and the rubber appliances without a qualm. She took notes. How do you spell the plural of *dildo*? she asked the policeman. With or without an *e*? The policeman said he didn't know. Probably like *tomatoes*, Rennie thought. Jocasta said it all looked very medical to her and she understood that in England it was the truss shops that used to sell under-the-cover bondage magazines, before sex supermarkets came in. The policeman said he wouldn't really know about that. He opened a cupboard and took out something even the police hadn't been able to figure out. It was a machine like a child's floor polisher, with an ordinary-looking dildo on the handle. He plugged it into a wall socket and the whole machine scooted around the floor, with the handle plunging wildly up and down.

But what's it *for*? Jocasta said, intrigued.

Your guess is as good as mine, the policeman said. It's too short for anyone standing up, and there's no place on it to sit down. Anyway, the way it runs around the room like that you couldn't keep up with it. We've got a private bet on here. Anyone comes up with some use for it that wouldn't take your guts out, we give them a hundred dollars.

Maybe it's for very active midgets, Jocasta said.

Maybe the police made a mistake, Rennie said. Maybe it really is just a floor polisher, with kind of a strange handle. Next thing you know you'll be raiding General Electric and seizing pop-up toasters.

Fifty percent of fatal accidents occur at home and now we know why, said Jocasta.

The policeman somehow did not like them laughing. He disapproved of it. He took them into a third room, which was set up with black-out windows and a video viewer and showed them some film clips, a woman with a dog, a woman with a pig, a woman with a donkey. Rennie watched with detachment. There were a couple of sex-and-death pieces, women being strangled or bludgeoned or having their nipples cut off by men dressed up as Nazis, but Rennie felt it couldn't possibly be real, it was all done with ketchup.

This is our grand finale, the policeman said. The picture showed a woman's pelvis, just the pelvis and the tops of the thighs. The woman was black. The legs were slightly apart; the usual hair, the usual swollen pinkish purple showed between them; nothing was moving. Then something small and grey and wet appeared, poking out from between the legs. It was the head of a rat. Rennie felt that a large gap had appeared in what she'd been used to thinking of as reality. What if this is normal, she thought, and we just haven't been told yet?

Rennie didn't make it out of the room. She threw up on the

policeman's shoes. Sorry, she said, but he didn't seem to mind. He patted her on the back, as if she'd passed a test of some sort, and took her arm, leading her from the darkened room. Politely, he did not look down at his shoes.

I thought that one would get to you, he said. A lot of women do that. Look at it this way, at least it's not for queers.

You need your head repaired, said Jocasta, and Rennie said she thought maybe it was time to leave. She thanked the policeman for being so cooperative. He was annoyed with them, not because of his shoes but because of Jocasta.

I can't do this piece, Rennie told Keith.

Why not? he said, disappointed in her.

It's not my thing, she said. I'll stick to lifestyles.

Maybe it is a lifestyle, he said.

Rennie decided that there were some things it was better not to know any more about than you had to. Surfaces, in many cases, were preferable to depths. She did a piece on the return of the angora sweater, and another one on the hand-knit-look industry. That was soothing. There was much to be said for trivia.

For a couple of weeks after that she had a hard time making love with Jake. She didn't want him grabbing her from behind when she wasn't expecting it, she didn't like being thrown onto the bed or held so she couldn't move. She had trouble dismissing it as a game. She now felt that in some way that had never been spelled out between them he thought of her as the enemy. Please don't do that any more, she said. At least not for a while. She didn't want to be afraid of men, she wanted Jake to tell her why she didn't have to be.

I thought you said it's okay if you trust me, he said. Don't you trust me?

It's not you, she said. It's not you I don't trust.

Then what is it? he said.

211

I don't know, she said. Lately I feel I'm being used; though not by you exactly.

Used for what? said Jake.

Rennie thought about it. Raw material, she said.

Later on, she said, If I had a rat in my vagina, would it turn you on?

Dead or alive? said Jake.

Me or the rat? said Rennie.

Feh, said Jake. You sound like my mother. Always worrying about the dustballs under the bed.

No, seriously, she said.

El sleazo, he said. Come on, don't confuse me with that sick stuff. You think I'm some kind of a pervert? You think most men are like that?

Rennie said no.

•

I ran into Paul in Miami, says Lora. At first he told me he was in real estate. I was down there with some guy, that was after me and Gary split up, and around that time if there was a free weekend going I took it. It wasn't the sex, I couldn't have cared less if a man ever touched me again or not, that's how I felt then. With Gary it was never that great anyway, it was a lot like going through a revolving door, in and out before you know it and if you sneezed it was all over except for washing the sheets.

Maybe I wanted it that way, maybe I wanted to be able to take it or leave it. Maybe I thought if I got to like it too much I'd be stuck. I wanted to think, Chuck you, Farley, there's nothing much I need *you* for, if I want to I can turn around and walk right through that door and the only one who'll be missing a thing is you. I thought it was just something you let me do to you. I don't think most of them even liked it very much either. They only did it because you were supposed to.

I guess I just wanted to be with someone. It wasn't the nights that were bad, it was the mornings. I didn't like to wake up in the morning and have nobody there. After a while you just want someone to like you. You want someone to maybe have breakfast with, go to the movies with, stuff like that. I used to say there's only two things that matter, is he nice or is he rich. Nice is better than rich but take it from me, you can't have both, and if you can't get nice take rich. Sometimes I said it the other way around. Not that there's a whole lot of either one hanging out there on the trees, you know?

At first I thought Paul was only nice. He wasn't mean like a lot of them, he was easy to be with, he wasn't a pain in the ass, you know? Then I figured it out that he was rich, too. He had this boat, he only had the one then, and he said why didn't I come down here for a couple of weeks, get a tan, relax, and there wasn't any good reason not to. Once I got down here I couldn't see any good reason to leave. Around that time I found out what he really did.

I worked on the boats for a while. Most of these boats have two or three crew and a cook, they really do run charters on the boats, it would look funny if they didn't, and the crew all knew what he was doing, they were in for a percentage, he had people he could trust. I was supposed to be the cook, what I knew about cooking on a boat you could stick in your ear, it's not like cooking in a real kitchen, but I picked it up. I was seasick as hell at first, I puked my guts out, but I figure you can get used to almost anything if you have to and when you're out in the middle of the ocean there's only one way off the boat, eh?

A lot of girls work the boats here, the straight boats as well, though you never really know if the boat's straight or not, you learn not to ask what they've got in the hold. Whoever runs the boat expects you to make it with them; if you don't like it you can always get off the boat. I never made it with the charters though, that wasn't part of the deal.

It's always them that get the maddest about it too. They think if they're renting the boat they're renting everything on it. Maybe I'm for sale, I'd tell them, but I'm sure as hell not for rent. How much? one of them said, an asshole. Hot-shot lawyer or something. You couldn't afford it, I said. Funny, you look pretty cheap to me, he said. I may be pretty but I'm not cheap, I said. I'm like a lawyer, what you're paying for is the experience.

Anyway you only had to do a few charters, maybe once a month, you could survive on that. The rest of the time I was living with Paul. Or anyway that's what it was called. We slept in the same bed and all, but there was something missing in him, it was like being with someone who wasn't there, you know? He didn't care what I did, anything I wanted to do was okay with him, other men, anything, as long as it didn't interfere with him. Deep down inside he just didn't give a shit. You know what the locals say about him? *He does deal.* With the devil, is what they mean, they don't mean the business. It's what they say about loners.

About the only thing that really turned him on was danger, as far as I could figure out. Once in a while he'd do this really dangerous stuff.

Like, a couple of months after I came down here there was this thing with Marsdon. That was before Marsdon went to the States. He was living with this woman, and he came home one day and caught her in the sack with one of his cousins, I forget which one. It could be anybody, sooner or later they all turn out to be cousins if you study it hard enough.

Of course Marsdon beat her up. If he hadn't beat her up, the other men would have laughed at him and so would the women. They expect it, for being *bad*, which is what they call it. But he went too far, he made her take off all her clothes, not that she had that many on when he found her, and then he covered her with cow-itch. That's like a nettle, it's what you do to people you really don't like a whole lot. Then he tied her to a tree in the back yard, right near an ant hill, the stinging kind. He stayed in the house, drinking rum and listening to her scream. He left her there five hours, till she was all swollen up like a balloon. A lot of people heard her but nobody tried to untie her, partly because he had a mean reputation and partly because it was a man-woman thing, they don't think that's anyone else's business.

Paul heard about it and he walked into the back yard and cut the rope. You just don't do that. Everyone waited to see what Marsdon would do, but he didn't do anything. He's hated Paul ever since. It was after that he went to the States and got into the army, or that's what he said he was doing. I wish he'd stayed there.

Paul didn't know the woman, he wasn't being noble as far as I could tell. He did it because it was dangerous; he did it because it was fun. Some fun if you ask me. You'd never know when he was going to pull one of those, you'd be washing your hair and you'd look out the window and there he'd be swinging from some goddamn tree, like Tarzan. He was like a little boy that way. He always said he knew what he was doing, but I knew some day he'd try it once too often and that would be that.

That's one of the reasons I stopped working on his boats. He was taking too many chances.

The stuff comes from Colombia, on the freighters. For the government there it's just another cash crop. Nobody can do anything about the freighters and once they're out in the ocean nobody can do anything about that either, except maybe hijack the boat. People have tried that but it's not too safe any more, they're shooting back. The U.S. knows which boats it's on, they follow everything by satellite, they can track the big boats by the sound of the motors; so they can't get it into the States that way. They bring it here, to one of these islands, and they split it up and put it onto yachts or private planes, they're using those more now, and they take it up to Miami or maybe in through the Virgin Islands. It's not just the U.S. and Cuba trying to control it here. The third group is the mob, and they're spending more money. It's a guaranteed multi-million-dollar business, so they can afford a top-level lobby in Washington, to keep them from legalizing it. Nobody wants it legalized, then you could grow it right there in your own back yard, the bottom would fall out of the market.

Ellis never stopped them, they were paying him off, but that may be changing, he may want in on the ground floor. He just made a big bust in the harbour over at St. Antoine. It seems some locals were growing it up there behind the bananas and smuggling it out on the fishing trawlers. A medium-sized operation but the big ones don't want any competition, and Ellis doesn't want the peasants marketing it themselves, he'd lose his cut. I'd guess it was the mob who put Ellis up to making the bust. Two to one he'll resell it himself.

At first they were just hiring Paul's boats, piecework, to make the run up from here to Miami. But then he went down there himself and bought his own army general. He figured why should he be the middleman when he could buy wholesale himself and sell retail, which makes sense except that then he had them all down his back, the CIA, the mob, Ellis, the works. No thanks, I said, I like my skin the way it is, only the holes God gave me. I told him I'd do the tourists, they'd trust me more because I was white and a woman, as long as he bought a few local cops for me, I'd do retail, but none of that other stuff.

The second reason I stopped was Prince. I just met him in a beach bar and it was love at first sight, that never happened to me before. I know you think it's weird because he's so much younger than me but that's the way it happened. I don't know what it was, maybe it was the eyes. He looked at you straight on, you felt that everything he was saying just had to be the truth. It wasn't always, I found that out, but he always believed it was. He even believed all that communist stuff, he really believed he could save the world. He couldn't tell you something and not believe it himself. He was so sweet. I was a real sucker for that.

He didn't want me going out on the boats with Paul, he didn't want me having anything to do with Paul in that way any more, he was jealous as hell. I guess I was a sucker for that, too. He wanted me all to himself, nobody else ever wanted that. He wanted us to have a baby. I never felt that important before.

As for Paul, you know what he did? He shook hands with me. That was all. I thought I was going to cry but instead I laughed. And I thought, that's what it's been like all along, sleeping with him and everything, there's been nothing more to it than that. Shaking hands.

●

Rennie wakes up in the middle of the night and Paul is still there, she can hardly believe it; he's even awake, he's a shape in the darkness, above her, resting on one elbow; is he watching her?

"Is that you?" she says.

"Who else would it be?" he says. She doesn't know. She reaches out for him and he's tangible, he doesn't go away.

It's early morning. Rennie can hear a sound outside the window, a bleating. She gets out of bed and looks: it's a goat, right beside the house, with a chain around its neck attached to a stone so it can't wander off. She wishes it would shut up. Two men are nearby, hacking at the shrubs with machetes. Gardeners. One of them has a transistor radio, which is thinly playing a hymn. Paul is still asleep, he must be used to it. She was dreaming there was another man in the bed with them; something white, a stocking or a gauze bandage, wrapped around his head.

When she wakes again Paul is gone. Rennie gets up and puts on her clothes, then wanders through the house looking for him. It's nobody's house, it could be a motel, it's empty space and he's left no footprints. It occurs to her that she's just spent the night with a man about whom she knows absolutely nothing at all. It seems a foolhardy thing to have done.

She goes outside. There's a tree beside the porch, covered with pink flowers, a swarm of hummingbirds around it. It looks arranged. The too-bright sunshine, the rock garden, the road below it along which two women are walking, one carrying a large tree limb balanced on her head, the foliage and then the blue harbour dotted with postcard boats, the whole vista is one-dimensional this morning, a scrim. At any moment it will rise slowly into the air and behind it will appear the real truth.

There's a noise coming from behind a clump of trees to the east, a desolate monotonous wail, a child. It goes on and on, as if this is a natural form of speech, almost like breathing. A woman's voice rises, there are thumps; the child's howling changes in intensity but not in rhythm.

Rennie looks through the telescope, which is focused on one of the yachts. There's a woman in a red bikini, lowering herself into the water; the telescope is so strong that even the roll of fat above the bikini bottom, even the striations on her belly are visible. Is this Paul's hobby, peering at distant flesh? Surely not. Yet the telescope confers furtive power, the power to watch without being watched. Rennie's embarrassed by it and turns away. She swings herself in the hammock, trying not to think. She feels deserted.

When Paul still doesn't come back, she goes into the house. She checks out the refrigerator for something to eat, but there's not much. Ice cubes in the ice cube tray, a tin of condensed milk with holes punched in the top, a small paper bag full of sugar, some yellowing limes, a pitcher of cold water. Noodles in the cupboard, a bottle of rum, a packet of coffee, some Tetley's teabags, a tin of Tate & Lyle golden syrup with a string of ants undulating around the lid. They skipped dinner last night and she's starving.

The logical explanation is that Paul has gone for food, since there isn't any. She wishes he'd left a note for her, but he doesn't seem like the note-leaving type. The house is very empty. She walks through the livingroom again; there aren't even any books or magazines. Maybe he keeps his personal things on the boat, the boats. She goes into the bedroom and looks into the closet: a couple of shirts, a spear gun and a mask and flippers, jeans folded on a hanger, that's it.

In the bureau there are some T-shirts, neatly stacked, and stuck at the back of the top drawer a couple of photos: colour snapshots, a white colonial house with a double garage, a green lawn, a yellow-haired woman in a shirtwaist dress, smiling to reveal slightly buck teeth; hair short and close to the head, an unsuccessful permanent growing out, two little girls, one blonde, one reddish-brown, both in pigtails with ribbons, it must have been a birthday. The mother's hands on their shoulders. The sun casts shadows under their eyes so that even though they're smiling they look slightly disappointed, the disappointment of ghosts. In the other picture Paul is there too, much younger, a crewcut but it must be him: a shirt and tie and pants with sharp creases, and beneath his eyes the same shadows.

Rennie feels she's prying but she's into it now, she might as well go on. It's not as if she'll use it for anything: she just wants to know, she wants to find something that will make Paul real for her. She goes into the bathroom and looks through the medicine cabinet. The brand names are unrevealing: Tylenol in a large bottle, Crest toothpaste, Elastoplast, Dettol. Nothing unusual.

There's another bedroom, or she assumes it's a bedroom. The door's closed but not locked: it opens as easily as all the other doors. It is a bedroom, or at least there's a bed in it. There's also a table, with what looks like a radio on it, a complicated-looking one, and some other equipment she can't identify. In the closet there's a large cardboard box standing on end. The address label's been torn off. It's full of styrofoam packing beads, but otherwise empty. It looks very familiar.

There's someone in the house, walking across the wooden floor. She feels as if she's been caught in a forbidden room, though Paul hasn't forbidden anything. Still, it isn't nice to snoop in other people's houses. She comes out, closing the door behind her as quietly as she can. Luckily there's a hallway: she can't be seen.

But it's not Paul, it's Lora, in a fresh pink dress with bare shoulders. "Hi there," she says. "I brought you some stuff." She's at the kitchen counter, taking it out of a straw basket: bread, butter, a carton of long-life milk, even a tin of jam. "He never has anything in the house. I'll make us some coffee, okay?"

She gets out the electric kettle, the coffee, the sugar; she knows exactly where everything is. Rennie sits at the wooden table, watching her. She knows she should feel thankful for all this attention, thoughtfulness, but instead she's irritated. This isn't her kitchen and she doesn't live here, so why should it bother her that Lora is acting as if she owns the place? And how did Lora know she'd be here? Maybe she didn't know it. Maybe she's in the habit.

"Where's Paul?" says Lora.

"I don't know," Rennie says. She's on the defensive: shouldn't she know, shouldn't he have told her?

"He'll turn up," says Lora lightly. "Here today, gone tomorrow, that's Paul."

Lora brings the coffee, a cup for each of them, and sets it down on the table. Rennie doesn't want to ask for food, though she's ravenous; she doesn't want to tell Lora about missing dinner. She doesn't want to tell Lora anything. She would like Lora to vanish, but instead Lora sits down at the table, settling in. She sips her coffee. Rennie watches her hands, the squat fingers, the rough gnawed skin around the nails.

"I wouldn't get too mixed up with Paul if I was you," she says. Here it comes, thinks Rennie. She's going to tell me something for my own good. In her experience, things that people told you for your own good were always unpleasant.

"Why not?" she says, smiling as neutrally as possible.

"I don't mean you can't," says Lora. "Hell, why not, it's a free country. Just, don't get mixed up, is all. Not that he gets that mixed up with most people anyway. Easy come, easy go. Around here there's a high turnover."

Rennie isn't sure what she's being told. Is she being warned off or just warned? "I guess you've known him a long time," she says.

"Long enough," says Lora.

Now there are footsteps and a shadow falls on the front window, and this time it is Paul, coming across the porch. He walks through the door smiling, sees Lora, blinks but keeps on smiling.

"I went for eggs," he says to Rennie. "I thought you'd be hungry." He sets a brown paper bag down on the table, proud of himself.

"Where in hell did you get any eggs, at this time of day?" says Lora. "The eggs aren't in yet." She's getting up, to go Rennie hopes, she sets down the coffee mug.

Paul grins. "I've got connections," he says.

●

Paul scrambles the eggs, quite well, they're not too dry; Rennie gives him three and a half stars for the eggs. They eat them with jam and toast. There's a toaster, though the only way you can get it to work, says Paul, is by short-circuiting it with a paring knife. He keeps meaning to get a new one, he says, but new toasters are smuggled in and none have come in lately.

After breakfast Rennie thinks she should offer to wash the dishes, since Paul did the cooking. "Forget that," says Paul.

"Someone comes in." He takes her hands and pulls her to her feet and kisses her, his mouth tasting of buttered toast. Then he leads her into the bedroom. This time he takes off her clothes, not too quickly, without fumbling. She takes his hand with their blunt practical fingers, guides him, they slide on to the bed, it's effortless.

Rennie comes almost at once, they're both slippery with sweat, it's luxurious, indulgent, gleeful as rolling around in warm mud, the muscles of her thighs are aching. He pauses, goes on, pauses, goes on until she comes again. He's skilled and attentive, he's good at it. Maybe she's just a quick fuck for him, a transient, maybe they're both transients, passing through, is that what Lora was trying to say? But she can live with that, it's something, and something is better than nothing after all.

After a long time they get up and take a shower; together, but Paul is absent-minded as he soaps her back and then her breasts, carefully enough but he's already thinking about something else. She passes her hands over his body, learning him, the muscles, the hollows. She's looking for something, his presence in his own body, the other body beneath the tangible one, but she can't reach him, right now he's not there.

Paul takes Rennie's arm above the elbow as they step out into the white light. She wants to ask what they're going to do now, but she doesn't, because it doesn't seem to matter. Go with the flow, Jocasta would say, and she's going. She feels lazy and unhurried; the future, which contains among other things an overdraft at the bank, seems a long way from here. She knows she's fallen right into the biggest cliché in the book, a no-hooks, no-strings vacation romance with a mysterious stranger. She's behaving like a secretary, and things must be bad, because it isn't even bothering her. As long as she doesn't fall in love: that would be more than secretarial, it would be unacceptable. Love or sex? Jocasta would ask, and this time Rennie knows. Love is tangled, sex is straight. High-quality though, she'd say. Don't knock it.

They walk down to the sea and along the beach. By now he's remote but friendly, like a tour guide. Part of a package.

"See that building?" he says. He's pointing to a low shed-like structure. It's painted green and has three doors. "That made a lot of trouble here a couple of years ago. Ellis built it, it was supposed to encourage the tourists."

"What is it?" Rennie asks, unable to see why it would be encouraging.

"Now they use it to store fishnets in," says Paul, "but it used to be a can. A public can; Men, Women and Tourists. The idea was that the tourists would get off the boat and need a place to shit, and it would be right there handy for them. But the people here didn't think a thing like that should be down on the beach, out in the open like that. They thought it was indecent. They filled it up with stones, Tourists first." He smiles.

"They don't like tourists?" says Rennie.

"Let's put it this way," says Paul. "When the tourists come in, the prices go up. The big election issue this year is the price of sugar. They say it's getting too high, the people can't afford it."

"Just as well, it's bad for you," says Rennie, who believes in roughage, more or less.

"That depends on what else you have to eat," says Paul.

●

There's music, coming along the beach, wooden flutes and a drum. It's a parade of some sort, a mob of people walking along on the sand. Even though it's morning they have torches, cloth wrapped on sticks and soaked in kerosene, Rennie can smell it. Behind the adults in the crowd, around the edges, children are jumping and dancing in time to the music. Two kids are carrying a banner made from an old sheet: PRINCE OF PEACE: HE WORKS FOR YOU NOT YOU FOR HIM. Out front is Elva, chin up, strolling rather than marching. She has a white enamel potty in one hand and an unfurling roll of toilet paper in the other. She holds these objects high, as if they're trophies.

Rennie and Paul stand to the side as the parade goes past. At the very end comes Marsdon, still in his boots; the heels sink into the sand, it's hard for him to walk. He sees the two of them but does not acknowledge them.

"What does it mean?" says Rennie. "The toilet paper."

"It's aimed at the government," says Paul. "It's what they'll need after the election."

"I don't understand," says Rennie.

"They'll be so scared they'll shit their pants," says Paul. "Roughly translated." He's indulging her again.

They walk up the beach to the main road of the town. The parade has turned around now and is coming back; people have stopped to watch it. There's a car parked also, with two men in mirror sunglasses in the front and a third in the back. He's wearing a black suit, like an undertaker.

"The Minister of Justice," says Paul.

Paul says a lot of the stores are closed because of the election. Knots of men are gathered here and there; sun glints on the bottles as they pass from hand to hand. Some of the men nod to Paul. Not to Rennie: their attention slides over her, around her, they see her but only from the corners of their eyes.

They go up the hill and along a back street. There's a persistent hum; as they walk north it becomes a throb, a steady heartbeat. Metal, a motor of some kind.

"The power plant," says Paul. "It runs on oil. That's the poor end of town."

224

They go into a store called The Sterling Emporium. Paul asks for some long-life milk, and the woman gets it for him. She's about forty-five, with huge muscled arms and a small neat head, the hair screwed into lime-green plastic curlers. She brings out a brown paper bag from under the counter. "I save it for you," she says.

"Eggs," Paul says. He pays. Rennie can't believe how much they cost.

"If they're that hard to get," she says, "why doesn't someone start a chicken farm?"

"You'd have to ship in the feed," says Paul. "They don't grow it here. The feed weighs more than the eggs. Besides, the eggs come in from the States."

"What's that got to do with it?" says Rennie. Paul only smiles.

"They catch the thief," the woman says to Paul as they're heading for the door. "The police take him on the boat today."

"He's lucky then," Paul says to her.

"Lucky?" says Rennie, when they're outside.

"He's still alive," says Paul. "They caught another man, last month, stealing pigs up at one of the villages; they pounded him to death, no questions asked."

"The police?" says Rennie. "That's terrible."

"No," says Paul. "The people he was stealing the pigs from. It's a good thing for this one he only stole from tourists. If it was locals they'd have kicked his head in or taken him out and dumped him into the sea. As far as they're concerned, stealing's worse than murder."

"I can't believe that," says Rennie.

"Look at it this way," says Paul. "If you get angry and chop up your woman, that's understandable; a crime of passion, you might say. But stealing you plan beforehand. That's how they see it."

"Is there a lot of that?" says Rennie.

"Stealing?" says Paul. "Only since the tourists came in."

"Chopping up your woman," says Rennie.

"Less than you might think," says Paul. "Mostly they beat or slice rather than chop." Rennie thinks of cookbooks. "There's no shooting at all. Not like in, say, Detroit."

"Why is that?" says Rennie, hot on the sociological trail.

Paul looks at her, not for the first time, as if she's a charming version of the village idiot. "They don't have any guns," he says.

●

Rennie is sitting on a white chair in the beach bar of the Lime Tree, where Paul has left her. Parked her. Stashed her. He has a boat coming in in a few days, he said, there are some things he has to take care of. Rennie feels peripheral.

Is there anything you need? he asked before he went off.

I thought most of the stores were closed, she said.

They are, he said.

Something to read, she said, with a touch of malice. If he's so good at it let him try that.

He didn't miss a beat. Anything in particular?

Anything you think I'd like, said Rennie.

Which will at least make him think about her. She sits at the wooden table, eating a grilled cheese sandwich. What could be nicer? What's wrong anyway? Why does she want to go, if not home, at least away? Paul doesn't love her, that's why, which ought to be irrelevant.

Don't expect too much, he said last night.

Too much of what? said Rennie.

Too much of me, said Paul. He was smiling, calm as ever, but she no longer found this reassuring. Instead she found it a symptom. Nothing could move him. He kissed her on the forehead, as if she were a child, as if he were kissing her goodnight.

Next you're going to tell me there isn't very much, said Rennie. Right?

Maybe there isn't, said Paul.

Rennie didn't know she was expecting anything until she was told not to. Now they seem vast, sentimental, grandiose, technicolour, magical, ridiculous, her expectations.

What am I doing here? thinks Rennie. I should take my body and run. I don't need another man I'm not supposed to expect anything from.

She's a tourist, she can keep her options open. She can always go somewhere else.

●

"I am disturbing you?" It's a statement, with the force of a question. Rennie looks up: it's Dr. Minnow, in a white shirt open at the throat, balancing a cup of coffee. He sits down without waiting for an answer.

"You are enjoying yourself at the home of your American friend?" he says slyly.

Rennie, who believes in personal privacy, is annoyed. "How did you know I'm staying there?" she says. She feels as if she's been caught by a high-school teacher, necking under the boys' gym stairs. A thing she never did.

Dr. Minnow smiles, showing his skewed teeth. "Everyone knows," he says. "I am sorry to interrupt you, but there are some things I must tell you now. For the article you are writing."

"Oh yes," Rennie says. "Of course." Surely he doesn't still believe she's going to do this, now or in the future; but apparently he does, he's looking at her with candour and assurance. Faith. "I don't have my notebook with me," she says, feeling more and more fraudulent.

"You can remember," says Dr. Minnow. "Please, continue with your lunch." He's not even looking at her, he's glancing around them, noting who's there. "We are seeing how the election is going, my friend," he says.

"Already?" says Rennie.

"I do not mean the results," says Dr. Minnow. "I mean the practices of this government. Ellis is winning, my friend. But not honestly, you understand? This is what I wish you to make clear: that Ellis will not have the support of the people." It's the same measured tone of voice he's always used, but Rennie can see now that he's far from calm. He's enraged. He sits with his thin hands placed one on the other, on top of the wooden table, but the hands are tense, it's as if he has to hold onto them to keep them from moving, lifting, striking out.

"The only votes Ellis is getting are the ones he buys. First they bribe the people with the foreign aid money from the hurricane," he says. "This I can prove to you, I have witnesses. If they are not afraid to come forward. He gives out the roofing materials too, the sewage pipes, the things donated. On St. Antoine this bribery is effective, but here on Ste. Agathe it does not work. Here the people take the money from Ellis but vote for me anyway; they think this is a good joke. Ellis knows this trick will not work here on Ste. Agathe, he knows the people are for me. So he has been playing with the voters' list. When my people go to vote today, they find they are not recorded. Even some of my candidates have been removed, they cannot cast a vote in their own favour. 'Sorry,' they tell them. 'You cannot vote.' You know who he put on? Dead people, my friend. Half the people on the voters' list are dead. This government is being elected by corpses."

"But how could he do that?" says Rennie. "Didn't your party see the lists before the election?"

Dr. Minnow smiles his crooked smile. "This is not Canada, my friend," he says. "It is not Britain. Those rules no longer apply here. Nevertheless I will do what the sweet Canadians would do. I will challenge the results of the election in the courts and demand another vote, and I will call for an independent inquiry." He laughs a little. "It will have the same results here as it has there, my friend. None at all. Only there it takes longer."

"Why do you bother?" Rennie says.

"Bother?" says Dr. Minnow.

"If it's as rotten as you say," says Rennie, "why do you bother trying to do anything at all?"

Dr. Minnow pauses. She's shaken him a little. "I agree with you that it seems illogical and futile for me to do so," he says. "But this is why you do it. You do it because everyone tell you it is not possible. They cannot imagine things being different. It is my duty to imagine, and they know that for even one person to imagine is very dangerous to them, my friend. You understand?" He's about to say something else, but there are screams, from over near the kitchen door, the yacht people at the tables are looking, getting up, already there's a cluster of them.

Rennie stands up, trying to see what it is. It's Lora. She has one arm around Elva, whose eyes are closed, who's silently crying. There are red splotches on her PRINCE OF PEACE T-shirt. Her face is streaked, mapped, caked, dark red.

●

Lora sits at a table, one leg crossed, ankle on her knee. In front of her is a rum and lime and a glassful of ice cubes and a white enamel basin full of dark pink water. Elva is sitting beside her, still crying, her hands in her lap. Lora is washing away the blood with a blue washcloth from the hotel.

"Maybe I should lie her down," she says to Rennie. "What do you think?"

"God," says Rennie. "What happened?"

"I don't really know," says Lora. "I hardly saw it, it was too fast. One minute Prince was outside this polling station, just talking to the people, and the next thing there was all this shouting. It was two policemen with guns and the Minister of Justice. They just pushed in and started hammering Prince. Don't ask me why."

"Is he all right?" says Rennie.

"I don't even know that," says Lora. "I don't know where he went. He'll turn up, he usually does."

"Did she get knocked down by accident or something?" Rennie says.

"Her?" says Lora. "Hell no. She had her hands around the Justice Minister's neck, she damn near strangled him. They hit her on the head with a pistol butt to make her let go."

"Is there anything I can do?" says Rennie, who isn't too comfortable: the sight of the blood in the white basin is making her feel sick. Maybe she can go for Band-Aids and then she'll be off the hook.

"Get me some cigarettes," says Lora. "Over at the bar, Benson and Hedges. Maybe we should take her home."

"Marsdon," says Elva. "Some time I kill that boy."

"What?" says Lora. "What's she saying?"

"Marsdon start it," says Elva. She stops crying and opens her eyes. "I hear him. He call the Justice Minister a bad name. Why he need to do that?"

"Shit," says Lora. "Marsdon thinks everybody has to die for the revolution. *His* revolution, is what he means. He'll do just about anything to make sure they do. I wish he'd take off those stupid cowboy boots, I bet he sleeps in them. He thinks he's God's gift, ever since he came back from the States. He was in the army up there, it did something to him. He saw too many movies and now he thinks he's a hero. If Prince gets elected, Marsdon gets to be the Minister of Justice. Shit, can you picture that?"

"I better now," says Elva. She takes an ice cube out of the glass and pops it into her mouth.

"She's still bleeding," says Rennie, but Elva's already walking away, steadily, as if there's nothing wrong with her. "Shouldn't you go with her?"

Lora shrugs. "What makes you think she'd let me?" she says. "She does what she likes. When you get to be her age around here nobody can tell you a thing."

"Does she have somewhere to go?" Rennie says. "Someone who can take care of her?"

"She has daughters," Lora says. "She has grandchildren. Not that she needs taking care of, mostly she takes care of them. This whole place runs on grandmothers."

A girl from the hotel comes and takes away the basin. Rennie feels a little better, now that there's no actual blood. The people are back in their chairs, voices are normal, the sun shines on the boats in the harbour. Lora has her cigarettes now; she lights one, blowing the smoke out through her nostrils in a long grey sigh.

"The whole thing was Marsdon's idea," she says. "Prince running in the election. He never would of thought it up himself. Marsdon would run for God if it was open, except who would vote for him? Nobody likes him, everybody likes Prince, so he had to talk Prince into doing it for him. Prince thinks the sun shines right out of Marsdon's ass and nobody can tell him any different, so what can you do?"

"Do you think he'll win?" Rennie says.

"Christ, I hope not," Lora says. "I hope he loses. I hope he loses so bad he never even thinks of doing it again. Then maybe we can get back to some kind of normal life."

●

Rennie trudges up the road towards Paul's house, because where else is there? She wishes Paul had told her when he was coming back, but she's hardly in a position to demand it. She's only a sort of house guest. A visitor.

There's no cool side of the road, and the asphalt is so hot it's almost melting. No one is sitting on the porches at this time of day; nevertheless, Rennie feels she's being watched. Halfway up the hill she's overtaken by a crowd of schoolgirls, ten or twelve of them, different sizes but all in heavy black skirts and white long-sleeved blouses, white bows in their hair, bare feet for the most part. Without asking or saying anything two of them take her hands, one on either side. The rest of them laugh and mill around her, examining her dress, her sandals, her purse, her hair.

"Do you live near here?" she asks one of them, the one holding her right hand. She's about six, and now that Rennie's speaking directly to her she's shy; but she doesn't let go of the hand.

"You have a dollar?" says the one on the left. But an older girl puts a stop to that. "Don't be so bold," she says.

"Are you cousins?" asks Rennie. One of them attempts to explain: some are sisters, others cousins, others cousins of some but not of others. "Her daddy the same, her mother different." When they reach Paul's gateway they let go of her hands without being told: they already know she's staying there. They watch as she goes up the stairs, giggling behind her.

Rennie has no key, but the door isn't locked. Until recently, Paul said, you never had to lock your door, and he's still not in the habit. She goes out to the hammock and rocks herself, waiting for time to pass.

Half an hour later a short brown woman in a green print dress with large yellow butterflies walks in through the door. She nods at Rennie but takes no notice of her after that. She wipes off the table, washes the dishes and dries them and puts them away, cleans off the top of the stove, and sweeps the floor. Then she goes into the bedroom and brings the sheets out. She carries them into the garden at the side of the house, where she washes them, by hand, in a big red plastic pail, using water from a small tap that comes out of the water tank. She rinses them and wrings them out and hangs them up. She disappears into the bedroom again, to make up the bed, Rennie assumes. Rennie swings herself in the hammock, watching. She ought to pretend to be doing something important, but she can't, she's too uneasy, she can almost smell what it feels like to be cleaning up after other people's feeding and sex. She feels superfluous and both invisible and exposed: something so much there that nobody looks at it. The woman comes out of the bedroom with Rennie's pink bikini underpants from the day before. Presumably she's going to wash them.

"I'll do that," says Rennie.

The woman gives her a sideways glance, of contempt, puts the underpants on the kitchen counter, nods again, and goes down the steps to the road.

Rennie gets up and locks the doors of the house and mixes herself a drink. She lies down on the bed, under the mosquito net, meaning to take only a short nap. Then someone is touching her neck. Paul. A faceless stranger.

●

It's raining; heavy drops like tacks patter on the tin roof. The huge leaves outside the window move in the wind, making a sound like the dragging of thick cloth across a floor. Something's loose out there.

Rennie's both avid and melancholy, as if it's the last time. More and more the emptiness of this house reminds her of a train station. Terminal, the place where you go to say goodbye. Paul is being too tender, it's the tenderness of a man boarding a troop ship. A man who can hardly wait. *Wait for me* would be the proper thing for him to say; he'd have no intention of doing the same himself. But she doesn't know where he's going. He's not giving anything away.

"If I were noble," says Paul. "I'd tell you to get the next boat out to St. Antoine and get the next plane out to Barbados and get the hell back home."

Rennie's kissing him beside the ear. His skin is dry, salty, the hair greying there. "Why would you do that?" she says.

"Safer," says Paul.

"Who for, you or me?" says Rennie. She thinks he's talking about their relationship. She thinks he's admitting something. This cheers her up.

"You," he says. "You're getting too involved, it's bad for you."

Rennie stops kissing. *Massive involvement*, she thinks. He smiles at her, looking down at her with his too-blue eyes, and she wonders whether she can believe a word he says.

"Take the plane, lady," he says, very sweetly.

"I don't want to go back," Rennie says.

"I'd like you to," says Paul.

"Are you trying to get rid of me?" says Rennie, smiling, fearing it.

"No," says Paul. "Maybe I'm just being stupid. Maybe I want there to be something good I've done."

Rennie feels she can make her own choices, she doesn't need to have them made for her. In any case she doesn't want to be something that Paul has done. Good or otherwise.

She thinks about going back. There will be the hedge-hopper to Barbados, the wait in the steamy airport among the secretaries, just-arrived or in transit, lonely and hopeful, with their vague expectations; then the monotonous jet and then the airport, sterile and rectilinear. It will be cold outside and grey, and the wind will smell of diesel fuel. In the city people will be hunched into their winter coats, scuttling heads-down along the sidewalks, their faces not flat and open like the faces here but narrow and pallid and pushed into long snouts, like the snouts of rats. No one will even glance at anyone else. What does she have to look forward to?

●

Jake came over to pick up his suits and his books and pictures. He had his new lady's car downstairs, his own was on the fritz. He didn't say whether or not the new lady was in it, and Rennie didn't ask. *Lady* was his own term, a recent one. He had never called Rennie his lady.

He made several trips, up the stairs and down again, and Rennie sat at the kitchen table and drank coffee. From the hooks above the stove there were now things missing, pots, frying pans, which had left round haloes of lighter yellow on the wall, penumbras of grease. From now on she would have to decide what to eat. Jake decided before: even when it was her turn to cook he decided. He brought home all kinds of things: bones, wrinkled old sausages filmed with powdery mould, rank and horrible cheeses which he insisted she had to try. Life is an improvisation, he said. Exploit your potential.

Rennie's potential had been exploited, she didn't have any left. Not for Jake, who stood awkwardly in the doorway, holding a dark blue sock, asking if she'd seen the other one. Domesticity still hung in the air around them, like dust in sunlight, a lingering scent. Rennie said she hadn't, but he might try the bathroom, behind the laundry hamper. He went out and she could hear him rummaging. She should have gone somewhere else, not been here, they should have arranged things differently.

She tried not to think of the new lady, of whom it was not right to be jealous. She didn't know what the new lady looked like. To Rennie she was just a headless body, with or without a black nightgown. As perhaps she was to Jake. What is a woman, Jake said once. A head with a cunt attached or a cunt with a head attached? Depends which end you start at. It was understood between them that this was a joke. The new lady stretched out before her, a future, a space, a blank, into which Jake would now throw himself night after night the way he had thrown himself into her, each time extreme and final, as if he was pitching himself headlong over a cliff. It was for this she felt nostalgia. She wondered what it was like to be able to throw yourself into another person, another body, a darkness like that. Women could not do it. Instead they had darkness thrown into them. Rennie couldn't put the two things together, the urgency and blindness of the act, which had been urgent and blind for her too, and this result, her well-lit visible frozen pose at the kitchen table.

Jake was in the doorway again. Rennie did not want to look at him. She knew what she would see, it would be the same thing he saw when he looked at her. Failure, of a larger order than they would once have thought possible. But how could there be failure, since failure had been outside their terms of reference? No strings, no commitments, that's what they'd said. What would *success* have been?

Rennie thought of telling him about the man with the rope. Meanly, since it would only make him feel guilty and that was why she would be doing it. What would Jake make of it, the sight of one of his playful fantasies walking around out there, growling and on all fours? He knew the difference between a game and the real thing, he said; a desire and a need. She was the confused one.

Rennie did not say anything, nor did she stand up and throw her arms around Jake's neck, nor did she shake hands with him. She didn't want charity so she didn't do anything. She sat with her hands clenched around the coffee cup as if it was a bare socket, live electricity, and she couldn't move. Was this *open*, was it grief? What had become of them, two dead bodies, what could you do without desire, without need, what was she supposed to feel, what could be done? She pressed her hands together to keep them still. She thought of her grandmother, hands together like that, head bowed over the joyless Christmas turkey, saying grace.

Keep well, said Jake, and that was the whole problem. He could not admit she wasn't. No fun playing games with the walking wounded. Not only no fun, no fair.

●

The day after Jake was gone, for good, Rennie did not get up in the morning. There did not seem to be any point. She lay in bed thinking about Daniel. It was true he was a fantasy for her: a fantasy about the lack of fantasy, a fantasy of the normal. It was soothing to think of Daniel, it was like sucking your thumb. She thought about him waking up in the morning, rolling over, turning off the alarm clock, making love with his pregnant wife, whose face Rennie did not picture, carefully and with consideration but somewhat quickly because it was morning and he had other things to do. His wife didn't come but they're both used to that, they love each other anyway. She'll come later, some other day, when Daniel has more time. Taking a shower, drinking a cup of coffee, black, no sugar, which is handed to him by his wife through the bathroom door, looking in the mirror while he shaves and not seeing at all what she saw when she looked at him. Daniel getting dressed, in those mundane clothes of his, tying his shoelaces.

At three in the afternoon Rennie called Daniel, at the office, where she thought he would be. She left her number with the nurse: she said it was an emergency. She had never done such a thing before. She knew she was being wicked, but thinking about Daniel brought out in her whatever notions of wickedness were left over from her background. Daniel himself had such clean fingernails, such pink ears, he was so *good*.

Daniel called her back fifteen minutes later, and Rennie did her best to give the impression of someone on the verge of suicide. She never actually said it, she could not go so far, but she knew the only way she could entice Daniel over would be to give him a chance to rescue her. She was crying though, that was real enough.

She wanted Daniel to hold her hand, pat her on the back, comfort her, be with her. That was what he was good at. She had given up expecting anything else. She got dressed, made the bed, brushed her teeth and hair, being a good child at least to this extent. When Daniel came he would give her a gold star.

He knocked at the door, she opened it, he was there. What she saw was not someone she knew. Anger and fear, and something else, a need but not a desire. She'd pushed it too far.

Don't do that again, he said, and that was all for the time being.

She thought he knew what was inside her. No such luck.

After a while Rennie was lying on her own bed, which was still more or less made, and Daniel was putting on his shoes. She could see the side of his head, the bent back. The fact was that he had needed something from her, which she could neither believe nor forgive. She'd been counting on him not to: she was supposed to be the needy one, but it was the other way around. He was ashamed of himself, which was the last thing she'd wanted. She felt like a vacation, Daniel's, one he thought he shouldn't have taken. She felt like a straw that had been clutched, she felt he'd been drowning. She felt raped.

This is what *terminal* means, she thought. Get used to it.

●

After they make love Rennie wraps a towel around herself and goes out to the kitchen. There's a lizard, sand-coloured, with huge dark eyes, hunting the ants that file towards the cupboard where the golden syrup is kept. Rennie eats three pieces of bread and jam and drinks half a pint of long-life milk. Paul says some people here think that because it says LONG LIFE on the carton, you'll have a long life if you drink it.

She goes back to the bedroom and steps over the clothes entwined on the floor. Paul is lying with his hands behind his head, legs flung out, looking up at the ceiling. Rennie climbs in under the mosquito net and curls beside him. She licks the hollow of his stomach, which is damp and salty, but he hardly twitches. Then she runs her hand over him, stroking. He blinks and smiles a little. The hair on his chest is grey, and Rennie finds it comforting, this sign of age: it's possible after all for people to grow older, change, weather. Without deteriorating; up to a point. It's the past, it's time that's stained him.

She wants to ask about his wife. It must be a wife, the house and the lawn and the shirtwaist dress wouldn't go with anything else. But she doesn't want to admit she's been going through the bureau drawers.

"Were you ever married?" she asks.

"Yes," says Paul. He doesn't volunteer anything else, so Rennie keeps on going. "What happened?"

Paul smiles. "She didn't like my lifestyle," he says. "She said there wasn't enough security. She didn't mean financial. After the Far East, I tried to go back and settle down, but when you've been living that way, day to day, never knowing when someone's going to blow you into little pieces, that other kind of life seems fake, you can't believe in it. I just couldn't get too excited about taking the car in for the winter tune-up or any of that. Not even my kids."

"So you're a danger freak," says Rennie. "Is that why you run dope?"

Paul smiles. "Maybe," he says. "Or maybe it's the money. It beats selling real estate. Second biggest dollar import commodity in the States; oil's the first. I don't take unnecessary risks though." He takes her hand, moves it down, closes his eyes. "That's why I'm still alive."

"What do you dream about?" says Rennie after a while. She wants to know, which is dangerous, it means she's interested.

Paul waits before answering. "Not a hell of a lot," says Paul finally. "I think I gave it up. I don't have time for it any more."

"Everyone dreams," says Rennie. "Why don't men ever want to say what they dream about?"

Paul turns his head and looks at her. He's still smiling, but he's tightened up. "That's why I couldn't hack the States," he says. "When I went back there, the women were talking like that. That's how they began all their sentences: *Why don't men.*"

Rennie feels she's been both misinterpreted and accused. "Is there something wrong with saying that?" she says. "Maybe we want to know."

"There's nothing wrong with saying it," says Paul. "They can say it all they like. But there's no law that says I have to listen to it."

Rennie continues to stroke, but she's hurt. "Sorry I asked," she says.

Paul puts a hand on her. "It's not that I've got anything against women," he says. Rennie supplies: *In their place.* "It's just that when you've spent years watching people dying, women, kids, men, everyone, because they're starving or because someone kills them for complaining about it, you don't have time for a lot of healthy women sitting around arguing whether or not they should shave their legs."

Rennie's been outflanked, so she retreats. "That was years ago," she says. "They've moved on to other issues."

"That's what I mean," says Paul. "*Issues.* I used to believe in issues. When I first went out there I believed in all the issues I'd been taught to believe in. Democracy and freedom and the whole bag of tricks. Those gadgets don't work too well in a lot of places and nobody's too sure what does. There's no good guys and bad guys, nothing you can count on, none of it's permanent any more, there's a lot of improvisation. Issues are just an excuse."

"For what?" says Rennie. She leaves her hand on him but stops moving it.

"Getting rid of people you don't like," says Paul. "There's only people with power and people without power. Sometimes they change places, that's all."

"Which are you?" says Rennie.

"I eat well, so I must have power," says Paul, grinning. "But I'm an independent operator. Freelance, same as you."

"You don't take me very seriously, do you?" says Rennie sadly. She wants him to talk to her, about himself.

"Don't start that," says Paul. "You're on vacation." He rolls over on top of her. "When you go back home, I'll take you seriously."

Once upon a time Rennie was able to predict men; she'd been able to tell exactly what a given man would do at a given time. When she'd known that, when she was sure, all she had to do was wait and then he would do it. She used to think she knew what most men were like, she used to think she knew what most men wanted and how most men would respond. She used to think there was such a thing as most men, and now she doesn't. She's given up deciding what will happen next.

She puts her arms around him. She's trying again. She should know better.

●

From the refrigerator Paul takes two fish, one bright red, the other blue and green, with a beak like a parrot's. He cleans them with a large black-handled knife, kneeling by the tap in the garden. Rennie can smell the fish from where she lies in the hammock; it's not her favourite smell. It strikes her that she hasn't yet been to the beach here. She would like to lie on the sand and let the sun wash out her head so that nothing is left in it but white light, but she knows the consequences, a headache and skin like a simmered prune's. She's gone so far as to put on a pair of shorts though.

There's a vine over the porch, large cream-white flowers, cup-shaped and unreal. From the porch railing two blue-green lizards watch her. The road below is empty.

Paul leaves the fish on the porch and shinnies up a nearby tree, coming down with a papaya. Rennie can't help it, but all this activity reminds her of Boy Scouts. Next thing you know he'll be showing her how well he can tie knots.

There's a sunset, a quick one; it's getting dark. Rennie goes inside. Paul is cooking the fish, with onions and a little water, but he won't let her help.

They sit across from each other at the wooden table. Rennie gives him four out of five on the fish. He's even got candles; a huge green locust has just singed itself in one of them. Paul picks it up, still jerking, and throws it out the door.

"So you thought I was with the CIA," he says, as he sits down again.

Rennie is not so much embarrassed as startled. She isn't ready for it, she drops her fork. "I suppose Lora told you that," she says.

Paul is having fun. "It's a strange coincidence," he says, "because we thought you were, too."

"What?" says Rennie. "You must be crazy!" This time it's not surprise, it's outrage.

"Look at it from our point of view," says Paul. "It's a good front, you have to admit. The travel piece, the camera. This just isn't the sort of place they do a lot of travel pieces about. Then the first person you connect with happens to be the man who has the best chance of defeating the government in the election. That's Minnow. Nobody watching would call that an accident."

"But I hardly know him," says Rennie.

"I'm just telling you what it looks like," says Paul. "Spot the CIA, it's a local game; everybody plays it. Castro used tourists a lot, and now all kinds of people are using them. The CIA is using non-Americans a lot; it's better cover. Locals and foreigners. We know they're sending someone else in; they may be here already. There's always one or two here, and in my business you like to know who it is."

"So it wasn't the Abbotts after all," says Rennie. "I didn't think so, they were just too old and nice."

"As a matter of fact it was," says Paul. "But they've been recalled. Whoever comes in next will be taking a more active role. It could be anyone."

"But *me*," says Rennie. "Come on!"

"We had to check it out," says Paul.

"Who is *we*?" she says. "Lora, I suppose." Things are coming clear. They picked her up almost as soon as she was off the plane. First Paul in the hotel diningroom; so much for eye contact. Then Lora, the next day on the reef boat. Between the two of them they'd hardly let her out of their sight. There must have been someone following her around and reporting back to them so they'd know where she was heading.

"Lora comes in handy," says Paul.

"Who went through my room?" says Rennie. It couldn't have been him, since he was having dinner with her at the Driftwood.

"Did someone go through your room?" asks Paul. Rennie can't tell if his surprise is real or not.

"Everything," she says. "Including the box. The one in your spare bedroom."

"I don't know who it was," says Paul. "I'd like to though."

"If you thought I was the CIA, why did you send me to pick up the box?" says Rennie.

"First of all," says Paul, "they don't care that much about the dope trade. They like to know what you're up to so they can maybe use it on you to get you to do something for them, but apart from that they don't care. It's the political stuff they care about. But the police hanging around the airport are something else. They'd seen Lora too many times, that was the sixth box we'd run through. We needed someone else and I didn't want it to be me. It's always better to use a woman, they're less likely to be suspected. If you weren't an agent, no harm done; unless you got caught, of course. If you were, you'd already know what was in the box but you'd pick it up anyway, you wouldn't want to lose contact by refusing. Either way, I'd have the gun."

"It was for you?" says Rennie.

"In my business you need them," Paul says. "People shoot at you and you have to be able to shoot back. I had some coming up from Colombia, you can often pick them up down there, serial numbers filed off but they're U.S. Army equipment, military aid, you get them from crooked generals who want to make a little money on the side. But I lost that boat and I lost the connection at the same time. Elva's the contingency plan. She really does have a daughter in New York, so it was easy enough to fly her there with the money. Those people like cash. She didn't know what it was for though. She didn't know what was in the boxes."

"Lost?" says Rennie.

"The boat got sunk, the general got shot," says Paul. "I've just replaced both of them but it took me a while."

"Who's shooting at you?" says Rennie, who is trying very hard not to find any of this romantic. Boys playing with guns, that's all it is. Even telling her about this is showing off; isn't it? But she can't help wondering whether Paul has any bullet holes in him. If he has, she'd like to see.

"Who isn't?" says Paul. "I'm an independent. They don't like people like me, they want a monopoly."

Rennie picks up her fork again. She lifts her fish, separating the bones.

"So that's what all this was about," she says.

"All what?" says Paul.

"All this fucking," says Rennie, pronouncing the *g* despite herself. "You were checking me out."

"Don't be stupid," says Paul. "It was mostly Marsdon's idea anyway, he's paranoid about the CIA, it's like a monomania with him. He wanted us to get you out of here as fast as possible. I never believed it myself."

This isn't the answer Rennie wants. She wants to be told she's important to him. "Why not?" she says.

"You were too obvious," Paul says. "You were doing everything right out in the open. You were too nice. You were too naïve. You were too easy. Anyway, you wanted it too much. I can tell when a woman's faking it."

Rennie puts her fork down carefully on her plate. Something is being used against her, her own desire, she doesn't know why. "I'll do the dishes," she says.

●

Rennie fills the sink with hot water from the teakettle. Paul is in the second bedroom, with the door closed. He says he's trying to find out who's winning the election. Local politics, he's told her. Nothing to do with her. She can hear blurred voices, the crackle of static.

She's scraping the fishbones off the plates when she hears footsteps on the porch. There are a lot more footsteps than she's prepared to deal with. Wiping her hands on the dishtowel, she goes to the second bedroom and knocks at the door. "Paul," she says. Feeling like a wife. Incapable.

Rennie's in the bedroom, which is where she wants to be and where Paul wants her to be. Out there, in the livingroom, there's a loud meeting going on. The results of the election are in, Ellis has seven seats, Minnow has six and Prince has two, and Rennie can add. So can everyone in the livingroom, but so far six and two still only make six and two.

It's nothing to do with her though. Paul said that and she believes it. She's reading the books he got for her somewhere, God knows where since they're museum pieces, Dell Mysteries from the forties, with the eye-and-keyhole logo on the cover, the map of the crime scene on the back, and the cast of characters on the first page. The pages are yellowed and watermarked and smell of mould. Rennie reads the casts of characters and tries to guess who gets murdered. Then she reads up to the murder and tries to guess who did it, and then she turns to the back of the book to see if she's right. She doesn't have much patience for the intricacies of clues and deductions.

"You goin' to let that bastard win?" It's Marsden, almost a shriek. "You let him fool you? So many years he betray the people, you goin' to betray the people too?"

Dr. Minnow is making a speech; his voice rises and falls, rises and falls. He, after all, has more experience as well as more seats, he will be the leader of the opposition, if nothing else. Why should he back down in favor of Prince? He cannot let the Justice Party swing in the direction of Castro.

"Castro!" Marsden yells. "All you tell me is Castro! Prince no Castro!"

Why here? Rennie asked. I'm the connection, Paul told her. Rennie wishes they would turn down the volume. She's not doing too well with the murderers, but she's eighty percent on the victims: two blondes with pale translucent skin, mouths like red gashes and swelling breasts bursting through their dresses, two tempestuous redheads with eyes of green smouldering fire and skin like clotted cream, each carefully arranged on floor or bed like a still life, not quite naked, clothing disheveled to suggest rape, though there was no rape in the forties, fingermarks livid around the throat – they loved *livid* – or a wound still oozing, preferably in the left breast. Dead but not molested. The private eyes finding them (two hot-tempered Irishmen, one Greek, two plain Americans) describe each detail of the body fully, lushly, as if running their tongues over it; all that flesh, totally helpless because totally dead. Each of them expresses outrage at the crime, even though the victim provoked it. Rennie finds it curiously innocent, this hypocritical outrage. It's sweetly outmoded, like hand-kissing.

●

After a while Rennie hears the sound of chairs being scraped back, and then it's quiet. Then Paul comes into the room and starts taking off his clothes, as if nothing at all has happened. He peels the T-shirt off first, drops it to the floor. Already it seems to her a familiar gesture. Rennie counts: she's known him five days.

"What happened?" she says. "What were they doing?"

"Dealing," says Paul. "Minnow won. As of fifteen minutes ago, he's the new prime minister. They've all gone off to have a party."

"Marsdon backed down?"

"No," says Paul. "He didn't exactly back down. He said he was doing it for the good of the people. There was some disagreement about who *the people* were, but you have to expect that."

"Did Prince just sort of abdicate?" says Rennie.

"Prince didn't do anything," Paul says. "Marsdon did it for him. Marsdon's going to be Minister of Tourism, and they sawed off at Justice Minister for Prince. That's why Marsdon didn't struggle too hard. He wants to see the look on the face of the current Justice Minister. They hate each other like shit."

He disappears into the bathroom and Rennie can hear him brushing his teeth. "You don't seem too happy," she calls.

Paul comes out again. He walks flat-footed, heavily towards the bed. He's older than she thought. "Why should I be?" he says.

"Dr. Minnow's a good man," says Rennie. This is true, he is a good man, and it's not his fault that goodness of his kind makes her twitchy. It's like being with someone on a diet, which always makes her lust for chocolate mousse and real whipped cream.

"Good men can be a pain in the ass," says Paul. "They're hard to deal with. He's a politician so he's a user, they have to be, but he's less of a user than most. He believes in democracy and fair play and all those ideas the British left here

247

along with cricket, he really does believe that shit. He thinks guns are playing dirty."

"What do you think?" says Rennie She's back to interviewing him.

Paul's sitting on the edge of the bed, as if reluctant to get into it. "It doesn't matter what I think," he says. "I'm neutral. What matters right now is what the other side thinks. What Ellis thinks."

"What does Ellis think?" says Rennie.

"That remains to be seen," says Paul. "He's not going to like it."

"What about Prince?" says Rennie.

"Prince is a believer," says Paul. "He supplies the belief. He thinks that's all you need."

Now at last he does get into bed, crawling under the mosquito net, tucking it in before turning to her. He's tired, no doubt of that, and Rennie suddenly finds this very suburban. All he needs are some striped pyjamas and a heart attack and the picture will be complete. He's not the one who's giving that impression though. It's her own solicitude, faked. She knows something he doesn't know, she knows she's leaving. She'll be on the afternoon boat tomorrow, and everything in between is just filler. Maybe she'll tell him she has a headache. She could use some sleep.

Still, doubt is what you should give other people the benefit of, or that's the theory. She owes him something: he was the one who gave her back her body; wasn't he? Although he doesn't know it. Rennie puts her hands on him. It can be, after all, a sort of comfort. A kindness.

"What do you dream about?" Rennie says. It's her last wish, it's all she really wants to know.

"I told you," Paul says.

"But you lied," says Rennie.

For a while Paul doesn't say anything. "I dream about a hole in the ground," he says finally.

"What else?" says Rennie.

"That's all," says Paul. "It's just a hole in the ground, with the earth that's been dug out. It's quite large, there are trees around it. I'm walking towards it. There's a pile of shoes off to the side."

"Then what?" says Rennie.

"Then I wake up," says Paul.

●

Rennie hears it before she realizes what it is. At first she thinks it's rain. It is rain, but something more. Paul is out of the bed before she is. Rennie goes into the bathroom for a large towel, which she wraps around her. The pounding at the door goes on, and the voice.

When she gets to the livingroom what she sees is Paul, stark naked, and Lora with her arms around him. She's dripping wet.

Rennie stands with her mouth open, holding her towel around her, while Paul grapples with Lora, pushing her away from him, holding her at arms' length, shaking her. She's crying. "Oh God, oh Christ," she says.

"What is it?" says Rennie. "Is she sick?"

"Minnow's been shot," Paul says, over the top of Lora's head.

Rennie goes cold. "That's incredible!" she says. She feels as if someone's just told her the Martians have landed. It must be a put-on, an elaborate joke.

"They shot him from behind," says Lora. "In the back of the head. Right out on the road and everything."

"Who would do it?" Rennie says. She thinks of the men, the followers, the ones with mirror sunglasses. She tries to focus on something useful she could do. Maybe she should make some tea, for Lora.

"Get your clothes on," Paul says to her.

Lora starts to cry again. "It's so crummy," she says. "The fuckers. I never thought they'd go that far."

Dr. Minnow is in a closed coffin in the livingroom. The coffin is dark wood, plain; it rests on two kitchen chairs, one at either end. On top of the coffin there's a pair of scissors, open, and Rennie wonders whether they are part of some ritual, some ceremony she doesn't know about, or whether someone's just forgotten them.

The coffin is like a stage prop, an emblem out of some horrible little morality play; only they've forgotten to say what the moral is. At any moment the lid will pop up and Dr. Minnow will be sitting there, smiling and nodding, as if he's pulled off a beautiful joke. Only this does not happen.

Rennie is in the livingroom with the women, who sit on chairs or on the floor, children sleeping in their laps, or stand against the wall. It's one o'clock at night. There are other women in the kitchen, making coffee and setting out plates for the food that the women have brought: Rennie can see them through the open doorway. It's a lot like Griswold, it's a lot like her grandmother's funeral, except in Griswold you ate after the burial, not before, and you did the hymn-singing in church. Here they do it whenever they feel like it: one starts, the others join in, three-part harmony. Someone's playing the mouth-organ.

Dr. Minnow's wife has the place of honour beside the coffin; she cries and cries, she makes no attempt to hide it, nobody disapproves. This, too, is different from Griswold: sniffling was all right, into a handkerchief, but not this open crying, raw desolation, this nakedness of the face. It wasn't decent. If you went on like that they gave you a pill and told you to go upstairs and lie down.

"Why this happen?" the wife says, over and over again. "Why this happen?"

Elva is sitting beside her, holding her hand, which she rubs gently between her own two hands, massaging the fingers. "I see him into this world," she says. "Now I see him out of it."

Two women come out of the kitchen, carrying a tray with mugs of coffee. Rennie takes one, and some banana bread and a coconut cookie. It's her second mug of coffee. She's sitting on the floor, her legs are going to sleep beneath her.

She feels guilty and useless, guilty because useless. She thinks of all the history that's lying there in the coffin, wasted, a hole blown through it. It seems to her a very tacky way to die. Now she knows why he wanted her to write about this place: so there would be less chance of this happening, to him.

"Should we be doing anything?" she whispers to Lora, who's sitting beside her.

"Who knows?" says Lora. "I never went to one of these before."

"How long does it go on?" says Rennie

"All night," says Lora.

"Why this happen?" says the wife again.

"It was his time," says one of the women.

"No," says Elva. "A Judas here."

The women stir uneasily. Someone begins to sing:

"Blessed assurance, Jesus is mine,
Oh what a foretaste of Glory divine,
Perfect salvation, sent from above,
Washed in his goodness, lost in his love."

Rennie is uneasy. It's hot in the room and too crowded, it smells of cinnamon and coffee and sweat, a sweet, stuffy, unhealthy smell, clogged with emotion, and it's getting so much like Griswold she can't bear it. *What did she die of? Cancer, praise the Lord.* That was the kind of thing they said. She stands up, as unobtrusively as she can, and edges towards the porch, out the door that stands mercifully open.

The men are outside, on the concrete porch that runs around three sides of the house. The drink here is not coffee; in the dim porch light the bottles gleam, passing from hand to hand. There are more men, down below in the garden, there's a crowd, gathering, some of them have torches, there are voices, tense, rising.

Paul is out there, a conspicuous white face, standing to one side. He spots Rennie and pulls her back against the wall beside him. "You should be in with the women," he says.

Rennie chooses to take this not as a put-down but as a social hint. "I couldn't breathe," she says. "What's going on down there?"

"Nothing yet," says Paul. "They're mad as hell though. Minnow was from Ste. Agathe. A lot of people here are related to him."

Someone's carrying a chair over to the porch railing. A man climbs up on it and looks down at the upturned faces. It's Marsdon. The voices quiet.

"Who kill this man?" he says.

"Ellis," someone calls, and the crowd chants, "Ellis, Ellis."

"Judas," says Marsdon, almost a shout.

"Judas. Judas."

Marsdon raises his hands and the chanting stops.

"How many more times?" he says. "How much more, how many more dead? Minnow a good man. We are going to wait till he kill all of us, every one? We been asking, many times, we get nothing. Now we gonna take."

There's shouting, an enraged cheer, then one clear voice: "*Tear down Babylon!*" In the dark below, bodies begin to move. Marsdon bends, stands up again; in his hands is a compact little machine gun.

"Shit," says Paul. "I told them not to do that."

"Do what?" says Rennie. "What are they going to do?" She can feel her heart going, she doesn't understand. *Massive involvement.*

"They don't have enough guns," says Paul. "It's as simple as that. I don't know where Prince is, he'll have to stop them."

"What if he can't?" says Rennie.

"Then he'll have to lead them," says Paul. He pushes off from the wall. "Go back to the house," he says.

"I don't know the way," says Rennie. They came in a jeep.

"Lora does," says Paul.

"What about you?" says Rennie.

"Don't worry," says Paul. "I'll be fine."

●

They go by the back streets, Lora first, then Rennie. The only place to be, in Lora's opinion, is out of the way. It's muddy here from the rain but they don't bother to pick their way around the water-filled potholes, there's no time and it's hard to see. The only light comes from the small concrete-block houses set at intervals back from the road. The road is deserted, the action is a couple of streets farther down towards the sea. They hear shouting, the smash of glass.

"Bank windows," says Lora. "I bet you anything."

They cross a side street. For a moment there's a glimpse of torches. "Don't let them see you is my motto," says Lora. "In the dark anyone's fair game. They can apologize afterwards but who cares, eh? There's going to be a few old scores settled, no matter what else they do."

Now they can hear gunfire, irregular and staccato, and after a minute the feeble lights in the houses flicker and go out, the underlying hum in the air shudders and cuts. "There goes the power plant," says Lora. "They'll take over that and the police station, there's only two policemen on Ste. Agathe anyway so it shouldn't be that hard. There isn't a hell of a lot else to take over around here. Maybe they'll smash up the Lime Tree and get drunk on the free booze."

"I can't see," says Rennie. Her sandals are muddy, the bottom of her skirt is dripping; she's more disgusted than frightened. Window-breaking, juvenile delinquency, that's all it is, this tiny riot.

"Come on," says Lora. She gropes for Rennie's arm, pulls her along. "They'll be up here in a minute, they'll be after Ellis's people. We'll take the path."

Rennie stumbles after her. She's disoriented, she has no idea where they are, even the stars are different here. It's slow going without a moon. Branches heavy with damp flowers brush against her, the smells are still alien. She pushes through the leaves, slipping on the wet earth of the path. Below them is the road. Through the undergrowth she can see moving lights now, flashlights, torches, and hurrying figures. It's almost like a festival.

When they finally reach the house it's completely dark.

"Damn," says Rennie. "We locked it when we went out and Paul's got the key. We'll have to break in."

But Lora's already at the door, pushing. "It's open," she says.

As soon as they're inside the door there's a sharp glare, sudden, against their eyes. Rennie almost screams.

"It's only you," says Paul. He lowers the flashlight.

"How in shit did you get back here ahead of us?" says Lora.

"Took the jeep," says Paul. To Rennie he says, "Get your things."

"Where's Prince?" says Lora.

"Down there being a hero," says Paul. "They've got the two policemen tied up with clothesline, and they're declaring an independent state. Marsdon's writing a proclamation and they want to send it out over my radio. They're asking Grenada to recognize them. There's even some talk of invading St. Antoine."

"You've got to be kidding," says Lora. "How the shit would they do that?"

"In the fishing boats," says Paul, "plus whatever other

boats they can grab. They've got a bunch of Swedish tourists in the police station, and those two German women who are making one hell of a fuss. They've requisitioned them. Hostages."

"Can't you stop them?" says Lora.

"You think I haven't tried?" says Paul. "They won't listen to me any more. They think they've won. It's way out of control. Go to the bedroom," he says to Rennie, "and get your stuff. There's a candle in there. I'm taking you over to St. Antoine, you can get the morning plane out. If you were smart," he says to Lora, "you'd go with her. You've still got your passport." Rennie lets herself be ordered. This is his scene after all, his business; he's the one who's supposed to know what to do next. She hopes he does.

She feels her way along the hall into the bedroom. There isn't much to pack. It might as well be a hotel room; it has the same emptiness, the same melancholy aura of a space that has been used but not lived in. The bed is tangled, abandoned. She can't remember having slept in it.

●

The jeep is parked on the road in front of the house. They go down the stone steps, hurrying, their feet in the strong beam of the flashlight.

Paul has one of the small machine guns; he carries it casually, like a lunch pail. To Rennie it looks like a toy, the kind you aren't supposed to give little boys for Christmas. She doesn't believe it could go off, and surely if it did nothing would come out of it but rubber bullets. She's afraid, but even her fear seems inappropriate. Surely they are not in any real danger. She tries hard for annoyance: perhaps she should feel interrupted.

Just before they climb into the jeep Paul heaves something overarm into the darkness of the rock garden.

"What was that?" says Lora.

"I killed the radio," says Paul. "I called my boats first. They're staying away. I don't want anyone calling St. Antoine, I don't want any welcoming committees in the harbour when we get there."

"Who'd do that?" says Lora.

"I've got a few ideas," says Paul.

The motor catches and the headlights go on and they drive down the road, which is empty. Paul doesn't go all the way into the town. Instead he parks beside a stone wall.

"Go down to the shore and wait beside the pier," he says. "I'll pick you up there in about fifteen minutes. I'll get us a boat."

"Your boats are all out," says Lora.

"I didn't say mine," says Paul. "I'll jump the motor."

He's younger, alive in a way he hasn't been before. He loves it, thinks Rennie. That's why we get into these messes: because they love it.

He helps them over the stone wall and passes Rennie's bags down to her. She feels stupid lugging her camera: what is there to take pictures of now?

"Don't talk," says Lora. Rennie sees where they are: they're in the garden at the back of the Lime Tree. They find the path and feel their way down it. The hotel is dark and silent; behind a few of the windows candles flicker. The bar is deserted, the patio littered with broken glass. Along the beach, towards the town, they can hear singing. It's men, it's not a hymn.

The tide's going out, there are several yards of wet beach. The waves are strangely luminous. Rennie wants to look at this, she's heard about it, phosphorescence.

"Crawl under the dock," Lora whispers.

"For heaven's sake," says Rennie, who doesn't like the idea of crabs and snails.

"Do it," Lora says; it's almost a hiss. This, apparently, is serious.

The dock is built on a foundation of split rocks that have

not yet been smoothed by the sea; the space between the rocks and the wooden slats of the dock is only two feet high. They crouch together, doubled over. Rennie's still clutching her bags and her purse. She doesn't know who they're supposed to be hiding from.

The moon comes up, it's almost full; the grey-white light comes through the slats of the dock, throwing bars of shadow. Rennie thinks how nice it would be to have a warm bath and something to eat. She thinks about having lunch with someone, Jocasta maybe, and telling this story. But it's not even that good a story, it's about on the level of being stopped at customs, since nothing more than inconvenience has happened to her.

At last they can hear a motor, turning over, starting up, moving towards them.

"That's him," says Lora, and they back out from under the dock.

Marsdon is sitting in one of the wooden chairs up on the patio, one leg bent, the ankle resting on his knee to show off his boots. He's got his machine gun pointed right at them. Two men stand silently behind him.

"Where you think you goin'?" he says.

The St. Antoine police motor launch is tied at the end of the Lime Tree pier, where it bobs gently up and down in the swell. Paul sits at the round wooden table facing Marsdon. He's soaking wet, from swimming out to the launch. Between them there's a bottle of rum. Each of them has a glass, each of them has a machine gun; the machine guns are on the ground under the table, but within reach. The two other men are over at the bar. There's a woman with them, very drunk, she's lying on the patio near them, in the broken glass, humming to herself, her skirt up over her thighs, opening and closing her legs. Rennie and Lora sit in the other two chairs.

Paul and Marsdon are arguing about them. Paul wants to take Rennie to St. Antoine, Marsdon doesn't want him to.

Marsdon doesn't want anyone leaving the island. Also, Marsdon wants more guns. Paul promised him more, says Marsdon, they've been paid for; now he should deliver. He's the connection.

"I told you about the problem," Paul said. "You should have waited. Next week I have some coming."

"How can we wait?" Marsdon says impatiently. "When they hear on St. Antoine that Minnow is shot, they goin' to blame us anyway." Slyly, he offers to trade Paul's own machine gun for a safe exit. Slyly Paul refuses.

Rennie can see what she is now: she's an object of negotiation. The truth about knights comes suddenly clear: the maidens were only an excuse. The dragon was the real business. So much for vacation romances, she thinks. A kiss is just a kiss, Jocasta would say, and you're lucky if you don't get trenchmouth.

She listens, trying to follow. She feels like a hostage, and, like a hostage, strangely uninvolved in her own fate. Other people are deciding that for her. Would it be so bad if she stayed here? She could hole up in the Lime Tree, call herself a foreign correspondent, send out dispatches, whatever those are. But maybe Paul just wants to leave, get out; maybe she's just the occasion.

"You think I'm more important than I am," she says to Marsdon.

"Don't bug him," Lora says in a low voice. Marsdon looks at Rennie, seeing her this time. His movements are slow enough, outwardly calm, but he's excited, his eyes gleam in the moonlight. Fragmentation, dismemberment, this is what he sees when he looks at her. Then he's ignoring her once more.

"You bring the guns, you can take her," he says.

"No deal," says Paul.

There are more men now, coming along the beach from the town; several carry torches. One of them comes over to the table and puts his hand on Marsdon's shoulder.

"I am ready to make the broadcast now," he says, and Rennie realizes that this must be Prince. She's never seen him before. His face is in shadow, but the voice is young, younger than she thought, he sounds about nineteen.

"I wouldn't do that yet," says Paul, "if I were you."

Prince's head turns towards him in the shadows. "Why?" he says.

"Have you any idea of what's going to happen next?" Paul says.

"We have won the revolution," says Prince, with the placid confidence of a child reciting a lesson. "Grenada has recognized us. They are sending men and guns, in the morning."

"Where did you hear that?" says Paul.

The outline of Prince's head turns towards Marsdon.

"The radio," Marsdon says.

"Did you hear it yourself?" Paul says to Prince.

Marsdon pushes his chair back. "You calling me a liar," he says. There are more men now, a circle; tension draws them in.

"Take a boat to Grenada," Paul says to Prince. "Anything you can get. Right now, before morning. If you're lucky they'll let you stay there."

"You an enemy of the revolution," says Marsdon.

"Bullshit," says Paul. "You just want an excuse to blow my head off the way you blew off Minnow's."

"What you tellin' me?" says Prince.

"Put it together," says Paul. "He's the new agent. You've been set up, right from the beginning."

There's a pause. Rennie closes her eyes. Something with enormous weight comes down on them, she can hardly breathe. She hears the night sounds, the musical waterdrip, the waves, going on as usual. Then everything starts to move.

Oh God, thinks Rennie. Somebody change the channel.

●

Rennie walks along the pier at St. Antoine. She's safe. It's almost dawn. The power plant here isn't on the fritz and there's a string of feeble bulbs to see by. She feels dizzy and nauseated, an hour and a half in the launch, not rolling with the waves but smashing into them, a collision, a sickening lurch downwards, then up like a roller coaster, thud, crunch of her bones, backbone against backbone, stomach lurching inside her with its own motion. She'd hung on, trying to think of something serene, keeping her head up, eyes on the moon, on the next wave, the water glowed when it moved, phosphorescent, sweating all over her body despite the wind, wondering when she was going to throw up, trying not to. After all she was being rescued.

Can't you slow down? she called to Paul.

It's worse that way, he called back, grinning at her. Even now he found her funny.

At the dock he idled the motor and practically threw her onto the shore, her and her luggage, before backing the boat out and turning towards the sea. No goodbye kiss and just as well, she didn't want anything against her mouth just now. They touched hands for a moment, that was all. What bothers her is that she forgot to thank him.

He's not going back to Ste. Agathe, he's heading south. He'll meet one of his boats, he says. There are other harbours.

What about Lora? said Rennie.

She had the chance, said Paul. She wanted to stay with Prince. I can't fight off the entire St. Antoine police force just for Lora. She can take care of herself.

Rennie doesn't understand anything. All she knows is that she's here and there's a plane at six and she wants to be on it, and she can't keep walking. She sits down on the pier with her head between her knees, hoping that the rolling under her feet will stop.

She can hear the sound of the motor launch, receding, no more significant than the drone of a summer insect. Then there's another sound, too loud, like a television set with a cop show on it heard through a hotel room wall. Rennie puts her hands over her ears. In a minute, when she's feeling better, she'll go to the Sunset Inn and pick up her passport and see if she can get a cup of coffee, though there's not much chance of that. Then she'll take a taxi to the airport and then she'll be gone.

She sits there until she's ready, ready enough; then she starts walking again. There are a few people about, men; only one of them tries to stop her, a simple request for fornication, and he's pleasant enough when she says no. There's no war on here, possibly they haven't heard anything about it yet, everything seems normal. Then there are more men, running past her towards the end of the pier.

It's light; close by there are roosters. After what seems a very long time she reaches the Sunset Inn and goes in through the archway. She climbs the stairs; now she will have to sign her name for all the time she hasn't spent here, all the meals she hasn't eaten. She won't even argue, she'll put it on her charge card. Enjoy now, pay later.

The Englishwoman is up and dressed, in an avocado-green shirtwaist, behind the counter as usual. Possibly she never sleeps.

"I'd like to check out," says Rennie, "and I'd like my passport, please, it's in the safe. And I'd like to call a taxi."

The Englishwoman looks at her with the gloating, almost possessive stare of one who enjoys giving unwelcome news. "Are you thinking of taking that morning plane?" she says.

Rennie says yes.

"It's been cancelled," says the Englishwoman. "All the planes have been cancelled. The airport's been shut down."

"Really?" says Rennie, cold within.

"We're in a state of emergency," says the Englishwoman proudly. "There's been an uprising on Ste. Agathe. But you must know all about that. Didn't you just come from there?"

Rennie lies on her bed. At least it's a bed. She's fallen on it without even taking off her clothes but she's too exhausted to sleep. Now she will have to stay here, at the Sunset Inn, home of beige gravy, until they start the planes again. She feels marooned.

Then it's full of daylight and the door, which was shut and locked, is open. Two policemen are standing in the doorway. Grins, drawn guns. Behind them is the Englishwoman, her arms folded across her chest. Rennie sits up. "What?" she says.

"We arrestin' you," says one of the policemen, the pinkish one.

"What for?" says Rennie. She feels she ought to act like an outraged tourist.

"Suspicion," says the other policeman.

"Suspicion of what?" says Rennie, who is still half asleep. "I haven't done anything." It can't be the box with the gun, they haven't mentioned it. "I'm writing a travel piece. You can phone the magazine and check," she adds. "In Toronto, when they're open. It's called *Visor*." This sounds improbable even to her. Does Toronto exist? They won't be the first to wonder. She thinks of her blank notebook, no validation there.

The two policemen come forward. The Englishwoman looks at her, a look Rennie remembers from somewhere, from a long time ago, from a bad dream. It's a look of pure enjoyment. *Malignant*.

VI

"I thought it was dumb," says Lora. "I always thought it was dumb. Anyone who'd die for their country is a double turkey as far as I'm concerned. I mean any country, but this one, well, that would make you a triple one. Shit, it's only three miles long. I thought they were all nuts, but what can you tell them, eh?

"You may think Ellis is an old drunk, I told Prince, you may think he's harmless because nobody's seen him for twenty years, but if you think he's just going to let you take over without a squeak, you're out of your mind. But then Marsdon would start talking about sacrifice for the good of all, and that stuff would get to Prince every time. He's a sweet guy, he's soft-hearted, it appealed to him, and though I wouldn't want to be part of a country Marsdon was the leader of, he's no dummy, he knew he was making me look like a selfish white bitch who didn't care and only wanted Prince to screw around with.

"Maybe I should of left, but the truth is I thought they were just having a good time, sneaking around at night, having secrets, sort of like the Shriners, you know? I never thought they'd *do* anything.

"Change the system, Marsdon used to say. Why would I want to do that? I said. It's working just fine for me. Stuff politics, I'd tell him. As far as I'm concerned the world would be a lot better off if you took the politicians, any kind at all, and put them in the loony bin where they belong. You can tell that junk to Prince if you want to but don't tell it to me, because I know what you really want. You want to shoot people and feel really good about it and have everyone tell you you're doing the right thing. You'd get a kick out of that. You make me sick.

"I always knew Marsdon would shove a knife in me as soon as look at me if he got the chance, or in anyone else for that matter, he's a mean bugger but I guess if you want to start a war you have to have someone who doesn't give that much of a piss about killing people, you can't make an omelette without breaking eggs.

"There just weren't enough of them and they weren't ready. They wouldn't of been ready in a month of Sundays. Paul used to tell Marsdon he just wanted to be Castro without putting in the time, and it would get to him because that was about the size of it. They wouldn't of even had any guns if Paul hadn't brought some in for them. That was Marsdon's idea too, the guns. Paul didn't know he was an agent. I don't think he knew, not until Minnow got shot.

"If you're thinking of hiding out in the hills, forget it, Paul said. Two helicopters and that's it, this is a dry island, you know there's no cover up there, it's just scrub. But they seemed to think it was enough for them to be right. Getting rid of Ellis, that was the point. Nobody's denying it would of been nice, but there's real life, you know? I mean, I used to think I'd like to fly like a bird but I never jumped off any roofs. I once heard of a man who blew himself up in the toilet because he was sitting on the can and he lit a cigarette and he threw the match in, except his wife had just dumped some paint remover into it. I mean, that's what it was like. Though once in a while I thought, well, they might just do it. You know why? They're crazy enough. Sometimes crazy people can do things other people can't. Maybe because they believe it."

Rennie wonders where her passport is. She feels naked without it, she can't prove she is who she says she is. But she believes that other people believe in order, and in the morning, once they find out she's in here, once they realize who she is, they'll let her out.

Lora slaps at herself. "Fucking bugs," she says. "They like some people and not others. You think you'd get used to them, but you never do. Anyway, we've got a roof over our head. There's lots worse things."

Rennie decides not to think about what these may be.

●

"There was a little shooting at the police station," says Lora, "but not that much, and the power plant was empty. The police did a sweep of the island, it's not that hard because it's not that big, and they picked up anyone they found hiding or running or even walking on the road. They had the names of the main ones and they wanted everyone related to them too but that would of been everyone on the island, everyone's related to everyone else around here.

"They tied the men up with ropes, those yellow nylon ropes they use a lot around here for boats and stuff, they tied them together in bundles of three or four and threw them on top of each other in the ship, down in the hold, like they were cargo. The women they just tied their hands together, behind their backs, two together, they let them stand up. When we got over to St. Antoine there was a big crowd at the dock already, the radio had been full of it all morning, communists and all that, they hauled the bundles of men off the boat and the people in the street were screaming *Hang them! Kill them!* It was like wrestling.

"The police took us to the main station, down in the cellar where there's a cement floor, and they tied the men together in a long line, there must've been fifty or sixty people, and they beat them up, sticks and boots, the works. The women they beat up some too but not as much. I wasn't there for that part of it, they had me in another room, they were asking me questions about Prince. They've got him in here somewhere.

"Then they threw buckets of cold water over them and locked them up, they were wet and cold, nowhere to piss, nothing to eat, and then they brought them here. They didn't lay any charges because they hadn't figured out what charges to lay. The Justice Minister went on the radio and said there hadn't been any violence, the people got the cuts and bruises from falling down when they were running away. And then they declared a state of emergency, which made everything legal. They can take anything of yours they want to, your car, anything, and there's a curfew too. Nobody knows for how long.

"They said Minnow was shot by the rebels, they said Prince killed him. People believe what they hear on the news and who's going to tell them any different? They'll believe Ellis because it's easier to believe Ellis.

"It's perfect for Ellis: now he's got an excuse to do it to everybody he doesn't like, plus nobody's going to say anything against him, for years. And think of all the foreign aid he'll get now. The hurricane was all right but this is a lot better.

"We're lucky. The others are all seven or eight to a cell. Some of these people have no idea why they're here, all of a sudden these police with guns just bashed into their houses and grabbed them. They didn't know what was happening, they don't have a clue, they were just in the way."

●

The room they're in is about five feet by seven feet, with a high ceiling. The walls are damp and cool, the stone slick to the touch as if something's growing on it, some form of mildew. The back of Rennie's shirt is damp, from the wall.

This is the first time she's been cold since coming down here.

The floor is stone too and wet, except for the corner they've been sitting in. There's a barred metal door fitted into the end wall and opening onto the corridor, which is lighted; the light shines in on them through the bars. Someone has written on the walls: DOWN WITH BABYLON. LOVE TO ALL. In the wall opposite the door, higher up, there's a small window with a grating. Through this window they can see the moon. There's nothing in the room with them except a bucket, red plastic, new, empty. Its use is obvious but neither of them has used it yet.

"How long do you think they'll keep us in here?" says Rennie.

Lora laughs. "You in any hurry?" she says. "If you are, don't tell them. Anyway it's not how long you're in, it's what they do to you." She inhales, then blows the smoke out. "Well, this is it," she says. "Tropical paradise."

Rennie wonders why they've left Lora her cigarettes and especially the matches. Not that there's anything here that could burn down, it's all stone.

Rennie wishes they had a deck of cards or a book, any book at all. It's almost bright enough to read. She can smell the smoke from Lora's cigarette and beneath that a faint after-smell, stale perfume, underarm deodorant wearing off; it's from both of them. She's starting to get a headache. She'd give anything for a Holiday Inn. She longs for late-night television, she's had enough reality for the time being. Popcorn is what she needs.

"You got the time?" says Lora.

"They took my watch," says Rennie. "It's probably about eleven."

"That all?" says Lora.

"We should get some sleep, I guess," Rennie says. "I wish they'd turn out the lights."

"Okay," says Lora. "You sleepy?"

"No," says Rennie.

They're scraping the bottom of the barrel. Rennie thinks of it as the bottom of the barrel, Lora thinks of it as the story of her life. This is even what she calls it. "The story of my life," she says, morosely, proudly, "you could put it in a book." But it's one way not to panic. If they can only keep talking, thinks Rennie, they will be all right.

Lora takes out her cigarettes, lights one, blows the smoke out through her nose. "You want a cigarette? I've got two left. Oh, I forgot, you don't smoke." She pauses, waiting for Rennie to contribute something. So far most of the contributing has been done by Lora. Rennie is having a hard time thinking up anything about her life that Lora might find interesting. Right now, her life seems like a book Jocasta once lent her, very *nouveau wavé*, it was called *Death By Washing Machine* although there were no washing machines in the book. The main characters fell off a cliff on page 63 and the rest of the pages were blank.

Rennie tells Lora about the man with the rope. She's certain that Lora will be able to produce something much heavier, a multiple axe murder at the least.

"Sick," Lora says. "They shouldn't even put those guys away, they should just hang a few cement blocks around their legs and drop them in the harbour, you know? Let them out in twenty years and they just do it again. I once knew this guy who wanted to tie me to the bedpost. No way, I said. You want to tie somebody up, I've got a few suggestions, but you're not starting with me. Try a sheep and a pair of rubber boots and work your way up. He come back?"

"No," says Rennie.

"I'd rather be plain old raped," says Lora, "as long as there's nothing violent."

Rennie feels there's been a communications breakdown. Then she realizes that Lora is talking about something that has actually happened to her. Without any warning at all.

"God," she says, "what did you do?"

"Do?" says Lora. "He had a knife. I was just lucky he didn't mess anything up, including me. I could of kicked myself for not having a better lock on the window."

Rennie sees that Lora is pleased to have shocked her. She's enjoying the reaction; it's as if she's displaying something, an attribute somewhere between a skill and a deformity, like double-jointedness; or a mark of courage, a war wound or a duelling scar. The pride of the survivor.

Rennie knows what she's supposed to feel: first horror, then sympathy. But she can't manage it. Instead she's dejected by her own failure to entertain. Lora has better stories.

●

Rennie watches Lora's mouth open and close, studies the nicotine stains on her once perfect teeth, it's a movie with the sound gone. She's thinking that she doesn't really like Lora very much; she never has liked her very much; in fact she dislikes her. They have nothing in common except that they're in here. There's nobody here to look at but Lora, nobody to listen to but Lora. Rennie is going to like her a whole lot less by the time they get out.

"But, Jesus, will you listen to me," says Lora. "Here we are, just sitting around on our asses talking about men, fucking men, pardon my French, like at high school only then it was boys."

"What else do you suggest we do?" says Rennie, with sarcasm; after all, it's Lora's fault they're in here. But it's lost on Lora.

"If it was two guys in here," she says, "you think they'd be talking about women? They'd be digging a tunnel or strangling the guards from behind, you know? Like at the movies." She stands up, stretches. "I need to pee," she says. "At least we don't have to do it on the floor, though ten to one somebody already has, it smells like it." She slips off her underpants, spreads her purple skirt over the red bucket like a tent, squats down. Rennie stares at the wall, listening to the patter of liquid against plastic. She doesn't want to know what Lora will wipe herself with; there are only two choices, hands or clothing.

Rennie has her knees drawn up, she's cold. If they lie down they'll be wet, so they're still sitting, backs against the wall. The light comes through the door, endlessly, it's impossible to sleep. She puts her forehead on her knees and closes her eyes.

"I bet you could see out the window," says Lora, "if I gave you a leg up."

Rennie opens her eyes. She fails to see the point, but it's something to do. Lora bends and cups her hands, Rennie puts her right foot into them and Lora hoists, and Rennie manages to reach up and grab the bars. She pulls herself up, she can raise her head to the opening.

It's a courtyard of sorts, with a wall around it and another building on the other side. Her eyes are almost at ground level; it's overgrown with weeds, a white jungle in the moonlight. The gallows platform rises out of the weeds, a derelict tower. Rennie knows where they are. On three sides of the courtyard it's a sheer drop to the sea, and the building they're in is the fourth side. There's a faint smell of pigs. No one is out there.

"There's nothing to see," she says when she's back down.

Lora rubs her hands together. "You're heavier than I thought," she says.

They sit down again. After five minutes or half an hour there's a sound above them, outside the window. A scuttling, a squeak.

"Rats," says Lora. "Around here they call them coconut rodents. Mostly they just eat coconuts."

Rennie decides to concentrate on something else. She closes her eyes: she knows that there are some things she must avoid thinking about. Her own lack of power, for instance; what could be done to her.

She can feel Lora's arm against her own, it's comforting. She thinks about refrigerators, cool and white, stocked with the usual things: bottles, cartons of milk, packets, coffee beans in fragrant paper bags, eggs lined up quietly in their shells. Vacuum cleaners, chromium plated taps, bathtubs, a whole store full of bathtubs, soap in pastel wrappers, the names of English herbs, the small routines.

●

Lora's still talking. But Rennie can't concentrate, she's getting hungrier and hungrier. She wonders when it will be morning. Surely they will bring something to eat, they'll have to, her stomach is cramping and she hopes it's only the hunger.

Her eyes feel gritty, she's irritated because she hasn't slept more, it's Lora's fault, she needs more sleep and she's thirsty too. It's like the time she was trapped all night in a bus station, by a blizzard, on her way home for Christmas, some town halfway there, the snack bar isn't open and the toilets don't work, there's a bad smell and no prospect of a bus out until dawn, maybe not even then, they have to wait for the wind to go down before they can plough the roads, people yawning and dozing, a few grumpy children, the coffee machine out of order. But it would be tolerable if only the woman packed beside her on the bench would quit talking, in a maroon coat and curlers, no such luck, it goes on and on, triplets, polio, car crashes, operations for dropsy, for burst appendixes, sudden death, men leaving their wives, aunts, cousins, sisters, crippling accidents, a web of blood relationships no one could possibly untangle, a litany at the same time mournful and filled with curious energy, glee almost, as if the woman is childishly delighted with herself for being able to endure and remember so much pointless disaster. *True Confessions*. Rennie tunes out, studies the outfit on the

273

woman asleep on the bench across from them, her head sideways: the corsage with the Christmas bells and silver balls and the tiny plastic Santa Claus held captive on her large woollen breast.

"You aren't listening," says Lora accusingly.

"Sorry," says Rennie. "I'm really tired."

"Maybe I should shut up for a while," says Lora. She sounds hurt.

"No, go on," says Rennie. "It's really interesting." Maybe soon they will come to question her, isn't that what happens? And then she can explain everything, she can tell them why it's a mistake, why she should not be here. All she has to do is hang on; sooner or later, something is bound to happen.

●

Rennie is walking along a street, a street with red-brick houses, the street she lives on. The houses are big, square, solid, some with porches, some with turrets and gingerbread trim painted white. These people take care of their houses, they are proud of their houses. Houseproud, says Rennie's grandmother, who is.

Her mother and her grandmother are with her. It's Sunday, they've been to church. It's fall, the leaves have turned, yellow, orange, red, a few drift down on them as they walk along. The air is cool, cold almost, she's so glad to be back, she feels safe. But nobody's paying any attention to her. Her hands are cold, she lifts them up to look at them, but they elude her. Something's missing.

Here we go, says her mother. Here are the steps. Easy, now.

I don't want to die, says her grandmother. I want to live forever.

The sky has darkened, there's a wind, the leaves are falling down, red on her grandmother's white hat, they're wet.

The window above them gets brighter and brighter, now it's a square of heat. Rennie thinks she can see mist rising from the floor and walls and from the red bucket. The lights in the corridor are still on. Lora's asleep, her head thrown back into the corner where she's propped, her mouth is open a little, she's snoring. Rennie has found out she talks in her sleep, nothing intelligible.

Finally there's a shuffle in the corridor, the clink of metal. A policeman is here, unlocking the door; in two-tone blue and a shoulder holster. Rennie shakes Lora's arm to wake her up. She wonders if they're supposed to stand at attention, as they used to in public school when the teacher came in.

There's another man with the policeman, dressed in shoddy grey. He's carrying a bucket, red, identical to the one that's fermenting by the door, and two tin plates stacked one on the other and two tin cups. He comes in and sets the bucket and the plates and cups down on the floor beside the first bucket. The policeman stays outside in the corridor.

"Hi there, Stanley," Lora says, rubbing her eyes.

The man grins at her, shyly, he's frightened, he backs out. The policeman with him locks the door again, acting as if he hasn't heard.

On each of the plates there's a slice of bread, thinly buttered. Rennie looks into the bucket. The bottom is covered with a brownish liquid that she hopes is tea.

She scoops some out in a tin cup, takes that and a plate over to Lora.

"Thanks," says Lora. "What's this?" She's scratching her legs, which have red dots on them, bites of some kind.

"Morning tea," says Rennie. It's the English tradition, still.

Lora tastes it. "You could've fooled me," she says. "You sure you got the right bucket?" She spits the tea out onto the floor.

The tea is salty. They've made a mistake, Rennie thinks,

they've put salt in it instead of sugar. She pours the tea back into the bucket and chews the bread slowly.

●

The cell heats up. Rennie begins to sweat. The stench from the bucket is overpowering now. Rennie wonders when she'll stop noticing it. You can get used to almost anything.

She's wondering when someone in authority will arrive, someone she can talk to, someone she can inform of her presence. If they only realize she's here, who she is, they'll get her out. The policeman did not look like someone in authority. She's convinced of her right to be released, but she knows that not everyone will see it exactly that way.

About midmorning, judging by the sun, two other policemen arrive outside the door. One is black, one brownish pink. They seem friendlier than the first one, they grin as they unlock the door.

"Take the bucket and come with us," says the pink one. Rennie thinks they're talking to her. She comes forward.

"I wonder if I could see the supervisor," she says.

"We not talking to you," the black one says rudely. "She the one."

"Hi there, Sammy," Lora says. "Hold your horses."

She goes out with them, carrying the bucket of piss.

Lora is gone a long time. When she comes back she has a clean bucket. Rennie, who's been imagining atrocities, says, "What happened?"

"Nothing to it," says Lora. "You just empty out the bucket. There's a hole in the ground out there. I saw some of the others, they were doing the same thing." She sets the bucket down in its old place and comes over to the dry corner to sit down.

"Prince is on the floor above us," she says. "They're fixing it up for me to see him, maybe in a couple of days." She's happy about this, she's excited. Rennie's envious. She would like to feel like that.

"Guess what?" says Lora. "They got Marsdon."

"Oh," says Rennie. "Is he in here?"

"I mean he's dead," says Lora. "Somebody shot him."

"The men on Ste. Agathe?" says Rennie. She thinks of Marsdon running through the scrub, up the hill in his slippery leather boots, nine or ten men after him, while the police boat comes into the harbour, they'd want to get him while they still had time.

"No," says Lora. "The story is it was the cops. Ellis."

"I thought he was working for the CIA," says Rennie. "I thought he was an agent."

"There's a lot of stories," says Lora. "The CIA, Ellis, what's the difference? Anyway Ellis didn't want him talking about how he set it up, Ellis wants everyone to believe it was real. Nothing like a revolution to make the States piss money, and they've done it already, Canada just gave a great big lump of cash to Ellis, they told me, it said on the radio. Foreign aid. He can use it to finance his dope trade." She pauses, keeping an eye on Rennie. "Some of them are saying that Paul shot Minnow," she says.

"You don't believe that," says Rennie.

"Who knows?" says Lora.

"Why would he do that?" says Rennie.

"CIA," says Lora. "He was the one bringing in the guns for Marsdon, eh?"

"Come on," says Rennie.

Lora laughs. "You believed it once," she says. "I'm just telling you what they're saying. Guess what else?"

"What?" says Rennie, not wanting to.

"They think you're a spy," says Lora. She chuckles, a little insultingly.

"Who does?" says Rennie. "The police?"

"Everyone," says Lora, grinning. "Just, they haven't figured out who for yet."

"How did you hear all this?" Rennie says. "It's ridiculous."

Lora looks at her and smiles. From the pocket of her skirt she takes out a fresh package of cigarettes, Benson and Hedges, and a box of Swedish matches. "Same place I got these," she says. "I told you I had my ass covered."

Rennie's tired of guessing games. "How?" she says.

"I'm a dealer, remember?" says Lora. "So I made a deal."

"Who on earth with?" says Rennie, who can't imagine it.

"Those two cops, the ones who came just now?" says Lora. "Morton and Sammy. I knew they'd be here sooner or later; it took them a while to work it out but now they're in charge of us. They don't want us in with the others. They were selling for me on St. Antoine, they were my protection. Nobody knew except Paul. They sure as hell don't want anyone else around here finding out about that." She lights one of her new cigarettes, tosses the match onto the damp floor. "They were in on the shipments. They knew what was coming in and when, they knew the guns were coming up from Colombia along with the grass, they knew what was in Elva's boxes, they didn't know all about it but they knew enough, and they didn't tell, how could they without blowing their own act wide open? Ellis wouldn't like that. He'd think that was treachery. A little dealing he could understand but not that. Dealing they'd just get canned. That, they'd get offed. So I've got them by the nuts."

"Can they get us out?" Rennie says.

"I don't want to push it," says Lora. "I don't want to make them jumpy, they're jumpy enough already. Anyway they want me here, they can keep an eye on me better. They don't want anyone else to get hold of me and start squeezing; who knows, the first hot cigarette on the foot and everything might come squirting out. They'll take good care of me though, they know I won't go down alone, I told them that. If I go I take somebody with me."

"What's to stop them from just burying you quietly in the back yard?" says Rennie.

"Nothing at all," says Lora. She finds this funny. "Pure bluff. I told them I had someone on the outside who's checking up on me."

"Do you?" says Rennie.

"Well," says Lora, "there's always Paul. Wherever he is."

Neither of them wants to talk about that.

●

They're eating, lunch, cold rice and chicken backs, boiled, Rennie thinks, but not enough. Pink juice runs out. Lora gnaws with relish, licking her fingers. Rennie doesn't feel too well.

"You can have the rest of mine," she says.

"Why waste it?" says Lora.

"Maybe we could ask them to cook it more," says Rennie.

"Ask who?" says Lora.

Rennie hasn't thought about it. Surely there must be someone to ask.

"It could be a lot worse, is what I always say," says Lora. "Where there's life there's hope. It's better than a lot of the people get at home, think of it that way."

Rennie tries to but without much success. Lora is eating the rest of Rennie's chicken back now. She aims a bone at the bucket, misses, wipes her hands on her skirt. The nails are grey, the skin around them nibbled. Rennie looks away. Now they will have stale chicken to smell, as well as everything else.

"We could ask them about the tea," says Rennie.

"What?" says Lora, her mouth full.

"The salt in the tea," says Rennie. "You could tell them they made a mistake."

"Hell, no," says Lora. "That wasn't a mistake, that was orders. They're doing it on purpose."

"Why would they do that?" says Rennie. The poor food she can understand, but this seems gratuitous. Malicious.

Lora shrugs. "Because they can," she says.

●

It's dusk. They've had supper, a piece of bread, the salty tea, water which tastes like rancid butter, a cupful each. The mosquitoes are here. Outside the grated window they can hear the pigs, up there in the yard; as Rennie watches, a curious snout pokes through.

Neither of them is saying anything. Rennie can smell their bodies, unwashed flesh, and the putrid smell from the bucket, Lora is out of cigarettes for the time being, she's picking at her fingers, Rennie can see her out of the corners of her eyes, it's an irritating habit, they've both run out, run down. She's having trouble remembering which day this is, they should have begun when they got here, scratches on the wall, perhaps this is the day her ticket expires, her twenty-one-day excursion. Maybe now someone will come looking for her, maybe she will be rescued. If she can only keep believing it, then it will happen.

She hopes they'll do it soon, she's deteriorating, she knows this because right now she's daydreaming about food, not even real food, not spinach salads with bacon and mushrooms and a glass of dry white wine, but Colonel Sanders chicken, McDonald's hamburgers, doughnuts filmed with ersatz chocolate and shreds of stale coconut, thick nasty cups of ancient coffee, the dregs, her mouth's watering at the thought of it, potato chips, candy bars from subway magazine stands, Mars, Rowntree's coated raisins, silently and voluptuously she repeats the names, how can she? She sleepwalks along Yonge Street, into one franchise after another. *No-frills Snak Pak*. Maybe she's delirious.

She switches to a jigsaw puzzle, in her head, the top border, the ones with the flat edges, it's always the sky, one piece fits into another, fits into another, interlocking, pure blue.

280

"Try getting a comb for us," says Rennie. "If you can."

"I tried before," says Lora. "People slash their wrists with them. They don't want any funny deaths in here, not if they can help it. Some church or other is poking around."

"How about a brush?" says Rennie.

"You got any money?" says Lora, with a small laugh.

Rennie looks at her, she's thinner now and filthy, there's no other word for it, the white blouse is grey, the purple skirt is damp and greasy, dark moons under the eyes, they both smell, there's a sore on Lora's leg that won't heal, her hair is matted. Rennie knows how she herself must look. She thinks they should do exercises, but when she suggested it, Lora said, "What for?" and Rennie doesn't have the strength to do them by herself. What she really wants is a toothbrush. A mirror. Someone who could get them out.

"I could braid it," she says.

"What?" says Lora. It's harder and harder to keep her attention.

"I could braid your hair," says Rennie. "At least that would untangle it."

"Okay," says Lora. She's restless, she's out of cigarettes again, the flesh around her nails is raw. "I wish we could get some news in here," she says. "You can't trust what they tell you. I'm tired of this place."

Rennie doesn't remember hearing her complain before. It seems like a bad omen. She begins on the hair, it's like pulling strands of wool apart.

"Go easy," says Lora. "At least we don't have lice."

"Yet," says Rennie. Now they're laughing, it's idiotic, they can hardly stop. There's no reason for it. When they finish, Rennie keeps going with the hair. She's making it into two long frizzy braids. "What do you dream about?" she says to Lora.

"Lots of stuff," says Lora. "Being on a boat. My mother.

Sometimes I dream about having a baby. Except I never know what to do with it, you know? I think I'd like it though. When I get out of here and I get Prince out maybe that's what we'll do. They think it's funny here if you have a baby after you're about twenty-five though. For them that's old. But I don't care, let them laugh. Elva will like it, she's always bugging me to have a son for Prince."

Rennie finishes with one of the braids and starts on the other. "If we had some beads," she says, "I could do you up like a Rasta."

"Tinfoil," says Lora. "Some of the girls use that on the ends. When you get out, can you do something for me?"

"What makes you think I'll be out any sooner than you?" says Rennie.

"Oh, you will," says Lora. She says this wistfully, fatalistically, as if it's just a fact of life that everyone knows about.

Instead of cheering Rennie up this makes her anxious. She winds the two braids around Lora's head. "There," she says. "You look like a German milkmaid. Except I've got nothing to pin them with."

"Tell someone I'm here," says Lora. "Tell someone what happened."

Rennie lets go of the braids. "Who should I tell?" says Rennie.

"I don't know," says Lora. "Someone."

Lora's face is streaked with dirt. Perhaps later they can take turns wiping off each other's faces with the salty tea.

●

Rennie can't remember what people are supposed to think about. She tries to remember what she herself used to think about, but she can't. There's the past, the present, the future: none of them will do. The present is both unpleasant and unreal; thinking about the future only makes her impatient, as if she's in a plane circling and circling an airport, circling and not landing. Everyone gripping the arms of the seat, trying not to imagine the crash. She's tired of this fear, which goes on and on, no end to it. She wants an end.

She wants to remember someone she's loved, she wants to remember loving someone. It's hard to do. She tries to conjure up a body, Jake's body, as she has before, but she can hardly remember what he looks like. How does she know he ever existed? There's no proof. Acts of the body, of love, what's left? A change, a result, a trace, hand through the sea at night, phosphorescence.

Of Paul, only the too-blue eyes remain. They don't talk about Paul much; nothing has been heard, according to Lora, nothing has been said on the radio. He's disappeared, which could mean anything. Rennie does not want to think about the noises behind her in the harbour, the machine-gun fire, the explosion. She doesn't want to think of Paul as dead. That would rule out the possibility of rescue. She would rather know nothing. Possibly she is the last person he touched. Possibly he is the last person who will ever touch her. The last man.

She switches to a yoga class she once went to with Jocasta. *Feel the energy of the universe. Now relax. Start with the feet. Tell your feet, Feet, relax. Now send your mind into your ankles. Tell your ankles, Ankles, relax.* Go with the flow.

She thinks about Daniel, Daniel eating his breakfast while listening to the news, which he doesn't really seem to hear, since his knowledge of world affairs is more or less nil, Daniel caught in rush hour, Daniel getting his feet wet because he didn't listen to the weather forecast. Daniel in surgery, a body spread before him, his hands poised for incision. Daniel leaning across his desk, holding the hand of a blonde woman whose breasts he has recently cut off. Who wants to cure, who wants to help, who wants everything to be fine. You're alive, he says to her, with kindness and duplicity, compelling as a hypnotist. You're very lucky. Tears stream silently down her face.

Daniel moves through the day enclosed in a glass bubble, like an astronaut on the moon, like a rare plant in a hothouse: a fluke. Inside the bubble his life is possible. Normal. Outside, what would become of him? Without food or air. Ordinary human decency, a mutation, a freak. Right now she's on the outside looking in.

From here it's hard to believe that Daniel really exists: surely the world cannot contain both places. He's a mirage, a necessary illusion, a talisman she fingers, over and over, to keep herself sane.

Once she would have thought about her illness: her scar, her disability, her nibbled flesh, the little teethmarks on her. Now this seems of minor interest, even to her. The main thing is that nothing has happened to her yet, nobody has done anything to her, she is unharmed. She may be dying, true, but if so she's doing it slowly, relatively speaking. Other people are doing it faster: at night there are screams.

Rennie opens her eyes. Nothing in here has changed. Directly above her, up on the high ceiling, some wasps are building a nest. They fly in through the grating, up to the nest, out through the grating again. Jack Spaniards, Lora calls them. In memory of what war?

Pretend you're really here, she thinks. Now: what would you do?

●

It's another morning, time has a shape even here. When the guards come, they have names, Sammy and Morton, and she knows now which name belongs to which, Morton's the pink one, Rennie stays in the background. She still has difficulty understanding what's being said, so she lets Lora deal with it. They have a hairbrush now, though not a comb; which is better than nothing. Rennie would like a nail file, but she knows better than to ask, it's too much like a weapon. Lora doesn't need one, her nails are bitten down to the quicks anyway.

"Try for some chewing gum," Rennie says to Lora. Where there are cigarettes there must be gum. It will give the illusion of toothpaste; her mouth feels as if it's rotting. Lora goes out with the bucket.

She's gone longer than usual, and Rennie begins to worry. At the back of her mind is the fear that Lora won't be able to restrain herself, her temper, that she'll do something or say something that will tip the balance, put them both in jeopardy. She herself, she feels, would have more control.

But when Lora comes back she's the same, there are no cuts or bruises, nothing has been done to her. She sets the empty pail on the ground and squats over it. Rennie knows that smell, the smell of bloodheat, seaweed, fishegg. Lora wipes with a corner of her skirt, stands up.

"I got your chewing gum," she says. "Next time I'll try for some toilet paper."

Rennie is disgusted. She thinks Lora should have more self-respect. "No thanks," she says coldly.

Lora looks at her for a moment. "What the shit's eating you?" she says.

"You're worth more than a package of gum," Rennie says. How many of them, she wants to ask, one or both? One at a time, or both? Lying down or standing up? It isn't decent.

Lora is bewildered for an instant. Then she laughs. "Goddammn right I am," she says. "Two packages. I got one for myself too."

Rennie doesn't say anything. Lora sits down and opens the gum. "Women like you make me sick," she says. "Tightass. You wouldn't put out to save your granny, would you?"

"Let's not talk about it," says Rennie. There's no point. They're in this room and it's a small one and there's no way out. All she can do is try to avoid a fight.

"Why in hell not?" says Lora, chewing. "What's wrong

285

with talking about it? What makes you think it's any different from having some guy stick his finger in your ear?"

"It is," says Rennie.

"Only sometimes," says Lora.

Rennie turns her head away. She feels sick to her stomach. She doesn't want to watch Lora's grubby hands, her bitten fingers as they strip open the pack of cigarettes, the cigarette between the drying lips, the corner of her mouth.

But Lora is crying, Rennie can't believe it, convulsive sounds from her throat, her eyes clenched. "Fuck it," she says. "They've got Prince in here. They won't let me see him, they keep promising. What'm I supposed to do?"

Rennie is embarrassed. She looks down at her hands, which ought to contain comfort. Compassion. She ought to go over to Lora and put her arms around her and pat her on the back, but she can't.

"I'm sorry," she says. *Women like you.* She deserves it. It's a pigeonhole, she's in it, it fits.

Lora sniffles, stops now, wipes her nose on the back of her hand. Grudging, resentful, forgiving, a little. "How would you know?" she says.

●

Rennie doubles over, stumbles for the bucket, crouches. It's sudden, she can feel the sweat dripping down her back, she's dizzy, she hates pain. She's been invaded, usurped, germs taking over, betrayal of the body.

She lies down on the floor, even though it's wet. She closes her eyes, her head is the size of a watermelon, soft and pink, it's swelling up, she's going to burst open, she's going to die, she needs water, even water tasting of chlorine, Great Lakes poisons, her sense of irony has deserted her, just when she needs it, any kind of water, an ice cube, sugar and fizz from a machine. What has she done, she's not guilty, this is happening to her for no reason at all.

"You okay?" says Lora. She's touching Rennie's forehead, her fingertips leave dents. Her voice comes down from a great distance.

Rennie tries hard. "Make them get a doctor," she manages to say.

"For that?" says Lora. "It's only *turistas*. Montezuma's Revenge, the tourists call it. Everyone gets it sooner or later. Take it from me, you'll live."

●

It's night again. Someone is screaming, quite far away, if you tune it down it sounds like a party. Rennie tunes it down. She can sleep now in the light from the corridor, she goes to sleep quite peacefully, no one has done anything to her yet, she goes to sleep hugging herself. The screaming is worse when it stops.

Rennie is dreaming about the man with the rope, again, again. He is the only man who is with her now, he's followed her, he was here all along, he was waiting for her. Sometimes she thinks it's Jake, climbing in the window with a stocking over his face, for fun, as he once did; sometimes she thinks it's Daniel, that's why he has a knife. But it's not either of them, it's not Paul, it's not anyone she's ever seen before. The face keeps changing, eluding her, he might as well be invisible, she can't see him, this is what is so terrifying, he isn't really there, he's only a shadow, anonymous, familiar, with silver eyes that twin and reflect her own.

Lora is shaking her, trying to wake her up. "For Christ's sake," says Lora. "You want every cop in the place down our necks?"

Rennie says she's sorry.

It's noon, Rennie can tell by the heat and the angle of the light, and then the rice arrives. How much she's come to depend on it, that tin plate. The day ends when it's empty and another day of waiting begins, right then, with the scrape of the bones into the red bucket. Her life is shrinking right down to that one sound, a dull bell.

Outside in the courtyard there's something going on; all of a sudden there are harsh voices, shouts, a shuffle and clank. Then there's a scream. Lora gets up, her plate drops and spills. "Christ," she says, "they're shooting people."

"No," says Rennie. There haven't been any shots.

"Come on," says Lora. She bends, holds out her cupped hands.

"I don't think we should look," says Rennie. "They might see us."

"Maybe it's Prince," says Lora.

Rennie places her tin plate carefully on the ground. Then she puts her foot in Lora's hands, is lifted, clutches the bars.

There are people in the courtyard, five or six men in uniform, the two blues of the police, then another group, they seem to be tied together, arm to arm, they're being pushed down, to their knees, among the dry weeds and snarls of wire, the police have sticks, cattle prods? The ones kneeling have long hair, long black hair standing out from their heads; at first Rennie thinks they're women, then she sees they are naked from the waist up, they have no breasts.

One man still wears a woolly tea-cosy hat; a policeman snatches it off and the hair tumbles out. A pig runs in panic through the archway, it zigzags among the men, standing and kneeling, the policemen laugh, two of them chase it with cattle prods while the others watch, it dashes under the gallows platform and then back through the archway again. The kneeling men turn their heads, follow it with their eyes.

Now Rennie sees that one of the policemen has a rifle, he's raising it, for a minute she thinks he's going to shoot them all, the whole line of them. He hesitates, letting them believe this, do they? But he detaches the bayonet and walks slowly around to the back of the line with it, strolling, hips rolling, taking his time, luxuriating. He's not doing this just because he's been ordered to: he's doing it because he enjoys it. *Malignant*.

"What's going on?" says Lora, whispering. Rennie doesn't answer.

The policeman grasps the hair of the first man in the line, gathers it almost lovingly into a bunch, a handful, then suddenly jerks the man's head back so that the throat is taut, it's going to be worse than shooting. Butchery.

But all he does is saw at the hair, he's cutting the hair off; that's all he's doing. Another man follows him with a green garbage bag, for the hair. It's chilling, this tidyness.

"What is it?" says Lora. "What're they doing?"

He's at the second man now, the courtyard is oddly silent, the noon sun beats down, everything is bright, the men's faces glisten with sweat, fear, the effort of keeping in the hatred, the policemen's faces glisten too, they're holding themselves back, they love this, it's a ceremony, precise as an operation, they're implementing a policy, he pulls the head back like a chicken's, the hair is grey, he slices again with the bayonet but he's not careful enough, the man howls, a voice that is not a voice, there are no teeth in his opened mouth, blood is pouring down his face. The man with the bayonet stuffs the handful of hair into the bag and wipes his hand on his shirt. He's an addict, this is a hard drug. Soon he will need more.

The kneeling man continues to howl. As if they've been waiting for it, two others come over and one of them kicks the howling man in the stomach. A third throws water over him from a red plastic bucket. The man falls forward, he's kept from hitting the pavement by the ropes that link him to

289

the other men, one of the policemen jams the cattle prod in between his legs, he's flung back, now it's a scream. Not human.

"Pull him up," says the man in charge, and they do. They continue along the line, the hurt man's face is on a level with Rennie's own, blood pours down it, she knows who it is, the deaf and dumb man, who has a voice but no words, he can see her, she's been exposed, it's panic, he wants her to do something, pleading, *Oh please.*

"Let me down," says Rennie The best they can do is avoid calling attention to themselves. She leans against the wall, she's shaking. It's indecent, it's not done with ketchup, nothing is inconceivable here, no rats in the vagina but only because they haven't thought of it yet, they're still amateurs. She's afraid of men and it's simple, it's rational, she's afraid of men because men are frightening. She's seen the man with the rope, now she knows what he looks like. She has been turned inside out, there's no longer a *here* and a *there.* Rennie understands for the first time that this is not necessarily a place she will get out of, ever. She is not exempt. Nobody is exempt from anything.

"Good God, what is it?" says Lora. She's still whispering, her hands on Rennie's shoulders.

"Prince isn't there," says Rennie. "They're cutting their hair off."

She kneels, picks up the chicken back Lora spilled, wipes the dirt from it with her fingers, puts it on Lora's plate. "You should eat it," she says. "We need to eat."

●

In the middle of the morning, at the usual time, the two guards come again. Today one of them is new, he's too young, skinny body, thin wiry arms, face smooth as a plum, eyes innocent. Rennie takes one look at him and sees that he knows nothing at all. Morton is frightened, he's got his arm across his chest, almost touching his pistol, things are no longer under his control. It's the innocence of the other one that frightens him.

They unlock the door. Lora's watchful but she bends over anyway to pick up the smelly red bucket.

"Her turn today," says Morton, pointing at Rennie with the other hand. "You been doin' it every time."

Rennie isn't prepared for this, she knows what will be expected of her and she's not ready for it, but Lora steps in front of her, she's going to dare him. "Why?" she says. "Where's Sammy?"

"I don't mind which one," says the boy. He's heard something then, he wants part of it, he knows what but not what for.

"Shut your mouth," says Morton. He's afraid of being caught out, the young kid's smart enough to figure it out but he's a fool, he'll tell, maybe not deliberately but one way or another. He wants Rennie to go rather than Lora because it's safer, that's what he thinks. "Sammy's grandmother got sick," he says to Lora.

"Yeah," says the young boy. "She sick bad." He has a high nervous giggle. "What you need Sammy for? I just as good."

"I'll go," says Rennie. She doesn't want a squabble, something's about to go wrong.

"No," says Lora. The barred door's partly open, she yanks it and pushes out into the corridor. "What's happened to Prince? Is that it? You don't want me to know, you don't want to tell me. Oh shit. Where did you put him?"

She's got Morton by the arm but he's the one who's sweating, it's not her, she's tight and cold. The young boy's looking at both of them, trying to untangle this. He giggles again. "Prince?" he says. "The big man, Prince of Peace? He never in here at all, man."

"Shut your damn mouth," Morton says to him.

"You tell her he still alive?" says the boy. "He dead a long time ago, man." He thinks this is a joke. Rennie wonders whether he's stoned, it's a possibility.

"When?" Lora says quietly, to him alone, not to Morton. She's dropped her hands down, she's no longer holding Morton's arm.

"What you need to tell her that for?" Morton says with disgust. The boy has completely blown it.

"He was caught in the crossfire," the boy says. He giggles some more. "That what it say on the radio. You tell her you got him in here, make her work hard for you, eh? Get some for your own self. You are a bad man." He's laughing now, not just giggling, this is the funniest thing he's heard in a long time.

"You pig," Lora says to Morton. "You knew all along. You were just afraid I'd crack up if I heard about it, right, and then they'd find out what you were up to. They shot him in the back, right?"

Morton puts his hand on her arm, soothingly, like a doctor almost. "You go back in," he says. "I doin' the best I can for you. You lucky you alive."

"Fuck you!" Lora screams. "I'll tell everyone about you, nobody screws me around like that, they can shoot you too for all I care!"

Tears are running down her face. Rennie heads towards her. "Lora," says Rennie, "there's nothing you can do," but Lora is beyond her. Morton is pushing her now, back towards the door.

"Fucking pig," she says, "take your fucking hands off me!" She kicks at Morton, aiming for the groin, but he's too fast for her. He catches the raised leg, lifts, tips her backwards towards the boy, who's quick enough, he's not stoned after all, he catches her and jerks her arms behind her. Morton knees her in the belly, he's knocked the air out of her. Now nobody needs to hold her arms and after the first minute she's silent, more or less, the two of them are silent as well, they don't say anything at all. They go for the breasts and the buttocks, the stomach, the crotch, the head, jumping, *My God,*

Morton's got the gun out and he's hitting her with it, he'll break her so that she'll never make another sound. Lora twists on the floor of the corridor, surely she can't feel it any more but she's still twisting, like a worm that's been cut in half, trying to avoid the feet, they have shoes on, there's nothing she can avoid.

Rennie wants to tell them to stop. She wants to be strong enough to do that but she isn't, she can't make a sound, they'll see her. She doesn't want to see, she has to see, why isn't someone covering her eyes?

●

This is what will happen.

Rennie will be taken to a small room, painted apple green. On the wall there will be a calendar with a picture of a sunset on it. There will be a desk with a phone and some papers on it. There will be no windows.

Behind the desk there will be a policeman, an older man, with short greying hair. In front of the desk there's a chair. Rennie sits down in the chair when the policeman tells her to. The policeman who's brought her here will stand behind her.

She is asked to sign a release form saying that while in custody she has not been harmed in any way and has not witnessed any other detainee being so harmed. She thinks of Lora, her pulped face. She understands that unless she makes a mark on this paper they may not let her out. She feels that she has forgotten how to write. She signs her name.

They have her suitcase here, from the hotel, and her purse. The older man says that perhaps she would like to change her clothes before meeting the gentleman from the Canadian government who is here to see her. Rennie feels this would be a good idea. She's taken to another small room, much like the first except that the calendar is different, it's a white woman in a blue bathing suit, one piece, again no windows. She knows the young policeman is standing outside the door. She opens her suitcase and sees her own clothes, the clothes that used to be hers. Alien reaction paranoia. She starts to cry.

Rennie knocks on the inside of the door, which opens. She walks out. She's just as dirty but she feels less dirty now, she feels decent, she's wearing a cotton dress, faded blue, and her hair is combed, as well as she could do it in the mirror from her purse. She's carrying the suitcase in her right hand, the purse is over her left shoulder. Her passport isn't in the purse or the suitcase either. So she's not really out, not yet. She's decided not to ask where her camera bag is.

She is taken up some stairs, along a stone hallway, then into a much larger room, one with windows. She can hardly remember what it's like to be in such a large room, to look out of windows that are so huge. She looks out. What she sees is the muddy field where the tents were; now it's empty. She understands that this is one of the rooms that are usually shown to tourists, the room where they were going to sell the local arts and crafts, a long time ago. There are two wooden chairs in the corner, and a man is standing beside them waiting for her. He's still got the tinted glasses and the safari jacket.

He shakes hands with Rennie and they sit down on the wooden chairs. He offers her a cigarette, a black one with a gold band, which she refuses. He smiles at her, he's a little nervous. He says she certainly has given them some uneasy moments. There wasn't a lot they could do when the region was destabilized and the government here was so panicky, overreacting he says, but the situation is normalizing now.

The government can't make a public apology of course but they would like her to know unofficially that they consider it a regrettable incident. They understand that she is a journalist and such things should not happen to journalists. It was an error. They hope she's prepared to consider it in the same light.

Rennie nods and smiles at him. Her heart is beating, she's beginning to think again. Of course, she says.

To tell you the truth, says the man, they thought you were an agent. Of a foreign government. A subversive. Isn't that absurd? It's the common charge though, in countries like this.

The man is uneasy, he's leading up to something, here it comes. He says he realizes she's a journalist but in this instance things are very delicate, getting her out of here has been more difficult than she may suppose, she doesn't know how these small southern countries operate, the people who run them are quite temperamental. Irrational. For instance, the Prime Minister was very angry because the Americans and the Canadians didn't send in their armies and their navies and their air forces to support him, over, let's face it, a completely minor insurrection, doomed even before it started. The Prime Minister seemed to feel that Rennie should be kept in a cell because these armies had failed to materialize. As a kind of hostage. Can she imagine that?

Rennie says she can. I suppose you're telling me not to write about what happened to me, she says.

Requesting, he says. Of course we believe in freedom of the press. But for them it's a matter of saving face.

For you too, thinks Rennie. Have you any idea of what's going on in there? she says.

The Council of Churches made an inspection and was satisfied with the conditions, he says, too quickly. In any case we can't interfere in internal matters.

I guess you're right, says Rennie. She wants her passport back, she wants to get out. Anyway it's not my thing, she says. It's not the sort of piece I usually do. I usually just do travel and fashion. Lifestyles.

He's relieved: she understands, she's a woman of understanding after all.

Of course we don't make value judgements, he says, we just allocate aid for peaceful development, but *entre nous* we wouldn't want another Grenada on our hands.

Rennie looks out the window. There's a plane, coming down at a sharp angle across the oblong of sky, it flashes, silver, up there in the viciously blue air. It must be the afternoon flight from Barbados, the one she came in on, only now it's on time. The situation is normalizing, all over the place, it's getting more and more normal all the time.

Actually I'd like to forget the whole thing as soon as possible, she says. It's not the sort of thing you want to dwell on.

Of course not, he says. He stands up, she stands up, they shake hands.

●

When they're finished, when Lora is no longer moving, they push open the grated door and heave her in. Rennie backs out of the way, into the dry corner. Lora hits the floor and lies there, limp, like a bundle of clothing, face down, her arms and legs sprawled out. Her hair's all over, her skirt's up, her underpants ripped and filthy, bruises already appearing on the backs of her legs, the heavy flesh of her thighs, massive involvement, or maybe they were there already, maybe they were always there. There's a smell of shit, it's on the skirt too, that's what you do.

The older one throws something over her, through the bars, from the red plastic bucket.

"She dirt herself," he says, possibly to Rennie, possibly to no one. "That clean her off."

They both laugh. Rennie's afraid it isn't water.

They go away, doors close after them. Lora lies on the floor, unmoving, and Rennie thinks *What if she's dead*? They won't be back for hours, maybe not until the next morning, she'll be alone here all night with a dead person. There should be a doctor. She picks her way carefully around the outline of Lora, the puddle on the floor, blood mixing with the water, it was only water after all. She looks out through the bars, down the corridor, as far as she can see in either direction. No one's there, the corridor is empty and silent, the lightbulbs hang along the ceiling with loops of wire in between, at regular intervals. One of them is burned out. I should tell someone, thinks Rennie.

●

Rennie is in the kitchen, making herself a peanut butter sandwich. There's a radio on somewhere, a soft blur of noise, or maybe it's the television, a blue-grey oblong of mist in the livingroom where her grandmother sits propped in front of it, seeing visions. Rennie cuts the sandwich in four and puts it on a plate, she likes small neat ceremonies like this, she pours herself a glass of milk.

Her grandmother comes through the doorway between the diningroom and the kitchen. She's wearing a black dress printed with white flowers.

I can't find my hands, she says. She holds out her arms to Rennie, helplessly, her hands hanging loose at the ends of them.

Rennie cannot bear to be touched by those groping hands, which seem to her like the hands of a blind person, a half-wit, a leper. She puts her own hands behind her and backs away, into the corner and along the wall, maybe she can make it to the kitchen door and go out into the garden.

Where is everybody? says her grandmother. She starts to cry, screwing up her eyes like a child, scant tears on the dry skin of her face.

Rennie's mother comes in through the kitchen door, carrying a brown paper bag full of groceries. She has on one of her shopping dresses, navy blue.

What's going on? she says to Rennie.

I can't find my hands, says her grandmother.

Rennie's mother looks with patience and disgust at Rennie, at her grandmother, at the kitchen and the peanut butter sandwich and the groceries she's carrying. She sets the bag down carefully on the table. Don't you know what to do by now? she says to Rennie. Here they are. Right where you put them. She takes hold of the grandmother's dangling hands, clasping them in her own.

●

The sunlight is coming in through the little window, it falls on the floor in squares, in one of the squares is Lora's left hand, the dirty blunt fingers with their bitten cuticles curled loosely, untouched, they did nothing to her hands, shining and almost translucent in the heavy light. The rest of the body is in darkness, in water, the hand is in the air. Rennie kneels on the wet floor and touches the hand, which feels cold. After a moment she takes hold of it, with both of her hands. She can't tell from holding this hand whether or not Lora is breathing, whether or not her heart is still moving. How can she bring her back to life?

Very carefully, this is important, she turns Lora over, her body is limp and thick, a dead weight. Dead end. She hauls Lora over to the dryest corner of the room and sits with her, pulling Lora's head and shoulders onto her lap. She moves the sticky hair away from the face, which isn't a face any more, it's a bruise, blood is still oozing from the cuts, there's one on the forehead and another across the cheek, the mouth looks like a piece of fruit that's been run over by a car, pulp, Rennie wants to throw up, it's no one she recognizes, she has no connection with this, there's nothing she can do, it's the face of a stranger, someone without a name, the word *Lora* has come unhooked and is hovering in the air, apart from this ruin, mess, there's nothing she can even wipe this face off with, all the cloth in this room is filthy, septic, except her hands, she could lick this face, clean it off with her tongue, that would be the best, that's what animals did, that's what you were supposed to do when you cut your finger, put it in your mouth, clean germs her grandmother said, if you don't have water, she can't do it, it will have to do, it's the face of Lora after all, there's no such thing as a faceless stranger, every face is someone's, it has a name.

She's holding Lora's left hand, between both of her own, perfectly still, nothing is moving, and yet she knows she is pulling on the hand, as hard as she can, there's an invisible hole in the air, Lora is on the other side of it and she has to pull her through, she's gritting her teeth with the effort, she can hear herself, a moaning, it must be her own voice, this is a gift, this is the hardest thing she's ever done.

She holds the hand, perfectly still, with all her strength. Surely, if she can only try hard enough, something will move and live again, something will get born.

"Lora," she says. The name descends and enters the body, there's something, a movement; isn't there?

"Oh God," says Lora.

Or was that real? She's afraid to put her head down, to the heart, she's afraid she will not be able to hear.

●

Then the plane will take off. It will be a 707. Rennie will sit halfway down, it will not be full, at this time of year the traffic is north to south. She will be heading into winter. In seven hours she'll be at the airport, the terminal, the end of the line, where you get off. Also where you can get on, to go somewhere else.

When she's finally there, snow will be on the ground, she'll take a taxi, past the stunted leafless trees, the slabs of concrete, the shoebox houses, they'll stop and she'll give the driver the correct amount of money and she'll walk up the stairs and through her own front door, into the unknown. She doesn't know who will be waiting for her, who will be there, in any sense of the word that means anything. Perhaps nobody, and that will not be fine but it will be all right.

Wherever else she's going it will not be quietly under.

She's drinking a ginger ale and thumbing through the in-flight magazine, which is called *Leisure*. On the front, up at the top, there's a picture of the sun, orange, with a smiling face, plump cheeks and a wink. Inside there are beaches, the sea, blue-green and incredible, bodies white and black, pink-brown, light brown, yellow-brown, some serving, others being served, serviced. A blonde in a low-riding tie-dye sarong, the splotches reddish. She can feel the shape of a hand in hers, both of hers, there but not there, like the afterglow of a match that's gone out. It will always be there now.

The ginger ale tastes the same as it used to, the ice cubes are the same, frozen with holes in them. She notes these details the way she has always noted them. What she sees has not altered; only the way she sees it. It's all exactly the same. Nothing is the same. She feels as if she's returning after a space trip, a trip into the future; it's her that's been changed but it will seem as if everyone else has, there's been a warp. They've been living in a different time.

There's a man sitting beside her. Although there's an empty seat between them he moves over, he says he wants to see out the window, one last glimpse as he puts it. He asks if she minds and she says she doesn't. He's standard, a professional of some sort, he's wearing a suit and drinking a Scotch and soda, he's selling something or other.

He asks how long she was down for and she says three weeks. He says she doesn't have much of a tan and she says she's not all that fond of lying around in the sun. She asks what he does and he says he represents a computer company. She wonders if he really is who he says he is; she'll wonder that about everybody now.

Vacation? he says.

She could pose as a tourist but she chooses not to. Working, she says. She has no intention of telling the truth, she knows when she will not be believed. In any case she is a subversive. She was not one once but now she is. A reporter.

She will pick her time; then she will report. For the first time in her life, she can't think of a title.

He asks her if she's a secretary. "I'm doing a travel piece," she says, and gets the usual reaction, a little surprise, a little respect, she's not what she looks like. She tells him where.

Where they had the trouble? he says. He says he's been there and it doesn't have a tennis court worth mentioning, and she agrees that it doesn't.

He asks her if she travels alone much and she says yes, she does, her work requires it. He asks her to dinner and she wonders what to say. She could say that her husband is meeting her at the airport or that she's a lesbian or that she's dying, or the truth. She says unfortunately she doesn't have enough time, she has to meet a deadline, and that's the end of him, he feels rejected, he's embarrassed, he moves back to his own seat and opens up his briefcase, it's full of paper.

She looks out the window of the plane, it's so bright, the sea is below and there are some islands, she doesn't know which ones. The shadow of the plane is down there, crossing over sea, now land, like a cloud, like magic. It's ordinary, but for a moment she can hardly believe she's here, up here, what's holding them up? It's a contradiction in terms, heavy metal hurtling through space; something that cannot be done. But if she thinks this way they will fall. *You can fly*, she says to no one, to herself.

There's too much air conditioning, wind from outer spacer blowing in through the small nozzles, Rennie's cold. She crosses her arms, right thumb against the scar under her dress. The scar prods at her, a reminder, a silent voice counting, a countdown. Zero is waiting somewhere, whoever said there was life everlasting; so why feel grateful? She doesn't have much time left, for anything. But neither does anyone else. She's paying attention, that's all.

She will never be rescued. She has already been rescued. She is not exempt. Instead she is lucky, suddenly, finally, she's overflowing with luck, it's this luck holding her up.

MARGARET ATWOOD

The Handmaid's Tale

In the Republic of Gilead, Offred has one purpose: to breed. If she deviates she will, like all dissenters, be hanged at the wall or sent out to die slowly of radiation sickness. But even a repressive state cannot obliterate desire – neither Offred's nor that of the two men on which her future hangs...

'Moving, vivid and terrifying. I only hope it's not prophetic'
Conor Cruise O'Brien,
The Listener

'*The Handmaid's Tale* is both a superlative exercise in science fiction and a profoundly felt moral story'
Angela Carter

'Compulsively readable'
Daily Telegraph

VINTAGE BOOKS
London

MARGARET ATWOOD

Life Before Man

Elizabeth, monstrous yet pitiable; Nate, her husband, a patch-work man, gentle, disillusioned; Lesje, a young woman at the Natural History Museum, for whom dinosaurs are as important as men. A sexual triangle, three people in thrall to the tragicomedy we call love...

'A modern saga... She has a fine ear for words and a quick wit for absurdities'
The Times

'An extraordinary imagination – witty, light-footed, realistic, yet with shooting insights into the nature of personality and love'
Financial Times

'A splendid work...superb'
Marilyn French

VINTAGE BOOKS
London